BERTRICE SMALL

THE SHADOW QUEEN

HARLEQUIN®

entertain, enrich, inspire™

Recycling programs
for this product may
not exist in your area.

ISBN-13: 978-0-373-77697-9

THE SHADOW QUEEN

Copyright © 2009 by Bertrice Small

To Abby Zidle, who began the journey with me through the World of Hetar, and hooked me on *The Amazing Race;* and to Tara Parsons, who continued the adventure at my side. Wonderful editors, and friends!

THE
SHADOW
QUEEN

PROLOGUE

MAGNUS HAUK, DOMINUS of Terah, lay dying upon the deck of his brother-in-law Corrado's new ship, the *Splendor*. Captain Corrado lay grievously injured nearby. The main mast for the vessel had snapped as it was being installed, hitting both men when it fell. Corrado had been quicker to leap aside, sustaining a shattered right leg as well as several other broken bones, but he survived. The Dominus, however, had been crushed by the great spar. Still, he managed to hold tightly on to the life remaining to him.

"Lara!" he managed to gasp. *"Get Lara!"*

He did not have to ask. Seeing the disaster unfolding, the ship's second mate had dashed down the gangway, and hurried to find the Domina. Yet before he had even reached the castle entry itself Lara came running forth past him, and headed directly for the scene of the accident. The second mate swore afterward that her feet never touched the ground as she moved swiftly up the gangway onto the deck of the ship.

As she knelt by her husband's side one look told her that his grasp on life was tenuous at best. "Magnus, my love," she said, brushing a lock of his thick, golden hair from his forehead. "I am here." There it was again staring boldly at her. *Death.* Damned death! She did not want to lose this man, but even she had not the power to heal such injuries. Only the Celestial Actuary could give life to mortals.

The turquoise-blue eyes opened at the sound of her voice. "Get my mother. Our son, Taj. Kaliq. *Now,*" he rasped urgently. "I cannot remain much longer."

"I will sustain you until you must go," Lara told him. That much she could do. She wanted to rail at the heavens, which were again taking another husband from her.

It wasn't fair! Wasn't she supposed to leave him to seek her destiny one day? Or had her destiny come calling upon her at last?

"Lara!" Corrado called to her. "Let me be by his side."

She shuddered at the sound of Corrado's pain. Then she transported him painlessly by means of her magic next to where her husband lay. Pushing aside her own grief, Lara used her magic to bring her mother-in-law, Lady Persis; her sister-in-law, Sirvat, who was Corrado's wife; and her son, Taj, to the deck of the vessel.

"Prince Kaliq, heed my plea. Cease all else, and come to me!" she cried aloud, and he was immediately there by her side.

For a moment the others stood confused. Then Sirvat knelt by her husband's side casting an anxious glance at Lara. Lady Persis cried out in despair recognizing death was about to claim her only son. Taj, the shock evident upon his young face, put a comforting arm about his grandmother, who was frail and elderly now.

"Hear me!" Magnus Hauk said. "Lara will rule for our son until she deems him ready to be Dominus of Terah. *Only Lara!* Her word is to be law in Terah."

"She is female," Lady Persis quavered. "Never has Terah been ruled by a female, Magnus, my son."

"Only Lara!" he repeated. "My dying words must be honored. Corrado, Kaliq, you are my witnesses. Swear you will uphold my last wishes."

They swore.

"Taj, my son, come to me," Magnus Hauk called, his voice discernibly weaker.

"I am here, my lord father," the boy said as he came to kneel by his sire's side.

"Swear to me you will obey and sustain my dying wishes. Your mother is to rule until she believes you are ready. *Swear!*" The Dominus grew even paler as he spoke.

Taj began to cry. "I am too young to be Dominus," he wept. "I swear, my lord father. My mother will rule until I am able to take up my inheritance. I will not question your wishes. I will not!"

"Mother, Sirvat, swear!" he demanded weakly.

"I swear, brother!" Sirvat said.

"Mother!"

"I…swear," Lady Persis said reluctantly. "But it goes against tradition," she could not refrain from adding.

"Kaliq, protect them!" the Dominus said, his voice beginning to fade away.

"With my own life, Magnus," the great Shadow Prince swore.

"You are immortal," Magnus Hauk said with a feeble smile.

"Not entirely," Kaliq responded. Then he, too, knelt by the Dominus's side. "Are you ready, my lord?" he asked him softly.

Magnus Hauk looked to Lara, his turquoise gaze locking on to her faerie green eyes. With the last of his strength he said, "I have loved none but you. I have never been happier than when I was with you. Mourn me briefly. Then find your destiny, Lara, my love, my life. You are surely meant for greatness. Now I must leave you."

Lara pressed her lips together to keep from crying out. She caressed his ashen cheek. Then, bending, she kissed him a final time letting loose her hold on him as she did. Magnus Hauk, Dominus of Terah, died softly, his last breath slipping from between his lips to be caught up by the south wind which bore it away.

Prince Kaliq, the great Shadow Prince, could see the Dominus's spirit as it hovered above them all, reluctant to depart. *Go, my friend,* he told Magnus Hauk in the silent language of the magical folk. *You know I will keep my word to you.* Then he watched sadly as the spirit rose up and disappeared. He looked to Lara, for his greatest concern now was for her. Magnus Hauk had left her with a terrible responsibility. He wondered how the Terahns, a people of ancient tradition, would react to their Domina assuming power for her son.

Without a word Lara stood up, taking Taj's small hand in hers as together they walked from the ship, returning to the castle to prepare for a funeral, and for the transition that was to follow. Kaliq shook his head. His fears were needless. Lara knew her duty, and the Shadow Princes had taught her well. He would be there for her, but he would not intrude. For all the faerie blood in his veins, her son had no magic about him. He was mortal, but Lara would teach him well.

CHAPTER ONE

LARA HAD BROUGHT the convenience of faerie post to Terah many years before. Now she marshaled the tiny messengers, sending them throughout Terah announcing the unexpected death of the Dominus Magnus Hauk. The leaders of all the villages were instructed to gather at a central meeting place assigned to each of the seven fjords, at a specific time on the day of Magnus Hauk's funeral. The headmen and -women of the New Outland families were also sent similar instructions. The mountain gnomes were also invited to participate. Her husband's funeral would be a grand one.

Lara thought back to the time she had managed the funeral of her first husband, Vartan, Lord of the Fiacre. She had been a young girl with two small children then, one a baby. Now her eldest son, Dillon, was a man grown with his own wife. Her eldest daughter, Anoush, was also grown. The three children she had borne Magnus Hauk were still fledglings. Well, perhaps not the eldest, Zagiri. At seventeen Zagiri was fully grown, wasn't she? Lara sighed sadly. She was finally beginning to understand the curse of being faerie with mortal offspring. Her children were aging. But she was not.

"Mother?" Anoush had come to stand by her side.

"Yes, my darling," Lara answered the daughter she had borne Vartan of the Fiacre twenty-one years ago.

"I have a crystal that will ease the pain," Anoush volunteered.

"Nay," Lara said softly. "Magnus Hauk's memory is more than worthy of my pain, but thank you." Reaching out, she patted Anoush's small, pale, blue-veined hand. This first daughter of hers was so fragile while the other two were healthy. Zagiri might even be called sturdy. How different they all were. There wasn't a magical bone in Zagiri's body despite her bloodline while Anoush had *the Sight* and was an instinctive healer of mind, body and soul. Her *gift* was both a joy and a sorrow to her, for she was so intuitive and sensitive herself she suffered along with those who sought her help.

As for her youngest daughter, Marzina, she was, like Dillon, extremely magical and had proven so at an early age. Born a twin to her brother, Taj, Marzina had not been sired by Magnus Hauk although it was generally believed she had been. The seed from which Marzina had blossomed was that of Kol, the Twilight Lord, who had forced himself upon Lara on the Dream Plain. For this crime Kol was now imprisoned, his kingdom in chaos. No one had ever questioned Marzina's paternity but for Lara's mother, who had been present at the twins' birth and declared she looked like a Nix relation.

Lara felt a tear slip down her cheek. She rarely wept, but now suddenly the tears flowed for Magnus Hauk, who had been so good to all of her children. Anoush wrapped her mother in her embrace, and, sobbing, Lara accepted her daughter's comfort as the girl's hand stroked her mother's pale golden head. "It isn't fair!" She voiced aloud her frustration and her despair over her husband's sudden demise.

"I know," Anoush agreed, "but when has life ever been fair, Mother? Was it fair when my uncle killed my father, Vartan?"

Lara drew away from her eldest daughter. "Nay, it was not fair then, nor is it fair now, Anoush. I shall not wed again. The men I marry seem to meet with untimely ends."

"You do not need to marry," Anoush replied, and suddenly her blue eyes glazed over. "You are loved without the bonds of marriage. And you have your destiny to consider. It draws closer, but you are still not ready to receive it. There is time yet." Then Anoush slumped against Lara. "Mother?" she whispered a moment later.

"It's all right, my darling," Lara comforted her. "It was one of your visions."

"Was it important?" Anoush wanted to know, for she never recalled these moments when she saw into the future.

Before Lara might answer Anoush her two younger daughters burst into her dayroom shrieking with terrible distress.

Zagiri threw herself into her mother's arms. "Is it

true?" she sobbed. "No! No! It cannot be true! Tell me our father isn't dead?"

Lara's sorrow evaporated as her anger arose. "It is true, Zagiri," she said. "Now who has usurped my right to bring you this awful news?"

"Grandmother Persis," Marzina quickly replied, for Zagiri was incapable of answering, so great was her grief. She had been Magnus Hauk's firstborn, and he had without meaning to tended to favor her.

"The old bitch!" Lara hissed softly. "Where is Taj?"

"With her," Marzina answered her mother. "She is most distraught."

"Not so distraught that she couldn't send your sister into hysterics," Lara said angrily. She turned to the weeping Zagiri, and gathered the girl into her arms. There was nothing she could say that would comfort this daughter of Magnus Hauk, but she cradled and rocked the girl until Zagiri's sobs subsided.

"How did Father die?" Marzina asked sanguinely, her eyes filled with tears.

Zagiri's woebegone face looked up at Lara now.

"The main mast of your uncle Corrado's new ship was being set into place. It shattered, broke and fell onto your father and uncle. Your uncle will survive. Your father's injuries were mortal. He called for me, for Kaliq, your grandmother and Taj so his last wishes might be heard, and swore us to uphold them."

"Couldn't you have saved him, Mother?" Zagiri asked Lara now, pulling away from her mother's embrace. "You are faerie! What good are all your powers if you could not save the life of the man you love?" she asked angrily, irrationally.

"Aye, I am faerie, but sustaining mortal life is beyond my powers. His wounds were fatal. It was all I could do to help him live long enough to make his last wishes known, Zagiri," Lara told her daughter. "I am sorry you had to learn of your father's death in this fashion. It was not up to your grandmother to tell you, and I can see that she did it badly. But we will survive, my darlings. We are together, and your father would want us to honor his memory by living our lives as he would want us to do."

Zagiri sniffed.

"You are so selfish," Marzina told Zagiri. "All you think about is yourself. How do you think our mother feels having to have watched our father die, and not be able to help him? Is her grief nothing to you, Zagiri? He was her husband. Her mate."

"Where is our mother's grief?" Zagiri said bitterly. "I do not see it."

"I have seen it," Anoush told her younger sister. "Before you entered this chamber I held our mother while she wept for Magnus Hauk. And she will continue to grieve in private I know. But now she must take up the duties of the Dominus if Terah is to survive. When word of our father's death reaches across the sea to Hetar do you think they will remain peaceful knowing my brother, the new Dominus, is yet a boy? Our mother has much to do if Terah is to remain strong. Her sorrow must be private, Zagiri. She needs her strength to save us all."

Zagiri was suddenly remorseful. "Oh, Mother, I did not realize..." Then she gasped. "A woman ruling Terah? What will the people say?"

"To all intents and purposes Taj will rule Terah," Lara answered Zagiri. "I will guide him as the Shadow Princes once guided me. When your brother is capable I will step aside, and he will rule without me."

"You will be a Shadow Queen then," Marzina said with just the hint of a smile.

Lara smiled. "Aye, I shall remain in the shadows so that the customs of Terah not be offended or disturbed. I promised your father that, and I will honor my promise."

"Grandmother Persis will not like it," Zagiri murmured.

"But she will accept it," Lara responded. "She gave your father her sacred word as he lay dying. So did Kaliq, your uncle and aunt. The last wishes of Magnus Hauk will be honored, my daughters. Now leave me. I have already sent faerie posts to the elders, and the New Outlands, but I must inform the High Priest Arik at the Temple of the Great Creator, and Kemina, High Priestess at the Temple of the Daughters of the Great Creator, of the Dominus's death. They will conduct your father's funeral service. Tell your brother to come to me, and see that your grandmother stays out of mischief."

"Dillon should be told," Anoush reminded her mother.

Lara nodded as her daughters left her presence. There was so much to do, she thought. And so little time in which to accomplish all that needed doing. By Terahn law Magnus Hauk's Farewell Ceremony had to be completed within three days. She had already decided that the burning vessel that carried his body out to the sea would be that very one that had been responsible for his death. She knew that Captain Corrado would agree, for no Terahn would ever sail upon the ship that had caused the demise of Magnus Hauk. Lara sighed. How much time had passed since her husband's death? An hour? Two? She was both numb and aching at the same time.

"Mother?"

She looked up to see her son Taj. His face was full of sorrow. "Come in, my lord Dominus," she replied to him. "Sit down. We must talk."

"It is too soon," the boy said tearfully.

Lara shook her head. "Nay," she told him. "You are your father's heir. There is no time for self-indulgence, Taj. You are Magnus Hauk's son, and you will be, *must* be, strong in the face of this tragedy. Once it is known that your father is gone, and you rule in Terah, our enemies will gather and plot, and seek to gain an advantage over us. You cannot let that happen. And I will help you with the aid of the High Priest Arik, and others, Taj. But never will I appear by your side. I will stand in the shadows behind your throne until you are old enough and wise enough to rule without me. Terah will see you, accept you as their Dominus from this terrible day forward."

"I do not know how to be Dominus," Taj responded.

Lara smiled. "Of course you don't," she told him. "It was never expected that you be Dominus so young. Your father and I wanted our children to have a happy childhood without the cares that accompany adulthood."

"Teach me," Taj said. "What must I do first?"

It pleased her that he had pushed his grief aside, and begun asking questions. "You will call the chief scribe, Ampyx, to you. Then you will dictate an official announcement of your father's death, and your right of inheritance. You will then order that it be sent by faerie post to be published throughout all of Terah. I have already notified the elders of the seven fjords, the religious, and the New Outlanders in your name. It was necessary, for by custom the Farewell must be done on the third day. I will bring them all here with my magic," Lara said.

"What will I tell Ampyx?" Taj asked her. "Will you be with me when I speak to him, Mother?"

"I will not be with you," Lara replied. "Remember it must appear from the start that you are in total charge, my son. Here is what you must dictate to Ampyx. You will say that it is with great sorrow you must bring the news of your father's death to his beloved people. That as his only natural-born son you have taken the right of inheritance. Then have Ampyx sign this document in the name of Taj Hauk, Dominus of Terah."

"I will go to the throne room now," Taj told Lara.

"Aye," she agreed. Then they both stood, and Lara embraced her young son. "Go," she said to him.

The boy strode bravely from his mother's apartments, and hurried through the castle to the official chamber where his father had formally received guests and dignitaries from other worlds. He climbed the dais to the throne of Terah, and, standing before it, called out, "Send for the chief scribe, Ampyx!" To his own surprise his voice did not tremble. And while the chamber appeared empty Taj knew there was always a servant discreetly in attendance there day and night.

"At once, my lord!" a voice called.

Taj sat heavily upon his father's throne. He wondered how long it would take for him to think of it as *his* throne. Then he composed himself, and considered the words he would utter to Ampyx. His mother had laid out the boundaries for him, but she knew he was an intelligent boy, and would want to speak from his own heart. Taj smiled. His mother was a very clever woman, and there was much he could learn from her. His grandmother had told him he should not listen to any woman, but rule in his own right. But Taj Hauk knew he needed his mother's counsel now. His father had with his dying breath put them all in Lara's charge. Magnus Hauk would not have done such a thing if he had not felt it was the right thing to do.

"My lord?"

Taj raised his head from his thoughts and stood up. "Chief Scribe, I would dictate to you," he said.

Ampyx immediately sat down cross-legged upon the marble floor and drew out his writing board, parchment, pen and a small stone bottle of ink. "I am ready, my lord."

"It is with deep sorrow that I announce the sudden death… No. Write, the sudden and accidental death of Dominus Magnus Hauk, this tenth day in the first month of the planting season. His Farewell Ceremony will be held as custom dictates on the third day following his demise. All of his beloved people who can attend are welcome at the castle." Taj stopped, and considered carefully his next words as the head scribe looked up at him. Then Taj continued. "As Magnus Hauk's only son I now formally claim the right of inheritance." He looked to the chief scribe. "Read my words back to me, Ampyx."

The tiniest of smiles touched the head scribe's lips, and then he read back the words that had just been dictated to him.

When he had finished the boy added, "Sign it Taj Hauk, Dominus of Terah." Then considering again he asked ingenuously, "Have I forgotten anything, Ampyx?"

"Nay, my lord. Your words are just as they should be." He arose from the floor and bowed to the boy. "May I offer you my own condolences, my lord Dominus, on the death of your great father?"

"You may," Taj replied formally. "I thank you." Then,

remembering, he said, "See my words are published this day throughout the kingdom from the Sea of Sagitta to the Obscura in the New Outlands."

"It will be as you wish, my lord Dominus." And, bowing, the chief scribe backed out of the throne room.

"It was nicely done," Lara said, stepping from behind the tall throne where she had been hidden listening. "And now Ampyx will gossip among the other scribes about the strength of the young Dominus. And they will gossip to their friends and families. It is a good start, Taj." She held out her arms to him, and he immediately went into them.

"I am so afraid, Mother," he admitted to her. "Dictating an announcement was easy. Ruling a land is not. Where do I even begin?"

"You begin where your father left off. Rebuilding our merchant fleet ship by ship. Your father wanted our ships to be able to defend themselves, especially now that the secret of our existence is well-known throughout Hetar. The Hetarians have not yet breached our shores. They tried once and failed, but sooner or later they will attempt it once more, my son. You are a boy ruler. Untried. There will be those even here in Terah who will seek to undermine you. You must be strong from this first day, and show no weakness. You are Magnus Hauk's son." Lara felt her voice quiver when she said his name. How long had he been dead now? Two hours? Three? She kissed her son's cheek. His face was smooth, not yet roughened by adulthood. Then she released him from her embrace.

"Where is my father's body?" Taj asked.

"It has been taken to the Farewell House to be processed for the ceremony," Lara answered her son. She found it difficult to look at him now, for Taj Hauk was his father's image. At thirteen he was already at least three inches taller than Lara. He had his father's long nose, high cheekbones and thin lips. Like Magnus his short hair was dark gold with lighter gold highlights, and his eyes his sire's turquoise-blue. Suddenly it hurt her heart to gaze upon him.

"I think we should use my uncle's new vessel," Taj said. "It will be considered unlucky now. Better to have it convey my father's body to the sea."

"I agree," Lara answered, keeping to herself the fact that she had already decided upon that course of action. Taj would always recall when he thought of this day that first decision he had made without her. She was proud he was beginning to think like a Dominus. And Magnus would be proud, too.

"My aunts must be informed before the official notification is cried," Taj remarked. "I would do it myself," he told his mother.

"I will transport you. Which would you visit first?" Lara asked.

"The eldest of my grandmother's children," Taj said. "At this time of day Narda will be in her hall working upon her tapestry while her husband, Tostig, plays an endless game of Herder with his eldest son."

Lara waved her hand. "So you are there," she said as her son disappeared.

He reappeared in Lord Tostig's hall, and the sight of the young boy stepping from a haze of green smoke caused his aunt Narda, the eldest of Lady Persis's children, to shriek with surprise and drop the needle she had been plying.

"Nephew!" she scolded him. "Could you not come to visit in a more conventional manner? This magical transport you have effected is most disconcerting."

"I come to bring you tragic news, Aunt," Taj began.

Lady Narda shrieked again, but this time it was a sound of distress. *"Mother,"* she cried, a hand going to her heart.

"Nay, my grandmother is in good health," Taj reassured her. "It is my father who was today killed on Captain Corrado's new ship when the main mast they were raising snapped, and crushed both my uncle and my father. Corrado will live. My father did not. The Farewell Ceremony is in three days as custom demands. I have claimed the right of inheritance. I am now your new Dominus."

His aunt stared at him both shocked and surprised. Then she burst into fulsome tears. "My poor, dear brother," she sobbed, but her tears were only partly sorrowful. She had not been close with her younger, only brother. Then as suddenly as they had begun her tears ceased, and she said, "You are very young to rule Terah, Nephew. You will need the guidance of men like my husband."

"My father's Farewell Ceremony will be held at the castle in three days as custom requires," Taj said, ignoring his aunt's remark. "Now I must go and inform my aunt Aselma of this news. Mother!" And he was gone from Tostig and Narda's hall in another burst of pale green smoke.

"He is too young to rule," Narda said to her husband, who had heard all, but said nothing while Taj was with them. "You must make certain you are chosen to be the boy's regent. My sister, Aselma, will certainly be encouraging her husband, Armen, to the position. And he dotes upon her. He will do anything to see she is happy. If worst comes to worst we can share the regency, but you must be first as I am the elder. I will not have Aselma and Armen lording it over us. You know how she is." Narda's deep blue eyes were concerned. She was an attractive woman who had been some years her brother's elder. Her dark blond hair was beginning to show streaks of silver.

"It is possible that Magnus made other arrangements," Tostig said in his quiet and pleasant voice. "We only know your brother is dead. We do not know if he lingered before he died, nor can we know if he had previously made arrangements in case of his early demise. I would not advise you and your sister get into a power struggle over the young Dominus. At least not before we know all the facts. And there is the Domina to consider, my love. You are not foolish enough to think that Lara would allow anyone to interfere with her son's rule." He was a gentleman of medium height and build, with fading brown hair, and mild blue-gray eyes that peered out on his world through a pair of wire-rimmed spectacles.

"Women have no place in governance," Narda said primly.

Her husband smiled. "I am not certain that now is so, my love," Tostig answered.

Narda gasped. "My lord! What a radical thing to say," she exclaimed, shocked.

"Your brother valued his wife's counsel," he replied. "He told me countless times that there were decisions he could not have made without her. And often it was Lara who suggested the solutions to the various problems a Dominus faced, and needed to solve."

"Certainly he was teasing when he said such things," Narda responded.

"Now, my dear," Tostig said with a smile, "there is no doubt that Magnus loved Lara, but he was not a man to misrepresent the facts. If he said his wife advised him, and gave him answers he could not find, then she did. I have often wondered why women are considered incapable of rule when they so obviously rule their homes, and do it well. Is not a kingdom just an extension of one's home?" He patted her hand.

"Sometimes you absolutely confuse me, my lord," Narda said. "But I love you nonetheless. Very well. We will wait to see what happens. But we must leave tomorrow for the castle if we are to be there in time for my brother's Farewell." Her blue eyes filled with tears. "We were not close," she said with a sigh. "But he was my blood, and always kind to me, and to our children. Poor Mother! She will be heartbroken. I suppose Aselma knows by now."

Aselma and her husband, Armen, had been eating their evening meal when Taj appeared in their hall. They blinked in surprise, but then Aselma waved her nephew forward inviting him to join them. "It's roast boar, Nephew," she said. "It has been marinated in apple cider and clove." Aselma was a plump woman who had always had a penchant for good food. Younger than Narda, but older than her brother, she had rosy cheeks, a head of blond hair that time seemed not to have faded and the same bright blue eyes as her siblings.

"I thank you for your hospitality, Aunt," the boy said, "but I am the bearer of sad tidings."

Like her elder sister had, Aselma cried out, "Mother!" as her hand flew to her plump bosom.

"Nay, it is my father, Aunt. He was killed this morning when the main spar from Captain Corrado's ship broke as it was being set into place. The Farewell Ceremony is in three days' time."

"You are the Dominus," Aselma said quickly.

"I am," Taj responded.

"You are too young," she said.

"But I am Dominus," Taj repeated. Then he bowed

to her, saying, "You are invited to the castle with your family to pay your respects to my father. Now I will leave you. Mother!" And he was gone.

"You must be regent!" Aselma said to Armen.

"If it will please you, my love," her husband replied.

"We must leave tomorrow for the castle," Aselma said as she cut herself another slice of the roast boar and began to eat it. "Narda will certainly be trying to get there ahead of us, and Tostig is too mild a man to be regent."

"There may already be a regent chosen," Armen murmured to his wife.

"Nonsense!" Aselma declared. "Magnus was young. He would have hardly expected to die in an accident. It is unlikely he had made any arrangements at all."

"What of the Domina?" Armen asked.

"What about her?" Aselma said. "She was his wife, nothing more. And she is faerie to boot. I thank the heavens that of the three children she bore my brother two have no magic in them at all. Zagiri is a lovely girl, and Taj as sensible a Terahn as any despite his foreign blood."

"And Marzina?" Armen said with a wicked smile.

Aselma shuddered delicately considering her large frame. "Do not mention that brat to me, husband. She is a wicked creature if there ever was one. Look what she did to my cat. It was terrible!"

He laughed. "It was partly your fault, my love. You said in her presence that you wished you could keep

Fluffy forever, for you loved her so. But you did want to keep her from birding in your garden, for the birdsong delighted you, as well. Marzina was but attempting to please you."

"She turned my cat to stone as it sat among the roses, Armen!" Aselma said, outraged. "She is a dreadful child!"

He laughed again. "There was no harm done, my love. Lara restored the beast."

"It has never been the same since," Aselma grumbled.

"But no longer birds in your garden," he remarked.

Aselma sniffed. "I do not care to discuss my niece," she said. "And tomorrow we leave at the break of day for the castle. You will be regent if I have anything to say about it, my husband."

"You will not," he murmured so softly that she did not hear him, but his gray eyes were considering as he wondered if his late brother-in-law had made any arrangements for his only son in the event of an unforeseen emergency. He rubbed his bald pate slowly, thoughtfully. As much as he loved his wife Armen did not wish the responsibility of a regency, and he suspected that neither did Tostig. They were both contented landowners with grown children. They were moving, slowly of course, toward old age. This was no time to be saddled with the responsibilities of a government, a nation, a people. It might have been better if things had remained the way they once were, and the men of Terah did not hear the voices of the women. Both his wife and his sister-in-law were always saying that women must be subservient to their men, and yet both of them were supremely ambitious women. It was an interesting conundrum. He wondered if his nephew realized the trouble he had left in his wake.

Taj, however, had returned to the castle as evening was slipping into night. He suddenly felt weary, and saddened beyond anything he had ever known. He was thirteen years old, and he was suddenly responsible for Terah and its people. "I cannot do it," he said aloud to himself, and his young shoulders slumped as he stood alone in his mother's dayroom. He felt tears pricking his eyelids.

"It does indeed seem more than one lad can bear," a sympathetic voice agreed.

"My lord Kaliq," Taj exclaimed as the great Shadow Prince stepped from the gloom. "What am I to do? I cannot be Dominus! I am but a boy yet."

The Shadow Prince came forward, and put a comforting arm about Taj. "Let us sit, my lord Dominus," he said as he led the boy to a settee. They sat. "You are your father's son, Taj Hauk. And your mother's son, as well. You have no magic in you despite your bloodlines, but you do have the strength of will that certain mortals have. It is instinctive in people like you. You knew just what to say to your aunts this day, and you did not permit their words to trouble you. You comforted your grandmother. You have already begun taking charge as the man of the family must do.

"There will be some who say you are not old enough to rule. You will not hear their voices, for mortals like that are quick to complain, but slow to put forth solutions. At your birth it was decided that this responsibility be set upon your shoulders at this moment in time, my lord Taj, even as the instant of your father's death was set out when he was born. And your father was a wise man. He refused to let go of the life force until he had set forth his wishes for you."

"My mother is to rule for me," Taj said, low.

"No, my lord Dominus, *you* are to rule. But you will do so under your mother's guidance. Her wisdom is great and she respects the customs of Terah. She will never permit it to appear as if you are not in total charge. And in a few years you will be, for you are intelligent, and will learn quickly. Already today you have realized that your uncle's ship is best used as your father's funerary vessel. It was a wise decision," the Shadow Prince complimented the boy.

"I did, didn't I?" Taj remembered proudly.

"Indeed, my lord Dominus, you did," Kaliq said. "Now, if you will permit me to direct you, I think you must go to your chamber where you will find a small meal waiting, for you must keep up your strength. Then you will sleep."

"I will bid my mother good-night first," Taj said.

"I am pleased by the respect you show her," the

Shadow Prince replied. "I will bid you good-night now, my lord." And with a bow Kaliq disappeared back into the shadows of the dayroom.

Taj went to the door of his mother's bedchamber and knocked. Hearing her voice bid him enter, he did, and went directly to her. "I have spoken with my father's two sisters," he said. "They both said I am too young to rule."

Lara smiled almost grimly. "I am certain they have pretensions of a regency, but I suspect their husbands have not. They will be on their way to the castle in the morning, but I shall slow their travels, for I am in no mood to cope with Narda and Aselma."

"My father said how it must be," Taj answered her. "I heard him as did others."

"And it will be as Magnus Hauk directed us with his dying breath," Lara told her son. "But I will still cause the rain to fall tomorrow, and the road to muddy. A day's trip shall become two. They will reach us the night before the Farewell Ceremony."

"Kaliq said that everything has happened as it should," Taj told his mother. "He said my father's fate and mine were decided upon the day we were born."

"Did he?" Lara sighed. "I suppose he is right. He is always right, damn him!"

"Will he help us, Mother?" Taj wanted to know.

"If we need him," she replied.

"Does my grandmother Ilona know of my father's death?" the boy asked.

"Aye. While you were gone I went to her," Lara responded. She did not tell her son that her mother, the Queen of the Forest Faeries, had been less than sympathetic.

"Sooner or later your mortal would have died," Ilona said sanguinely. "Better it happen now than you be forced to see him become old, and as white-haired and grizzled as his own mother is. You have had your children by the men you have loved, Lara. Now for goodness' sake embrace your faerie heritage fully, and take no more husbands. Lovers are far more satisfactory, and so easily discarded. A husband is generally nothing more than an encumbrance."

"Is that what you think of Thanos?" Lara asked of her stepfather.

Ilona's laughter tinkled gaily as she tossed her pale golden hair, and her green eyes twinkled. "Gracious no! Thanos is the perfect husband. He sired a son and heir upon me, and then found an interest that keeps him away from me most of the time. And bless him, he takes lovers to feed his appetite for passion. But unless you wed a man of the magical realm you would not have such latitude. So better you just take lovers from now on, my daughter."

"Try to be respectful when you come to the Farewell Ceremony, Mother," Lara had said dryly. "If not for my sake, for Taj's."

"Oh never fear, I shall be properly mournful. Magnus Hauk was, after all, a good mortal, and he loved you completely even overlooking your time with Kol, the Twilight Lord," Ilona said.

Lara had departed her mother's home at that. Now she looked at her young son. "Your grandmother Ilona was shocked by the accident, and she will be here for the Farewell Ceremony, Taj," Lara told her son.

The boy nodded. "I am weary," he told her.

"Go and eat, and then sleep," Lara said to him. "I will see you in the morning, my darling. While it is my duty to make all the preparations for the Farewell Ceremony, I should appreciate you being by my side, and approving my actions." Lara put an arm about her son and kissed him softly on his cheek. "Good night, my dearest Taj."

The boy hugged her hard. "Good night, Mother," he said and then left her.

Alone. She was alone. How long had Magnus Hauk been dead now? Ten hours? Eleven? Lara felt the tears come again. She had been wed almost twenty years to Magnus Hauk. Her life had become a comfortable round of seasons that had blended into one year, and then another, and another. She had never been bored, and while she waited for the destiny foretold for her to unfold she had been happy. She had been content in his arms, and in this life. Oh, there had been an occasional adventure. But Magnus Hauk was always there waiting when the adventure was over. But now she was alone. Lara sank down upon their bed, and wept bitterly once more.

KALIQ WATCHED HER from the shadows, and fought back his urge to go to her. To take her into his arms and comfort her. But now was not the time. She needed to vent her grief in this lonely privacy, and then reach deep down into the well of strength he knew she possessed. She would need to be strong for her son. She would need to be strong to convince Magnus Hauk's family and the religious community of Terah that her late husband's wishes must be followed at all costs. She was the only one who could aid the young Dominus so that when the danger came he would be strong enough to withstand it.

Still her weeping clawed at his heart. It was rare that a Shadow Prince fell deeply in love, but Kaliq of the Shadows did love the faerie woman, Lara, with every fiber of his being. He had for years. She was his single vulnerability. He wished he might transport them immediately to his desert palace of Shunnar to console her, but, cloaked in his invisibility, he instead stepped near to the bed where she now lay sobbing with her grief. Moving his hand gently above her body from her head to her toes, he set her into a deep and dreamless sleep. Her sadness would not abate, but at least come the morning she would awaken rested, able to face the responsibilities that were now hers.

Her body relaxed. The pitiful sounds of her mourning suddenly ceased. Her breathing grew regular and even. Kaliq smiled to himself as he stood next to Lara's bed watching her sleep. He considered what would happen next. Hetar, of course, would be involved somehow once word of Magnus Hauk's death reached them, but how quickly he was not certain. He had already set a watch to see if any among the tiny faerie post folk was a spy, for he was certain there would be one or two subverted by Hetar's rulers.

Kaliq frowned thinking of Hetar. They had been making great strides toward the equality of its citizenry until recently. The two Shadow Princes currently serving on the High Council had reported that something was disturbing the rhythm of Hetar's being of late. They had not yet been able to pinpoint it, but they were listening. Still, even unsubstantiated rumors had been scarce. A sure sign that something wicked was being brewed, Kaliq thought. He would speak with Lara soon about this latest development. Neither Terah nor the young Dominus needed to be dragged into Hetar's problems whatever they turned out to be. The great Shadow Prince bent and kissed Lara's cheek as she lay on her side, her pale golden hair tousled and spread across the pillows. *Sleep well, my love,* he told her in the silent language of magical folk. Then he was quickly gone from the chamber.

When the morning came Lara awoke. Her heart ached. With a sigh she encased it in ice. She could show no weakness now. She was faerie, and yet magic had little to do with what she was about to undertake. She arose from her bed feeling well rested, to her surprise. She had dreamed no dreams in the night. Indeed nothing had disturbed her slumbers despite her great grief.

How had that happened? And then she smiled to herself. Kaliq, bless him! She had sensed him as she wept for Magnus Hauk, but had not wanted his company. He had understood, of course, and had not intruded upon her physically. But he had, she was certain, given her the gift of restful sleep and Lara was grateful to him for it.

"Mila," Lara called to her serving woman. "I am ready to bathe."

Mila appeared looking properly somber. "They are ready for you, Domina. Shall I lay out your garments?"

"Aye. Does everyone in the castle have purple mourning bands for their arms?" Lara wanted to know.

"Aye, Domina, and there are enough for any who come," Mila informed her lady.

Lara nodded, and then went to her private bath. The serving women were silent, and she was glad. She was not quite ready to deal with anyone else's sorrow but her own. But the moment she left her own apartments it would be a different matter. When she had completed her ablutions, she returned to her bedchamber and got dressed. Mila had laid out a pale lilac-colored gown trimmed at its round neck, and the cuffs of its round sleeves with an embroidered band of gold threads and tiny violet crystals. The serving woman fastened the deep purple mourning band about her mistress's upper right arm as Lara slipped her feet into her flat-soled lilac kidskin slippers. Sitting, she let Mila brush her long hair, and then weave it into a thick single plait. Then, standing again, she left her apartment, hurrying to the small family dining chamber where she discovered her five children and her daughter-in-law awaiting her.

"Dillon! Cinnia!" she exclaimed with genuine delight.

Dillon immediately enfolded his mother into his embrace and kissed her cheek. "Are you all right?" he asked tenderly. "This has to have been a terrible shock for you, Mother. I am so sorry. Magnus was a good stepfather to me. We came as soon as Kaliq came to tell us. He says that Grandmother and Cirillo will be here later today."

Lara felt a brief moment of weakness, but then she returned her son's kiss. "My faerie heart has turned to ice, Dillon," she told him. "I cannot believe any of this although I know it is true. Yes, it has been an awful shock."

"Tell me what happened?" he said gently.

And she told him quietly, dispassionately, of how Magnus Hauk had died.

Dillon said nothing. He just nodded.

"Magnus made them all swear as he lay dying that they would honor my rule," Lara told her firstborn. "It shall, of course, appear as if Taj is ruling for you know how the Terahns are about women. I do not wish to change their customs, but Magnus knew what would happen if he ordered a regency."

Dillon laughed briefly. "Aye," he agreed. "But how will you placate those who see themselves grasping the reins of Terahn power?"

"I intend forming a special group of advisors for the

new Dominus," Lara said. "It is possible some of them may have good ideas, but of course the last word, the final decision, is that of the Dominus."

"Clever," Dillon agreed, "but how will they take to having a woman overruling them, Mother?"

"I will remain as much in the background as possible. Marzina says I will be a Shadow Queen. It must appear publicly as if Taj is in firm control of Terah at all times," Lara explained. "And eventually the council of advisors will actually forget I am even there which is what I want. Magnus's elder sisters will, of course, want their husbands involved. And I want Corrado. I think it is better to keep this group small and manageable, don't you? No one but the Dominus's three uncles."

"Agreed!" her eldest said. "Will you tell Tostig and Armen the truth?"

"Aye, I will. Whether they tell their wives is, of course, up to them," Lara said with a mischievous twinkle in her green eyes. "Now if you are through questioning me let us sit down and eat. We have a busy day ahead of us. I must have everything done by the morrow, for it will be my duty to sit at the foot of Magnus's bier and accept the condolences of all who come until the burning vessel upon which he will take his final voyage is sent off to the sea." She turned to her daughter-in-law. "Thank you for coming, Cinnia." Then she looked to her own daughters, and gave them a small smile. "We are together, my daughters, and that is all that is important for now. Taj, take your place at the head of the family table. You are not just the Dominus of Terah now. You are also the master of this household. I will sit in my usual place opposite the Dominus until the day he takes a bride. You, Dillon, will be at your half brother's right hand."

"And I will sit at my twin's left hand," Marzina spoke up before her mother might say another word.

"You are the youngest of us all," Zagiri noted, but she did not complain.

"We all share blood," Marzina replied, "but I share with Taj what none of you shared with him. I shared our mother's womb."

"Sit in your place, Marzina," Lara instructed her daughter quietly. "Anoush and Zagiri, sit on either side of me, and Cinnia will sit next to her husband. Now let us thank the Great Creator for Magnus Hauk, and the time we had with him, and the wonderful memories we share. Let us thank him that we are all together," Lara said, and everyone in the chamber including the servants bowed their heads.

CHAPTER TWO

MAGNUS HAUK'S TWO older sisters arrived at the castle of the Dominus within moments of each other. Their ships raced each other up the fjord, beneath the morning sunshine, Narda's vessel reaching the stone dock but a moment before Aselma's.

"It is as it should be," Narda told Tostig. "I am, after all, the eldest of our mother's children." She walked regally down the gangway onto the pier. "Hurry! I want to get to the lift before my sister does." Narda attempted to appear as if she were just strolling toward her destination. Tostig had to take large steps to keep up with her.

The Dominus's castle was built into and above the great cliffs that bordered the fjord. Of dark stone, it was surprisingly graceful and beautiful for such a large structure. Its tower peaks of gray slate soared high into the bright blue sky. Greenery trailed over, and grew up along its terrace walls behind which were beautiful gardens. At the end of the quay was an entrance into the cliffs.

"Look at her! Pretending she isn't practically running so she can reach our nephew before we do," Aselma grumbled to Armen as their own ship was tied fast. "Can they not hurry with that damned gangway?"

Armen hid his smile, for it wouldn't do to have his wife throw a temper tantrum now. She and her sister might scheme all they wanted. What was going to happen next had already been set into motion. He was as shocked as everyone was at the sudden and certainly unexpected death of his brother-in-law, but he instinctively knew that the reins of power in Terah were not meant to rest in either his or Tostig's hands. Silently he followed his wife down onto the stone pier and walked toward the castle.

Aselma and Armen walked quickly through the entry but the wooden gate to the lift was closed. They could see the bare hairy legs of the Mountain Giant drawing the wooden platform up to the castle. They could see the bottom of the platform, and Aselma's sharp ears could hear her sister's voice as the lift rose higher.

"You could have waited for us!" she shouted, tilting her head up.

Narda's head looked down over the platform's rail. "Is that you, Aselma?" she called out in a deceptively sweet voice. "I didn't realize you were that close behind us. It seemed to me your vessel was still in the middle of the fjord when we disembarked. I'll meet you in the family hall, dear."

"Old cow!" Aselma muttered.

Above them the lift came to a stop, and then it was quickly lowered again. Aselma and her husband stepped onto the platform, which was raised once again to the correct level of the castle. The couple exited into the brightly lit corridor, following it to the family hall. Entering, they found Narda sobbing in her mother's arms. Not to be outdone in her grief Aselma screamed, and ran to her parent weeping. Tostig and Armen shook hands, and would have stepped into the background but that Lara, coming into the chamber, beckoned them from it.

In the corridor again she greeted them cordially. "Please come with me, my lords. There is a matter I wish to discuss with you."

They followed her down another hallway and into a beautiful library with tall arched windows looking out over the fjord. There they found their other brother-in-law, Corrado, Sirvat and the young Dominus awaiting. They greeted one another. Both Tostig and Armen noted that their sister-in-law looked drawn with her grief. Lara was, it seemed to them, as beautiful as ever. Her faerie green eyes, however, were swollen with her sorrow.

"My lords," she said to them, "I have asked you here because you should know what my husband's dying wishes were. Corrado, Sirvat, Lady Persis and my son can attest to the truth of my words."

"We should never doubt your word, lady," Tostig said.

Lara smiled. "Thank you, my brother, but Magnus has done something that will shock you. He named me regent for our son."

To her surprise Armen chuckled. "Shocking by

Terahn custom, I will agree, but knowing you both it is not so unexpected." Tostig nodded in agreement.

Lara nodded, amused. Armen was a far cleverer fellow than he was given credit for by those who knew him. "Taj is certainly too young and inexperienced to rule Terah, my lords, as he will tell you himself. But Terah must believe that he is in full charge, counseled by wise advisors. While I will rule Terah from behind my son's throne, I am asking the Dominus's three uncles to serve as the Dominus's Council. You understand that my word is the final word in all matters, but for the sake of continued tranquility in Terah this will not be public knowledge. I'm sure that both Narda and Aselma will be pleased at this honor you have been given," she concluded, a small twinkle in her eyes.

"My lady Domina, you have saved both Armen and me from much distress with our wives," Tostig said with an exaggerated sigh of relief.

Lara could not contain her laughter, but then she said, "I cannot blame them for being ambitious for their husbands, my lords. But Terah can only have one ruler. You understand fully what I have told you. I alone will rule Terah for my son. His best interests, and those of Terah, are my priorities. I will not allow this to degenerate into an internecine family war which would surely spill over into Terah itself. Our strength lies in our unity, for be certain, my lords, that when Hetar learns of what has happened they will be considering ways and means of conquering us. The Lord High Ruler Jonah is no fool.

He has been to Terah. He knows of its riches. The fever for acquisition runs in Hetar's blood. In their eyes Terah is a great prize."

"Lady Domina," Armen said quietly, "Tostig and I are content being landowners. Corrada we all know loves his ships, and being captain of all captains. Let all of Terah believe we rule for our nephew. We gladly leave that onerous task to you. You are far wiser and more sophisticated than we are. You will know how to hold Hetar at bay."

"What will you tell your wives?" Lara asked Tostig and Armen.

"Nothing but that we three are the Dominus's Council," Tostig said emphatically. "If either of us says more than that Aselma and Narda will quarrel over which of us should have precedence so they may have precedence over each other. Nay, Armen, Corrado and I are equals by the Dominus's command. But what if the Lady Persis should tell her older daughters of Magnus Hauk's dying wishes?"

"She will not," Lara said. "The Dominus Taj Hauk has personally commanded that she keep the secret of his father's request that there be peace among us. Persis is no fool. She knows the dangers involved in such an indiscretion."

"And she is used to obeying a male's orders," Sirvat said mischievously. "My nephew's age matters little to her. He is a male, and he is the Dominus."

Lara smiled at her sister-in-law's observation. "Then

it is settled, my lords. The first day of each month I will bring you by means of my magic to the castle, and we will meet. That will allay any suspicions that your wives may have in this matter. Now, let us join the Lady Persis."

They rejoined Magnus Hauk's mother, and her two older daughters. Sirvat went to her elder sisters, kissing each one and greeting them. Lara waited for Aselma and Narda to acknowledge her, but only when Taj spoke sternly to his aunts did they do so.

"You have not greeted my mother, my father's widow," the young Dominus said.

"Our brother is gone. What importance can this faerie woman have in Terah now?" Aselma said rudely. "Will she not go from us soon?"

Lara was astounded by the woman's words. She had never been particularly friendly with her husband's two older sisters, but the antipathy in Aselma's words surprised her.

"Where would I go?" she asked Aselma in an icy voice. "Terah is my home. My son is its ruler. Until he weds I am yet the Domina."

"Aye! Still you have no real importance here now. My brother is dead. But the boy is too young to rule!" Aselma quickly replied. "He needs the guidance of an older man. He must not be corrupted by you as Magnus was. Women are not meant to rule."

"My son has already in his young wisdom chosen his three uncles to be the Dominus's Council," Lara responded. "I will bring them here to the castle at least once monthly to meet with my son and conduct the business of government."

"Once a month?" Aselma screeched. "One of us should at least live here at the castle to guide the boy each day."

"And I suppose you think you should be the one chosen," Narda cried angrily.

"Cease your arguments, Aunts," Taj Hauk said. "I do not choose to have either of you moving into my mother's house, and this castle is indeed my mother's home. Look to my uncle's injuries. My mother's magic has managed to heal his bones, but his bruises will take weeks to heal. She left them so that Terahns might see that he, too, was injured. His broken heart may never heal. Two days ago my father was killed. Tomorrow we will bid him farewell. If you cannot keep from your petty quarreling in these sorrowful times then I will send you home today." The boy had drawn himself up to his full height. His turquoise-blue eyes were fierce with his determination.

Narda and Aselma were suddenly properly cowed into obedience. The two sisters bowed their heads. Like their mother they accepted male dominance.

"Greet my mother properly now," Taj Hauk said, and they did. "You are all dismissed now but for the Domina. I will see you at the evening meal." He waved them off with a firm hand.

When the chamber was empty Lara turned to her

son. "I can see you have already learned from your father," she said.

The boy grinned. "Father would have been harder on them for their rudeness to you, but I understand they are grieving, too. Still, I know that had I not shown a firm hand with them at once their behavior would have escalated. They are old-fashioned, but the truth is they are both as ambitious as any for power. They shall not, however, have mine."

"Nor should anyone, my son," Lara told him. "I know there are many who think that I ruled over your father. I did not. But your father was willing to listen to what I had to say, Taj. And he was not ashamed to take my advice when it was good. I hope one day you will give your wife that same courtesy."

"In many cases," her son answered, "you made him believe your advice was his."

Lara smiled. "You are clever to have seen that," she replied. "He never did."

Taj chuckled. "Of course he didn't, Mother. He loved you beyond all else."

The tears came swiftly and unbidden at the boy's words. Lara turned away quickly, wiping the evidence of her grief with her two hands.

"Mother! I am sorry," her son cried. "I shall not speak of my father again."

"Nay!" Lara said. "Nay! You must always speak of him, for as long as people speak of Magnus Hauk he is yet with us. His memory must remain, Taj. He was a great Dominus. Only a great man would have listened to me when I realized the men of Terah had been cursed by Usi. Only a great man would have had the courage to fly in the face of Terahn tradition and trust a woman to correct a bad situation, but your father did. His loss is so new, my son. And I will weep for him easily now. In time I will grow stronger, and my cold faerie heart will be hard once more. I have encased it in ice already, but the ice seems to melt at the mere mention of Magnus Hauk." She brushed the tears that continued to flow away again. "I suppose it is that small bit of me that is mortal." She sighed, and gave a watery little chuckle.

The boy put an arm about her shoulders. "It pleases me to see you grieve so for my father," he said.

Lara almost laughed aloud at Taj's pronouncement. It was just the sort of thing Magnus Hauk would have said to her. "You are truly your father's son," she told him as he hugged her close.

"You must rest now, Mother, for tomorrow will be a big day for all of Terah," Taj said to her, but she shook her head.

"Nay. I will go and don the finest robes I have. Then I will sit at the foot of your father's bier in the Great Hall of the castle until the morrow. The people have been coming all day to pay their respects. We must open the doors to them soon," Lara told him. "It is tradition that a Domina sit at the foot of her husband's coffin and greet his people as they come to mourn him. I will not neglect that tradition." She kissed Taj's cheek. "Come into the hall while I am there, and greet the people."

"I will," he promised her.

She left him, and went to her own chamber where Mila, her serving woman, was waiting for her. Lara was surprised to see that Mila had laid out a simple white silk robe, its round neckline and long full sleeves edged in shining gold threads. "You think this appropriate?" she asked the servant.

Mila nodded. "He has been dressed in his finest and richest robes, Domina. You in a simple gown will show all of Terah your respect for Magnus Hauk by your lack of ostentation. It is the Terahn way, Domina, but as you have never attended to the death of a family member before you would not know that. All of them, even the young Dominus, will dress plainly so as not to take anything away from Magnus Hauk, for this is his time."

Lara felt the tears coming again. She collapsed briefly into a chair and wept softly. Finally drawing a long, deep breath she arose. "I will bathe first, Mila."

"Of course, Domina," the serving woman replied.

The women in the bath were ready for their mistress. Lara was too weary and sad for conversation, and they understood. When she had finished her ablutions she returned to her bedchamber, where Mila helped her dress and brushed out her long golden hair. The servant fit a narrow gold band about her mistress's head. The band had a small bloodred ruby in its center. Mila lastly fit a pair of golden kidskin slippers on

Lara's dainty feet. "Stand up, Domina, and let me see if all is right," she said.

Lara stood. The silk in the loose gown felt cool against her legs. It would be a comfortable gown in which to sit, she thought. Turning, she looked at herself in the tall mirror. It was indeed a modest gown, and if Terahn custom demanded it then she was content to wear it. "Tell the majordomo that the doors to the hall are to be opened to the people at the noon hour."

"I'll go immediately, and you eat something from that tray." Mila pointed to the sideboard where the tray sat. Then she hurried out.

Lara lifted the napkin covering the tray. Then she let it fall back again. Her appetite was practically nonexistent at this moment. She knew in time that she would eat again, but right now she could not entertain the thought. She did sip a cup of Frine. Then, leaving her apartments, Lara went to the Great Hall, where Magnus Hauk's body now lay in state. The hall was empty, to her relief, for the coffin and its bier were newly arrived. A single small plain wooden throne had been placed at her husband's feet.

Lara walked to where her husband lay. They had indeed dressed him in robes of incredible richness such as she had never seen. She did not recognize them at all. From where had they come? Lara looked upon the body. It looked like Magnus Hauk, and yet it didn't. That spark that had given her mortal husband life was no longer there. His body was but a shell, and Lara sensed if she touched it it might shatter. Reaching out, she straightened one of his short golden curls. His eyes were closed, veiling forever the bright turquoise-blue of his wonderful eyes.

"Ah, my love," she murmured softly. "It was a cruel and unfair end. What shall I do without you?" Then she bent and kissed his cold lips before taking her place in the throne at his feet. She could hear the bells in the castle's clock tower tolling the noon hour, and as the last strike sounded the great wooden doors to the hall opened. Lara sat straight up in her chair.

Slowly, hesitantly, the first of the mourners entered respectfully. Their eyes noted the Domina who sat quietly on her throne at her husband's feet. Looks of approval passed between the people as they noted her simple garb, her swollen eyes. Many of them had never seen Magnus Hauk's faerie wife before this day, for Terah was a great land of plains, mountains and seven fjords all opening onto the Sea of Sagitta, but they had heard much good of her.

They had traveled from their scattered farms and villages when the word had reached them of Magnus Hauk's death. Many of them for two days, coming in from the countryside by foot and in carts. Sailing up the Dominus's Fjord in their small boats. They had waited outside the castle for their opportunity to mourn their ruler. They did not know the Dominus personally, but they did know that in his reign there had been peace, and prosperity, that in the reign of Magnus Hauk the curse of Usi had been lifted from them. It was public opinion that Magnus Hauk had been a good ruler.

Lara sat for the next several hours in silence as the mourners filed by her husband's bier. Afternoon slipped into evening and evening into night. There was a small stir as Lady Persis entered the Great Hall. The crowd parted for her as she made her way to where Lara sat. Embracing her daughter-in-law she said softly, "You are a Domina to be proud of, Lara. I am glad that my son was so fortunate in his wife."

"Sit by me for a time," Lara invited Lady Persis. "You are his mother, and you once wore the Domina's crown." She moved from the center of her throne to make a place for the old woman.

Lady Persis's eyes filled with quick tears. Nodding, she accepted the invitation so graciously tendered and sat beside Lara for the next two hours. An audible murmur of approval had arisen from the mourners at the sight of the two women seated on the single throne at the foot of the coffin. Finally the young Dominus entered the hall, and escorted his grandmother out.

The night deepened. And then among the mourners there appeared familiar faces as the clan chiefs of the New Outlanders came into the hall. Liam of the Fiacre, Vanko of the Piaras, Imre of the Tormod, Roan of the Aghy, Floren of the Blathma, Rendor of the Felan, Torin of the Gitta and Accius of the Devyn. Floren had brought with him a magnificent display of flowers from his own fields, which he now set about the bier. Lara wept at the tribute, unable to help herself. With Magnus's permission she had brought these clans from Hetar where they had been preyed upon by the government there. They had been resettled on the far side of the Emerald Mountains where there had been no inhabitants. The clans of the New Outlands had made the land their own, and had been ever grateful and loyal to Magnus Hauk for his generosity. Now they came to mourn him. The native-born Terahns again nodded at one another favorably.

The night began to wane, and during a brief lull Mila came bringing a cup of Frine Anoush had mixed with strengthening herbs for her mother. Lara was numb with her weariness and sorrow. She went to wave Mila away but then the voice of her guardian spirit, Ethne, chided her gently in the silent language from the crystal star she inhabited that hung around Lara's slender neck.

You are far from death yourself, my child. You must keep your courage high at this time. You have done well so far but a new day is dawning, and at its end you will bid a final farewell to Magnus Hauk. But with every ending comes a new beginning. You know this to be so. Now drink the Frine that your daughter has prepared for you.

Lara took the carved silver goblet from Mila. "Thank you, and tell Anoush I thank her, as well," she said. Then, putting the cup to her lips, Lara slowly drank its contents. Almost immediately she felt her spirit lighten, and the strength pouring back into her. She almost smiled. Anoush did not have her magic, but she certainly had her own where herbs were concerned. That and the special sight she possessed made the girl very special. But Anoush had a fragile spirit that concerned her mother.

The sun rose. It would be a beautiful day. The crowds of mourners began to thicken once again. And then as the bell tower struck the midday hour sixteen men came to carry the open coffin of the Dominus down to the ship that would carry him on his final journey. The men chosen as coffin bearers were the eight clan chiefs of the New Outlands; Magnus Hauk's four brothers-in-law Corrado, Tostig, Armen and his wife's brother, Prince Cirillo of the Forest Faeries; the great Shadow Prince Kaliq; Master Ing, Corrado's older brother; Fulcrum, Chief of the Jewel Gnomes; and Gultopp, Chief of the Ore gnomes. Each was dressed in deep blue and sky-blue striped breeches topped with tunics of grass-green and short capes fashioned from cloth of gold and cloth of silver. The colors represented the sea that surrounded Terah, the sky above it and the green of its mountains and plains. The cape colors depicted the sun and the moon that shone on Terah. Beside each of the coffin bearers walked a representative from the villages on the seven fjords.

The bearers hoisted the coffin onto their shoulders. Then, led by Lara and the young Dominus, Taj Hauk, they walked with measured cadence to the lift. The wooden boards of it creaked as they all stepped on it.

Then the Mountain Giant who operated the lift began to slowly lower the platform. It was so heavy they could hear him grunting with his effort, but finally the platform came to a smooth halt. The coffin bearers stepped from the lift and, led by Lara and Taj Hauk, moved with a dignified rhythm down the long stone quay to the vessel that was tethered at its end.

Lara hardly recognized the ship as the one that had killed her husband. The cracked main mast had been replaced by a straight new spar that was hung with fresh sails. They were not the lavender-colored sails that Terah's Captain of all Captains, Corrado, favored. These sails were deep purple with starbursts of silver and gold. It was a beautiful boat, and Corrado had personally overseen its construction. Its color was a sparkling white. The glass in its bow cabin window sparkled in the sunlight reflecting the water below it. Its brass railings were polished to a high sheen. And on the prow of the ship had been affixed the figure of a winged faerie in a lavender gown, the fabric of the garment carved to appear as if it were blowing in the wind.

The bearers solemnly marched up the gangway and set the coffin down on the deck midship. The stone quay had been lined with mourners. There were many others crowding the hillsides on both sides of the fjord. Waiting at the gangway had been Lady Persis and her three daughters, along with Lara's mother, Ilona, Queen of the Forest Faeries, and her consort, Thanos, Arik, High Priest from the Temple of the Great Creator, and his female counterpart, Kemina. Each reached out to touch the body in a final farewell as it passed them. Once the open casket bearing Magnus Hauk's body had been delivered to the vessel, those accompanying it left the ship. Lara and Taj came to escort Lady Persis back up into the castle. They would be hosting a feast in the Great Hall for all who had come to bid their Dominus goodbye.

In the Great Hall they celebrated the life of Magnus Hauk. Accius of the Devyn, whose people were bards, had written a saga of the Dominus's life. Now the New Outlander entertained everyone gathered by singing his creation. He sang of the Terahns who believed their women mute, and had never heard a woman's voice until Lara arrived. He sang of how she had captured the heart of Magnus Hauk, and lifted the curse of Usi, which had really been on its men, and not the women. He sang of the Dominus's generosity in saving the clan families from enslavement in Hetar; of how Magnus Hauk's heart and mind had come to be open to change; of how he had become a strong leader for his people. He had been a good son to his mother; a good brother to his sisters; a sire to all the children who called him Father; and a great lover and husband to his faerie woman wife. Now the era of Magnus Hauk was ended. Accius of the Devyn sang of how Magnus Hauk's son, the Dominus Taj, was a young man of great promise. A true tribute to his noble father.

"May he rule in peace and prosperity as did his sire before him," Accius ended his tribute, bowing first to the young Dominus, then his mother and the rest of the guests.

There was much appreciative clapping as the Devyn bard took his seat again.

"There is something I must do before we conclude this," Lara said softly to her young son. "I will leave my image behind so that no one knows I am gone." She touched his cheek gently, and then was gone. Materializing first in her own chambers, she took down her sword, Andraste, which hung above the hearth. Then she reached for her staff, Verica. Verica had been away from her for a few years while he accompanied Lara's eldest son to the desert kingdom of the Shadow Princes. Kaliq had returned him to her when Dillon had gone to Belmair. Her two companions in her firm grasp, Lara magicked them into the stables, where she hurried to the stall of her great white stallion, Dasras. Browsing in his oat bucket, he looked up, recognizing her footsteps.

"Mistress, my condolences," he said, and bowed to her.

"Thank you," Lara said. "Now you three must go and pay your farewells to Magnus Hauk. He has sheltered you all these many years."

"Indeed," Dasras replied. "It is only right, Mistress."

"We must hurry, for his vessel will set sail at sunset," Lara told them. Then, grasping a handful of the stallion's thick, silvery-white mane, she vaulted onto his back, reaching for her sword and staff, which she had leaned against the stall wall.

There was no one in the stables as all were at the feast, but had there been no one would have been startled by the stable doors which opened before them. Lara rode out onto the stone quay, and up the gangway onto the deck of the ship. It bobbed gently in the flat sea about it. Lara slid off Dasras's back.

The stallion bent his head, and touched the forehead of the dead man with his velvety muzzle. "May your journey be a safe one, Magnus Hauk. May your destination be all that you could imagine. I thank you for your kindness and your generosity to me."

The wood staff, Verica, opened his eyes, staring down at the Dominus. *"Be at peace, mortal,"* he said.

Lara's sword, Andraste, began to sing softly, her ruby eyes glowing. Usually when Andraste sang it was in a deep voice, and her song was one of threatening terror and imminent doom to all who heard it. Now, however, the voice she sang with was sweeter than honey, her words reassuring. *"You have earned your place among those few especial mortals, Magnus Hauk, Dominus of Terah. Your progeny will honor your name forever. Walk in the light you have made yourself by your good deeds and your good heart. I bid you farewell!"*

Lara's eyes misted briefly. Andraste's tribute to Magnus Hauk had come from the very core of the magic weapon. Andraste did not suffer fools, or give praise lightly. "Thank you all," she told her closest companions. Then, using her magic, she sent them back to their places. Alone on the ship Lara sank to the deck next to the open coffin. "I have done everything that was expected of me, and more, my lord," she told him. "I am not Terahn born, but I have kept Terahn customs better than any Terahn. No one will question our son's blood, my love. And in these few days I have certainly seen how much like you he really is. Did you see how he put Narda and Aselma in their places?" She laughed softly. "He is pure mortal Terahn, Magnus. He will be a good Dominus, but I would have preferred it if he were older." She sighed. "I have prevented any challenge to Taj's rights by appointing our brothers-in-law as the Dominus's Council. They say they will leave me in peace to do what I must, but I wonder, Magnus. I wonder."

Lara reached out and touched her husband's lifeless face. "I do not think I can bear it without you, but I have to, don't I?" A tear slipped down her cheek. "Taj needs me, and so do Anoush, Zagiri and Marzina." She sighed again. "My mother warned me that giving my faerie heart to a mortal would bring me eventual sorrow. At least now you do not have to grow old while I remain as I am. Oh, Magnus! There wasn't enough time. There just wasn't enough time!" And Lara wept.

"You cannot stay here any longer." The voice of the Shadow Prince, Kaliq, pierced through her grief. "Your image is beginning to waver, and you will cause a panic if it disappears entirely. Your hall is full of mortal beings who are not used to your faerie magic, Lara, my love. Have mercy upon them, I beg you."

She looked up to see him standing by her side. "Nay,

I don't want them remembering Magnus Hauk's Farewell as the time his faerie wife disappeared before their eyes." She stood up. "Return!" she said and found herself back in the hall in her seat. Reaching out, she touched her son's cheek with her fingertips to let him know she was returned. "The sun is close to setting, my lord Dominus," she told him.

Taj Hauk stood up, and immediately the Great Hall grew silent. "It is time," he told them all. Then he stepped from the dais and led his mother from the High Board through the crowds in the large chamber.

"Give us a blessing, faerie woman," some dared to beg as they passed by, and when they did Lara would smile sweetly and say that they now had it.

"They love her," Lady Persis said to her daughters.

"I don't know why they should," Narda muttered.

"Nor I," Aselma agreed.

"It is because you do not know her," Sirvat told them. "If you did you would not be so spiteful, sisters."

"She bewitched our brother, and held him in her thrall, yet she could not save him from death," Aselma said bitterly.

"It is not within a faerie's powers to keep death away for long," Sirvat responded. "She did what she could so Magnus might make his last wishes known. And she healed my husband of grievous wounds."

"Well," Narda said, "at least our husbands will be in charge of directing our nephew's path. Terah will be as it has always been."

"Aye!" Aselma echoed.

"How ignorant you both are," Sirvat answered. "Terah will never be as it was. Not now that Hetar knows us. Magnus knew that, and was wise enough to raise a defense force to keep us strong and safe."

"And that would have never had to happen if *she* hadn't come here," Narda replied. "*She* has brought the misfortune of strangers upon us."

"If Lara hadn't come our men would still be deaf to our voices, although I imagine there are times Tostig would be happy not to hear your discontented carping," Sirvat said sharply. "Terah is the better for Lara. Our brother is gone, but she gave him a fine son who has taken his place as our Dominus. Now see if you can both cease your bitterness long enough to honor our brother as he leaves us."

"Your sister is correct in all she says," Lady Persis said quietly.

"What, Mother? Do you take Lara's side now?" Aselma wanted to know.

"When Lara came I will admit I was not happy, for I expected my son to wed a Terahn girl, but the truth is none suited him. Lara, however, did suit him. She has been a good wife to your brother, giving him children, and while she is bolder than Terahn women, it pleased your brother that she was. Look at all that has happened since his death three days ago. Could any Terahn-born Domina have acted more suitably, my daughters? She has honored the customs of this land scrupulously. I know now more than ever how fortunate my son was in his choice of a wife. Now cease your meanness."

Narda and Aselma were surprised by their mother's words. They grew silent, and now, joined by their husbands, came down from the castle and walked in procession to the great vessel whose sails had all been raised now. Arik, High Priest of the Temple of the Great Creator, came forward joined by the High Priestess from the Temple of the Daughters of the Great Creator, Kemina. They held their hands up to the evening sky.

"As death follows life, and night the day, we give thanks, Great Creator, for the life of Magnus Hauk," Arik said in a strong voice that carried throughout the entire crowd, and even across the fjord.

"For three days his essence has hovered near the body that housed it. It is now time for Magnus Hauk to begin his journey into the next life, Oh Great Creator," Kemina said, her own voice carrying well.

"May he be at peace, and leave us contented in the knowledge that in his time here he did well, and that the fruit of his loins will follow in his footsteps," Arik said. The High Priest presented the young Dominus with a flaming torch.

A small cry of surprise arose from the crowd when Taj Hauk handed the burning brand to his mother. A murmur of approval followed as Lara reached out to take her son's hand and place it on the hand that held the torch. Together they stepped forward setting the coffin of Magnus Hauk afire. Priests from the temple quickly came aboard to see that the entire ship was torched. Taj Hauk sliced through the ropes holding the boat to the stone quay. A light wind sprang up, and the flames began to leap higher as the vessel slipped out into the fjord and began to move downstream.

The young Dominus in the company of Corrado, the men of the family and specially chosen male guests would follow the ship out to sea, escorting it until it was burned to the waterline and sank. Lara invited the women of the family to return to the castle and watch the burning boat until it was no longer visible. They came, of course, but only Lara stood watching from a garden terrace until the flames were no longer visible. She struggled to sense his presence, but Magnus Hauk had truly gone for good. He had not lingered. Once more she wept softly, alone, for she wanted no comfort now. She needed to release her grief entirely so that she might be clearheaded, and better able to aid her son as he began his rule.

Corrado's ship did not return that night. The mourners began to return to their own homes. Aselma and Narda would have remained waiting for Armen and Tostig, but their mother told them no. She promised them that Lara would return their husbands to them by means of her magic, but they must go. "I am going, too. And Sirvat, as well."

As she saw her mother-in-law off Lara thanked her.

Lady Persis smiled the first kind smile she had ever smiled at Lara. "You need time to gather your strength, my daughter. Remember I know the truth of my son's last wishes, and will keep your secrets. I will return when Taj is formally crowned." Then she kissed Lara upon both cheeks with her cold, dry lips.

"She puts me to shame by her example," Lara's mother, Ilona, said sourly. "Come back to the forest with me. The old witch is right. You do need to gather your strength."

"Your realm has never given me strength," Lara replied. "I need to be here. Terah is from where I take my strength."

"Let me have Marzina, then, for a brief time," Ilona said.

"Not yet, Mother. Marzina needs to be with her brother and sisters now. I will send her to you in time," Lara promised.

"You are so protective of that child," Ilona complained. "I am her grandmother, after all. She is pure magic, and I have much to teach her, Lara."

Lara felt a stab of irritation. "I wish you had been as thoughtful of me when I was her age," she said. Then she relented. "Marzina is fortunate to have you, Mother."

"Of course she is," Ilona said calmly. "Do you think Persis can teach her anything of value? Persis would teach her to be obedient to male domination, and how to make conserves, and sugared violets. Bah! Marzina is magic, and I will teach her how to use it. With her bloodline she will be a great sorceress when she is grown."

"She is Magnus's daughter, a Terahn princess," Lara replied in an even voice.

Ilona laughed. *We know better, you and I,* she said in the silent language.

Lara grew pale. *You are cruel to remind me, Mother. Marzina must never know that the Twilight Lord violated me upon the Dream Plain when I was carrying Taj, and set his seed to bloom in me so that she was born when Taj was. You told everyone who would listen when I birthed her that she favored a Nix ancestress. No one has ever questioned her birth. Aye, magic courses through her veins, but the Twilight Lord was an evil being. I will not deny Marzina her talent, but I want it used only for good. Once you begin to teach her serious magic who knows what will be unleashed in her,* Lara said.

And only you or I can educate her to control any wickedness that may arise in her, the Queen of the Forest Faeries replied.

"She is still too young," Lara answered.

"She is thirteen," Ilona responded.

"Let our lives settle themselves back into a normal pattern. I will send her to you before the next Icy Season," Lara promised her mother.

"It is agreed, then," Ilona said. "Farewell, Daughter." And she was gone in a burst of purple smoke.

Lara sighed with relief. But for her daughters the castle was now empty of all guests. Everyone had returned home but for those with Corrado. She sought for her daughters, finding them in her private garden. It was a small, pretty space on a promontory that overlooked the Dominus's Fjord. On three sides of the garden high, vine-covered walls offered a view of the water. On the fourth side a castle tower soared into the skies above. Lara slipped off her shoes before walking out onto the fresh green grass where Anoush, Zagiri and Marzina were now seated near a bed of bright yellow and white spring flowers. A small nearby miniature almond tree was in bloom, its pink blossoms delicately scenting the air. Lara came and sat with them.

"It seems strange without Father here," Zagiri said softly.

"I cannot sense him at all," Marzina agreed.

"He has gone," Lara told them. "Sometimes spirits will linger, but his did not. I do not know why that is, but it is."

"It hurt too much to stay," Anoush told her companions. "He told me that before he went. He did not want any of us to stand still as if waiting for his return. He wanted us all to move forward with our lives."

"Can you sense him at all?" Lara asked her eldest daughter.

Anoush shook her head. "He is gone, Mother."

"His vessel must have gone far that those accompanying it are not yet back," Zagiri noted. "It was a magnificent Farewell. I wonder that more Terahns do not do it."

"Not all Terahns have access to the sea, or have vessels to burn," Lara replied. "Usually such Farewells are reserved for a Dominus and his family."

"What will we do now?" Marzina wondered.

"Our lives will continue as they always have," Lara told her daughters.

"How can they without Father?" Marzina responded anxiously. "Nothing will ever be the same again, Mother! *Nothing!*"

"You are correct," Lara said. "Nothing will ever be the same as it has been with Magnus Hauk in our midst. It will be totally different, and yet it will also be familiar. Although your father has left us, it does not mean we will change the pattern of our days. Tomorrow you and Zagiri will begin your lessons once again, and Anoush will prepare for her annual trek to the New Outlands to visit her father's family. If Taj is back then he will resume his studies once more. Your father would not want us to stop living because he is no longer living."

"Taj is the Dominus now," Marzina replied. "Why should he need to continue studying? He is his own man."

"Taj is still a boy, and his capacity for knowledge will never be satisfied, for he is like his father," Lara said. "Besides, no man, or woman for that matter, should rule from a position of ignorance, Marzina. And none of us should ever stop learning."

"You don't know half of what you will need to know to be a good Terahn wife," Zagiri remarked. "Even I still have much to learn, and I am four years your senior."

"I do not need to know any more about cooking and soap making," Marzina said scornfully. "I want to learn more magic. Grandmother Ilona has promised to teach me."

"And provided your behavior is exemplary over these next few months I shall allow you to go to her just before the Icy Season," Lara said quietly.

Marzina's eyes widened with surprise and delight. "Oh, Mother!" she gasped. "Really? Truly? I can go to Grandmother soon?"

"If you show me that you are mature enough to be taught by your grandmother, Marzina, then just before the Icy Season begins you may go to the Forest Kingdom. *But not a moment before.* If, however, you act the spoiled princess as you sometimes do, if you play wicked magic tricks on the servants, then I shall decide that you are not yet old enough to be away from home. Your grandmother will not be an easy taskmistress."

"I will be good," Marzina promised.

"Hah!" Zagiri said scornfully. "I shall be amazed if you are." She mischievously stuck her tongue out at her younger sister. "Want to turn me into a toadstool, brat?"

Marzina's purple eyes narrowed dangerously. "Not at all," she said sweetly, "but I might make your careless tongue sprout with toadstools, sister dear."

Zagiri shrieked, horrified, for she knew Marzina could do exactly what she threatened to do.

"This is not the kind of behavior that will gain you

the privilege of going to your grandmother's, Marzina," her mother said quietly.

"I didn't say I would, Mother. I just said I might," Marzina answered pertly.

Lara had to laugh. "Well, threatening is as bad as doing it, so control your anger in the future. You must learn that or else your magic will control you, and not the other way around." She turned to Zagiri. "You are happy being what you are, my golden daughter. Please let Marzina be what she is meant to be. You should help one another. Now I would be alone in my garden. Leave me, my darlings."

They all arose from the soft lawn, and the three sisters hurried back into the castle. Lara walked to the end of her garden, and, reaching a wall, looked down the Dominus's Fjord and out to the sea. Suddenly she could just make out a faint smudge of lavender upon the horizon. It would be the sails of Corrado's vessel, and it was headed home. A wave of sadness overwhelmed her briefly. It was finished. Magnus was gone. She felt the ice about her cold faerie heart harden with her admission of fact. The small bit of mortal within her retreated, cowed by the magic thundering through her veins now. There was no time for mortal weakness anymore.

But her brief mourning had weakened her. She needed to go where she might regain her strength again, and she knew just the place. But first she must set her household in order. Taj would return by nightfall. She could not escape until everything was as it should be.

She would ask Corrado to stay at the castle while she was gone, for she could not leave her children without proper supervision. But she needed a few days to herself. She needed to draw deep from her well of strength. Even a faerie woman had her limits though few would consider that.

Lara felt a soft breeze touch her face. It smelled of both the sea and the spring flowers that grew on the cliffs around them. She breathed deep, and felt a wave of peace flow over her. A smile touched her lips. She would have a small respite before she would be needed. Her instincts told her that, and Lara was both glad and relieved. Looking out toward the sea, she could see the lavender smudge taking on the shape of sails. The return of Corrado's ship meant a whole new era was beginning. And once again Lara's destiny was moving closer.

CHAPTER THREE

THE OASIS OF Zeroun sat amid the rough golden desert sands. Above it was a cloudless blue sky with its bright, hot sun shining down. The sun felt good on her shoulders. Little had changed in the years since she and her giant friend, Og, had stopped at the oasis. The great tall trees with their curving, rough brown trunks capped by crowns of green fronds still towered over it. The stone well still stood at its center. And that wonderful oddity in the midst of the desert, a crystal pool with a soft sandy bottom and a waterfall amid the rocks of the oasis. Lara smiled as she looked about her. There was nothing in sight but desert. Once she had thought the sight both beautiful and frightening, but that was before her faerie powers had fully manifested themselves. Now as Lara gazed upon the world about her she simply thought it beautiful.

A wave of her hand, and a pale turquoise-blue silk tent with a striped turquoise and coral silk awning was erected. Lara stepped inside, and waved her hand once more. A large platform covered with a lime-green silk feather mattress appeared, and above it another awning striped in lime-green and gold. A single low ebony table materialized, a polished brass bowl filled with succulent fresh fruits in its center along with a crystal decanter of Frine. Multicolored pillows in shades of blue, coral and green popped from the air itself, and surrounded the table. An ebony trunk banded in brass appeared at the foot of the bed. Lara smiled. It was perfect.

Shedding her single white robe, she walked from the tent and into the cool waters of the pool. The sand beneath her feet was as soft as she remembered it. She swam slowly about the pool, emerging beneath the waterfall and letting the icy stream soak her pale golden head. Swimming back to the edge of the pool, she emerged to let the sun warm her naked body. Lara sighed deeply. It was perfect. For the next few days she would be free of all cares. Alone. She would rest and regain her strength in this place she remembered so fondly from her girlhood. Returning to the tent, she lay down, and slept for the next several hours.

When she awoke the night was falling. Lara stepped outside the tent and placed a small protective spell about the oasis. She might have raised a fire in the old stone fire pit that was still there, but she chose not to do so. While the Oasis of Zeroun was off the beaten track, she still did not want a fire attracting the attention of anyone wandering the desert at night. She magicked a brazier to heat her tent. Then she conjured a small loaf of warm bread, and a bit of cheese that she ate with her fruit. Having satisfied her appetite, she fell back into bed, and slept until midday of the following day.

For the next three days she followed the same routine. She ate, she slept, she swam, and now and again she let the hot desert sun bake her for a few minutes. Lara could feel the strength flowing back into her from the moment she had awakened that first morning. Stepping through her tent on the fourth evening, she found Kaliq waiting for her. "My lord!" she said, surprised to see him. Lara walked to the ebony trunk, and drew forth a pale green silk gauze gown which she slipped on over her head.

"Did you really think you could come into the Kingdom of the Shadow Princes, and I would not know you were here?" he asked her, smiling his seductive smile.

"Did I need your permission to come to Zeroun?" Lara asked him as she reached for a small bunch of magenta-colored grapes, and began plucking them one by one, putting them into her mouth and eating them.

"Why did you not tell me you were here?" he asked.

"I wanted to be alone. I was worn-out both emotionally and physically with the shock of my husband's death," Lara told him honestly. "Sometimes that small bit of me that is mortal overcomes me, Kaliq."

"I would have had you come to Shunnar," he said.

"But I did not want to go to your palace," Lara told him. "I wanted to be alone to regain my strength, my equilibrium. I wanted to be able to think without all the distractions of my family, of my responsibilities, of Terah."

"He put too much on your shoulders," Kaliq said. "You are faerie, not mortal."

Lara laughed, and, walking across the tent, she sprawled down on the bed next to him. "Will you always persist in trying to protect me, Kaliq?" she teased him gently.

"Aye," he told her. She smelled of sunlight and fresh air. "Will you always persist in trying to tempt me?" the Shadow Prince countered.

"I don't have to try," Lara told him boldly. "Do I?"

"Nay, you do not," he admitted. He touched her shoulder with a single fingertip, and her silk gauze robe dissolved.

Smiling up into his intense gaze, Lara magicked his white robes away. "And now, my lord?" she asked him softly.

His mouth met hers in a scorching kiss that seemed to go on and on and on. He seemed to absorb her with his lips. Her body arched, her full breasts meeting his hard, smooth chest. "Aah, my love, is it too soon?" he asked, ever thoughtful.

"I am faerie, Kaliq, and you know we cannot live long without passion. My husband is dead. He will not return to me. Nor would he, knowing my nature, expect me to deny myself pleasures." She caressed his jawline, and ran her fingers through his dark hair as his deep blue eyes devoured her. "Make love to me, my lord," she said softly.

He smiled down into her green eyes. Within the magical realm he was considered a powerful creature. He had his whole existence enjoyed the female race, but never until Lara had he truly given his heart. "Faerie witch," he murmured against her lips. "Do you think to command my obedience? Remember who I am."

Lara smiled up into his sapphire eyes. "I know who you are, my lord. You are a deliciously lustful being with whom I have always enjoyed taking pleasures. How long has it been, Kaliq, since you last sheathed yourself within me?" Reaching down, she caressed his hard cock. Her fingers ran up its length, and then back down again.

"You think I do not remember?" His head dropped to one of her breasts, and he licked the nipple slowly, the pointed tip of his tongue encircling the thrusting nub of flesh. "Was it not when I brought you back from the kingdom of the Twilight Lord?" He shuddered as she cupped his sac, retaliating by nipping at the tender flesh of her nipple, then sucking it hard.

"You took shameful advantage of me, Kaliq," she purred as she slipped from his embrace. Twisting her body about, her charmingly rounded buttocks facing him, Lara grasped his length, and licked its taut head. Then, taking him into the warmth of her mouth, she began to slowly suckle upon him.

His big hands fastened about her hips, and he drew her back just enough so that he might avail himself of her pouting slit. Her nether lips were already swollen with her desire. He ran the tip of his tongue between the twin halves, and Lara whimpered. He licked at her, encouraging her juices to flow copiously. He was already dizzy with the scent of her sex. Pushing his tongue between the puckered flesh, he found with unerring aim the heated source of her sex. Peeling her nether lips apart he gazed on it, watching as it swelled before his eyes. Kaliq licked at the sensitive flesh. Then he sucked upon it, and groaned as she drew even harder upon his love rod.

"Do not milk me dry, my faerie witch," he told her. "I would release my juices into your hidden garden, beloved."

She immediately released him, and Kaliq put her upon her back, thrusting two fingers deep inside her. She gasped with open pleasure as the fingers moved slowly at first, then faster and faster within her until Lara cried with her small pleasure. Now he swung himself over her, pushing himself deep. And when he had sheathed himself he grew still more, letting her feel his throbbing male member thicken even further inside her.

"Ooh!" Lara sighed softly. "No lover I have ever had is like you, Kaliq." She twined her fingers into his. "Give me pleasures as only you can, my dear lord."

Smiling, Kaliq began to ride the woman beneath him. His lust for her burned so hot he was not certain he could give her what she craved before he took his own release. He had never been celibate, even in the years in which she was unavailable to him. And the females he made love to never had cause for complaint. But something was different when he took pleasures with Lara.

Her head swam with delight as his manroot filled her. Her heated passage enclosed him tightly as he probed her strongly. Her husbands had both pleased her in their bedsport, but with Kaliq it was always incredible. Lara wrapped her legs about his torso so he might thrust deeper, and he did. Her passions flamed, and she raked her nails down his long back.

"That's it, my faerie witch," he groaned in her ear. "Mark me with your claws as I will mark you with my kisses." His mouth closed over hers, and he kissed her deeply, hungrily, his tongue dancing sensuously with hers.

Lara could feel her desire rising more than she believed it could. "Give me pleasures, my lord," she demanded of him. "I need those pleasures that only you have ever been able to give me! Please, Kaliq! Do not hold back! *I need you!*"

Deeper and harder. Harder and deeper. The Shadow Prince thrust over and over again into his lover. Her head thrashed back and forth. She crested with a soft scream, and the pleasures came and came and came as she had never known them. Her body arched up against him as her legs fell away. He forced her down as he drove her harder.

Starburst after starburst exploded behind Lara's eyelids. She wasn't certain that she was breathing. She was awash in a pleasure that kept coming and coming and coming until she cried out a second time. "You're killing me, Kaliq!"

His body shuddered briefly, and then as if he had gained additional strength he pushed her further into a world of unbridled passion. "Do you want me to stop?" his voice ground out harshly. *"Do you?"*

"Nay! Nay! I need more, my love. *More!*" Lara half sobbed.

He redoubled his efforts. His great manhood seemed to thrust into her so deeply that she was certain it touched her heart. He fell into a hypnotic rhythm that both soothed and excited her further. His kisses covered her face, her throat, her chest. The heat from his lips scorching her, branding her in a way he never had before. Lara could feel her heart beating wildly. Then suddenly it happened. The pleasure surrounding her exploded throughout her body like nothing that she had ever experienced before. *"Kaliq!"* She cried his name but once, and then she was being pulled down into a throbbing darkness that reached out to enfold her. Lara's last memory of that moment was the triumphant sound of his voice shouting, and the feel of his creamy love juices rushing forth to cool her heated passage.

When she finally emerged from her stupor Lara found herself within his tender embrace. She could hear his heart beating with a measured rhythm beneath her ear. His big hand was stroking her long, pale, golden hair. She sighed with contentment, realizing that all her sorrow and fears were gone. And she felt strong once again. His passion had given her new strength. She knew this was not something he did for other women. "You still love me," she said softly.

"I will always love you," he said quietly. "You do not have to ask me that, for you know it is true, faerie witch."

"I am not certain I am worthy of such a love," Lara responded with a sigh.

"The love is mine to give to whom I choose, my darling," the Shadow Prince told her. "Now sleep. When you awaken I shall be gone. And it is time that you returned to Terah. The young Dominus needs you, Lara. And be warned. Hetar has learned of Magnus Hauk's death. Even now they consider their options."

Lara wanted to engage him in conversation regarding this news, but she could not seem to remain awake. She fell into a deep and restful sleep, and when she awoke she was alone once more. From the way the light was falling outside her tent she could see it was late afternoon. They had spent the previous night making love, and she had slept the day away, but she felt wonderful. Arising she went to bathe in the pool with its sandy bottom, stepping beneath the waterfall to rinse her long hair. Then, seating herself on a smooth rock ledge by the pool, she brushed her hair dry in the sunlight, plaiting it into a single thick braid.

Returning to the tent, she opened the ebony trunk, and drew forth a soft cotton chemise, as well as a beautiful high-waisted turquoise-blue silk gown with long, full sleeves, and a deep square neckline. Reaching into the trunk a second time, she pulled out a pair of matching kid slippers, and slipped them on her feet. A small box at the bottom of the chest held the Domina's ring. Taking it out, she put it on her finger. Other than the chain with the crystal star about her neck she wore no other jewelry.

Lara stepped from the tent to stand beneath its awning. It was almost sunset at the Oasis of Zeroun, which meant it was almost sunrise in Terah. She would be home when her children awoke. These few days away from her responsibilities had given her new strength and a great clarity. Lara spoke a small silent spell. *Invisible to all but me, this shelter no one else shall see.* Then with a wave of her hand she commanded a golden passage to open that would connect the Oasis of Zeroun with her castle in Terah. Stepping into it she walked a short distance, emerging into a small windowless room in the castle she used for this sort of magic.

"Good morning, Domina," her servant, Mila, greeted her as Lara entered her apartments. "You appear well-rested. The children are all well." Mila knew that thought would be foremost in Lara's mind. "Shall I bring your breakfast?"

"Aye, I am ravenous," Lara told her. "While you fetch it I will tell the Dominus that I am returned." She hurried from her chambers to her son's apartment. Taj was not yet fully awake as she bent to kiss him. "Good morrow, sleepyhead," she greeted him.

His turquoise-blue eyes flew open. "Mother! You are back!"

"I am, my lord. Did anything happen while I was gone that requires our attention?" she queried him.

"A faerie post arrived late last night from Hetar," Taj said as he sat up in his bed. "I said I would review it in the morning."

"To whom was it addressed?" Lara wanted to know.

"To me," the boy told her.

"Excellent!" his mother approved. "Trust the Lord High Ruler to follow proper protocol. Jonah is taking no chances at offending us, and because he does not know who the regent is he is being careful." Lara smiled.

"But he knows who my mother is," Taj replied ingenuously.

Lara laughed lightly. "Aye, he knows," she responded. Then she gave him another quick kiss, ruffling his dark gold hair. "I must go and have my breakfast, my lord Dominus. Come to me when you have had yours, and we will see what Hetar wants."

Her energy was high, and Lara could not believe how well she felt. Scarcely more than a week had passed since Magnus Hauk had been killed. While there was an underlying sadness within her, that sorrow no longer absorbed her. She wondered if death affected everyone this way, or was it just her cold faerie heart that allowed her to put the past behind her, and move on? Whatever the answer she was glad, for weighed down with grief over Magnus Hauk, she could not have managed to do what she must do, and her husband had entrusted her with the fate of their son, and of Terah. She would not fail him, but then she never had failed him.

She ate her meal, and shortly afterward her son joined her carrying the message from Hetar. Taj handed the rolled parchment to his mother. "You open it," he said.

"Nay," she told him. "You are the Dominus. You will open it, and you will read it first. Then you will hand it to me for my perusal."

He was still a boy. He knew he was much too young for the responsibility that had been thrust upon him, and he was afraid. But his natural-born Terahn male pride appreciated the fact that his mother would defer to him in this manner. Women in general might be inferior, but not his mother. His father had told him that. Taj knew Lara was seeking to teach him, and so he opened the message from Hetar, his eyes swiftly scanning its contents. Then he handed it to her.

"What does it say?" she asked him without looking at the scroll in her hand.

"The usual diplomatic language of regret on the death of my father," Taj said.

Lara now looked at the message. *It is with great regret we learn of the untimely death of the great Dominus Magnus Hauk, ruler of the Kingdom of Terah, our most valued ally,* it began. *Please tender our condolences to your mother, the Domina Lara, your siblings and all of Magnus Hauk's family. If there is any way in which your friends in Hetar may be of help, you have but to send to us.* It was signed, *Jonah, Lord High Ruler of Hetar.* Lara set the parchment aside upon a table.

"It seems a harmless message," Taj said.

Lara smiled. "It is. Yet there is menace behind it, my son. You will reply, of course. Hetar may be a dangerous world, but they do value manners above all. How one is perceived is most important to Hetarians. Remember that, my son. Now, have you chosen a secretary, Taj?"

"I thought to raise the chief scribe, Ampyx, to that position," he answered her. "What think you, Mother?"

"I believe him capable, and loyal," Lara said. "Will you allow me to appoint him to his new post? Ampyx is no fool, and it will tell him without telling him what your father wanted. He is an old-fashioned Terahn, but he is also intelligent and intuitive."

"Let us go to the throne room," Taj said. "And you will stand next to my throne."

They went to the throne room, and Taj sent a servant for Ampyx. The boy sat himself upon the throne of Terah, which was fashioned of gold with a high pointed back, and studded with gemstones. It had a wide seat with a purple silk cushion upon it. He looked so young and vulnerable sitting upon his seat of office. Lara stood half in the shadows to his left. She briefly let her eyes wander to the tall arched windows that looked out over the green cliffs, the fjord and the sea beyond. She had loved this land from the moment she first saw it.

The door to the throne room opened, and the chief

scribe entered. Seeing Taj, Ampyx hurried forward and bowed. He did not notice the Domina until she spoke.

"Master Ampyx," Lara said in a strong and authoritative voice, "my son has expressed a desire that you become his First Secretary. I have approved his wish. You will begin your duties immediately."

"I am honored by your trust, my lady Domina," Ampyx said, bowing to her.

"You will be privy to many secrets, and you will have to keep them," Lara told him. "Can you do this? Answer honestly, for if you fail the Dominus, *or me,* the punishment will be terrible," she warned him.

"My late uncle served the Dominus Enjar, our young Dominus's grandfather, in the capacity of First Secretary," Ampyx said. "And before him several of my antecedents served in the Dominus's household. Service to this family is in my blood, Domina. I know how to keep secrets." He paused. "May I have your permission to speak freely to you, and to the Dominus?"

"You may," Lara said, wondering what it was Ampyx needed to say to her.

"It is said that the late Dominus put the Kingdom of Terah in your charge alone," Ampyx responded slowly. He was a tall man of undetermined age with a large hooked nose, and a completely bald pate. His dark gray eyes showed nothing at all.

"Is it?" Lara replied softly. "And yet it was the Dominus who dictated to you the announcement of his father's death to be published throughout the kingdom, was it not? And I speak to you today only at the Dominus's request. It is Dominus Taj Hauk who rules in Terah, Ampyx, and you will certainly tell any who ask you that, will you not?"

Ampyx bowed to Lara again. "Indeed, Domina, I will tell any who ask that such is truth." And his fathomless eyes shone briefly with his admiration.

"You will help your master to compose a reply to the Lord High Ruler of Hetar. This will be your first duty."

"Will the Domina wish to see a copy of this missive before it is sent off?" Ampyx asked politely even though he knew the answer she would give.

Lara nodded. "Thank you. That is most courteous of you." She stepped down from the dais. "See to your duties, then. The Dominus must now return to his lessons."

The letter to the Lord High Ruler Jonah was composed, and, reading it over, Lara had to admit she could not have done any better herself. *My lord Jonah,* it began. *Your condolences are graciously accepted in the same spirit in which they were given. Terah will mourn the unexpected death of Dominus Magnus Hauk for some time. However, we are a peaceable kingdom, and no help is needed from Hetar. Our ships will continue to trade with yours.* And Taj had signed it with a flourish. Lara was pleased. Ampyx was going to prove a valuable asset.

A faerie post messenger was sent for, and carried off the rolled parchment to be delivered to the Lord High Ruler of Hetar. Scanning it, Lord Jonah's coal-black eyes narrowed as he attempted to read between the lines, but there was nothing upon which he could fasten. Thank you. We don't want your help. Our trade continues. Nothing! He walked to his wife's bedchamber. Vilia had been ill for several months with some kind of wasting sickness, but her mind was still sharp. He handed her the parchment. "Can you make anything of this?" he asked her.

"There is nothing," she said, reading it.

"Does he really rule Terah, I wonder?" Jonah said.

"Not unless he is some sort of genius, but with Lara for a mother who knows. He is, after all, our Egon's age. Be glad of that, Jonah, my love. The Terahns won't let a woman rule them, and so there is certainly some sort of regent's council overseeing the boy. We need to know who these men are. Then we may set about to subvert them. Terah will be a rich prize, my love, and it is you who will gain it for Hetar." Then she fell into a fit of coughing that left her breathless and weak. Her beautiful amber eyes were faded, and her dark brown hair had thinned and was lackluster in color.

"Terah is a rich prize," Jonah agreed with his wife. "Perhaps if we could gain some kind of serious alliance with the Terahns we could stop the talk of the imminent coming of the Hierarch. The rumors have even reached the High Council, Vilia."

"The Hierarch is nothing more than a fable," Vilia said. "A tale to make people feel better in the bad times. He doesn't exist, Jonah." She grimaced. "Give me some of that Razi, my love. The pain has returned, and is unbearable."

He poured some of the liquid narcotic into a goblet for her and handed it to her.

Vilia drank deeply. The Razi was quick to work and masked her pain. "Jonah, you must listen to me. I do not have much time left. I must help you plan now, and if you follow my plan you will be victorious," she promised him.

"You are not dying," he told her, but he knew better and so did she.

"We must try again to make a marriage between Egon and the Dominus's twin sister, Marzina," she said.

"They will refuse us as they did before," Jonah said.

"Perhaps not this time," Vilia replied. "Magnus Hauk is dead. The new Dominus is young, and his regent's council may decide giving us Princess Marzina as a bride for our son is a good way of keeping us at bay."

"The Domina Lara will never agree to it," Jonah said, "and no council of mortal men can stand against her will if she says nay."

"Then," Vilia said softly, sitting up again, "you must take one of the Terahn princesses for *your new wife*. The Dominus's twin is too young, but Princess Zagiri is not. She is seventeen if my memory serves me correctly. And with the parents who bred her she is certain to be very beautiful, Jonah. Would it not please you to have a succulent young thing like that in your bed? And she could give you more children. Children are valuable bargaining chips, my love. Marry them into the right families and if the Hierarch actually is not a myth and came, you would have the power to combat him."

"Do not speak to me of dying, Vilia!" But she was dying, and even he could not escape the fact. And yet she was looking out for his best interests as she always had. No man could have had a better wife in that respect, Jonah thought, although she had failed him as a breeder, and their only child was physically weak.

"It is a good idea, my love," Vilia said.

"I know," he admitted reluctantly, for he did have a certain loyalty to this dying woman who had been his wife, whose wealthy, important family had supported him so staunchly. But the thought of a young, nubile wife caused his cock to twitch beneath his robes. This Terahn princess was likely to be as fertile as her mother. She could give him strong sons, and beautiful daughters. "Does she have magic, I wonder?" he said aloud.

"My spies tell me not," Vilia replied. "Neither she nor her younger brother exhibit any signs of it."

"There is an older daughter, Vartan's get," Jonah said.

"I am told she is frail, and she has *the Sight*. While that has a certain value, as does her bloodline, her frailty would make her a poor breeder," Vilia pointed out.

"You amaze me as always," Jonah told his wife. "How did you get spies into Terah, my love?"

Vilia laughed weakly but she did not answer him. Instead she said, "The same way the Domina Lara gets her spies here in Hetar, my love. How is not important.

My informants have been told that at my demise their loyalty is to come to you. Now, I will personally open negotiations with the Dominus and his council else they think you insensitive. There is nothing wrong with a wife seeking to see her husband is in good hands when she is gone. I believe we have a better chance of obtaining Princess Zagiri for you than obtaining Princess Marzina for our son, Egon."

"Lara needs no alliance with Hetar," Jonah reminded his wife.

"Nay, she does not, but Terah's ruling council may feel differently," Vilia said.

"And if they refuse us?" he asked.

"Then we must steal your bride, Jonah, for Terah must be bound to Hetar. We cannot afford another war. With the Domina's magic we have no chance of winning."

"But if I am forced to steal her daughter she will surely retaliate," Jonah said.

"If the girl is compromised, and I certainly expect you to compromise her, then the Domina has no choice but to accept you for her son-in-law," Vilia replied with a cruel smile. "If you steal her you can hide her in your mother's Pleasure House until a proper marriage agreement can be made between the Dominus and you. She is a virgin, Jonah. She has not taken any lovers yet, I am assured by those who know. You will have her First Night privileges, my love. Think about it, my love. A sweet, tight love sheath that has never known the pleasures of a manly cock. What joy you will bring her, and she you!" Vilia smiled at her husband. She knew from the look he sought to conceal from her, from the way his robes moved, that he was indeed thinking of a new wife. Jonah was an exceedingly clever and ambitious man, but of late he was not as daring in his actions as he had once been. He needed encouragement, enticement, and the thought of a beautiful young wife was certainly that.

When her husband had left her Vilia called her secretary to her, and dictated a letter to the Dominus Taj Hauk of Terah. Several days later the Dominus read her letter to his mother and his council.

"My lord Dominus, forgive me for intruding upon your mourning, but as I, myself, am nearing my end of days, time is very much of the essence. When you and your twin were born my husband sought a marriage alliance between our son, Egon, and your sister Marzina, which your parents wisely refused. Now I propose a marriage between your sister Princess Zagiri and my soon-to-be widowed husband, Jonah, Lord High Ruler of Hetar."

"Never!" Lara exclaimed. "Why did you not tell me of this communiqué from Hetar, my lord Dominus?"

"It was addressed to me, Mother," Taj replied, and she was taken aback by his tone so reminiscent of his father's tone when annoyed. "Let me continue."

What had happened to the boy who just several weeks ago had cried in her arms, and claimed he was too young to rule? It was obvious that all the deferential treatment being lavished on her son had turned his head. But she would not embarrass him publicly. However, when they were alone she would speak most firmly to him.

"The physicians tell me I will live but a few more weeks. It would comfort me in my last days to know that my beloved husband will have a proper new wife, and my sickly young son a good stepmother. I do not have to tell you, my lord Dominus, of the advantages such a marriage alliance between Hetar and Terah would have for both of our kingdoms. And your sister will have the privilege as I have had of being wife to Hetar's ruler, a position for which she is eminently suited. I will eagerly await your thoughts on this proposal..."

"No," Lara said. "Zagiri will not be married to that man. He is old enough to be her father, my lord Dominus."

"An older husband is no disadvantage for a young woman. Zagiri needs a firm hand, Mother. He's young enough to give her children, which could guarantee us peace for years to come," Taj said to his mother.

His council remained strangely silent.

"We have no quarrel with Hetar now. We should have none in the future, and we are strong," Lara reminded her son. "Jonah is an evil man. He will not love her, and every woman should be loved by her mate. Why would you condemn your sister to such a fate, my lord Dominus?"

"I am Dominus of Terah, Mother. The decision is mine to make," Taj replied.

Lara could no longer contain her anger. "You are a Dominus by birth, Taj, but your father placed me in your stead until I deemed you old enough and wise enough to rule. What you propose is both foolish and heartless. *We* will refuse the offer."

"I have already told Zagiri of this offer of marriage, and she is not reluctant," Taj surprised his mother by saying. "My sister knows her duty to Terah."

"Your sister is as foolish as you are!" Lara snapped. "She sees herself as Queen of Hetar, but she will not be. She would be nothing more than a wife whose husband happened to be in charge. This offer will be refused, Taj."

"Let us hear from my council," Taj countered, flushing.

"My lords?" Lara looked to the three men.

"The offer is intriguing, especially as it comes from the Lord High Ruler's dying wife," Armen said. "Why do you suppose that is?"

"Vilia is even more manipulative than Jonah," Lara responded. "The idea is hers I am certain. If Jonah had approached us it would seem unfeeling of his wife's condition. But by Vilia coming to us she portrays herself as a woman seeking to do a final service for the man whom she has loved and to whom she has been so loyal. You are touched by her caring, are you not, my lords? You are meant to be."

"Why would she approach us at all when there is peace between us?" Tostig asked. "Can this Lord High Ruler not find a wife of his own?"

"There have of late been rumors in Hetar of the coming of the Hierarch," Lara said. "Many think the Hierarch a myth. Others believe in him wholeheartedly. The Hierarch would, of course, challenge the rule of the Lord High Ruler. Vilia seeks to make Terah her husband's ally in the event of such an occurrence," Lara explained.

"Who is the Hierarch?" Taj asked his mother.

"It is said in Hetar that when things change for the worst, and things become too difficult for the people, that the Hierarch will come, and return everything to as it was before the troubles. He is believed to be like the navigator on a ship. He is supposed to put everything back on its proper course."

"Why now?" Taj said.

"Because Hetar is going through great changes now, but those changes are not responsible for their difficulties. Their troubles have been caused by a previous government that was both corrupt and greedy. The late Gaius Prospero led Hetar into two ruinous wars. His alleged conquest of the Outlands has been a disaster with only the wealthy profiting. The Midland farmland is worn-out. There is a scarcity of food, and Razi has rendered the poor even more helpless. These are not problems that can be corrected easily, simply or quickly. It takes time, and frankly, despite the few women now getting elected into the Hetarian Council, the government is slow to act, which is very frustrating for the women who see the needs of the people and would correct them.

"Now these rumors of the Hierarch have begun among the citizens of Hetar. For the Hierarch to come and return Hetar to the way it was means the women will once again be subjugated. But the myth suggests that he will also return Hetar to its former prosperity and glory. The people believe this will happen with a wave of the Hierarch's hand. But this creature is not of the magical world. That I know. He is a mortal whoever he may be, and the truth is it is unlikely he can perform miracles. But desperate people in desperate times are apt to believe anything they are told that offers them a way out of the darkness. Lady Vilia seeks an alliance with Terah in hopes we can prevent the Hierarch, if indeed he exists, from toppling her husband from his lofty throne. She believes if your sister were wife to the Lord High Ruler that we would not want her driven from her own small pinnacle of importance, for it would reflect badly on Terah as well as Hetar."

"We should not put Princess Zagiri in such a precarious position," Armen said slowly. "With all due respect to you, my lord Dominus, I believe such a marriage alliance would bring nothing of value to Terah. I deem it inadvisable as a member of your council to offer the princess to the Lord High Ruler."

"Indeed," Tostig echoed, "it is likely Terah would suffer in more ways than one should we agree to such a marriage."

"Let us take a vote on the matter," Corrado, who had been silent until now, said. "All in favor of refusing the Lady Vilia's proposal speak out. Aye!"

"Aye!" Armen said.

"Aye," Tostig agreed.

"Your council has declined to give your sister in marriage to the Lord High Ruler, and I concur with them. Now, my lord Dominus, what say you?" Lara asked him.

"I will agree with the council, my lady Domina. I did not know all the facts," Taj said loftily in an effort to save face.

Lara was not of a mind to let him off easily. "You acted rashly, my lord. You behaved like the boy you are. You saw what you believed to be a golden prize, and you reached for it greedily without realizing there was rot beneath. Never allow anyone to press you into a decision until you have examined all the facts of the situation. Now you must accept the responsibility of your actions. Go and tell your sister of the council's decision, and why they have made it. Then return and dictate a refusal to the Lady Vilia," Lara told her son sternly.

The young Dominus arose from his place at the head of the table, and bowed to them all. He was flushed with his embarrassment as he hurried from the chamber.

"Forgive me, my lords, for acting so harshly with my son," Lara said, cleverly knowing that the three men in the chamber, while realizing she was correct, were still in sympathy with Taj. Males were, after all, in most cases the superior beings in Terah, but in Hetar that was changing, which the Dominus's Council disapproved of and found threatening. "He must learn, and I could see no other way of making my point. As I have said before, Hetar is a danger to us. But perhaps under these circumstances it is time for us to find a husband for Zagiri. May I rely upon your advice in such a matter?"

Corrado refrained from chuckling aloud. His sister-in-law had just neatly turned the irritation of his fellow council members away from her angry words to her son. He could see her sly flattery pleased them.

"She will need a husband who cannot be cajoled by her willfulness," Lara murmured. "And of course his birth must be impeccable, and his wealth without question. You will take your time, my good lords, seeking out such a paragon. It would please me if Zagiri could love her husband, and he her. The candidates you present to me will be winnowed down, and then I will invite them to the castle so Zagiri may come to know them, and they her. If something happy should come of it then we may count ourselves fortunate, eh?" She smiled a dazzling smile at Armen and Tostig.

"I think you are very wise, my lady Domina, to consider seeking a husband for Princess Zagiri," Armen said. "But what of the Lady Anoush?"

"My eldest daughter is fragile, and with her gifts it is better she pick her own husband, for he will understand her, know her, and not be intimidated by her talents. I suspect she will choose a husband from among her father's people in the New Outlands," Lara told her companions. "She prefers living among them."

Armen nodded. "How wise you are, my lady Domina, that you know your children so well," he said.

Lara laughed. "Your praise, my lord, is appreciated. Now it is time for me to return you all back to your homes. I thank you for coming this day. I believe the Dominus has learned a good lesson, and you have seen how adroit Hetar's wickedness can be." She lifted her hand and spoke the spell. *"Return, Lord Armen, from whence you came. Lord Tostig, Captain Corrado, do the same!"* And they were gone.

Lara sank back into her chair with relief. What on earth had convinced her son to make a decision without asking her first? Had he not realized the seriousness of playing with his sister's life? Someone had obviously been encouraging him, and she knew it had to be her mother-in-law. Taj was very fond of the old lady, and visited her regularly several times a week. Lara sighed. She would have to speak with her and the sooner the better. And with the thought and the need she found herself in Lady Persis's hall.

Her mother-in-law was sitting working a tapestry. She looked up, slightly startled, at Lara's appearance. It wasn't often her daughter-in-law visited. "Good afternoon, dear," she greeted Lara.

"Good day to you, Lady Persis," Lara responded.

"What brings you to my hall, for you visit only with

a purpose," Lady Persis said astutely. But she did smile a genuine smile.

"You have been encouraging Taj to assert himself," Lara began.

"He is the Dominus," Lady Persis replied.

"He is a thirteen-year-old boy whose father died less than a month ago, madame. Today he almost gave his sister in marriage to the soon-to-be widowed Lord High Ruler of Hetar. Do you know what a disaster that would have been?"

"I certainly never told him to do that!" Lady Persis exclaimed. "Which of his sisters? Not Zagiri! Not my beautiful golden girl!"

"Well, what did you tell him then, madame?" Lara demanded to know. "And, aye, it was Zagiri. What is worse is that he told her he was making the arrangement. Now I have sent him to tell her it is not so, and she will be furious having already seen herself in such a high place."

"I did not mean to cause any trouble," Lady Persis quavered. "But my grandson is now the ruler of Terah. I just wanted him to behave like a Dominus. I still cannot believe that his father appointed you the regent. You are a woman."

"Persis, I know it is difficult for you to understand that Magnus came to respect my opinion, and frequently asked my advice, but he did. I have appointed Corrado, Tostig and Armen, Taj's uncles, to advise me and to advise him. There has been no official announcement regarding my position, and there will be none. I respect Terah's customs far too much although I hope one day we can make some changes. As far as the average Terahn is concerned Taj is Terah's ruler. And it is his wisdom that will publicly prevail. As Marzina has so cleverly pointed out I am a Shadow Queen. Taj is young, and this is not the same kingdom his father inherited. Terah is no longer isolated and unknown. Hetar looks to us like a greedy wolf eyeing a fat ewe sheep. My son, for, Persis, he is my son, too, needs to learn that a Dominus must be thoughtful, must have knowledge of all that affects his kingdom, must be clever. Taj has the capacity to learn these things, but until a month ago he was a carefree lad. Magnus was just beginning to teach him what he needed to know. Now I must pick up where my husband left off.

"Magnus was not a child when his father died. He had experience because his father had seen to his education as a future Dominus. Taj needs time to cultivate that experience and learn. You have encouraged him to swagger and make decisions he is not ready to make, Persis. If you expect to receive regular visits from your grandson you must cease this behavior. Taj is Dominus in name only right now, but as long as Terahns believe that he alone rules them they are content. Surely you do not want your grandson's position challenged, Persis? Both of your daughters have sons, and they would gladly plunge Terah into a civil strife to gain power for their own."

The old woman had become very pale now. "I did not realize…" she began. "I only wanted to see that Taj was confident in his place."

"He's still half child," Lara replied. "He thinks giving orders is being Dominus."

"Hetar wants Zagiri for their ruler's wife?"

Lara carefully explained the situation to her mother-in-law.

"And his own dying wife has importuned you," Lady Persis said. "She must love him dearly to seek another wife for him as she lies dying."

"Vilia is a clever woman," Lara said dryly.

"But you will not let Zagiri make this marriage, Lara, will you?" Lady Persis made no secret that Zagiri was her favorite grandchild.

"Your golden girl is going nowhere," Lara assured her mother-in-law. "The council agrees, knowing all the facts, that it would be a bad idea, and now that Taj knows he agrees, too. I have, however, made him tell his sister of *his* change of heart. She will not be happy, but I have also asked the council to seek out prospective candidates for Zagiri's hand in marriage. I think it is time."

"Oh, that is a fine idea!" Lady Persis responded. "I might even have a few suggestions to make in that direction myself."

"Please do," Lara encouraged her. If the old lady was busy considering husbands for Zagiri she would be less apt to encourage her grandson to behavior he was not yet ready to exhibit. Lara realized that Lady Persis was lonely, and she was grieving Magnus as they all were grieving Magnus. Let her put her energies to something happy. No parent should outlive her child, Lara thought, even though she probably would. "I must return to the castle now, Persis. Taj may need a little bit of help with his sister."

"You tell my golden girl that I want her to wed in Terah. I cannot lose her," Persis said. "Goodbye, Lara." She turned back to her tapestry.

Lara magicked herself back to her apartments. She could hear Zagiri sobbing bitterly, and crying for her as she entered her dayroom. "What are you howling about, Zagiri?" Lara asked although she already knew. Still, Zagiri could be very dramatic when she chose to be, and that was usually when she was not getting something she wanted or thought she wanted.

"Taj said I was to be Queen of Hetar, and now he says I can't," Zagiri cried, flinging herself at her mother.

"Hetar has no queen, my darling," Lara told her as she disengaged her daughter from her person.

"The Lord High Ruler's wife isn't his queen?" Zagiri said, surprised.

"She is his wife. Nothing more," Lara informed her daughter dryly. "And Jonah has a wife who still lives. It would be considered in very bad taste to announce a betrothal while Lady Vilia yet breathes. Besides, Jonah is much older than you are, Zagiri. He wants an alliance with Terah because he stands in danger of losing his throne at the moment. He thinks if he marries you I will use my magic to help him keep that throne. He had no interest in you at all. I want you to wed a man who will love you, and whom you can love. Taj was foolish to tell you he was planning a match with Hetar's current ruler. He did not understand the entire situation, I fear. Now he does. We will decline Hetar's offer for your hand, my golden girl. Even your grandmother was distressed to think you might be sent from us. She has begged me not to do it. A request I find easy to accede to, Zagiri. Now dry your eyes. We have already begun a search for a proper mate for you, my darling."

"I would have liked to be a queen," Zagiri said slowly, "but I should prefer to be loved, Mother." The tears were suddenly gone. "I want a man who will love me as Father loved you. Do you think there is such a man out there for me?"

"We shall look for him, Zagiri, but you will know him when you meet him," Lara promised her daughter.

"Marzina said I was foolish to weep over not being able to marry a man I had never met," Zagiri informed her mother. "Sometimes Marzina is wiser than I am."

"Aye, your little sister has good instincts," Lara agreed.

"Will you find a husband for her one day, Mother?" Zagiri asked.

"Marzina has magic about her," Lara said slowly. "It takes a special man to love a woman who is magic. Magical women are not easy."

"Father thought you were wonderful, perfect," Zagiri answered.

He hadn't really, Lara thought to herself, but he had been a patient man, for Magnus Hauk had loved her totally and completely. *How can I do all this without you, Magnus?* She spoke to him in her head and heart once again. *I miss you so much.* "I am not perfect, Zagiri, and your father knew it. He just loved me, and that is what I want for you, my golden girl. I don't want a marriage of convenience for you, or for dynastic purposes. I want you to be loved, and to love. When you find a man who can do that, then you will marry. And marry happily. And unless I give you permission to wed, Zagiri, you cannot. Remember that, my daughter."

"I will, Mother," Zagiri promised.

CHAPTER FOUR

"THEY HAVE REFUSED us!" Jonah, Lord High Ruler of Hetar, was not pleased. Angrily he held out the parchment to Vilia, almost shaking it in her pale face.

She took it from him, and read the contents, frowning. "The boy was eager for the match I am told," she said slowly. "It is obvious now that he is not as much in charge as I believed. Nor is his council it would appear."

"Then it is the faerie woman who rules!" Jonah said. "Has she managed to spread her seditious movement to Terah?"

"Terah would never accept a woman ruler," Vilia replied. "She manipulates the boy from behind his throne. Any mother in her position would do so. Do you think Egon could rule Hetar by himself if you were gone, my love? I would certainly be behind my son's throne instructing him, teaching him. That is what the Domina does."

"Why does she refuse me? It was your first husband, Gaius Prospero, who was her enemy, not I. Her daughter would be wife to a great ruler. Does she think she can do better for the girl? Who, then? Surely she cannot believe the son of some wealthy Terahn a better match for her daughter than me?"

"Perhaps the Domina is uncomfortable with the fact I still live," Vilia murmured. "Or perhaps she seeks a title for the girl. You are Lord High Ruler, my husband, but I am just your wife. A princess cannot go from being a princess to just a plain wife." It had always annoyed Vilia that despite all the help she had given Jonah raising him to ultimate power, he had never seen fit to share that power with her. "Or mayhap she does believe the son of a wealthy man who would actually love her daughter would be a better husband to Princess Zagiri than you, Jonah."

"Then the Domina is a fool, except we know she is not," he replied irritably.

"Be patient, my husband," Vilia advised him. "I will try again, and this time I will send a small miniature of your face for the girl to see."

"They will hardly show her a miniature of me if they mean to refuse me again," he snarled at her. "Do you enjoy my embarrassment, Vilia? Does it give you pleasure in your last days to see me humiliated by the faerie woman and her ilk?"

"Jonah, Jonah," Vilia lamented. "Have you learned nothing from me? Offer to give the girl a title. One that will make it appear as if you are sharing your power with her, but that actually means nothing. Princess Zagiri will be known as the *First Lady of Hetar*. Is that

so difficult for you to do? The girl is worth it I promise you. She is very beautiful. Would you like to see?"

His black eyes narrowed speculatively. "What is it
you keep from me, Vilia? Of late you have been privy to
much information of a sort not available to me. How is
this so, my wife?" Reaching out, he took her thin hand
in his, his fingers tightening about her fingers.

"Let me go, Jonah," she said in a suddenly hard voice.
She pulled her hand from his rough grasp. "You know
of my secret heritage," she reminded him. "That I descend from Ulla, and the great sorcerer, Usi."

He nodded.

"When our son began to sicken I reached out to any
who would aid me," Vilia told her husband. "A Darkling —her name is Ciarda—answered my call. On my
death Egon will grow strong again, and fulfill the destiny meant for him as a mighty conqueror. Ciarda has a
sister among the faerie post who brings her information
from Terah, which is how I know the things I do. She
gave me a miniature of Princess Zagiri, to show you,
Jonah." Vilia reached beneath her coverlet and drew
out the small oval, which she handed to her husband.
"Isn't she lovely?"

Jonah stared at the heart-shaped face with its fair
skin and soft, rosy cheeks. The girl's mouth was lush.
Seeing it, he considered the many uses those lips could
have. Her eyes were green edged in dark gold lashes.
Her hair was a mass of luxuriant golden curls that tum-
bled over her shoulders. He stared, mesmerized by her

beauty. And then before his eyes the small miniature began to change, darkening first, and then growing light once again to show him an entirely different view of the painting's subject.

Jonah's mouth fell open with surprise as the picture now revealed the completely naked form of the Terahn princess. Her breasts were small but full with dainty coral-pink nipples. The figure in the miniature frame lifted one of those breasts as if holding it out to him while her other hand moved down her torso to rest suggestively at the smooth junction mounding between her shapely thighs. He licked his lips anticipating what it would be like to have the girl beneath him moaning with her need.

"Beautiful, isn't she?" Vilia remarked once again. "She would be worth a fight, wouldn't she, Jonah? If Terah will not give her to you then you must take her."

"If Egon grows strong again with your sacrifice, Vilia, then why do I need a young wife to give me more children?" he asked her.

"I have told you that your offspring will be bargaining chips not just to solidify your power, but their brother's, as well. His best allies will be his kinsmen and -women."

"Has the Darkling fixed the time of your death?" Jonah asked Vilia. His mind was filled with lustful thoughts of the girl in the miniature. He couldn't keep his eyes from it, and now the golden beauty was spreading her nether lips open with her fingers to reveal to him her hidden treasures. Her love bud was swollen, and pearly with her juices. The picture was so real that he could almost sense the taste of her on his tongue. Jonah had to turn away, for his lust was close to boiling over. The manhood beneath his robes was swollen and throbbing. He wanted Zagiri as he had never wanted another woman. And he would have her! Nothing, not even the faerie woman, would stand in his way.

"I cannot let go of my tenuous hold on life until I am certain that you will take this Terahn princess for your wife, Jonah," Vilia answered him. "Bring her to Hetar. Let me see her, and I will be satisfied, but you must not delay, for our son grows weaker with every passing day. We will send your miniature to Terah, and ask once again for Princess Zagiri. If they refuse us then you will take her by force. Who are these Terahns that they dare to deny the Lord High Ruler of Hetar?" Vilia held out her hand. "Give me back the princess's miniature."

"Nay," Jonah replied. "I would keep it."

She laughed. The Darkling Ciarda had told Vilia that the picture held an enchantment that would make Jonah lust after Zagiri of Terah. And the miniature they would send secretly to the innocent girl would also be enchanted. Zagiri would fall in love with Jonah in spite of herself. She would want him, too, and would become his loyal minion. And the faerie woman Lara would have no choice but to ally with Hetar then. Jonah would be safe against the Hierarch if indeed he actually existed. *I will die happy,* Vilia told herself. *Jonah and Egon will be safe. And Terah will be ripe for the plucking when my son is old enough to take it. Did not my cousin Kol promise me that night on the Dream Plain that Egon would be a great conqueror?* "Aye, keep your miniature," she told her husband. "It will keep your appetite whetted for the girl, won't it, Jonah?" And Vilia laughed weakly. Then she closed her eyes, listening as he retreated from her bedchamber and closed the door behind him.

He shoved the small magical painting into the pocket of his robes. A young serving wench was sweeping the carpet in the dimly lit corridor. Striding up to her he said in a harsh voice, "Lift your gown, wench, put your palms against the wall and bend over for me." She did not argue or even speak but obeyed his rough commands instantly. Jonah was grateful that Vilia had taught their servants total obedience. Pulling up his robe, he directed his aching manhood, thrusting into the serving girl, pumping her hard as he imagined her to be Zagiri of Terah. He pushed deeper and deeper. The girl moaned as she shared pleasures with him. Finally satisfied he released his juices, withdrew from the servant and, pulling down his robes, hurried off down the hallway.

The encounter had taken the edge off of his lusts for now. Jonah was surprised by his reaction to the painting of the young princess. He had always been a careful man. A man who retained complete charge over himself, and those about him. But seeing the girl's beautiful face, and then her even more beautiful body, a body that was obviously filled with passion, he had found himself helpless to his own lusts. He had to regain control of himself again. He would not be like his predecessor, Gaius Prospero, who had found himself ensorcelled by a young and beautiful wife, and lost all of his abilities to rule in his desire to be with her. Nay! This beautiful, royal young wife would bring him prestige among the magnates of Hetar, and the people. He would convince them all that his marriage to Princess Zagiri of Terah would be the beginning of a new and prosperous era for Hetar. He would miss Vilia. But her sacrifice would not be in vain.

Once again the Lord High Ruler of Hetar applied to the young Dominus of Terah for his sister Zagiri's hand. Taking Vilia's advice, he told the Dominus that his sister would be known as the *First Lady of Hetar,* a title created especially for her. She would have a home in The City, and a villa in the Outlands on the sea. She would have vineyards, horses and cattle that would be hers. And all the slaves and servants she desired. He would treat her with respect and honor.

"If this came from any other man," Lara said, "I should seriously consider it, but not Jonah. The man is wickedness personified. His persistence disturbs me."

"He has sent a miniature of himself," Ampyx said, holding it out to his mistress.

She looked at it. "He does not flatter himself," she noted. "I will give him that. Dispose of it, and send the

Lord High Ruler a final refusal. Be less diplomatic this time, Ampyx," Lara instructed him. "Polite, but firm."

"I will attend to it, Domina," Ampyx replied, taking the miniature and bowing himself from her library. In his own small chamber the First Secretary set the miniature down on his writing table and wrote the Lord High Ruler of Hetar. Then, calling an undersecretary to him, he dispatched the missive not noticing that the miniature had disappeared from his large writing table.

ZAGIRI AWOKE THE following morning to find the miniature upon her pillow. Picking it up, she gazed into the dark eyes of the man pictured, and an odd feeling she could not put a name to overcame her. He could not be called handsome. His long face was perhaps a bit too severe, but there was a distinguished air about him. "Who are you?" she wondered aloud, and turned the miniature over. *Jonah, Lord High Ruler of Hetar* were the words inscribed upon the reverse of the little painting.

Surprised, Zagiri turned the oval in her hand back again to look upon his face. His dark eyes compelled her and when his thin lips twitched with a small amused smile Zagiri gasped with surprise, dropping the miniature in her hand. It fell toward the floor of the chamber, and then jumped back up directly into her palm again. Her fingers closed about it as if to protect it from further misadventure.

Suddenly the picture went dark, and when it grew light once more it pictured the dark-eyed man upon a large bed making love to a golden-haired girl Zagiri recognized as herself. She could not turn away from the tableau playing out before her eyes. The man was slender, but well muscled. His male member was quite large. He reached out to caress the breast of the naked girl and Zagiri could feel that hand caressing her breast. His mouth closed over a nipple, and Zagiri felt the tug of his lips, the swipe of his tongue as he licked the warm flesh of her bosom. She sighed with pleasure as those lips touched hers. She felt the pressure of them, the heat of them. Oh, it was wonderful! She had been kissed before, but never quite like this. A little moan escaped her, and, startled, she turned away from the miniature. When she looked back again it was his face she saw.

Had she imagined that erotic scene? Of course she had! Pictures of people didn't become alive. Zagiri laughed weakly. How had the miniature gotten into her bedchamber, and upon her pillow? She somehow knew her mother would not approve. Why did Lara dislike the Lord High Ruler of Hetar so much? Oh, she said he was wicked, and indeed the man in the painting did look a bit wicked. But he fascinated her, too. She was seventeen, and not a baby like Marzina who was four years younger. Shouldn't she be allowed a say in her future?

The search was on for a suitable prospective husband for her. Her mother and her grandmother were both involved in it. They would undoubtedly be parading a group of handsome, wealthy young men before her sooner than later. Suddenly Zagiri didn't know if she wanted to be married to a handsome, wealthy young man. She glanced down at the miniature again. The Lord High Ruler of Hetar had a seductive face that hinted at a very sensual nature, and while Zagiri was the most mortal of Lara's daughters she had her mother's passionate and fierce sexual nature. Jonah of Hetar looked like a far more interesting bed partner than the respectable scion of any wealthy Terahn family.

I want a man for a husband, not a boy, Zagiri thought to herself. Then she wondered again from where the miniature had come. She would ask Marzina about it. Her younger sister was good at keeping secrets, and usually knew everything that went on in the castle.

"Mother got another offer from Hetar for your hand yesterday," Marzina was pleased to tell her elder sibling. She very much enjoyed knowing what Zagiri did not.

"Why wasn't I told?" Zagiri said, annoyed. "I am not a child. Why does Mother insist upon treating me like one?"

"There was a miniature with the missive, but Mother told Ampyx to dispose of it," Marzina cheerfully volunteered.

"This miniature?" Zagiri said, holding it out for Marzina to see.

"Where did you get *that?*" the younger girl asked.

"It was on my pillow when I awoke this morning," Zagiri replied.

Marzina looked at the portrait. "He is not young,"

she noted. "And I feel the wickedness about him even just looking at his picture."

"I think he is very attractive. He looks like a man who knows how to rule," Zagiri said. "I would not mind if they made me his wife."

"You would have to leave Terah, and go to live in Hetar," Marzina responded.

"Terah is quiet and dull," Zagiri answered her younger sister. "Hetar, I think, would be exciting." She took the little portrait back from Marzina. "Don't tell anyone I have this. It is probably the closest I will ever get to Hetar," she said with a sigh.

"You need to take a lover," Marzina remarked wisely.

"I do not want a lover. I just want a husband," Zagiri said.

"But if you don't take a lover or two before you must wed then you will never know what other men are like," Marzina said. "It is not forbidden to take lovers once we reach the age of fourteen. Don't tell me you would go to your husband a virgin, Zagiri? If you have no experience, and do not know how to give and share pleasures you will disappoint him greatly. A woman should know how to offer pleasures, sister."

"There are none who have attracted me," Zagiri replied. *Until now,* she thought. "I should like to take pleasures with the Lord High Ruler of Hetar. I think he is probably the only man I should ever want."

"Oh, you just think that because Mother says you can't have him." Marzina chuckled. Then she grew serious. "If our mother says this man is wicked, and not suitable, sister, then she is right. Remember Mother comes from Hetar. She knows these people, and we do not. If she believed this man was the right man for you, Zagiri, she would let you have him."

"If I married this man I should be on an equal footing with Mother," Zagiri said. "I should be the wife of a powerful ruler of a great kingdom. Indeed, Mother is merely the widow of a ruler, and parent to a Dominus. I should hold a higher position now."

"Well, since you aren't going to marry the Lord High Ruler of Hetar there is no need for us to have this discussion, is there?" Marzina said. She wasn't sure she liked the attitude that her sister was suddenly taking.

"You will not tell anyone I have this miniature, will you?" Zagiri said.

"Nay, it is harmless enough, and if it amuses you…" Marzina answered.

During the nights that followed Zagiri began to dream of Jonah, the Lord High Ruler of Hetar. To Zagiri's surprise she found herself upon the Dream Plain each night, and he was always there. The first night it happened she asked him, "How has this come to be, my lord Jonah?"

"Do you think your mother is the only one with magic at her command, my golden girl?" Jonah answered Zagiri.

"Do you have magic?" she asked him.

"I have it at my beck and call," he told her, "but I am but mortal as you are."

"But you brought me here tonight," she reminded him.

"Aye, I did. I want to know you, Zagiri, and they will not allow it. But they do not know, shall not know, that we will meet upon the Dream Plain in the nights to come. And then you shall become my bride, my golden girl."

"My mother says you are old," she told him.

Jonah laughed. "I am not a youth," he admitted. "But I am yet young enough to give you pleasures such as no other man can, and I can give you children."

"She says you are wicked," Zagiri continued.

"I prefer to believe that I have done what I must for Hetar," he said. "I am a man who has never shirked from his duty to himself or his kingdom."

"Why do you want me?" she asked softly.

"It was my dying wife, Vilia, who has chosen you for me. Vilia has always put my best interests first and foremost. She has been an excellent wife. She says you will take up where she leaves off. That you will put my interests first because you will love me as she has loved me. Is she right, Zagiri? Will you love me?" His coal-black eyes scanned her small face. Then he bent and gently kissed her lips. "Love me, my little golden girl," he pleaded with her. *"Love me!"* His arms went around her.

"Oh, yes!" Zagiri whispered breathlessly. "Oh, yes,

Jonah!" Her heart was hammering wildly. This was the most exciting thing that had ever happened to her. She looked up into his stern face and was lost to him. This was a man! A real man. She sensed the danger about him, but was not afraid. He needed her, and she was going to be there for him. But then she remembered his wife, Lady Vilia. "Your wife?" she said, low.

"Will release her hold upon life as soon as she knows you will come to me," he told her softly, and his hand caressed her face.

In the nights that followed Zagiri met Jonah upon the Dream Plain. He would kiss her, and he would caress her, but he would not take pleasures with her because she was a virgin.

"We shall have a wedding night like no other," he promised her. "I shall have from you what no other man has ever had. And you will belong to me alone, my golden girl. You are mine. *Mine!*"

"But how can we wed?" Zagiri asked him. "My mother has forbidden it. Both my brother, the Dominus, and his council are in agreement that you shall not have me."

Jonah smiled at her, and it was the first full smile she had ever seen him smile. His teeth were very white, she noted. "How brave are you, my Zagiri?"

"I do not know," she answered him candidly. "I do not believe I have ever really had to be brave. What is it you are proposing?"

"Tomorrow night you will go to sleep in your own

bed. You will join me upon the Dream Plain, but we shall not part. You will awaken in Hetar, my golden girl. I have the magic at my command to make it happen. Would you like that?" he asked her, and he dipped his head to kiss the nipple of her breast.

"Will we marry quickly?" she asked him. "My mother will swiftly realize what we have done. And if she does not her mentor Prince Kaliq surely will."

"Vilia would speak with you before she dies, Zagiri. She would be certain that you will take her place in my life, and in our son's life. Then she will die. I will mourn her publicly for nine days. And after that I will be free to wed you, and we shall marry. You will be titled the *First Lady of Hetar,* my golden girl. Will that please you?"

"How can you be certain that your wife will die after meeting me and satisfying herself that I am suitable?" Zagiri asked cleverly.

"You have told me yourself that your father clung to life with your mother's help so he was able to dictate his final wishes," Jonah said. "So Vilia, with the aid of magic, clings to life. She has told me herself that once she sees and speaks with you that her death is imminent. I believe her." Leaning forward, Jonah kissed Zagiri's lush mouth. "Will you come to me tomorrow night, my golden girl?"

"I will come," Zagiri promised him. "And then I will be your wife, and we shall take pleasures together. I hope you are good at giving pleasures, for you shall be the only man I know. My appetites are great, for I am my mother's daughter in that respect."

"I will see you are well satisfied, Zagiri," Jonah promised her. She would come to him tomorrow! The Darkling Ciarda would make it possible as she had made these visits to the Dream Plain possible. "Until tomorrow," he told Zagiri and then she awoke.

Was it possible? Was it really possible that she could be transported to Hetar from the Dream Plain? Was it really possible that tomorrow night she would go to sleep in her own bed in her parents' castle, and awaken in a bed in Hetar next to the man she had come to love? Zagiri knew her mother would be frantic, but it was to be hoped that by the time she discovered the whereabouts of her daughter Zagiri would be Jonah's wife. Lara would be angry, of course, that Zagiri had flouted her wishes, but she would forgive Magnus Hauk's eldest child. She would forgive her daughter. And Hetar would be bound to Terah by this marriage. She was really doing a great service for her kingdom, Zagiri decided. She was making a peace that would last between the two kingdoms.

The summer was upon them. It was the day Anoush would leave for the New Outlands. Lara had decided to go with her eldest daughter for a few days. They would take Lara's great winged white stallion, Dasras. Dasras was eager to visit the many mares belonging to the Aghy Horse Lord, Roan. He had sired many a foal on Roan's mares, and the Horse Lord was always happy to see him visiting although Roan's breeding stallion was not.

Anoush was eager to leave the castle. Her heart had always been with her father's people. This time she knew she would have to ask her mother to let her remain with the Fiacre clan family. No Terahn male had taken her fancy. Indeed most of the Terahn men were wary of the girl. Her gifts of healing and especially of sight frightened them. While they found her fair to look at, and gently spoken, she was not the sort of woman a Terahn man wanted for his wife despite her lofty connections.

And Lara knew she would lose this eldest daughter of hers to the Fiacre this summer. But she would not forbid it. She could not. She would see Anoush had her own fine stone house with a garden, and a herd of cattle to call her own. There were serving women eager to serve in the house of the daughter of the great Fiacre hero, Vartan. Anoush had family in the New Outlands. Her foster parents and their children, who were her blood kin, among others. And perhaps there would be a husband for Anoush among the Fiacre. A man who would dare to make this special girl his own.

"I will miss you very much," Zagiri said to her eldest sister.

"You will come and visit in late summer with our siblings like you always do," Anoush replied.

"Perhaps not this year," Zagiri replied.

"And why not?" her mother wanted to know.

"Mayhap I shall have something else to do," Zagiri answered.

Lara laughed. "I can see your sister is looking ahead to perhaps some young man to come courting her."

Anoush said nothing, but she was suddenly troubled. Zagiri was hiding something, and that was not at all like her sister. Zagiri was usually an open book.

Lara's children walked to the stables with her where Dasras was already saddled, and waiting for the two women. The Domina hugged her children, cautioning Taj not to make any decisions in the next few days without her. He grinned and agreed. "Now both of you, do not quarrel with each other, I beg you," Lara said to Zagiri and Marzina.

"Would it be all right if I went and visited Grandmother?" Zagiri asked in innocent tones. "I have not seen her in several weeks, and I know she gets lonely."

"That is most thoughtful of you, Zagiri," Lara said. "Aye, go and visit Lady Persis if it would please you. It will please her, I know."

Zagiri smiled sweetly, and secretly congratulated herself on being particularly clever. If everyone thought she was at her grandmother's she would not be missed until her mother returned. By the time they sent for her and the word was returned that she had never been at her grandmother's it would be too late. Vilia would be dead and mourned her nine days, and she would be Jonah's new wife. Zagiri almost hugged herself with her delight.

Anoush looked at her sister strangely as she was

helped up onto Dasras's broad back. There was something wrong. She sensed it, but whatever it was her sister's mind was such a jumble of thoughts Anoush could not get a grasp of it. Should she say something or was it just Zagiri's usual racing thoughts? Finding herself seated upon the great horse, Anoush suddenly thought of the New Outlands, and how eager she was to get there. Putting her arms about her mother's waist, she put everything from her mind but the happiness she felt at leaving the castle.

The great stallion unfolded his beautiful wings. He trotted from the stable yard beneath a stone arch, and then began to gallop across a long green meadow until finally his wings began to gracefully flap, lifting him and his passengers into the air. He turned, soaring over the castle and the fjord. Then, crossing the fjord, he set his direction toward the Emerald Mountains, and the New Outlands beyond.

Magnus Hauk's three children watched them go.

"Anoush won't come back except for a visit now and again," Taj said.

"She's happier with the Fiacre," Zagiri remarked.

"We have to get back to our studies," Marzina reminded them, and together the trio walked from the stable yard back into the castle.

That evening as they sat finishing their meal Taj noted, "It is odd without both Father and Mother, isn't it?"

"They've both been away before," Marzina said.

"But now Father isn't coming back," Taj said softly. "I miss him."

"So do I," Marzina admitted.

"It is the nature of things to change," Zagiri told them. "Remember Dillon is gone, then Father, and now Anoush. I will leave you next. Then Marzina. Only Taj will remain here at the castle, for he is the Dominus."

"You aren't going anywhere for a long time," Marzina said.

"She's going to Grandmother's tomorrow," Taj noted.

"But only for a few days," his twin quickly responded.

"And you and I shall be left alone," Taj said.

"We shared our mother's womb. I think we can share a castle without getting into too much trouble," Marzina said mischievously. "My behavior must remain above reproach for Mother has promised me that if I don't get into any trouble I shall go to the Forest Kingdom to our queenly grandmother for training in magic soon."

"I have noticed," her brother teased, "that you haven't turned any of the servants into frogs, butterflies and birds of late."

"I always turned them back," Marzina said defensively.

"You and your magic are so childish," Zagiri said. "When are you going to grow up, little sister? Men do not like women who are too clever."

"Father liked our mother well enough," Marzina said pertly. "I doubt I shall ever wed a mortal man. I will need a man who understands my great talents."

"You will need a miracle, then," Zagiri said and Taj laughed aloud.

Marzina's face darkened briefly but then she laughed, too. "I'm too young to wed, anyway. But you aren't, Zagiri. I wonder what kind of husband they will find for you."

"I will find my own husband," Zagiri replied.

"Hah!" Her younger sister snorted derisively. "You know as well as I do that our mother must approve any match we make."

"It is bad enough to be treated like a child by Mother," Zagiri said irritably, "but to be spoken to like one by my little sister is not to be tolerated!" She stood up from the table. "I am going to bathe, and then go to bed."

"It is early yet," Taj noted.

"I am leaving early for Grandmother Persis's house. As it is not far I shall walk," Zagiri told her siblings. "When I return I hope you two younglings will have remembered that unlike you I am grown." Then with a toss of her golden curls she left them.

"What is the matter with her of late?" Taj wondered. "All this talk of being a grown woman while we are but children. I am the Dominus, and she has no respect for my position," he grumbled. "When she returns we shall have to have a little talk about that." Then he smiled at his twin. "At least you understand me, but then of course you would even if we are different in so many ways."

Marzina leaned over and kissed her brother's cheek. "It would have been wonderful if we had both been given the gift of magic, Taj. Just think what we could have accomplished together."

"You have the magic of two, sister," he said. "You will work it for both of us. It is better that I am more mortal, for magic is difficult for many Terahns to accept."

Marzina nodded, more than well aware of the truth he spoke. "It is early yet," she remarked. "Will you play a game of Herder with me?"

"Only if you promise not to move the pieces by magic," he told her. "I prefer to at least attempt to use my own skills to beat you."

"Oh, very well," Marzina agreed, and then she giggled. "Remember the first time I moved my pieces by magic. The look on your face, Taj, was priceless."

The young Dominus laughed at the memory. She had indeed startled him, for they had just been nine at the time. "I wasn't certain I could believe the evidence of my own eyes," he said, still chuckling.

"Mother couldn't believe what I had done, but Father thought it quite amusing," Marzina recalled. Then her beautiful little face crumpled, and she began to cry. "Oh, brother, I miss our father so much!"

Taj put comforting arms about his twin. "I miss him, too, Marzi. I am too young for this responsibility that has been thrust upon me, and I do not think I shall ever be the Dominus that our father was. And poor Mother walks such a fine line so that Terah may remain safe from all predators. Yet I cannot help but wonder if her natural prejudice against Hetar's rulers hasn't blinded her judgment."

"Nay, Taj, you must believe in Mother completely. She is right not to trust Hetar. Their own recent history does not speak well of their intentions," Marzina said. She could not tell him of the miniature of the Lord High Ruler that had appeared so mysteriously upon Zagiri's pillow. She had promised to keep her sister's secret, but now she worried if she should have made that promise. Her older sister had suddenly changed. She had become defiant, moody and even distracted. Marzina had never seen Zagiri behave in such a manner. She wondered if anyone else had noticed the change, or if she was even imagining it. What had happened to Zagiri? Well, perhaps a few days in the company of their Terahn grandmother would calm Zagiri. The sorrow that had so suddenly overcome her vanished. With a leftover sniffle she said, "You get the game table, Taj, and I will fetch the board and the pieces."

The twin siblings played several games of Herder, and the evening deepened into darkest night. There were no moons, for the skies had become dense and overcast. Finally Taj and Marzina admitted to one another that they were weary, each going to their bedchamber. Marzina could not help but look in on her elder sister. Zagiri was already abed and sleeping, a smile upon her beautiful face. Relieved to see her so Marzina went to her own bed.

Zagiri had just been about to enter the Dream Plain

when she had heard the door to her chamber open. The faint noise had drawn her back briefly, and through slitted eyelids she had seen the anxious face of her little sister. It had caused her to smile. Then Marzina had retreated, and Zagiri had heard her footsteps as they faded down the hall. She concentrated upon gaining the Dream Plain once more.

"Zagiri, my golden girl, where are you?" Jonah's voice called to her.

"Here I am, my lord!" Zagiri called back to him. Then the mists of the Dream Plain parted, and she saw him waiting for her. Zagiri hurried into his arms.

"Are you ready to be brave, and to come with me, my golden girl?" Jonah asked.

"I am ready!" Zagiri said eagerly. This was so exciting, she thought. She would awaken in Hetar, and she could hardly wait. Her heart was beating wildly with her anticipation. Soon she would be this powerful man's wife.

"Are you certain, Zagiri?" he asked her. "You must be certain that you are ready to come with me. This must be of your own free will, my golden girl."

"I am sure, my lord. I love you!" she told him. "I must be where you are!"

"Then come, Zagiri of Terah. Come with me to Hetar. Come and be my bride," he said to her. His arms enfolded her strongly now. "Awaken now, my golden one! Awaken in Hetar!" And his lips came down on hers, crushing her mouth in a hard, fierce kiss. His body pressed against hers.

Zagiri reveled in the touch of his mouth, the feel of his body against her, but then her head began to swim. She struggled to hold on. She could hear an unfamiliar voice whispering in her ear, bidding her to let go of her reality, and join theirs. The voice was dark and sweet, but at the same time it frightened her. Briefly she drew back, and when she did she felt his lips again on hers. Feeling secure once more, she slipped into the warm darkness beckoning her. Then suddenly she saw light ahead of her. She willed herself toward it, opening her eyes to discover herself in a strange room.

"Ah, my dear, you are with us at last," an unfamiliar female voice said to her.

Zagiri's green eyes focused themselves. Turning her head in the direction of the voice, she saw an older woman with ebony-black hair, skin like a gardenia and black eyes rising up from a chair next to the bed where she now lay.

"I am Lady Farah, the mother of the Lord High Ruler of Hetar. You are in my house for your protection."

"Where is my lord Jonah?" Zagiri asked the woman, attempting to sit up, but falling back when a wave of dizziness overcame her.

"Oh, my child, do not attempt to arise quite yet. You have made a great journey, and will be weakened by it," Lady Farah advised. "My son is safe in his own bed in his own home. When you are rested I will take you to

Lady Vilia so she may see you are safely with us. It is time for her to release her hold upon life. She has lingered overlong."

"Do you not like her, lady?" Zagiri asked, having recognized a disapproving tone in Lady Farah's voice.

"I do not dislike her," Lady Farah replied. "But the truth is she was never good enough for my son. She was the cast-off wife of the late emperor. She seduced him when she saw he was coming into power. She held on to him by giving him a son. Now you, my child, the daughter of a great ruler, will make my son a perfect wife. You have beauty, and you have breeding. And I will be your friend. Did you know that you have blood kin in Hetar?"

"I never thought of it," Zagiri responded, "but my mother does have half brothers, doesn't she?"

Lady Farah smiled toothily. "I am delighted that your mother has not forgotten from whence she sprung. Aye, my dear, you have several uncles and a grandmother in Hetar. Your eldest uncle, Mikhail, sits on the High Council as representative from The Quarter. He is a most educated and respected man who represents the finest that Hetar has to offer. You will meet him soon."

Zagiri attempted to sit up again, and this time her head swam but briefly, and then quickly cleared. "When can I see Jonah?" she asked.

Lady Farah smiled again. "How eager you are for my son," she purred approvingly. "You will give him many children. There is where Vilia and I always agreed. Children are most valuable commodities. Here in Hetar trade and wealth are most important. When you are wed to my son your mother will, of course, want to turn over your dower portion to him. As a princess you will surely have a great value. But gracious, I am rattling on like some old woman. Let me have the servants bring you some food and Frine. Then I will take you to meet Lady Vilia." Lady Farah stood up and hurried from the room.

Wealth was important, Jonah's mother had said. But would her mother turn over a dower portion to a daughter who had run away, and married a man in defiance of her mother's wishes? Zagiri was suddenly uncomfortable with the idea that her mother would disown her. What had she done in disobeying? And even if she wanted to return home to Terah how could she? What would happen to her? Would Jonah continue to love her if Lara would not provide a dower? They had never discussed a dower.

Servants came bringing her food, and sweet Frine. Zagiri found her appetite had disappeared. Lady Farah returned, and, seeing the girl picking at the food, chided her gently, and asked if she was well.

"I am excited yet weary," Zagiri answered her not knowing what else to say. She suspected this woman who was to be her mother-in-law would be more than disappointed if there was no dower portion for a princess of Terah forthcoming.

"Of course you are," Lady Farah said. "I can but

imagine how thrilled you must be to be marrying the Lord High Ruler of Hetar. It is a great honor."

"He should be equally honored to have a princess of Terah for his wife," Zagiri said, deciding that she had best be firm with this woman as her mother was firm with Lady Persis. After all, she was no longer a child. She would soon be the *First Lady of Hetar,* and her rank was certainly higher than this woman's in any case.

"My son tells me you are a virgin," Lady Farah said, stung and needing to change the subject so she might regain the upper hand over this girl. "That simply will not do, my child. How can you give him pleasures when you have no idea what pleasures are all about? I shall speak to Jonah, and have you properly broken in before your wedding night. You are seventeen, are you not? I was told Terahn girls were allowed to accept lovers once they turned fourteen."

"We are allowed to accept lovers if we want them. I never did. I wanted no man until my lord Jonah came into my life," Zagiri said earnestly.

"Shocking!" Lady Farah said. "And your own mother did not encourage you to take pleasures? I cannot imagine what the Domina was thinking." She tsked.

"Jonah says he wants to be the only man who knows me," Zagiri said.

Lady Farah looked aghast but then she laughed. "You have turned my son into a romantic. How quaint. It shall pass, however, with familiarity. Still, I shall suggest to him that you be properly trained in the amatory arts sooner than later. After all, as head of the Pleasure Guild I have a reputation to uphold. I cannot have you boring my son too quickly. Well, let us get you properly dressed. Vilia is waiting."

Silent serving women brought a selection of gowns, and Lady Farah chose a gown of soft peach color for Zagiri. The girl was dressed. Little matching slippers with gold buckles were fitted on her feet. Her golden curls were brushed out, falling over her shoulders and tumbling down her back. Lady Farah nodded her approval. A peach-colored brocade cloak lined in ivory silk was settled over her shoulders, and Jonah's mother led the way from the bedchamber down the stairs and into the cobbled courtyard where a large gold litter awaited the women.

Zagiri's eyes widened at the sight of the bearers. They were the tallest men she had ever seen, and they were all perfectly matched blonds. Their totally naked bodies were bronzed and oiled. The muscles of their arms and backs rippled. Their buttocks were tight. Their groins were shaved smooth, and their manhoods were neatly encased in bejeweled golden tubes of considerable length. Around their thick necks they wore collars fashioned from both gold and silver, and studded with pearls. They were barefoot.

"Get in, my child," Lady Farah said, gently pushing Zagiri into the litter, which was padded in silk, and filled with cushions. When they were both comfortably ensconced she drew the green silk gauze curtains. "I see you like my bearers. If you like I shall arrange for you to have a similar set. They were frightfully expensive, of course, but then you are to be the *First Lady of Hetar.* You should have nothing but the best. My lads have other talents, as well. Would you like to try one of them?"

"For what?" Zagiri asked.

"Why, for pleasures, you silly girl!" Lady Farah exclaimed, laughing lightly.

"No, thank you," Zagiri responded, feeling like a fool. Did everyone on Hetar behave in this fashion? "Tell me about Lady Vilia, please."

"I don't know why you want to know about her," Lady Farah said. "She is my son's past while you are his future."

"I was taught kindness, and this woman will die shortly," Zagiri said. "What harm is there in my knowing about my predecessor?"

Lady Farah shrugged. "She was the second wife of Gaius Prospero, the Master of the Merchants, who afterward became Hetar's emperor. He shed his first wife to marry her. She is of the family Ahasferus, a very prominent clan here in Hetar. She gave Gaius Prospero three children, two daughters and a son. My son was her husband's slave, and served as his confidential secretary."

"*Slave?* My Jonah was a slave? Why was that?" Zagiri demanded to know. What else were they keeping from her? She was a princess of Terah, and she could not wed a man of low birth no matter how exciting and powerful he was.

"My son is of noble birth. His father, Sir Rupert Bloodaxe, was a great Crusader Knight as was your own grandfather, John Swiftsword. But I was not Sir Rupert's wife. His wife had given him daughters, and he wanted a son of me. I gave him that son, and he treated Jonah with love, and devotion. But he neglected to free him before he died for children born to a man's Pleasure Woman are considered the property of their male parent. His father's wife, in a puerile effort to revenge herself upon me for giving her husband the son she could not, took advantage of the law, and sold my son into slavery. Fortunately Gaius Prospero purchased him, and Jonah, being clever, made himself indispensable. As for Vilia, she seduced him, and made him her lover. Later when Gaius Prospero fell in love with a beautiful woman he wanted to rid himself of Vilia, but was afraid of offending the family Ahasferus. Jonah offered to wed Vilia, and revealed at that point his heritage, making him a more than suitable match for her. Of course she was delighted. Why wouldn't she be? She could see that Jonah was meant for greatness. She has been a devoted and faithful wife to him, always putting his interests before hers. I will give her that," Lady Farah said. "And she did manage to birth my grandson, Egon, but he is frail. You must give my son strong sons, Zagiri."

"Of course I will give him strong sons!" Zagiri said. Now that she knew a little more about this man she was so eager to wed she would ask him about his past, and about the poor lady who would soon die. It was obvious Lady Farah didn't like Lady Vilia, but Jonah seemed devoted to her.

The litter came to a stop, and the curtains were drawn back by a servant. The two women exited their transport, following the servant into the house.

"You are now in the Golden District where the Lord High Ruler lives," Lady Farah told Zagiri. "This is the house where Lady Vilia has lived in her last days. She did not want to die in the palace lest it be tainted. Come along, Zagiri." And Lady Farah hurried briskly up a flight of marble stairs to an upper hallway.

A plump young man hurried forward. "Is this she?" he asked.

"Aubin Prospero, I present to you Princess Zagiri of Terah. This is Lady Vilia's elder son, my dear," Lady Farah said.

"I am so sorry about your mother," Zagiri said to Aubin Prospero.

"It isn't your fault," he told her. "My half brother will get her life force shortly, and be strong again. She gives her life for him. That is the kind of mother she has been. She has chosen you to be her successor. Know that I hold no ill will toward you, Princess. And you will have the loyalty of the Merchants Guild. We honor your grandfather John Swiftsword of famed memory."

"Thank you," Zagiri replied. She knew little of her mother's father but that he had sold her mother in order to further his career, and he had won his place in Hetarian society with his skills.

They had reached the door of a chamber at the end of the hallway.

"Go in," Aubin Prospero said. "She is waiting for you. Nay, not you, Lady Farah. My mother specifically asked that the princess come alone." He opened the door to the room and ushered her through, closing the door behind her.

Zagiri walked slowly to the curtained bed where Lady Vilia lay pale and gasping. "I have come, my lady, as requested," she said.

"Come closer, and let me see you." Vilia beckoned with a clawlike hand. "Aah, you are even more beautiful than I imagined. You will make Jonah very happy. Now, Zagiri of Terah, you must promise me that you will take the finest care of my husband and my son, who will shortly belong to you."

"I promise, Lady Vilia," Zagiri said earnestly.

"Why, you love him already," Vilia said, surprised. "That is your innocence, and loving upbringing. Tell your mother that I thank her for that."

"Why me?" Zagiri asked softly.

"Harder times are coming to Hetar, little princess. My Jonah will need a good woman by his side advising him, supporting him, if he is to survive, if Hetar is to survive. No ordinary woman will do, and we may need Terah's aid. With you the *First Lady of Hetar,* your mother and brother are more apt to help. He already cares for you, Zagiri of Terah. He has given you a title. I have never had one despite all the years I have looked after his interests." Vilia grew very pale, and slumped deeper against her pillows. "Watch over my son, Egon. It was foretold that he would be a great conqueror one day."

"I will!" Zagiri said.

"I will die shortly, little princess. Take that small lavender crystal bottle from the table. Catch my life's essence quickly, and see that my little son, Egon, drinks it. Aah! My time is finished," Vilia cried suddenly.

Zagiri gasped as the light faded slowly from the older woman's eyes. She quickly took up the container, blinking as a thin wisp of fog seemed to stream slowly from between Vilia's blue lips. Zagiri captured whatever it was in the bottle as she had been instructed. When no more of the substance came forth she stoppered the vessel, tucking it into the pocket of her gown. Then she ran to the door. "Someone! Quickly!"

Lady Farah hurried forward, putting an arm about Zagiri. "Quickly. You must leave this house."

"Wait! I have something from his mother for your grandson. He must have it now. Is the boy here?" Zagiri asked anxiously.

"Aye. Very well, we shall find him." Taking Zagiri's hand, Lady Farah led her through the house until finally they came to a pleasant apartment where a young boy sat quietly reading.

He was very pale and slender. Looking up, he smiled

as they entered the chamber. "Grandmother, how nice. Have you come to visit me?"

"Your mother has departed," Lady Farah said without preamble. "This is Princess Zagiri. She brings you something from your mother."

"What is it?" the boy asked. His dark eyes had grown large with the news of his mother's death, but he did not cry.

Zagiri withdrew the crystal bottle from her pocket. "Open your mouth, little one," she told him, and when he obeyed without question she poured the foglike substance from the vessel into his open mouth.

The boy swallowed it eagerly. "It tastes like berries," he told them when he had finished it all up. "Leave the crystal, Zagiri, for I shall retain it as a keepsake from my mother. Thank you."

"Now we must go!" Lady Farah said. "You cannot be seen here. Your half brother is here, Egon. Go and find him. You must send to your father now." She practically dragged Zagiri from the chamber, through the house and to her litter. "Quickly, quickly!" she told her bearers. "We must not be here when word gets out," she said to Zagiri. "The simple people are so superstitious. When they learn that the Lord High Ruler has taken the Domina of Terah's daughter to wife, and she was with his dead wife when Vilia died..." She paused. "Well, you know the rumors that will arise. Especially since the common folk are not privy to certain information."

Zagiri was surprised by what Lady Farah said. Hadn't

she been told that poor Vilia could not die until she had met the Terahn princess? Did the people of Hetar not realize that Vilia had done a noble thing in order to preserve her son's life? That she had personally chosen Zagiri of Terah for Jonah's new wife? Why would anyone suspect her of…of disposing of Jonah's old wife so she might be his new one? Her mother had not wanted any marriage between Terah and Hetar.

And then Zagiri began to recall little things that her mother had said when, curious, they would ask her to tell them about her girlhood in Hetar. Lara would tell them of the riches and magnificence of the Hetar of her youth. But she would also warn them that often the most beautiful things covered up the ugliest. Hetarians are manipulative, she'd said, and Zagiri was certainly seeing it in Lady Farah. For whatever reason Vilia could not die until she had met and spoken with Zagiri. And the longer she lingered the weaker her little son became. Why was that? What dark force was at work here? It had been powerful enough to bring her from the Dream Plain to Hetar. Suddenly Zagiri was afraid.

"I want to see Jonah," she said.

Lady Farah did not notice that the girl had become pale with fright. "He will probably come to see you tonight," she said. "And when he does we must sit together and discuss what to do with this foolish virginity of yours, my child. Vilia has a marvelous sex slave, Doran, who will be without a mistress now. He might be of help unless, of course, Jonah wants to sell him

off. We have several Pleasure Houses that now cater to
women here in The City. My son could make quite a fine
profit on Doran. But we shall see what he wants to do.
Gracious, you have become very pale, Zagiri. I imagine being transported via the Dream Plain from Terah
to Hetar must have been quite exhausting. We're almost
back to my house. You must have a nice rest when we
get there. You will want to be at your best when you see
Jonah tonight." And she smiled at her young companion, but the smile, Zagiri noticed, did not quite reach
to her dark eyes.

CHAPTER FIVE

ZAGIRI TRIED TO sleep, but she could not. She needed to see Jonah. She needed his reassurance that everything was going to be all right. She did love him. She did! But suddenly she was beginning to wonder if she had perhaps acted too hastily in agreeing to come to Hetar. Everything was so different here. She already knew she was not going to like her mother-in-law. But she would hide her dislike. The woman was too aggressive, and her constant nattering on about Zagiri's virginity distressed the girl. In Terah women did not give themselves quite so freely as they obviously did here in Hetar. Nor were they as consumed with sensual matters as in Hetar. Finally she fell into a restless sleep, but she did not dream.

A serving woman awoke her. "Princess, the Lord High Ruler is below in his mother's private salon. He wishes you to come to him," the servant said.

Zagiri's head ached, and her mouth was dry. "Frine," she said, and drank down the goblet the woman handed her. "I need to bathe my hands and face," she said, and the servant brought a basin of water and a cloth. Zagiri felt slightly restored after washing her face and hands. She smoothed the wrinkles from her gown.

"Let me brush the tangles from your hair, Princess," the servant said.

Zagiri sat down, and, picking up a brush, the woman tended to the girl's beautiful golden curls. "There isn't a woman in this house that has hair like yours, Princess," she said. "Men would pay a fortune just to touch such hair."

Zagiri said nothing, but she gave the servant a small smile. Finally, her hair once again in order, she arose. "Will you take me to your mistress?" she said.

"Please follow me, Princess," the servant said, leading the girl from her chamber and down a gracious flight of stairs.

They passed several beautiful women coming up the stairs with gentlemen. All of the men stared at Zagiri but she ignored them. *How rude!* she thought.

"Here we are," the servant said, opening a door and gesturing for Zagiri to enter.

She saw him at once. "Jonah!" Zagiri ran toward him.

"My beautiful golden girl," he greeted her, and, taking her into his arms, kissed her. "Aah, how sweet your lips are, my lovely princess. Let me drink my fill of you." He set her back, and his black eyes surveyed her. She was lovelier in reality than she was on the Dream Plain. "You are perfect, Zagiri. And I am so proud that you were brave enough to come to me. In just days we shall marry. Come now, and sit by my side."

"I told them I was going to my grandmother Persis for a visit. I shall not be missed for several days," Zagiri told him. Reaching up, she stroked his stern face. "You are everything that I dreamed, my lord. I was frightened earlier. I thought perhaps I would want to return to Terah, but now that I am with you all my concerns are gone." She lowered her voice so that only he might hear her. "Your mother is a forceful lady."

Jonah barked a harsh laugh. "You are kind in your judgment, Zagiri. However, you are a virgin. You have no skills at giving pleasures. If you are to be my bride you must know how to please me. Tonight, if it pleases you, we shall enjoy each other's bodies for the first time. Then my mother shall have you trained properly so that on our wedding night you and I may enjoy each other fully."

"What do you mean *have me trained,* my lord?" Zagiri asked him nervously. Coupling with him did not frighten her, but this talk of training her did.

"You will be taught how to please a man with your hands, your lips, your tongue and your most intimate female parts," Jonah told her. "On our wedding night you will show me all you have learned, my golden girl, but tonight I shall have your virginity of you. We call it First Night rights. A beautiful, well-trained virgin commands a high price, Zagiri, here in the Pleasure Houses of Hetar."

"I do not know..." Zagiri began. Then she gasped. "I am in a Pleasure House?"

"My mother is a Pleasure Mistress," he replied. "She is head of her guild. As such she has access to many resources. She will see you attain perfection for me," Jonah told the girl. "Only the most skillful of male Pleasure Slaves will be chosen to tutor you."

Zagiri was at first speechless. Then she said, "But I am a virgin, my lord, and I want only you for a lover!"

"You are sweet, my golden girl," he responded. "But once I have taken your maidenhead you are no longer virginal. Ignorance in the bedchamber is a great sin."

"Why can you not teach me what I need to know?" Zagiri asked of him.

Jonah laughed. "I am the Ruler of Hetar, my precious girl. I have no time, nor do I have the patience to teach."

"But if I know other men, I may find one that is preferable to you," she said to him. "I should be unhappy then, and so should you," Zagiri cried.

"I am considered a lover without peer," he reassured her. "And if you are truly unhappy with my performance then I shall buy you the sex slave who best pleases you," Jonah promised her. Then, standing, he took her hand. "Let us go now to your chamber, my golden girl, and we shall rid you of your troublesome virginity. Tomorrow you will begin your lessons in pleasures. All Hetar will be fixated on mourning Lady Vilia. No one will pay any attention to you. Then when the mourning is over I shall announce our wedding. You will come to the palace then. For now you will live in my mother's Pleasure House." He led her from the chamber where they had been speaking and up the stairs and to a different wing of the house. "Would you like to see?" he asked her as they moved past various doors.

Truly curious, Zagiri nodded. She was suddenly very excited. He was going to make love to her. And when he did she would convince him that this *training* nonsense was ridiculous. It had probably all been his dreadful mother's idea, anyway. Why kind of mother wanted her son's bride used by other men? It was unthinkable!

Jonah stepped before a door and carefully undid a small panel. He drew Zagiri to stand before the panel while he stood behind her. Zagiri peeped through the panel to see a beautiful woman with long, dark red hair kneeling before a man. As the girl watched the redhead took the male's manhood in one hand. She kissed it tenderly, and then her tongue encircled the mushroom-shaped tip several times. She ceased briefly to look up at her partner, smiling. He smiled back. The redhead began to take the manhood into her mouth. Soon she had absorbed it all, and from the way her cheeks were working Zagiri realized the woman was sucking on the manhood. She turned away, confused.

"Why is she doing that?" she asked Jonah.

"Because it gives him pleasure," he answered her. "It is a woman's duty to give a man pleasure when they enjoy each other's bodies." He closed the panel and drew her before another door opening the panel in it. "What do you see here, Zagiri?" he asked her.

Zagiri peeped into the room. Another beautiful woman lay spread wide upon a bed. There were two men with her. One had crawled between her legs and was licking at her mound. The other man was kissing the woman while fondling her breasts. Zagiri felt Jonah's hands slip up to cup her breasts. Even covered by her gown his actions excited her, and she pushed her buttocks back against him. "She is entertaining two men," Zagiri whispered breathlessly. The tableau before her was exciting.

"Aye," he responded, his fingers taunting her thrusting nipples. "Both will have her in a variety of ways, and they will all gain pleasure." He turned her so that she was facing him. "I will watch you take two men before you complete your training, my beautiful golden girl. But once we are wed, other than your personal sex slave, you are mine, and mine alone, Zagiri." His mouth came down hard on hers. Zagiri almost swooned in his arms, and, feeling her weakness, he picked her up and hurried down the hallway, kicking open the door at its end as he entered the chamber with her.

He set her down, and then to her great surprise he began ripping her gown from her. Zagiri cried out, shocked, and he slapped her lightly. Then he pushed her upon the great bed in the chamber, tearing the remaining shreds of her garment from her. "Lie still!" he said sharply. "The first thing you will learn is obedience to your lord." Then he began to remove his own garments slowly, setting them carefully aside. "Spread yourself, Zagiri. I want to look at your treasures as I disrobe."

To her own amazement, Zagiri obeyed him. In her

imagination she had always considered lovemaking a slow and elegant process where one kissed, and caressed, and finally joined. This wasn't anything like she had imagined. It was rough with a tinge of cruelty. She was both excited and fearful, but she spread her nether lips so he might view her, gasping when he reached out to finger her dainty love bud. She squealed as, standing over her, he began to tweak it until she was squirming uncontrollably.

"You will remain perfectly still while I play with you," he said in a hard voice.

"I cannot! It is too exciting," she half sobbed.

"Obedience, Zagiri, and discipline are two of the most important facets of taking pleasures," he told her as he removed his finger so she might recover herself. When she lay still again he said, "I will begin to touch you again, my golden girl. This time you will not wiggle. You will allow your feelings to burgeon until they burst. Trust me." His finger began to once again play with her.

Zagiri closed her eyes, and struggled with all her might not to move. What he was doing was pure torture, but then suddenly that tiny nub of flesh began to burgeon and burgeon until just when she thought she could stand no more a burst of perfect, pure pleasure drenched her. "Oh! Oh! Ooh!" she cried as wonder lit her face.

She heard his laughter, and then suddenly his head was between her thighs, and his tongue was lapping up the juices she had released. He groaned with his obvious delight. When he had satisfied himself he looked up into her shocked face. "Your first juices," he told her. "Virgin juices! They are rare, and nothing tastes like them." Then he put his head back between her legs, and sucked on the nub of flesh until she was shaking with what she realized was her own desire.

"Oh my good lord, please couple with me," Zagiri begged him. "I believe I am now ready to shed my troublesome virginity."

"Nay, not yet," he told her. "This is why you need training, my lovely one. You are like a child eager to have a sweet. You want to grab with both your hands at the bowl held out to you. When you are trained you will learn how to prolong the little pleasures so that you and I may enjoy greater pleasures. Tonight I will enjoy your innocence, but on a wedding night our coming together will be entirely different for you will have learned how to give pleasure, not just receive it."

She pouted up at him, and he chuckled. "I want to know your manhood," she said to him. "Why do you deny me?"

"Hush, my golden girl," he replied. Then without another word he pushed a long finger into her passage.

"Oh! Oh!" Zagiri's green eyes widened with surprise. The finger began to move back and forth, and her juices flowed again.

He withdrew the finger, sucked upon it for several moments, then drove two fingers into her passage, moving them back and forth while she strained against his hand. He played with her like this for several minutes, but then he abruptly ceased, saying to her, "I want you to take my manhood in your hand, Zagiri, and caress it."

Her nether regions were throbbing with their need. "Why are you being so cruel to me?" she asked him.

"Obedience, Zagiri. Take my cock, and caress it," Jonah told the girl sternly.

"No!" she said defiantly.

Without a word Jonah sat up, yanking Zagiri over his lap. Then he began to spank her while she shrieked and swore at him. Her bottom was small, round and plump. As he brought a fine pink sheen to the fair skin he was surprised to find himself becoming very excited by her struggles and cries. He was sophisticated enough to know that a certain amount of pain could sometimes be considered pleasurable, but he had never really considered it something he would enjoy. But he certainly was enjoying punishing Zagiri's disobedience. His manhood was now hard, aching and ready to be satisfied.

He shoved the girl from his lap and onto her back. Her pretty face was tearstained. "Spread yourself, Zagiri!" His knee pushed between her closed legs.

"I...I hate you!" she sobbed. "No one has ever dared to spank me. I am a princess of Terah! I hate you!"

He levered her legs apart. She struck out at him with her small fists. He caught her wrists, and yanked her arms above her head, imprisoning her with a single hand. His other hand pinched her nipples, causing her to squeal and buck. She was the most exciting creature he had ever known. "You are my beautiful golden girl," Jonah said as he now positioned his manhood at the mouth of her channel, "and your juicy virginal little cunt is ready to be plundered by your master." He pushed into her slowly.

Zagiri's eyes widened. She felt as if she were being split asunder. "You are too big!" she gasped.

"I have but inserted the tip," he told her. Then he pushed into her farther.

"Oh! Oh!" Zagiri exclaimed. She had not imagined anything like this, she thought, but then she could not remember at all what she had thought having a manhood pierce her would be like. She had envisaged a heavenly floating sensation when two bodies were joined so intimately. This was nothing like that. And when he pushed into her again she gasped at the feeling of fullness, wincing as he reached the barrier of her maidenhead. "You are too big!" she repeated.

"Your body will adjust to accommodate me in a moment or two," he promised her. "Tell me when you are ready to give me your virginity, Zagiri." He pressed his mound down against her.

The fur upon it was dark and rough, but as he pushed himself onto her soft, smooth mound a bolt of desire shot through her, and Zagiri's eyes widened again, and she gave a little gasp as she felt the manhood within her throbbing lustfully. Her breasts felt tight, and her nether regions ached with need. "Yes!" she hissed at him. "Yes, my lord Jonah! I need you! I need you!"

With a cold smile of triumph Jonah thrust hard into the girl beneath him, and she screamed as he shattered her virginity and buried himself deep. After a moment he began to move back and forth within her. And then he growled in her ear that she was to raise her legs. When Zagiri did, he pushed them back over her shoulders, bracing himself on the backs of her thighs as he thrust deeper and harder.

The pain had been ferocious, but then it faded to a burning sensation that slowly disappeared as he skillfully fucked her. Being one with this powerful man was the most wonderful thing that had ever happened to her, Zagiri thought, as she began to revel in each push of his loins against her as he plunged deeper and deeper. Unable to help herself, she screamed softly, meeting his downward drive by thrusting her hips up to meet his. "Yes! Yes! Yes!" she moaned in his ear. "Don't stop! Don't!"

"What a greedy little bitch you are, my golden girl!" Jonah groaned. "Now I must take my pleasure of you!" And he released his boiling juices.

Watching him from behind a hidden panel, Lady Farah shook her head in despair. Her son hadn't given the girl pleasure. He had only taken it. He was a fool. The girl had been nicely primed, and he left her hanging. "Go in and make this thing right," she said to the tall naked man standing with her.

"Yes, mistress," the male sex slave said, and, touching a button in the wall, the panel sprang open so he might step through.

Jonah lay upon his back breathing heavily with his satisfaction while the girl still lay spread, looking dazed. Virgin blood stained her milky thighs. The Lord High Ruler looked startled at the sex slave's entry.

"Your mother says I must complete what you began, my lord, lest the girl be unhappy," the slave explained as he climbed onto the bed. "With your permission, of course, my lord?"

Jonah nodded. "I lost control," he said. "She is too delicious."

The slave nodded. "It happens, my lord." He straddled Zagiri, and rubbed his manhood against her soft lips. "Open up, little one, and suck me sweetly," he said.

Startled, Zagiri turned to look at Jonah. "Go ahead, my golden girl," he said. "I did not give you the pleasure you deserve. The slave will. I shall not fail you again."

Half-conscious and still dazed, Zagiri obeyed, taking the slave's pale cock into her mouth. It was soft, having the faint taste of musk. Remembering the red-haired woman she had seen earlier Zagiri began to suck the slave.

"Use your tongue, little one," the male slave said. "That's it! Very good! You have an aptitude for this. Suck harder. You cannot harm me."

Zagiri sucked him harder, and soon she felt the slave's manhood swelling until she was unable to contain him within her mouth any longer. She gasped, choking.

"Release me!" the slave barked at her. Then he caressed her face with a gentle hand. "When the cock becomes too difficult to contain it is ready to give pleasures," he explained to her. Then he moved to kneel between her thighs, and drove carefully into her as he expected she would still be slightly sore from her first experience. The slave was well trained, and was frequently used by his mistress to train new Pleasure Women after their First Night rights had been taken.

"Ooh!" Zagiri exclaimed as she realized she was being taken a second time, and by this slave, not Jonah. She turned her head to look at him and he nodded encouragingly to her. "My lord!" she cried.

"Let him show you pleasures, my golden girl," Jonah told her. "I want to hear you cry out with delight when he brings you to the peak, Zagiri."

The sex slave bent, and kissed her lips tenderly. "Don't be afraid, little one," he whispered into her ear. "Let yourself go, and I will teach you the wonders of passion."

She was still shocked to realize what was happening to her, but the slave's skill was such that Zagiri found it difficult to think of anything except the fact she was starting to enjoy this activity. She closed her eyes, and let herself concentrate on the fact the slave's cock was not as thick, but was certainly longer than Jonah's. And it was making her feel wonderful. She moaned, and the sound was sensual, inviting.

Jonah's manhood twitched hearing it. He watched

Zagiri, obviously beginning to experience real pleasure for the first time. He moved around, leaning above her head, saying, "Open your mouth, Zagiri. You must suck me as you are being pleasured."

Zagiri whimpered, but she opened her mouth and, taking him, began to draw on his burgeoning flesh.

"You may come in her, but do not bring her to culmination," the Lord High Ruler commanded the sex slave. "I wish her to taste her first pleasures on my cock."

"Yes, my lord," the sex slave answered. "Tell me when you are ready."

"Ease yourself now," Jonah said.

The sex slave drove faster and faster into Zagiri, relieving his own lusts while holding the girl off from her peak. She whimpered and protested, but he whispered into her ear again. "Let your master show you paradise, little one." Then he came, and after a moment or two withdrew from her.

Jonah quickly mounted Zagiri a second time, and, feeling the entry of his wonderful, thick cock into her body, she opened her eyes, and wrapped her arms about him. He kissed her, his tongue moving in her mouth, in perfect time with his cock, which drove back and forth in her now well-lubricated channel. This time he had a mastery of himself, and brought her to a screaming perfection before releasing his own juices into her again. When he came to himself again he saw that the slave had gone. He arose from the bed, and, after bathing his male parts, began to dress himself again.

"What are you doing?" Zagiri said softly.

"I must leave you now, and return to the palace, my golden girl," Jonah told her. "The word of Vilia's death will be spread throughout Hetar by dawn. My part is that of the bereaved husband, and I do mourn her. She was a good wife and mother."

"Lady Farah says she seduced you in your slave days," Zagiri told him.

Jonah laughed. "She did, but I had been intending to seduce her. I just hadn't figured out how to do it in safety so her husband would not catch us."

"When will I see you again?" Zagiri asked him.

"On our wedding day," he told her. "Until then you will live in my mother's house away from prying eyes. You will obey Lady Farah's every dictate, Princess. And you will study hard so that on our wedding night you may surprise me with your newly acquired skills. You are no longer a virgin, Zagiri, but neither are you really a woman. You must be a woman to be my wife, my golden girl."

"Do not leave me," she begged him.

"You are a princess, Zagiri, and you know duty. I know duty, too." He bent and kissed her lips. "I will see you in a few days." Then he hurried from the chamber. He found his mother in her private salon where earlier he had greeted Zagiri. "You observed us," he said, irritated.

"And a good thing I did, my son, else Zagiri would have had no pleasures at all although I will admit you recovered most satisfactorily. Did you like Casnar? I thought I would make him one of her tutors. He has a lovely way about him. You saw that Zagiri was not frightened by him."

"I will send you Doran for her, as well," Jonah said. "He is extremely skilled. I want her ready and willing to accept a manhood in all her orifices. Do you have a young woman who can show her the pleasures of sapphic love? I want her ready for anything. And I want her mother to have to accept the fact that Zagiri is now mine."

"You are asking for a miracle in a short time. Of course she must be totally cooperative, Jonah. She seems intelligent enough."

"I'll send Doran today," the Lord High Ruler said, and then he left his mother.

Doran arrived, and the Pleasure Women of Lady Farah's house giggled and sighed with delight.

"I don't know how long I will be allowed to keep him," Lady Farah said. "But you will each get a turn with him, ladies, I promise you." She turned to the sex slave called Doran. "Will you enjoy all those pretty girls, Doran?"

Doran nodded, giving her a broad smile. He was mute but for a grunting noise he made when using a woman, but he could hear. Then he pointed at Lady Farah, and cocked his head questioningly.

She was surprised, but then she laughed. "Perhaps. We shall see," she said. "But you must be a very good

boy, Doran, if you want to settle into my nest." Lady
Farah tittered coyly.

"Who is the new girl?" one of the Pleasure Women
asked at supper that night.

"I cannot tell you right now," Lady Farah said to her
women. "She is to be trained for a very important person. In a brief while I will tell you everything, ladies.
Be patient, and inquire no further of me. And speak to
no one about this girl. No one must know she is here."

"Her virginity must have been lodged tightly," one
Pleasure Woman said. "She screamed so loudly when
it was taken from her that the lord with me lost his concentration. It took me a full hour to restore it."

"A true virginity can only be taken once," Lady Farah
said dryly. "The house will remain quiet again as it always is."

Her women laughed for some of the men coming to
take pleasures with them were noisy lovers and it was
not unusual to hear shouts and groans erupting from
behind closed doors. The magnates and other clientele
began to arrive for the evening. When she was certain
everything was as it should be Lady Farah went upstairs
to the chamber where Zagiri was being kept. She had
been given a potion that would keep her asleep until the
following morning, for her transportation from Terah
and her activities of the previous evening had worn the
girl out. But come the morrow Zagiri's lessons in how
to give pleasures would begin in earnest under her future mother-in-law's eye.

Satisfied that Zagiri was sleeping and safe now, Lady Farah made her way to her own chamber where the sex slave Doran stood waiting attendance upon her. Slipping off her robe with casual grace to reveal a well-toned body, Lady Farah looked Doran over with a critical eye. Her well-manicured hand ran up and down his goodly length. Reaching beneath him, she fondled his heavy sac. Bred to the right female, he could produce marvelous progeny who could be trained as future sex slaves. There was profit to be had from Doran, and it wouldn't come from selling him away. She must talk to her son about it. They must look for a few beautiful but sturdy girls from the Midlands. Squire Darah would certainly know the right families to visit.

"Vilia raved about you enough," Lady Farah said. "Frig yourself, and let me see what you have to offer."

With a smile he reached down, grasping his manhood, and began to rub himself. He was quickly hard, and Lady Farah nodded, impressed at the sex slave's girth and length. "You show well," she said dryly. "Now give me pleasures so I can see that you are worth your keep, Doran."

She moved toward her bedchamber behind the salon, but the sex slave grabbed her by her long dark hair, and forced Lady Farah down over the rolled arm of a couch. She protested his action, but, ignoring her, he kicked her legs apart, and drove into her without further ado. Then he proceeded to use her most thoroughly for a full hour, his thick rod plunging in and out of her channel until she was dizzy with delight, and almost ready to gain pleasures. Each time she reached that point he would pull back so that the sensations waned, and then he would begin all over again. He withdrew from her female channel at one point and pushed firmly into her ass. Farah groaned, but she did not forbid him. She squeezed the cheeks of her buttocks about his thick rod.

When he finally withdrew from that second orifice he held her down, a hand about her neck, as he bathed his member. Then he thrust into her female channel once again and gave her pleasures such as Lady Farah had never known. When she fainted away from the sheer joy of it he carried her into her bedchamber, laid her down upon her bed and then sat at her feet to await her further commands.

WHEN THE NEW day dawned Zagiri awoke slowly, stretching her limbs, feeling a soreness between her thighs. Briefly she thought of Terah, and her family. But then she put it from her mind. She was going to be the *First Lady of Hetar* soon, and she was in love with the man who would be her husband. Certainly her mother could understand that. Her mother had been in love at least twice. She considered her sexual initiation. And realized in retrospect how ignorant she had been in her innocence. Now she was eager to learn all the things that would give Jonah pleasures.

"Good morning, Princess," the same servant who had tended to her before said as she came into the bedchamber. "Are you now well rested? Lady Farah says that when you have eaten and bathed she will see you in her private salon."

"What is your name?" Zagiri asked the servant.

"Alka, Princess," came the answer.

"I will bathe first," Zagiri said. "See that my tub is brought to me."

"But, Princess," Alka responded, "this is a great house. We have a bathing chamber. Come, and I will bring you to it."

"We have several bathing chambers in my parents' castle," Zagiri replied. "I did not think Hetar would be as civilized. I am pleased to see it is."

"Not civilized?" Alka was shocked by the girl's words. "Princess, Hetar is certainly the most civilized kingdom in all the worlds known and unknown."

"My brother is King of Belmair," Zagiri volunteered. "It is a beautiful world."

"Belmair is a star, Princess," Alka pointed out.

"And when you are on Belmair it is Hetar that is the star," Zagiri told her.

Alka looked as if she didn't believe the girl but she said, "If you say so, Princess."

"You are ignorant," Zagiri remarked. "It is not your fault."

The bathing chamber was actually several tiled rooms. In the first one Zagiri was stripped of her sleeping garment and rinsed with warm water. Then she was scrubbed down with a fragrant soap and a rough cloth before being rinsed thoroughly a second time. Her long golden hair was washed, her fingernails and toenails carefully pared. Then she was told to soak in a small fragrant tub while a bath attendant toweled and brushed her hair dry. A massage with scented cream followed. She was re-dressed in a lovely pale green silk gown, and taken to Lady Farah.

"I have no shoes," she protested as she left the bath.

"You do not need them indoors," Alka said.

Lady Farah was waiting for Zagiri. She welcomed the girl, kissing her on both cheeks, and then dismissed Alka. "How do you feel, my dear?" she asked.

"I slept well last night," Zagiri answered.

The older woman laughed. "You have slept two nights and a day," she told her. "I felt it best you do so. Your initiation not to mention your trip across the Dream Plain had to be exhausting. Now, are you ready to begin your lessons?"

"Aye, I am," Zagiri said. "I want to know everything you can teach me that I may please my lord Jonah. I am not afraid of pleasures, and, like my mother, my lusts run hot."

Lady Farah smiled broadly. "I knew you were a sensible girl, and once we rid you of that silly maidenhead of yours you would understand. I think you will be pleased with the tutors I have chosen for you, Zagiri." She clapped her hands, and two men emerged from an alcove. "You will remember Casnar, of course, and this other fine specimen is Doran. He is mute, but he hears, and he is very talented. Casnar, however, will be in charge. Doran will assist him. Casnar will teach you what pleasures a man, and will therefore pleasure you. He will answer any questions you need to ask him. Go along now, my dear. You have much to learn, and little time in which to learn it."

"Come along, little one," Casnar said, taking Zagiri's hand. Both he and Doran were naked but for gold breech clothes. Where Casnar was tall and slender Doran was of medium height with a heavier build. Both men, however, were well muscled, and had very impressive manhoods, from the looks of the fabric.

"Where are we going?" the girl asked him. "I have not eaten yet."

"To your chamber. We will begin by examining each other's bodies. There are several erogenous zones that when touched properly give pleasure. You must learn them all, and learn how to touch them in the correct manner. When you can satisfy me that you have educated yourself and have gained the skill of touch you will be rewarded."

"What will you give me?" Zagiri wanted to know. "I'm hungry!"

"You will receive a most thorough reaming from one of us. It will be your choice, little one, as to which of us receives that privilege," Casnar told her. "Food later!"

"What if I want to be reamed by both of you?" she asked teasingly.

Casnar's blue eyes twinkled. "We shall see, my greedy little one." He chuckled.

When they reached Zagiri's bedchamber and had entered, Casnar told the girl to remove her silk garment, which she did. The men set aside their breech clothes.

"We will all recline together upon the bed," Casnar said.

"Are these sensitive places the same on both sexes?" Zagiri asked Casnar.

"You are quick," he said, pleased. "No, little one, they are not. I will show you those places that best please a woman, and then a man."

"Nay," Zagiri told him. "Let me learn the places that best please me in our lovemaking. But I would learn what pleases a man first."

"Take your hand, then," he told her, "and move it beneath Doran's twin sacs. Then, using the middle finger only of that hand, stroke it between the sacs."

Leaning back against the pillows, Doran spread himself open for the girl. His large manhood was limp, and lay lazily against his left thigh. She reached beneath him to cup the large pendulous sac in her hand. It overflowed her palm, and was cool to her touch. Zagiri separated her middle finger from its companions and reached out to seek where the sacs could be separated. Finding it, she began to stroke the soft flesh with her finger and within a very short time Doran groaned.

"Am I hurting you?" Zagiri asked, looking up into his face.

The sex slave shook his head and smiled.

"Continue, little one, and notice how his cock is now beginning to awaken from its slumber. That small area of flesh is very sensitive as you can see. Now crawl between his thighs, little one, and take the twin sac into your mouth. Use your tongue, and gently play with him. You may suck, but not too strongly."

Zagiri did as she was bidden, kneeling between Doran's legs and lowering her upper body so she might reach her desired target. The twin sacs were slightly downy with a soft growth. The girl licked them, taking them into her mouth, rotating her tongue about them, sucking lightly. The man began to groan, but the sound was not one of pain. Then suddenly Zagiri felt the tip of a finger sliding between the twin halves of her buttocks to rub softly at her rose hole. Instinctively she arched her back, and heard Casnar chuckle. She would have broken off her sucking, but Doran put a hand on her head to keep her in place.

"This, as you have realized, is a very sensitive spot for the female," Casnar said as he rubbed the tight little hole, which was now beginning, in spite of Zagiri's surprise, to relax. "Now I think you have teased Doran quite enough, little one. You may suck his cock, and enjoy his juices while I continue to attend to your most delicious ass. Of course, with just one man to attend to you will not yourself receive quite as much pleasure as you do with two, but we have little time in which to teach you what you must learn to please your future husband and master. You must be perfection for him, and an example to all the women of Hetar."

Zagiri heard his words, and was proud as she realized the responsibility she would have as Hetar's *First Lady*. She took Doran's extra-large manhood in her mouth. He was so big her lips were stretched to aching, but she gamely absorbed the thick peg of flesh, and sucked hard upon it. His fingers tangled in her hair kneading her head, encouraging her as he drew near to releasing his juices in her mouth. He came with a groan, and Zagiri swallowed, and swallowed, and swallowed his cream until she thought she could swallow no more. But then it was done, and he withdrew his manhood from between her pretty lips.

As he did the finger that had been arousing her, causing her nether regions to twitch with excitement, pushed into her body. Zagiri squealed, but Casnar reassured her with soft words. And then the finger was withdrawn to be replaced by his sturdy cock as his big hands first held her steady as he inserted the fleshy peg into her fundament, advising her not to struggle as he did so lest he hurt her. Zagiri wasn't sure she was breathing, but she gasped when he sheathed himself fully, then remained perfectly still, allowing herself to experience the sensation. Reaching beneath her, he began to play with her love bud, and she came upon his fingers as he throbbed within her.

"You see how even more sensitive the bud of your sex is when you are primed in other areas. Now Doran and I will show you how we three can have pleasures together." Still within her body, he gently eased Zagiri onto her side.

The girl was amazed to see that the other sex slave had, using his own hand, brought his manhood to a hard stand. He moved next to her, raising her leg and positioning it over his shoulder while he began to push himself into her female channel.

"You cannot!" Zagiri cried. "My lord Jonah cannot do something like this alone."

"But he can, little one, using a fine ivory dildo in either of your channels. You are going to give him a nice assortment of toys on your wedding night. And there might come a time when he will want to honor someone from whom he needs a great favor, so he will share your favors with his guest. This is not unheard of, Princess," Doran told her. "For now, however, I want you to just enjoy being taken by two men. Dildos are fun but not nearly as nice as the real thing."

Then together the two men began to use Zagiri vigorously. Her head spun as she concentrated first on the manhood plunging in and out of her female channel, and then upon the other one plundering her alternate channel. The two men were but separated by a thin membrane. The friction they created was incredible. They gave her pleasures twice and beyond anything she had ever imagined before the three of them came in an outpouring of orgiastic splendor that left them breathless and briefly weakened.

When they were all finally conscious again Casnar opened the door to Zagiri's chamber, and called to a servant. "Bring food!" he commanded. "We are all ravenous."

The food came. A half-barrel of oysters, the shells opened and ready for consumption; a large, juicy capon roasted to a golden-brown, stuffed with bread, sage, celery and onions; four ribs of rare beef set in a platter of its own juices; a bowl of new peas; another of fresh strawberries; bread, butter and a small wheel of hard yellow cheese. There were two decanters. One contained a heady red wine, and the other a peach-flavored Frine which was a mixture of wine and fruit juice. Both decanters were well-laced with aphrodisiacs so that the trio might continue.

Zagiri was starving, but Casnar would not allow her to eat right away. "Remember what the Lord High Ruler told you, little one. Obedience first. Lie back now, and learn." He covered her breasts, torso and mound with the cool gray oysters, which he tipped from their shells and onto her body. Then he and Doran began to eat the oysters off of her. They sucked the mollusks from her breasts, sucking the juices from her nipples. They nibbled them from her belly, licking her as they did so. They delved between her slit, seeking out every bit of oyster juice until she was wiggling with her rising desire, and they laughed wickedly. Then they sponged her with scented water to rid her of the sea scent.

Casnar sat Zagiri up. "Open your mouth, little one,"

he said, and when she did he fed her the half-dozen remaining oysters.

The two men fed her capon and beef with their fingers. They taught her to lick their fingers, and suck all the juices off of them in a sensual, suggestive manner. They made her close her thighs, pouring peas in the indentation she had made. Then they each ate from that natural bowl. When they had finished Casnar made a small hollow between his thighs, and Zagiri ate peas from it, licking his manhood free of the butter with which he had topped the vegetables.

"What a grand way to eat!" Zagiri told them.

"It keeps the passions alive and eager when one must stop to restore one's strength," Casnar explained. Then he had her lie back again and open her legs for him. Carefully he pushed a dozen fat hulled strawberries into her female channel. Then he began to suck each berry out one by one, licking the juices from her flesh. Zagiri was moaning with open desire at the conclusion of his exercise. Doran covered her breasts and torso with more strawberries, and began to pick them up, and eat them one by one, licking her breasts, her nipples, the taut flesh of her body as he did so. And while he delicately ate the berries, Casnar pushed two fingers into Zagiri, frigging her gently to help ease her excitement. Before his companion had finished his strawberries, Casnar was licking the girl's copious juices from his fingers, and she smiled at him.

When the lusty meal had been concluded the trio repaired to the baths. Afterward Zagiri was made to nap, for she had spent more than half the day in sensual pursuits, and she would be spending much of the night engrossed in these studies, too. Casnar went to seek out his mistress, and report to her on the girl's progress.

"Does she take to training?" Lady Farah asked the sex slave.

"Very well considering she was only recently a virgin," he replied. "Of course, we have concentrated on the most pleasurable facets of pleasures so far. May I ask if the Lord High Ruler enjoys giving and receiving pain in varying degrees?"

"Perhaps a little, like all men," Lady Farah said slowly. "I have never asked it of him, but Vilia never said anything, nor have any of the Pleasure Women registered a complaint against him for undue cruelty. And to my knowledge he has never visited any of the Pleasure Houses catering to those tastes. Still, his wife should know a little about such things. Spanking, of course, and he has already done that. She was indignant but did not hold it against him. I would suggest chaining her, using a blindfold, the tawse and a dog whip applied very lightly. Make certain she understands obedience, and will obey without question. If Jonah does anything other than spank her I should be surprised, but at least Zagiri should know there are greater consequences for disobedience. You will not, of course, have time to introduce her to toys, but see she is conversant with them all. I will help her to pick those she thinks will please him."

"I shall do everything as you command, mistress," Casnar replied.

"Has Doran had her? Was she able to take that wonderful cock of his?"

"She has been made familiar with it, aye, mistress. As a matter of fact, she took both of us at the same time. He had her female passage, and I the other," Casnar said.

Lady Farah sighed regretfully. "What a shame my son is so enamored of her. If she were just an ordinary girl I would make her a Pleasure Woman. A female who can take both your cock and Doran's at the same time would bring me a fortune. Be careful you do not stretch her so she cannot give her husband the pleasures he deserves."

"Yes, mistress. We were careful, and her passage seems to restore itself quite nicely. The Lord High Ruler will have no complaints."

"Excellent," Lady Farah said. Then she dismissed him, telling him to send Doran to her. She had done nothing all day but think of the sex slave who had belonged to her late daughter-in-law, Vilia. He was quite a perfect creature. Vigorous. Creative. And able to plow her without ceasing. *And he did not talk.* A man who did not swagger and brag was truly a treasure.

Lady Farah smiled to herself. Her life, for all the trouble Hetar was now facing, had taken on a rosy glow. They had stolen the Terahn princess for her son to wed, which would surely force the faerie woman, Lara, into being their ally. And the prestige the girl would bring to

Hetar would certainly quiet these unpleasant rumors of a Hierarch. And she had found a lover without par, who, if she could convince the Lord High Ruler to sell Doran to her, would bring her a fortune. She had already sent to Squire Darah requesting he seek out healthy young women in his Midlands Province so she might begin her breeding program. Aye, life was very good for the Head Mistress of the Pleasure Guild these days. Very good indeed.

CHAPTER SIX

LARA RETURNED FROM the New Outlands to be greeted by her twins. She had been gone for eight days now. Coupled with her sojourn at the Oasis of Zeroun she felt more rested than she had in several months. Anoush had told her mother as they traveled to the New Outlands that she did not want to return to Terah to live.

"I am Fiacre, Mother. I am Vartan's daughter, and I am happiest with my clan family. I want to remain with them. I will come and visit you, and you will come to see me, but I will not make the castle my home any longer. I had spoken to my stepfather before his death on this matter, and he said I must be where I was happiest," Anoush said.

Lara sighed but she had known this moment was coming. "I will have a house built for you," she told her eldest daughter. "Until it is constructed you will live with Liam and Noss."

"Aye, I should like my own home," Anoush responded. "It will make me a good marriage prospect despite my un-Fiacre talents." Then she laughed softly. "But most of my clan folk are now used to me."

"You wish to wed?"

"When I find a man whom I can love, aye, Mother. And I want children, too," Anoush surprised her mother by saying. "Despite my talents I am really just a clanswoman."

"I will see you have livestock and grazing land," Lara told her eldest daughter.

"Thank you," Anoush replied.

And so Lara had made the necessary arrangements for her child's comfort. Vartan's daughter would rejoin her father's clan family. She would be a young woman of property, and even before Lara had departed the New Outlands young men were beginning to visit Liam's hall. Mildri, Liam and Noss's young daughter, knew all the gossip, and happily expounded to Anoush what she knew of the young men.

Lara could see how happy and relaxed her daughter was to be among her father's people again. She saw how eagerly they welcomed Anoush, and realized that, as Anoush had assured her, they were used to the girl's talents now. And, too, Anoush was not faerie as her mother had been. They saw her first as Vartan's daughter, and that was good enough for the clan folk of the Fiacre. She left Anoush filled with a mixture of both happiness and sadness. She had but three children left.

But now as she hugged Taj and Marzina her eyes were sweeping the room looking about for Zagiri. "Where is your sister?" she asked her twins.

"She is still at Grandmother's house," Taj told his mother.

"And she is not yet back?" That was strange. While Lady Persis adored Zagiri, the girl did not usually remain with her grandmother more than three days when she visited. "Zagiri does not usually stay that long."

"I think she was just avoiding her lessons," Taj replied. "Marzina and I have studied hard in your absence, Mother. And we have not fought once! My twin is most respectful of my position and my high office."

"Your twin is clever and wise," Lara said dryly. Then she called a servant to her. "Send a messenger to Lady Persis's home saying I have returned and would like Zagiri to come home immediately," she instructed the servant.

"Yes, Domina," the servant replied, and bowed himself from the chamber.

An uneasiness overcame Lara. It was very unlike Zagiri to stay so long at her grandmother's house. But perhaps Persis had attempted to put forth a candidate for Zagiri's hand in marriage. Perhaps she had invited him to visit while Zagiri was with her and Zagiri actually liked her grandmother's choice, and remained. Could it actually be that simple?

An hour later the servant returned. "Domina, the messenger has returned. Lady Persis says she has not seen Princess Zagiri in many days."

Lara had no sooner heard the words he spoke than in a puff of lavender smoke she disappeared from the servant's sight. Reappearing in her mother-in-law's hall, she found Lady Persis actually expecting her.

"What is this all about?" the older woman queried Lara.

"I took Anoush to the New Outlands," Lara said.
"Zagiri said she wanted to come and visit you while I
was away. I gave her my permission. I just returned this
afternoon. I was gone eight days. You have not seen her
in that time?"

Lady Persis shook her head. "Nay, I have not. What
can have happened to my darling golden girl? Did she
ride?"

"Nay, Marzina says she said she would walk because
the weather was fair, and the distance short," Lara said.

"Could she have fallen from the cliffs?" Lady Persis quavered.

"I will send searchers, but Zagiri was like a mountain goat on the fjord paths," Lara replied. "I do not
believe she would have fallen, but we will look." Then
in another puff of smoke she was gone from Lady Persis's hall.

It was but two miles between the castle and Lady Persis's home. The cliffs were searched for the remainder
of the daylight. Two of the Forest Giants helped, walking in the fjord and searching the cliffsides carefully,
but no trace of Zagiri could be found. Lara was beginning to become frantic in her worry. Finally she knew
she had no choice.

"Prince Kaliq, heed my plea. Cease all else and come
to me!" she called aloud.

He appeared immediately in a swirl of his snow-white robes. "What is it, Lara, my love?" he asked her.

"Zagiri is missing! She said she was going to visit her grandmother, but she never did, Kaliq. No one has seen her in over a week," Lara cried.

"Have you asked your twins what they know?" he inquired.

"They know nothing! They thought she was at Persis's house," Lara said.

The Shadow Prince turned to look at Taj and Marzina. "The Dominus knows nothing," he told Lara. "But your princess daughter does, don't you, Marzina?"

"I promised not to tell," Marzina said softly.

"But you will tell us now because you understand how serious this situation may be, don't you, Marzina?" Kaliq said quietly.

Marzina nodded slowly, and then she spoke. "A few weeks ago Zagiri awakened to find a miniature of the Lord High Ruler of Hetar on her pillow."

Lara drew a sharp breath.

"She showed it to me. She thought him handsome. I thought him old," Marzina said. "Zagiri didn't know how the miniature had gotten on her pillow, but she didn't want anyone else to know of it. She was a little angry because you would not let her marry this man so she could become the ruler of Hetar's wife." Marzina did not tell her mother that Zagiri had boasted that as *First Lady of Hetar* she would rank above her mother, who was merely the widow of a Dominus. "She seemed intrigued and fascinated by the face in the miniature. She said it was a strong face, the face of a real ruler. If she had not been normal otherwise I would have thought her bewitched."

"She was," Kaliq informed the girl.

"How could she be?" Marzina asked, surprised.

"The spell was on both the portrait and Zagiri," Kaliq explained. "When she looked upon Jonah of Hetar's face she became ensorcelled. She was meant to desire him so greatly that she would find a way to go to him."

"No!" Lara cried out.

Kaliq sighed reluctantly. "The Lady Vilia has died," he told Lara. "Word came several days ago from the Shadow Princes on the High Council. It was not unexpected."

"He has taken my daughter!" Lara cried out. *"But how?* How did he manage to steal Zagiri away?" She turned to her twins. "Tell me exactly the last time you saw your sister. What time was it?"

"It was early evening," Marzina said. "We had finished our meal. Taj and I decided to play a game of Herder. Zagiri said she was going to bed. That was the last we saw of her. She had earlier told us she would walk to Grandmother Persis's house so when she did not appear for the first meal of the day we thought she had already gone."

"And so she had," Kaliq said humorously.

"This is not amusing, my lord," Lara cried. "How

has Hetar managed to gain possession of my daughter? *How?*"

"I would think it was obvious, my love," he answered her. "They have somehow managed to use magic, but from where they obtained this magic I do not know. But I will, I assure you. You must accept, however, that the Lord High Ruler has probably already taken your daughter for his bride. Vilia's mourning period would be but a week or so, Lara. The question is, if Zagiri is content to remain with the Lord High Ruler, do you want to bring her back to Terah?"

"You say she has been bewitched," Lara said slowly. "Then none of it is of her own free will. I will not have her enslaved in Hetar as I was once enslaved!" She was struggling to hold back her tears. Her daughter! Magnus's daughter! Their beautiful golden girl! Jonah of Hetar would not have her! No! No! No!

Kaliq could see the anger, the fear, the despair as it lit her face. "Lara," he said gently. "They have taken Zagiri to Hetar by means of magic, it is true. And the portrait of Jonah was enchanted to enchant her. But once she saw him then the magic would be gone. She would regain her free will. If she wants this man then you have no cause to bring her back. She is seventeen, my love. Do you really think a nice Terahn lad will do for Zagiri now? What could such a young man offer a girl who is in love with a powerful man? And who surely by now has been given pleasures beyond her wildest dreams by that man. You know better."

"Jonah has done this to gain Terah's allegiance," Lara replied.

"You are undoubtedly right," Kaliq agreed.

"Why does he need us?" Lara wondered. "What threatens him that he would go to such lengths to steal a Terahn princess? Why does he need Zagiri?"

"I do not know, but I think we had best find out," Kaliq told her. "Let me visit our council members, and see what I can learn." And before she might answer Kaliq was gone, disappearing into the shadows of the chamber. He reappeared in the apartment of the two Shadow Princes currently on the Hetarian High Council. "Lothair, Eskil, good evening to you both."

"Kaliq! What brings you to Hetar?" Lothair arose to greet his old friend. "You have just caught us. We are shortly to go out."

"There is magic in Hetar that there should not be," Kaliq said. "Over a week ago Princess Zagiri of Terah was stolen away. The culprit is, I am certain, the Lord High Ruler himself. He had sought her hand, but been refused not once, but twice. Only magic could have taken this girl from Terah, and as we know, the Hetarians don't have enough magic of their own to have done this. What have you heard, my brothers?"

"Lara must be furious and devastated by turns," Lothair said. "She will not be pleased by what I am about to tell you. Listen, Kaliq. Do you hear the music in the streets? Hetar celebrates this night the marriage of the Lord High Ruler. The bride's identity has not been revealed, however. Eskil and I had intended to later join the wedding party as we were invited. Come with us."

Kaliq nodded. "I will, but I will remain invisible to all but you and the bride. That way I can bring Lara my own eyewitness account."

"Then let us be gone," Lothair said and the three Shadow Princes stepped into the shadows of the chamber to emerge in the midst of the wedding feast.

Seeing them a majordomo hurried to lead the two princes to their table. The hall was lit by the light of a thousand beeswax candles and tapers. The air was heavy with the scent of rose and lily. There were flowers everywhere. There was a High Board, and below it a dozen trestles were set. All the tables were covered in a fine white linen edged in golden lace. Gold candelabra decorated with flowering vines were set at intervals along the tables. The guests ate upon silver plates with silver cutlery. They drank from silver goblets. Liveried servants stood behind each guest. Kaliq, invisible except to his brothers, sat on the very end of a bench. Eskil had spread his robes over it so no one else would attempt to sit there. Light music was being played by musicians in a gallery above the hall where the feast was being held.

There was a flourish of trumpets, and the doors of the hall opened to reveal the Lord High Ruler of Hetar. He was garbed in a black and gold robe, its wide sleeves and hem furred in golden fox fur. Upon his dark head he wore a thin circlet of gold studded with small gemstones. He led by the hand a beautiful young woman in a gold and white silk brocade gown with flowing sleeves, and a low square neckline that revealed her pretty round breasts. Her long flowing hair looked as if it were of spun gold. Upon the third finger of her left hand all could see a heavy red-gold marriage ring.

A gasp arose from those assembled, for they had only been told they were invited to a great feast to celebrate a most special occasion. There had been rumors that Jonah would be quickly taking a new wife so some had thought it would be a betrothal feast, and they wondered who the woman would be. Others thought perhaps that Jonah was giving a final feast to commemorate the life of the Lady Vilia. Her family had been quite certain of it. Now that they saw the young woman the Lord High Ruler led in so proudly they knew that they were wrong. And the marriage ring on her finger hinted at something else entirely, especially with Lady Farah following the couple and looking most smug.

They mounted the dais, and stood at their places at the High Board. The room grew silent with anticipation. It was at that moment Prince Kaliq chose to walk quietly from the bench where he had been seated and into the line of vision of Zagiri. Her green eyes widened slightly but she quickly realized that no one else could see the prince, and so she held her peace as Jonah began to speak.

"Good friends," he said. "Several days ago I lost my beloved wife, Vilia, to death. Vilia was a good wife, a model of perfection. And so it was before she died she chose for me my new wife. I introduce to you Princess Zagiri of Terah." Jonah drew the girl forward. "My bride. She is the daughter of our late friend Magnus Hauk, Dominus of Terah, and his wife, Lara, daughter of our own John Swiftsword. Her brother now rules in Terah, guided by the wisdom of his mother. Good friends, please greet Princess Zagiri, the *First Lady of Hetar*."

A great cheer arose from those assembled, and they clapped wildly as Zagiri stood before them. The girl with a proud smile on her lovely face stared out into the crowd of guests, but her eyes focused briefly upon Prince Kaliq, who stood leaning against one of the marble pillars of the hall, an amused smile upon his face. What was he doing here? Why could no one else but her see him? She looked away, not daring to say anything to Jonah. If Kaliq wanted to speak to her he would find an opportunity. Then suddenly everyone in the hall froze before Zagiri's startled eyes.

"What have you done, you foolish girl?" Kaliq asked her as he came forward.

"I have married a great ruler," Zagiri said defiantly. "What is so wrong with that, my lord Prince? Jonah is a wonderful man, and I am proud to be his wife."

"Your mother forbade this alliance, and yet you dared to go against her will," the prince said sternly. "And just how did you get to Hetar?"

Zagiri laughed. "I was brought across the Dream

Plain, my lord Prince. You and my mother aren't the only ones to have magic."

Kaliq shook his head at her. "You are such a mortal, Zagiri. You have no real idea what lives in the realm of magic. Or the power that some of us command. You think because you have grown up with a faerie mother, because your grandmother Ilona comes and goes in a puff of smoke that that is all there is of magic. Ask yourself why Jonah wanted you for a wife. Why he was so desperate to bring you to Hetar with all possible haste. Ask him if you dare."

"Jonah loves me," Zagiri said. "He calls me his golden girl, and says I will bring peace to Hetar," the girl declared.

"Where is there discord in Hetar that peace is necessary? Hetar is at peace because the Dark Lands are tamed for the interim, and Terah wants nothing to do with Hetar," Prince Kaliq said scornfully. "Jonah wants you for his wife because you bring him prestige and honor among his own people. And those people have become restless of late. It is said that the Hierarch's coming is imminent. Jonah does not want to solve Hetar's problems. He wants to distract the people so they will forget the problems that beset this land. What better distraction than a beautiful princess for a wife?"

"You are wrong!" Zagiri cried. "Lady Vilia chose me to follow in her footsteps, and Jonah fell in love with me at first sight."

"Lady Vilia had to die because Jonah could not put

such an openly loyal wife aside if he was to take you as a wife," Prince Kaliq said.

"Lady Vilia died to save her child," Zagiri told him. "I caught her essence in a bottle, and fed it to her son, Egon, who has for months been sickening. Within two days he was well again, my lord Prince! That good woman died so her child might live. And she picked a wife for Jonah who would follow in her footsteps. No matter what you say I will defend my husband, and stand by his side. I love him! Tell my mother that! Tell her I shall never return to Terah! That I rule a greater land than she does by the side of a husband who loves me!"

And Prince Kaliq was suddenly gone, and the hall noisy with congratulations again. Jonah looked down at his new wife and smiled. Zagiri smiled back at him. She was *First Lady of Hetar* now. She would not allow anyone to take that or this man away from her. Not all the magic in the world would part them.

LARA WEPT WHEN Kaliq returned and spoke with her. "She is not enchanted," he said. "She knows exactly what she wants, and she knows what she is doing. What I want to know is who brought her across the Dream Plain, and I mean to find out. There is dark magic at work here, my love."

"How did she look?" Lara asked him.

"Beautiful. Proud. Young," he answered her.

"If Magnus were here…" Lara began. Then she put her head in her hands. "Oh, Kaliq! I have failed Magnus.

Zagiri was our first child, and she was born out of great love. She has known nothing but love all her life. What will happen to her when she realizes that her husband is interested in preserving his own status, and has no heart despite his protestations to the contrary? Zagiri will soon feel the lack of love. It will destroy her, and I can do nothing to help.

"You tell me that my daughter has made this decision of her own free will. If indeed she did then how could I have known her so little? She is the first child I bore Magnus. She was created from our love, and yet now I find the child we loved and raised together is a stranger. Zagiri is gone from us now, from Terah. The daughter I knew, the sister her siblings knew never really existed."

"What if she seeks your help for Hetar?" Kaliq asked Lara.

"I don't know," Lara said. "My instinct is to say Terah will not give Hetar any aid of any kind. We want nothing to do with them. But what if this Hierarch appears? What will he want? How will he accomplish his mission? I always thought the Hierarch was nothing more than a legend. And when Hetar learns that Terah will not help them what will happen to my child, Kaliq? What will happen to Zagiri?"

"I must return to Shunnar and consider this," the prince told her. "Events both great and small happen for a reason, Lara. You know that is so. Now there are two questions I must answer. Who helped Jonah, and why is Zagiri so important to him? Where there are questions there are usually answers." He reached out and drew her into his arms. "Sometimes I wish life were simpler, don't you?"

Lara laughed weakly. "Aye," she agreed, "I do, but life isn't simple, Kaliq. For people like us it is convoluted, and ofttimes difficult." With a sigh she closed her eyes, and accepted the gentle kiss he pressed upon her lips. Then she said, "Oh, Kaliq, do you think he loves her?"

"I do not know," the Shadow Prince answered, "but she believes he does, and she loves him, Lara. Right now she will not leave him willingly, but you can be comforted knowing that she is safe. Zagiri possesses your passion, and your loyalty. Whatever Jonah really wants of her he does not have it yet."

"I am only just realizing that my daughter is recklessly ambitious," Lara responded slowly. "That will be Lady Persis's influence, but the old woman always spoiled Zagiri far more than her siblings. She will be heartbroken when she learns what has happened to her favorite grandchild."

"Let me leave you now, my love. We need to learn what is behind all of this," Kaliq told Lara. Giving her a quick kiss, he disappeared to reappear in his own palace of Shunnar where he found his brother Lothair waiting for him in his privy chamber.

"You have been with Lara?" he asked. "How is she?"

"Devastated, angry," Kaliq answered. "We must learn why the Lord High Ruler was so determined to have Lara's daughter as his wife. It certainly goes beyond his desire to gain Terah as an ally. Zagiri told me she was transported across the Dream Plain. Only magic could accomplish that, and as no one in Hetar has to my knowledge that kind of magic we must learn who did this great favor for the Lord High Ruler, and why. And, having granted such a boon to Jonah, they, whoever they are, will expect payment in kind," Kaliq said. "I thought we had closed off the darkness."

"Kaliq, Kaliq, there is always darkness lurking, and seeking to wreak havoc," Lothair responded. "Your concern for Lara clouds your vision, my brother."

"You are probably right," Kaliq admitted ruefully. "Now tell me what you have heard of the one they call the Hierarch."

"It's a legend that has no basis in fact," Lothair said. "But belief among the poor and the desperate often defies fact. It is said that when Hetar comes into its darkest days the Hierarch will appear to lead them back into the right path, and that path will bring Hetar back to prosperity and greatness. I cannot learn where this legend originally sprang from, but I believe we must know the source if we are to dispel it. I must go back into the history of Hetar to learn the truth."

"Go then, my brother," Kaliq said with a nod. "And while you take that direction I shall take another. I will seek out the magic that has been used here."

With a flourish of his white cape Lothair disappeared into the shadows.

Kaliq sat down at a large wooden table he used as a desk. Leaning back, he closed his blue eyes, and began to consider the possibilities. Who would have had the power to transport a mortal girl from one realm to another using the Dream Plain? No faerie from any of the kingdoms would have taken Ilona's granddaughter. The Queen of the Forest Faeries was not a being to be trifled with under any circumstances. The giants were not clever enough, and besides, Lara had no quarrel with any among them. Who then was responsible for this mischief? *It came to him suddenly!*

Only a Darkling could do what had been done, but Darklings were few and usually kept to the Dark Lands where they were under the control of the Twilight Lord. But Kol, the Twilight Lord, was imprisoned for his crimes against Hetar, Terah and Lara herself. And the twin sons Lara had borne him were hidden away by the factions that had grown up about them and now fought an endless civil war over which of these two young men would rule in his father's place. They would be fifteen now, Kaliq realized, surprised. The time had gone much too quickly. He should have been looking toward that realm. The darkness was obviously beginning to rear its head again.

Kaliq reached out, saying the words of a spell as he did. *"Darkling, Darkling, come to me. Though you would rather hidden be. A Shadow Prince calls you his way, and you cannot help but obey."* He felt the creature struggling to evade him. "Appear or suffer my wrath!" Kaliq said harshly. *"Now!"*

There was a small flash, and a beautiful woman appeared before him. "My lord Prince," she said in a smoky voice, and she swept him a mock bow. Her hair was as black as a moonless night. Her eyes were purple, and her skin milky-white. She was tall and slender. "What is it you want of me?" she said.

"Tell me your name," Kaliq answered.

The Darkling laughed. "If I tell you my name you will have power over me."

"I already have power over you," he said, "so tell me your name, Darkling."

"Why have you called me to you?" she countered.

"Your name, or I shall drag it from you," Kaliq replied.

"I had heard that you were masterful, my lord Prince," she taunted him. "How will you impel me to reveal what I choose not to reveal? Will you impale me upon your great lance forcing me to pleasures?" Her smile was wicked, and her breasts swelled just slightly over the low neckline of her violet silk gown.

"You are beautiful, and I should certainly enjoy sharing pleasures with you, but I never make love to a woman I cannot address by name," he told her, amused at her blatant attempt to seduce him.

The Darkling stamped her foot. "You mock me!" she cried out. "Yet I am worthy of your respect, for I can cause such havoc in Hetar and in Terah as has never been seen."

"Why would you do that?" he inquired of her.

"Because I can!" she responded childishly.

She was young, he realized then. "Tell me your name, Darkling," he said with a small smile. "You know mine."

Now the Darkling smiled an arch almost coquettish smile at him. "My name is Ciarda," she said. Then she clapped her hand over her mouth. "I did not mean to say it!"

"I told you I should have your name from you," Kaliq told her.

"How did you do it?" she wanted to know. "I should like to learn how to do such a thing."

"You are too young for such knowledge," Kaliq told her. "But tell me, Ciarda, why did you bring the Princess Zagiri to Hetar?"

"Because the Lord High Ruler wanted her," Ciarda responded. "The Hierarch is coming soon, and the Terahn girl will be necessary to help him keep his place as ruler."

"Indeed," Kaliq remarked dryly. "Your powers are great for one so young."

"I have been given the loan of all my sisters' powers," Ciarda said, proudly tossing her head so that her long ebony hair moved gracefully.

She was lying, and he knew it, Kaliq thought. "Why do you seek to harm Hetar?" he asked her.

"I shall not tell you why, my lord Prince," Ciarda said, and then she disappeared.

Kaliq cursed softly. He had underestimated Ciarda because he had believed her both young and naive. Her beauty had misled him. What in the name of Limbo was the matter with him? It was not like him to reveal his thoughts so easily. He might force her back to him, but she was prepared to resist him now, and he had lost the advantage. He was letting his passion for Lara weaken him, and he didn't like it. And he knew Lara would not have liked it, either. She would scold him for behaving like a boy, Kaliq thought with a small smile. And she would be right.

If he was to aid Lara then he had to pull himself together. He needed all of his strength and his powers to be of use. Allowing emotions to cloud his judgment and to weaken him was unlike a Shadow Prince. But the death of Magnus Hauk had allowed him to dream once again of having the faerie woman all to himself for eternity yet he had never thought such a thing possible. Indeed he believed it an impossible situation.

"Brother!" Lothair was once again in his presence. "I have found the source for the legend of the Hierarch. On her deathbed, Ulla, who had been Usi the sorcerer's concubine, the one who bore the daughter from whom Vilia Ahasferus descended, is said to have spoken these words. *'There will come a time in the future when Hetar grows weak and loses its path. When that time comes a leader will arise to bring Hetar back into*

*the way of righteousness. He will be called the Hier-
arch.'* I stood by Ulla's bed as she spoke these words,"
Lothair told Kaliq.

"Was Ulla known to be clairvoyant? Or was this
some mischief of Usi's?" Kaliq wondered aloud. "And
Vilia was descended from Ulla's daughter, and the chosen one in her generation. Still she loved Jonah, and
would have done nothing to harm him."

"Perhaps she was threatened," Lothair said thoughtfully. "She was happy with both her husband and the
son she bore Jonah. The only thing that irritated her was
that despite the strides the women of Hetar have made
Jonah would not give her the title of consort. What if
some dark being wished to bring Jonah down so that
the Hierarch could arise, and take power here in Hetar?
Despite her bloodline Vilia was not truly touched by
the darkness. She was greedy and ambitious, it is true,
but she was loyal to those loyal to her. If she was approached to help destroy her husband she would have
refused. So *they* reached out to harm her son in an effort to force her to their will."

"But instead Vilia warned Jonah of what was coming,
and chose an important bride for him that his stature
be increased among the people of Hetar." Kaliq took up
the thread of Lothair's idea. "And then using her own
small powers healed her child with her own life force.
I must admit to admiring such a bold tactic. It was both
clever and brave."

"Still," Lothair said, "it was the Darkling who

brought Zagiri across the Dream Plain. If the Darkling is the one who threatened Vilia in the first place why would she help her? There is more to this, brother."

"The Darkling's name is Ciarda," Kaliq said.

"The word itself means *dark*," Lothair remarked. "Is she beautiful?"

"Very," Kaliq replied. "I should have enjoyed taking pleasures with her but that she is an enemy. Her aura is violet, and it shimmers around her. She told me that her sisters had given her their powers, and then she was gone." He sighed. "I need to know more of this creature. I can scent wickedness in the very air, Lothair. It has penetrated even here to Shunnar. Gather those of our brothers who are strongest now, and go forth to seek any who would call himself the Hierarch. It is not like us to be caught off guard. Something evil is brewing, and I would know what it is."

"Agreed," Lothair said. Then he was gone from Kaliq's presence.

The great Shadow Prince sat for some time considering his next move. He could sense that this was the most dangerous game he had played in some time. He drew his cloak tightly about him and in the silent language of magic he spoke the spell. *Take me to where the Darkling lies. Reveal me not before her eyes.* He found himself in a small room. Ciarda sat brushing her long dark hair. Her beautiful coloring reminded him of Lara's youngest daughter, Marzina. And suddenly

Kaliq knew. Ciarda was either a daughter or a sister of Kol, the imprisoned Twilight Lord.

Ciarda laid the hairbrush aside. She shrugged her diaphanous lavender robe aside, and said aloud, "Rolf, Rolf, hear my plea. Cease all else, and come to me."

And a young Wolfyn appeared before Ciarda. Yanking her into his arms, he kissed her greedily while his paw hand kneaded at one of her breasts. "Prepare for me!" he growled, and when she fell upon her hands and knees he quickly mounted her, thrusting into the Darkling, leaning forward to bite her neck. Ciarda moaned with open pleasure.

Hidden in the shadows, Kaliq watched impassively. Wolfyn were more animal than anything else. The creature would not be long, and then perhaps Kaliq would overhear something of interest. The Darkling continued to whimper, her cries finally rising with her needy satisfaction, and finally the Wolfyn howled his satisfaction before releasing Ciarda. He was young, Kaliq noted, and handsome for his kind.

"How are my brothers?" Ciarda asked her lover.

"Their factions cannot keep from quarrelling and causing trouble," Rolf replied. "You will have to return to the Dark Land, Ciarda, and correct this. Old Alfrigg has his hands full, and he just isn't up to the job. Did you get the princess for the Lord High Ruler? Remember you promised me I might have her when we destroy Hetar."

Ciarda drew on her robe again. "You will have her, Rolf," she promised. "And yes, he has made her his wife.

Zagiri is Lord Jonah's weakness. He actually loves her. As for the girl, she is besotted by him, and so eager to please. She studies with two rather delicious sex slaves so she may give him the finest pleasures."

Rolf licked his lips with his long tongue. "I shall look forward to having her one day," he growled. "Let me see her, Ciarda! Please!"

Ciarda laughed, but she reached up and took down a small crystal globe from a shelf, handing it to him. "Gaze into it, and behold," she said.

Rolf looked down into the ball cradled in his hands. He could see the beautiful golden princess as she made love to, and was given pleasures in return by, Lord Jonah. He licked his lips again several times imagining the softness of her skin, the scent of her. His male member twitched eagerly.

Seeing it, Ciarda snatched the crystal globe away from the young Wolfyn. She was in no mood to be plundered by him again tonight. "Tell Alfrigg that I want a meeting with my brothers, Rolf. The sooner the better. It is almost time for me to bring the Hierarch out into the open. It will cause a war between his followers, and those who follow Jonah. And then we will take Hetar with virtually no loss to ourselves. They will not triumph over the darkness this time."

"Your father would be proud of you, Ciarda," Rolf said.

"My father had no real use for any of his daughters," she replied. "Only the birth of the next Twilight Lord was of interest to him. Then that damned faerie woman he insisted upon mating with caused us chaos by birthing twin sons. And when she escaped him he would not let it go. He had to invade her consciousness upon the Dream Plain. We all know how that turned out," Ciarda said bitterly. "We are unable to release him, Rolf. The Shadow Princes have made it impossible. But I will complete what he began. The conquest of first Hetar, and then Terah."

"I tell you again, Ciarda, that your father would be very pleased with you. It is unfortunate that you are a female. You would make a great ruler," Rolf said.

She smiled at him. "Thank you," she said, and with a wave of her hand she sent him back to his own time and place.

Kaliq had heard enough. He willed himself back to his palace in Shunnar. So the Darkling was the daughter of Kol. Kaliq chuckled to himself. He had seen the quick look on Ciarda's face when the young Wolfyn had said she would be a great ruler. There was no doubt in the Shadow Prince's mind that that was exactly what the girl meant to do. She would use her twin brothers' forces to take Hetar after they had been weakened by their own civil war. The brothers would perish before it was all over, and the beautiful Darkling would attempt a coup. She would probably succeed, too. Kaliq chuckled again. Ciarda was worthy of his admiration. It was a very clever plan. The trick, of course, would be to keep Ciarda bottled up in the Dark Lands.

Oddly her observation about Jonah and Zagiri was, he considered, good news. Lara might not think it so, but the fact that the Lord High Ruler of Hetar, an ambitious and ruthless scoundrel, loved Zagiri was encouraging. Not that Kaliq believed that the girl's love for Jonah would change him. It wouldn't. But unless Zagiri grew disillusioned with her husband and rebelled against him, she would be safe, for Jonah would protect her. He would attempt to convince Lara of that fact, but his beloved faerie woman retained a mortal's emotions where her children were concerned. She had lost her firstborn to Belmair, her second to the New Outlands.

To lose the first of the children she had borne Magnus Hauk so soon after the other two was difficult for her, especially as she had promised Marzina that she might go to her grandmother in the Forest Kingdom when the Icy Season came. Now she would not want to allow Marzina to leave, Kaliq knew, but he must convince her otherwise. Marzina, like her mother, was extraordinarily magically talented, and, like her mother, would certainly have a destiny to live out. As the Shadow Prince had anticipated, Lara was not happy with the news he brought her.

"How can she be happy with *that* man, Kaliq? *How?* Jonah is a vicious snake!" Lara's beautiful gilt-colored hair swirled about her as she paced back and forth.

"I cannot disagree with you regarding Jonah's character," Kaliq said quietly. "But Zagiri has fallen madly in love with him, and he is utterly besotted by her. There is no enchantment here. Hetar suits your daughter. She appears to adore the many luxuries it offers her, and Lady Farah has seen her trained to both give and receive pleasures. Her passions, like yours, my love, run very deep. She is content, and she is safe."

"For now," Lara answered him. "What else have you learned, my lord?"

Kaliq told her about Ciarda, and the plans she had.

"Indeed," Lara said softly. "So Kol sired a daughter before his sons."

"Several, it would appear, though how many I do not know. I would have thought him more prudent," the Shadow Prince observed.

"And so he may have been," Lara responded. "Ciarda probably lied to you, but then again there might be others. And this Darkling would kill Kol's sons, would she? Interesting, my lord. Is it possible that we can alert Alfrigg to her plotting?"

"Not yet, my love," Kaliq said. "I am not certain if he sides with one of the twins, or if he has decided to support Ciarda."

"Alfrigg is a man who believes strongly in the traditions of the Dark Lands," Lara told Kaliq. "I do not think he would favor Kol's daughter over one of his sons. He probably has not chosen a side at all. He will remain neutral until one of Kol's sons triumphs over the other. Then he will declare his loyalty to the victor."

"They are your sons, too," Kaliq reminded Lara. "Have you no feeling for them at all, my love?"

"None!" Lara told him. "Kol forced his spawn upon me. Turning the one into two was the only way I managed to triumph over the darkness for us all. And I could not have done it without your help, Kaliq. 'Twas you who got the Munin to return my memories to me, else I should have perished in the Dark Lands."

"It matters not to you that your sons will be murdered by the Darkling in her attempt to grasp her father's power?" Kaliq asked quietly.

Lara shook her head stubbornly. "Do not ask me to care about them, Kaliq. I do not know them, nor they me. They are their father's sons, not mine. And as Kol's sons it will take more than a Darkling to destroy them. Remember their birth was meant to cause chaos in the Dark Lands."

"But if their lives are taken, and Ciarda can make good her ambition to rule in her father's place, both Hetar and Terah once again stand in danger from the darkness," Kaliq said. "You know we cannot let that happen, my love."

"Then what would you have us do, my lord?" Lara demanded of him.

"First," he said, "Marzina must go to Ilona, for only her grandmother can protect her from what may come. Your daughter will be needed in the future."

"I have lost my three oldest children, Kaliq, and now you would have me part with my youngest?"

He laughed aloud at her outrage. "Think, beloved! Do not let that tiny bit of you that is mortal rule your cold faerie heart. Marzina longs to go to her grandmother to learn all that Ilona can teach her about magic, and you promised her that she could. Perhaps after you have returned from The Gathering rather than waiting for the Icy Season," he suggested. "Then we only have Taj to protect. As both of us will be going back and forth to manage this situation, one boy is easier to manage than three children. And there is the matter of the Hierarch. I do not know enough yet about him, and he represents a danger to Hetar."

"I will speak to Taj and Marzina," Lara agreed finally, sitting down next to him. "How can you be so calm about all of this, Kaliq?"

The Shadow Prince chuckled. "These past few years have been quiet, my love. Are you not ready for a few more adventures? Has your life not been just a bit dull while you played at being a wife and a mother to your five children?"

"I never played at being either a wife or a mother. I loved being Magnus's wife. I loved mothering my children," Lara said softly.

"And you almost forgot that fate has a destiny planned for you," Kaliq told her.

"Every step of my life has been a part of my destiny," Lara responded.

"You have been but marking time," the Shadow Prince said. "Now the wheel of life has begun to move again for you."

She sighed deeply. "I know. I sense the changes coming. I will not be allowed to simply live quietly like a mortal." She reached up, and touched the crystal star she had worn about her neck her entire life. "I can feel Ethne, my guardian spirit, growing restless within her crystal. And Andraste has of late begun to hum above the hearth in the Great Hall where she waits for me," Lara said. "When Magnus was killed I knew the time was near when my life would begin to shift once more. Yet I hoped it was not so. I have been so happy in Terah, Kaliq."

"If you choose, Terah can always be your home, my love," he said to her. "I had hoped that you would consider Shunnar your home."

Lara looked sharply at him. "That you still love me after all these years," she said. "I have let two mortal men into my cold faerie heart, Kaliq. Both are dead too soon."

"But I am a Shadow Prince, and I have lived forever," he replied with a small smile. He leaned forward to kiss her lush mouth.

Lara melted into the kiss. No one had ever kissed her quite like Kaliq, and she sighed happily. She had never really been able to resist him. He was the ultimate in pure magic. They broke off their embrace, and her green eyes looked into his blue ones.

"One day," he told her.

"One day what?" she queried him.

"One day you will be mine forever, my love," he answered her.

"Did you not once tell me that such a thing was not meant to be?" Lara said.

"I also told you I could not father children," he replied with a wicked smile. "Yet we have a son who rules in Belmair, do we not? If I had not lied to you then you should not have gone forth from Shunnar as you were meant to do. You were so very young then, Lara, filled with both passion and idealism. You would have never discovered your greatness as it was intended you do, nor accomplished all you have accomplished. I could not allow you to stay, and so I lied to you then. Now, however, is a different time."

"And now," she answered him, "I am not quite so idealistic, my lord Kaliq. As the truth of my heritage has been revealed I have become more faerie with but a touch of mortal. I do not know if I have it in me to love again as I have in the past."

"You love me now," he said with just a hint of arrogance in his voice. "One day you will admit it, Lara, my love. And then you will make Shunnar your home again."

She laughed, for suddenly she felt as if she were almost on an equal footing with the great Shadow Prince. "But until that time I may take lovers," she said.

He shrugged. "As will I," he returned playfully. Then he grew more serious. "I must set my brothers in Hetar to seek out all they can learn about the Hierarch."

"Aye, for if we can stop him before a civil war is

begun we can stop Ciarda from moving out of the Dark Lands and into Hetar," Lara said.

"You might have to choose sides in the Dark Lands," Kaliq told her.

"Why?" Lara wanted to know.

"Ciarda must be destroyed, and one of your sons must triumph over the other," Kaliq replied. "Whichever of them takes up the throne of the Dark Lands will be kept too busy consolidating his power to cause trouble in Hetar. I think you must decide which of your sons is the lesser of two evils. Then we will aid him to gain the ascendancy, my love."

"This is a terrible choice you give me, Kaliq," Lara said, low.

"Do you think you can recognize the one you created from the first?" he asked her. "Perhaps he will be the least dangerous."

"I have not seen them since several weeks after their birth," Lara replied. "Can you find them for me, Kaliq? Can I see and study them?"

He nodded. "It can be done, my love."

"Then do it," Lara told him. "Do it before this situation breaks my cold faerie heart. I have not thought of Kolbein and Kolgrim in years. I never wanted to think of them, or their wicked, black-hearted father. Now they are men, almost grown, and I must choose which one will live to reign over the Dark Lands, and which of them will die so the other may rule in relative peace. No mother should be forced to this kind of a decision,

Kaliq. But I am faerie, and I know what will happen if I allow that drop of mortal blood in me to overrule my common sense. Find me a way to observe Kol's twin heirs, and I will pick so that our worlds may be safe." His arm about her was comforting, and seemed to imbue her with an iron strength.

"They are both well hidden," Kaliq said. "It will take time to ferret them out, my love. Keep to your summer schedule—go to the New Outlands to visit the clan families. Now more than ever it is important that Terah have their loyalty. Take Taj with you so he may make friends among those his own age."

"He already has many friends there, but renewing those friendships now that he is the Dominus is wise. First, however, he must go to the Temple of the Great Creator where the High Priest will see that he is anointed formally. After that we will travel to the New Outlands. I will be there when you need me, my lord Kaliq."

They both arose, and he smiled into her eyes again. "Continue to be brave, my love," he said to her, and then he stepped back into the shadows of the room and was gone.

A faint smile touched Lara's lips as she breathed in the sandalwood scent that clung to his cape. She was still not happy with Zagiri's marriage. But she had no time for Zagiri now. There was much to do, and much at stake in the weeks to come.

CHAPTER SEVEN

LARA ALWAYS ENJOYED visiting the clan families of the New Outlands. Each summer she would decamp from her castle and spend several weeks with them. One summer many years past, Kol, the Twilight Lord, had kidnapped Lara, stealing her memories from her so that she believed she was his wife. He believed she was the female who would give him the single son that was born to his kind. What Kol had not known was that the Shadow Princes had planned the entire episode, and when Lara was pregnant they had regained her memories for her. Then they had explained why she had been chosen to give Kol his son. Her magic would change the child in her womb into two sons. And after their birth Lara would be brought back to Terah.

As it was forbidden to kill any son born to a Twilight Lord, the birth of twins did precisely what the Shadow Princes had intended. It caused chaos and a civil war in the Dark Lands that raged to this day. The Twilight Lord was imprisoned. His sons were hidden away, and factions favoring each of the boys grew up around them. But Kol had had his revenge upon Lara, assaulting her upon the Dream Plain when she was carrying Magnus Hauk's only son, and implanting a daughter who was born with Taj, and believed to be Magnus Hauk's child. Lara's husband had never known, for his mother-in-law had claimed Marzina's exotic coloring was that of a Nix ancestor.

It had been difficult at first for Lara to love this youngest child of hers, but Marzina had proven so genuinely sweet natured and dear that her mother could not resist her. She was also, next to her elder brother, Dillon, the most magical of Lara's children. It was a bond that drew them closer as the years passed by. Now Lara prepared to send her beloved daughter to her mother in the Forest Faerie Kingdom of Hetar. After what had happened to Zagiri she feared she could not protect Marzina properly as she needed to concentrate upon teaching her youngest son to rule his domain of Terah. Her destiny, Lara realized, was once again leading her forward whether she would go or not.

And, too, Lara's mother, Ilona, Queen of the Forest Faeries, longed to take charge of her favorite granddaughter in order to teach her faerie magic. Appearing in her daughter's apartments in her usual puff of smoke, she embraced Lara. "I am so glad you have decided to send Marzina to me sooner," she said in her musical voice.

"Kaliq has convinced me it is important she leave Terah now rather than a few months from now," Lara replied. "I hate it when he gets all mysterious."

Ilona laughed. "He knows much of what is to come,

but is forbidden from disclosing it lest he change the history of our worlds. Are you off to the clan families?"

Lara nodded. "I left Anoush several weeks ago, but did not remain. Now I would spend some time making certain that the clan families do not forget the debt they owe to Terah, and to me. Liam and his generation are growing older. Those following them must be made to remember. It doesn't matter that a mountain range separates us. If we leave the clan families to themselves they will become a law unto themselves, and forget their loyalty to Terah. It is the way of mortals to eventually forget their past."

"You are wise, daughter," Ilona said. "And Anoush has definitely decided to remain with her father's people?"

"Aye. They accept her *Sight* now, and revere her healing skills. Some young man will eventually seek her love, and take her for his wife. Anoush prefers being Fiacre, and there is little of me in her, which is perhaps for the better, Mother."

"Aye, I believe you are right," Ilona agreed. "Well, daughter, it would appear you have but one duty now. That is to Taj, and to Terah. Anoush and Zagiri have both made their choice of how they would live their lives. Dillon rules Belmair. Now Marzina, the most talented of your three daughters, will come with me so she may fully embrace her faerie heritage. I will take good care of her as I would have of you had I had that opportunity, Lara. She will be safe in the Forest Kingdom. Our people will guard her with their own lives."

"What of my brother, Cirillo?" Lara asked her mother.

"Impetuous boy," Ilona said in an annoyed tone. "He spends more time with his lover on Belmair than in the kingdom he will inherit one day." She shook her head. "A female dragon! Where did I err in raising him? I blame his father, of course. Thanos is the one who is so enamored with the natural world. It is all his fault!"

Now Lara laughed. "Oddly I think Nidhug the perfect mate for Cirillo. Oh, he will please you one day, and sire an heir on some sweet faerie lass, but Nidhug is the female he will love above all others, Mother. Be glad he will do his duty by your kingdom. Besides, it will be centuries before you fade away."

"Indeed it will," Ilona agreed. "Now where is my darling Marzina?"

"Here, Grandmother!" Marzina said, appearing suddenly.

"How long have you been eavesdropping on us?" Lara asked her daughter. "You know I have asked you not to do that." She turned to Ilona, who was beaming with pride at her granddaughter's aptitude. "Marzina lacks discipline, Mother, and even you will agree that good magic requires strict discipline."

"Aye, it does," Ilona agreed, "but do not scold the child, Lara. She is just eager."

Lara sighed. "You spoil her, Mother. Try not to make

her too impossible. Remember that she is a princess of Terah as well as faerie born." Lara reached out and took Marzina's face between her two hands. "I love you, little one. I will miss you. Were times not so dire I should keep you with me, Marzina. Remember you are my daughter, and the sister of Terah's Dominus. Obey your grandmother without question. If you prove worthy she will teach you the magic you need to know. Do not be impatient or imperious with others as you sometimes are." Lara kissed her daughter on both of her rosy cheeks. "There is change coming, Marzina, and it brings great danger with it. Do not leave the Forest Kingdom unless you are with your grandmother, your uncle Cirillo or Prince Kaliq. Do you understand me, my daughter?"

"I understand, Mother, and I thank you for this wonderful opportunity," Marzina said earnestly. "I will not fail you, or my brother."

"He may need you and your magic one day," Lara told her youngest born. "Remember that you have an obligation to Terah, the land of your birth. Study hard with your grandmother." She smoothed a lock of Marzina's dark hair from her face and sighed. "Go now before I allow my love for you to overrule my common sense," Lara said, and she struggled to hold back the tears that threatened to well up in her green eyes.

Ilona came forward, kissed Lara upon the cheek and then, putting an arm about her granddaughter, disappeared with them both in a poof of lavender smoke.

Goodbye, darling girl, Lara heard her mother call in the silent language of the magic world. A single tear ran down Lara's cheek. She brushed it away impatiently. Marzina was not a mortal child. She was magic, and it was time she learned how to control her magic and use it for good.

The day after her youngest child had departed Lara took her son with her upon Dasras, and they left for the Temple of the Great Creator where Taj would be officially anointed as Dominus of Terah. Dasras descended several miles from the temple, and galloped the rest of the distance as was his custom. They were greeted at the gates by the High Priest Arik, who was Taj's great-uncle.

"Welcome, my lord Dominus, my lady Domina," he said, coming forward smiling. He looked at Lara. "You are well, my daughter?"

She nodded. "I miss him, but aye, I am well. Painful as it is even I know that it is as it should be at this point in time, my lord Arik."

"The guest house is ready for you," Arik replied. "Tomorrow at the exact moment of sunrise we will annoint young Taj. Will you stay with us for a few days?"

"Nay, it is our time for the New Outlands, and they are expecting us," Lara told him. "Changes are coming, my lord, and we need to be ready for them."

"Is Terah safe?" he asked anxiously.

"To my knowledge for now, aye," Lara responded. "But you must know that my daughter Zagiri was lured away to Hetar. She has of her own free will married the Lord High Ruler. They believe it will force us to aid them in any time of trouble."

"Will it?" Arik queried her.

"I want to say nay, but the truth is I do not know now. I suppose it will depend upon the situation. I am not happy that Zagiri has put Terah in this position, my lord."

"Nay, you would not be. You refused such a match, did you not?" he said.

Lara nodded. "I did. There is more to this tale than I would tell you, my lord Arik. I know you will trust me to do what is best for Terah, and for my son Taj."

"I will, Domina. My nephew trusted you, and Magnus was no fool despite his deep love for you," the High Priest said. "Now I would take my great-nephew from you. He must be bathed, purified and spend the night in prayer and contemplative thought before he is anointed at dawn. Can you find your own way now, Domina? You will find an old friend awaiting you. You and she will be the only females allowed to witness the anointing." He bowed respectfully to Lara.

"Kemina!" Lara exclaimed. "How wonderful! Aye, I can find my way to the guest house, my lord Arik. I remember it well." She turned to Taj. "Make your father proud, my son," she told him, and she kissed him upon his forehead. "Now go with the High Priest while I attend to Dasras, and then find Kemina."

The young Dominus returned his mother's kiss,

touching her cheek with his cool lips. Then with a small nod of compliance he went off with Arik.

"He wears the mantle of his office well for one so young," Dasras noted.

"I know," Lara replied to the great stallion. "Magnus would be pleased to see it." She took his bridle and led him toward the stables.

"This place makes you sad," Dasras said softly.

"Magnus brought me here so I might lift the curse of Usi from the priests. I had not been in Terah long. The old High Priest Aslak was both horrified and scandalized by me," Lara recalled. "When he died in the night I wasn't so certain the shock of hearing my voice hadn't killed him. Fortunately Magnus's uncle had already been chosen his successor. I performed my magic, and the rest you know. Still it has been several years since I last came to the Temple of the Great Creator. And I never come without remembering that first time," she finished. "Ah, here we are at the stables."

"Greetings, Domina," the young priest tending the stables said. "Greetings, Lord Dasras. Your stall awaits you. I have brought a bucket of fresh water from our spring, there is fresh hay and your oats are newly poured. Is there anything else I may do for you?" the priest asked anxiously. He had never before served this magical beast although he had heard of him from others who had.

"My shoulders ache," Dasras said. "A light massage would be appreciated."

"Before or after you have eaten?" the priest inquired.

Dasras considered carefully. "After, I think," he said.

"I will see you on the morrow. Rest well," Lara told the great beast. Then she hurried off through the temple compound, crossing over the square stones that formed a bridge over the pond leading to the guest house. Stepping up onto the porch of the building, she smiled into the welcoming face of Kemina, High Priestess of the Daughters of the Great Creator, who awaited her in the open door. "Kemina!"

"Domina, it is good to see you again," Kemina said, embracing the younger woman. "You look well, I am happy to see."

The two women entered the dwelling. Kemina had brought two young novices with her to serve them. The young women moved silently about, instinctively anticipating the needs of their mistress and her companion. They were in awe of this service, for while they had heard of the faerie woman who had been Magnus Hauk's wife, they were simple girls from ordinary families who would have never hoped to see let alone meet Lara.

The widowed Domina and the High Priestess spent a pleasant afternoon and evening recalling old times shared. The two novices brought them a simple supper of capon, salad, warm bread, sweet butter and fresh fruit. They drank Frine, and toasted the memory of Magnus Hauk, and then they toasted Taj.

"Tell me of your daughters," Kemina finally asked.

Lara told her of Anoush's desire to return to her father's people, of Zagiri's runaway marriage and of Marzina being put for safety's sake with her faerie grandmother. "Something is brewing. I sense it like one senses an impending storm, Kemina. I don't know yet what will happen, but my entire energies must focus on Terah, and Taj."

"The rumors," Kemina said. "They are barely dared to be whispered, and are faint. Are they true?"

"What rumors?" Lara replied.

"That Magnus Hauk left you as regent for his son," Kemina murmured softly.

Lara nodded. She would not lie to Kemina. "He did, but such a thing must never become public knowledge, or even be admitted. I asked Corrado, Armen and Tostig to become the Dominus's Council to defuse any rumors. They have accepted that I am in charge until Taj is skilled enough to take control for himself. Terahn customs must not be broached for the sake of peace. There are always those who would cause trouble. Corrado and Persis were there when Magnus died as were Sirvat and Taj."

"Persis?" Kemina laughed. "Poor lady. How difficult hearing her son hand you the power must have been for her. She is so traditional in her manner."

"It was difficult, but her loyalty to both Magnus and to custom has required her compliance," Lara said. "And giving Taj a public council of male family members has helped her to overcome any qualms she may have struggled with, Kemina."

"You walk a fine line," the High Priestess said with a sympathetic smile.

"I do," Lara admitted, returning the smile. "But if it were not meant to be then it should not be."

"Nay, it would not," Kemina agreed.

The two women talked until moonrise, and then they retired to their beds. In the hour before the dawn they were awakened by the two novices so they might bathe prior to attending the anointing. Together they walked to the Temple of the Great Creator. Above them the sky was light, neither gray nor white. It would shortly turn to blue with the coming of the dawn. Both women were dressed in the simple white robes that had been supplied them by the priesthood. The necklines were round and high. The sleeves were long and flowing. The waistlines were beneath their breasts, and the fabric falling from that point was narrow and pleated. Sheer white gauze veils covered their heads, and they were barefoot.

Arriving at the temple, they were escorted inside and led up a flight of stairs to a small balcony that overlooked the main chamber of the temple, which was empty but for the young Dominus, who stood in prayer, naked, his back to them. At the sound of a gong the priesthood belonging to the Temple of the Great Creator entered the chamber led by Arik. They were chanting in the ancient Terahn tongue, their voices low. They formed a circle around Taj, who now stood before a simple marble altar. Arik stepped forward, and as the sun crept over the horizon spilling its light into the open temple, the High Priest poured the holy oil of Terah over the golden head of the young Dominus. The oil ran down his neck, over his bare shoulders, threading its way down his back and chest. Not a word was spoken, and only the hum of the chanting priests broke the silence. Finally Arik took a robe from the altar and draped it over Taj. Then he led the Dominus from the great chamber.

Kemina took Lara's hand, and together the two women descended the staircase back down to the main floor of the temple. The High Priestess led the Domina back to the guest house where they found their morning meal awaiting them. Fresh bread, hard-boiled eggs, butter and a honeycomb. The silent novices served them, bringing hot cups of green tea to their mistress and the Domina.

"Did you enjoy the ceremony?" Kemina asked Lara.

"Aye. It was simple and beautiful," Lara said. "The coronation will, I expect, be more lavish."

"Nay, it will not. While you will arrange that there be celebration feasts throughout Terah on that day paid for at government expense, Taj will be crowned here in this temple. Only his family, specially chosen representatives from the Seven Fjords and the New Outlands, along with the priesthood, will be allowed to attend the actual ceremony. It is as simple an affair as today's anointing was. And the day after life will continue onward as any other day after a celebration," Kemina explained.

"How lovely, and how perfect. In Hetar they would have the most lavish of crownings, and the feasting would go on for a week," Lara said.

"Such a thing breaks the rhythm of life," Kemina noted. "It is not good to break the rhythm of our passage."

They ate their meal, and then prepared to depart. Lara changed from the white robe into her leather trousers, white shirt, leather vest and boots, braiding her hair into a single plait. She strapped her sword, Andraste, onto her back. Then, embracing Kemina and thanking the two young novices for their service, she left the guest house for the stable yard where Dasras was saddled, and awaiting her.

"Good morrow, Domina," he greeted her.

"Good morrow, Dasras," she responded.

"Mother!" Taj hurried into the courtyard dressed for travel. His dark gold hair still bore the traces of holy oil. Lara smelled the sweet freesia as she embraced her son. "Did you see my anointing? My great-uncle Arik said you would be there with the High Priestess, but I glanced about, and did not see you."

"We were in the balcony above the chamber, and saw all," Lara assured him. "Are you tired, my son?"

"I prayed all night," the boy replied. "Or I tried to pray, but sometimes my mind went to my pleasurable memories and thoughts. Do you think the Great Creator was displeased with me, Mother?"

"Nay, he was not displeased," Lara said. "He understands that young men, even those who have become the Dominus of Terah, cannot yet focus only on serious matters."

"I did try, Mother," Taj said earnestly. "I really did!"

"Of course you did," Lara responded. "Now, my lord Dominus, let us mount Dasras, and be away for the New Outlands. Our companion is eager to visit Lord Roan's meadows, and see the mares who will undoubtedly be eagerly awaiting him."

Dasras neighed enthusiastically and pawed the ground with one hoof, causing both Lara and Taj to break out in laughter. They climbed aboard the big stallion, Taj sitting before his mother in the saddle for as Dominus he had official precedence over her. But it was Lara who controlled the reins of her horse. The High Priest and Kemina both came to see them off. With Dasras's permission the boy wrapped his hands in the magical beast's thick mane as he trotted from the courtyard of the Temple of the Great Creator out onto the road that led across the meadows.

Picking up speed, Dasras's great wings unfolded, and he rose up into the cloudless morning sky, circling the temple and then turning toward the high mountain range that separated Terah Prime from the New Outlands. Soon they left the open fields behind, and gentle hills appeared beneath them. Dasras flew on, rising as the hills became the Emerald Mountains. He felt the boy begin to relax, and called softly to his mistress to secure her son so he would not fall.

"If only one of your offspring were winged," Lara said. "It was easier to bring the children when they were smaller, and we could keep them in saddle baskets."

"Indeed it was," Dasras agreed. "We are almost there, however, mistress. See, the mountains are giving way once more to hills, and the plains beyond. How long will we remain this time?"

"Perhaps the remainder of the summer," Lara said. "I do not know. It will depend upon the information that Kaliq brings to me. But it would be nice to remain until The Gathering is over, wouldn't it?"

"Aye, mistress, it would," Dasras agreed. He began to drop down as they approached the meadows of the Aghy Horse Lord Roan, scanning the mares below. "A fine group of pretties," the stallion said with a small snort. "I think I shall join them as soon as I have delivered you and the Dominus to New Camdene."

Lara laughed. "You are as randy as a Shadow Prince," she told him.

Dasras galloped on through the late-morning skies and then below them livestock in the meadows became cattle, and Lara knew they had reached the territory of the Fiacre clan family. From her vantage point she could see the head village, New Camdene, in the distance. Dasras dropped down lower and lower. Then when they were but a short distance from the village, his hooves touched the ground so he might gallop the rest of the distance into New Camdene.

Lara gently shook Taj awake. "We are almost there, my son," she said.

The boy snapped awake immediately. "Thank you, Mother," he said.

His father, Lara remembered, had been able to awaken quickly and fully as Taj just had. But she had no time to grow sad with the memory, for there were already shouts of welcome reaching her ears as Dasras reached the village proper. Sitting straight before her, Taj was returning the greetings. Reaching the hall of the head of the Fiacre clan family, Lara was pleased to see Liam, Noss and their children waiting for them.

Dasras came to a stop, and Liam hurried forward. "Welcome, my lord Dominus. Welcome, Domina," he said. His red hair was showing bits of silvery copper as it faded with age, and there were deeper lines about his blue eyes.

Noss, his wife and Lara's best friend, pushed her husband aside. "Lara!" She hugged the faerie woman. "It is so good to see you, dearest one." She turned to young Taj. "Welcome, my lord Dominus, to New Camdene. You will find Sinon and Gare awaiting you in the hall," she told him.

Suddenly the Dominus was a boy again. "Thank you, Noss," he said, dashing off.

Lara smiled, and then she sighed. "He is really too young for his office," she said to Noss as, linking arms, the two women strolled to Noss's garden where they would spend much of this morning talking. "Thank you for asking his friends to come. Yesterday was very busy for him, and this morning he was officially anointed," she told her best friend. "He will be officially crowned on the first anniversary of his father's death according to Terahn custom."

"But you rule Terah, do you not?" Noss asked.

"The Dominus Taj Hauk rules Terah," Lara told her, and Noss nodded her understanding.

"Tell me of the girls," Noss said. "Why are they not with you?"

Lara explained and again Noss nodded.

"Zagiri was always a bit wild," she told Lara. "You, and especially Magnus, spoiled her terribly. A lovelier girl there has not been, but headstrong."

"Mayhap it is not unfortunate, then, that she is Jonah's new wife," Lara replied dryly. "She will certainly keep him on his toes."

"You do not mean that," Noss said as, reaching the garden, they sat down upon a padded bench. A serving woman immediately brought them goblets of cool Frine. "You were probably heartbroken when you learned what that naughty child had done."

Lara laughed. "You know me too well, but Kaliq convinced me that as Jonah actually cares for her, Zagiri will be safe as long as Hetar is safe. Now with the shock of my husband's death easing, our son upon his throne and my daughters safe I have returned to the New Outlands to rest, and consider what is ahead, Noss."

"Anoush's home has just been completed," Noss said. "She will be moving into it shortly."

"Where is my daughter? Why did she not come to greet me?" Lara wondered.

"She had been traveling to the other villages commissioning furnishings for her house, and talking with the various cattle holders about breeding her bull. She planted an herb garden on her property even before the house was finished. I have never seen her happier, Lara. She is Fiacre despite your blood," Noss told Lara. "Several young men are interested in courting her, but while she is charming with them she seems disinclined to pick a husband right now."

"Let her be then," Lara replied. "When the right man comes along she will show no reluctance whatsoever, Noss."

"Agreed," Noss said. "It was that way with us, wasn't it?"

"Aye, and it was so long ago," Lara answered softly. "The years have flown."

"You grow no older," Noss noted. "I am plump with age, and the brown hair that Liam so loved when I was younger grows thinner, and is beginning to be streaked with a gray that is most unattractive. It is not the lovely silver that some get, but rather a dull faded color. I hate it!"

"I will outlive many," Lara admitted to her best

friend. "That is the curse of faerie blood although that drop of mortal blood in my veins will eventually bring my life to an end sooner than if I were a full-blooded faerie woman. Would you like me to fix your hair for you, Noss? I can, you know."

"I just want it to be the way it was," Noss said plaintively.

"Then so be it," Lara said with a quick wave of her hand. "I hope Liam won't be too surprised." And she smiled.

Noss ran her fingers into her hair. It was thick again, and the hair was not coming out each time she touched it. She pulled a lock of it, and smiled happily. It was a rich brown once more, free of dullness. "Thank you!" she said, hugging Lara.

Anoush returned from her visits to the other Fiacre villages, and she was radiant and serene by turns in her new life. She invited her mother to stay with her, but Lara demurred, explaining that she was enjoying being with Noss again. She would stay with Anoush on her next visit, she told her daughter. Anoush agreed with a sweet smile. It made Lara happy to see her eldest daughter finally so content.

It was, Lara would recall in later years, an almost perfect summer. While she missed Magnus Hauk, Zagiri and Marzina, Lara delighted in seeing Taj running, riding, hunting with his two best friends, Sinon and Gare. All the cares of his office had dropped away. Boyish laughter filled the air as the trio roughhoused and joked with each other.

Dasras had decided to remain with the herd of mares belonging to the Aghy Horse Lord, Roan, unless Lara needed him. Usually Roan was content to allow Lara's stallion to roam freely, mounting his mares whenever the magical beast wished. This year, however, the Horse Lord had a new stallion he wished to use as a breeder. Dasras had set the young stallion into a frenzy as he casually moved among the mares, cutting those out who pleased him. The Horse Lord rode to New Camdene from his Aghy lands, greeting Liam as he entered his hall.

"Roan, I had not thought to see you until The Gathering," Liam said.

"I must speak with Lara," Roan replied. "Where is she?"

"In Noss's garden, beneath the pergola," Liam answered. "She meditates there every day at this hour. You know the way. Go and find her. You will stay the night, of course. Noss would be angry at me if you did not."

"We cannot have Noss angry." Roan chuckled. Then he went to find Lara. Seeing her as she sat quietly, Roan felt a bolt of lust race through him. She was as beautiful as she had ever been, and she was widowed now. He held no illusions that she would marry again, and Roan knew she was not likely to remain in the New Outlands, but would she be averse to taking pleasures with him? He had always desired her. "Lara," he said, coming up to her and bending from his great height to kiss her cheek.

"Lord Roan! I had not thought to see you so soon," Lara answered him. He was as handsome as ever, she considered. His eyes had always fascinated her. They were so deep a blue as to appear almost black like summer cherries. The flaming red hair that had crowned his head forever was still bright although perhaps it was fading just a little.

"You must ask Dasras to return to you, Lara," Lord Roan said.

"Why?" She overlooked the fact that Roan had addressed her familiarly. He was not a man who was easy with rules and formality.

"I have a new young stallion who shows promise, and I wish to see the kind of colts he will breed. Since Dasras arrived he has been in a frenzy for the mares all flock to your magical beast. I have penned my animal, but sooner or later he will break out of his confinement, and challenge Dasras," Roan said. "I do not want the creature slain by your stallion, Lara. Ask him to return to you."

"Why do you not ask Dasras to choose six favorites and then drive them to a far pasture?" Lara asked the Horse Lord.

"I did, and he was most amenable. But the mares not chosen by your horse refuse to mate with my breeding stallion. They will not settle down until they believe

Dasras is gone for the year and their companions returned," Roan said, running a big hand through his hair.

Lara giggled, and when he looked aggrieved she laughed. "I am sorry, Roan, but it is very funny. Really it is. Why did you not tell Dasras he was not welcome in your meadows this year? He would have stayed away, and been content with his mate, Sakira, who resides among the Fiacre. You know two blooded stallions cannot live peaceably together when a herd of mares is involved."

Roan looked abashed. "I know," he admitted, "but the truth is I always enjoy seeing Dasras's enthusiasm for my mares. And I did not think you would come this year, Lara. I do not know how Terahns mourn."

"In very much the same way as the clan families. Magnus's funeral pyre was escorted to sea three days after his death," Lara said. "My husband would have expected me to continue on as if he were here. Taj needed a carefree summer with his friends. He has taken his responsibilities as Dominus most seriously, and it is a heavy burden for a boy of thirteen," she said.

"But you rule for him, do you not?" Roan asked.

"The Dominus rules," Lara replied. "I but advise him, and I do so from the shadows behind the throne, for Terahns do not have female rulers."

"Aah," Roan replied, understanding dawning in his dark blue eyes. Then he grinned mischievously at her. "I have always liked dominant women," he told her.

"Pah! You like all women, Roan of the Aghy," Lara

mocked him. "How many women do you call wife now?"

"Eight," he replied, "yet none satisfy me as I know you could."

Lara looked at the Aghy Horse Lord. He had always lusted after her from the first moment he had met her. She remembered Vartan, her first husband, warning his friend off. What kind of a lover would Roan be? Lara wondered. He probably lacked finesse, but would be as lusty and enthusiastic as his stallion. She had to admit she was curious.

"Do you want to take pleasures with me, Roan?" she asked him.

His mouth dropped open with surprise, but he quickly recovered. "Aye!" he said. "You know I have always wanted you, Lara. Do you want to take pleasures with me?"

"Perhaps. Perhaps not," Lara answered him. "If the moment is right it will come. And then it will go, for I am not of a mind to keep a permanent lover, Roan."

"Nor I," he told her. "And I need no more wives. I already have too many," he said with a rueful smile.

"You could hardly take the Domina of Terah for a wife." She reminded him gently of her status. "But mayhap we will enjoy each other's company during the weeks I am here visiting my daughter and her family."

He knelt before her, smiling. "Do you not age at all, Lara? You are more beautiful than ever if such a thing is possible," he said. His big hands slipped beneath the soft cotton gown she wore, sliding slowly up her legs to her thighs. "Your skin is like the finest silk, *Domina*." Then, bending his fiery head, he began to follow the path his hands had taken, kissing and licking his way to the junction of her closed thighs. He could smell her female scent, and it was intoxicating to him. He nuzzled at her, and her legs slowly opened to him. Pushing his head between her legs, he peeled her nether lips open with his thumbs, staring at her sex with admiration and awe, licking at her juices, which were already beginning to flow for him.

"May I suck you, *Domina?*" he asked her softly, and when she nodded his mouth closed over her love bud, and drew upon it.

Lara closed her eyes, the better to enjoy the tugging sensation upon that most sensitive part of her anatomy. She had not expected such delicacy and elegance from the Horse Lord. His teeth nibbled gently upon her, then he sucked several hard tugs on her flesh, and she murmured with her appreciation. He brought her to a perfect wave of pleasures that flowed over her, leaving her relaxed and sated. "That was very nice, Roan," she complimented him. "May I return the favor?"

"Nay, it is not necessary," he told her. "I can give a woman a taste of pleasures to come without needing to rut like a boy, Lara. I enjoyed the interlude. Next time, however, we will take pleasures of each other."

"We will indeed," Lara told him. "You surprise me. I had not expected such finesse from you, my lord."

Roan chuckled as he rose to his feet, drawing her gown back down again. "I have had many years of practice, Lara. I know how to give a woman pleasures, and I know you are skilled in giving a man pleasures. I will look forward to our coming together tonight."

"I will recall Dasras on the morrow," Lara said to him. "You mean to remain the night, then? If you wish to return home now I can easily send you, my lord."

Roan laughed. "You will scream for me, *Domina*," he told her softly. Then he left her in the garden where he had found her.

Now it was Lara who laughed. Roan had always been supremely confident where passion and pleasures were concerned. It would be fun to have a lover for a brief time. She was faerie, and her desires ran hot. Soon enough they would return to the castle, and she must take up her duties as the Domina, as the Shadow Queen behind the throne of the young Dominus. But it was summer now, and the New Outlands were rich with growth as the cattle of the Fiacre and the horses of the Aghy fattened themselves in rich green meadows. The moment was ripe with possibilities, and the air lush with the anticipation of a new lover. She hoped he would not disappoint her but the little demonstration he had just offered her was certainly encouraging.

Noss rejoined her. "Roan was whistling when he returned to the hall," she said.

"I think I shall take him as a lover while I am here," Lara said casually.

"You must tell me then if he is as good as he claims he is," Noss replied with a rich chuckle. "He has desired you for years, but you know that. Why now?"

"It pleases me now," Lara responded.

"Something is coming," Noss said, suddenly serious. "You pleasure yourself because it gives you strength for the hard times. I know you, Lara. What is it?"

"Kol had a daughter by one of his women. A Darkling named Ciarda. She seeks to destroy Kol's sons and rule the Dark Lands herself. Her magic is strong. If she is allowed to have her way she will reach out her hand to wreak havoc in Hetar first and then Terah. There is a rumor there now that the Hierarch is coming."

"The Hierarch is a myth," Noss said. *"Isn't it?"*

"I honestly don't know," Lara said, "but I do know Ciarda must be stopped. Kol's sons are practically grown, and they continue to battle for supremacy in the Dark Lands. I must seek them out, and learn which of these two evils is the lesser. Then I will destroy the other that Ciarda may be exposed. Her half brother will control her once he has the Dark Lands firmly in his grip. It will take years, and the darkness will be kept at bay."

"You must destroy your own child?" Noss gasped.

"I birthed them, but they are not mine," Lara said. "They are Kol's sons. You know I was entrapped into having them. Few know my connection with the Dark Lands, Noss, but you are my friend, and know what I went through."

Noss nodded. "I was honored that you could confide

in me," she remembered. "I cannot imagine what you suffered then, and must now suffer." Noss reached out and took Lara's hand.

Lara squeezed the hand in hers. She and Noss had a long and deep bond even if their lives had gone in different directions. "It will be easier, I think, for not knowing them," she told her friend. "I hope it will be easier, but even my cold faerie heart quails at the thought of condemning someone to death. Still it must be done."

"Could not someone else do it?" Noss asked her. "Why did the Shadow Prince make you the responsible party for such a heinous act?"

Lara sighed. "Is it monstrous to condemn a monster?" she asked. "And Kol's sons will be monsters you may be certain. Those who have been responsible for raising them will have seen to that. They will have vied with each other to produce the most atrocious and shockingly evil creature."

"Do not think about it," Noss said. "It is too awful to even contemplate."

"Nay, I shall not think about it. I shall think of the Horse Lord instead," Lara said with a small smile. "Tonight I shall enjoy his passion, and tomorrow he will be gone. He will be a perfect divertissement, and I will not consider what is to come."

"They say his manhood is as big as a stallion's." Noss laughed softly. "You will tell me if it is so tomorrow, Lara."

"I will," Lara promised, and then she chuckled.

"You are like a pair of young maidens, heads together, giggling," Noss's husband, Liam, leader of the clan family Fiacre, said as he joined them. "What is it that amuses you two? What mischief are you up to this afternoon?"

"We are speaking on the subject of men," Noss told her mate. "Lara has decided to take pleasures with Roan."

"Good!" Liam replied. "Now maybe he will stop mooning about each time he learns you are here in the New Outlands."

"Or maybe he will moon even more," Lara teased Liam pertly.

Liam threw back his head and laughed heartily. "Be gentle with the fellow for all our sakes, my lady Domina," he said.

At the evening meal Roan could hardly keep his eyes from Lara, and when his hand went to his cup once too often she laid her own hand over his saying softly, "It is impossible that a man of your years and experience could disappoint me, unless of course he grew too drunk to enjoy what we both anticipate. After this afternoon's little demonstration I am eager to be with you tonight, my lord Roan."

"I yearn for you, and yet you terrify me now that what I have so longed for is to become a reality," Roan admitted, low.

"Then we shall not wait any longer, my lord," Lara said. "Come," she said, rising from her seat at the High Board and leading him from the hall.

He stumbled after her wondering what had happened to his confidence. How long had he desired this woman? Years! And now that he was to obtain his heart's desire he was actually frightened of what was to come. What if he didn't measure up to her other lovers? What if he disappointed her? Was the anticipation to be better than the reality?

Lara brought him to the small chamber that was hers when she visited the Fiacre. Closing the door behind her, she turned the key in the lock. A mattress upon a slightly raised platform took up most of the space. On the narrow wall a small window was open to the evening sky. Lara shrugged off her pale green cotton gown, saying as she did, "I do not want you tearing one of the few summer garments I keep here." Then she rotated about so that she was facing him. "Is everything as you expected, Roan?" she asked him.

The Horse Lord's mouth fell open as his dark blue eyes devoured the female before him. He was not used to women taking the initiative when it came to pleasures. He was not certain as he viewed her perfect form if he liked her boldness, but then she smiled at him.

"Oh, Roan, I have startled you, haven't I? I am sorry." Stepping up to him, she brushed her lips across his. "Will you let me undress you? Or do you prefer to do it yourself?" Lara smiled again.

"Nay," he managed to say. "You do it."

"Oh, I am glad you will let me," she purred as her fingers undid the horn buttons on his soft leather jerkin. Beneath he wore a cotton shirt, and she unlaced it, sliding her palms across his smooth chest as she pushed the shirt off over his shoulders and down his sinewy arms. Bending, she licked at his nipples. Then, kneeling, she helped him to pull off his boots before undoing the close-fitting leather pants he wore and sliding them over his tight buttocks. Her hands lingered on his flesh, caressing him teasingly.

He was on fire. His heart was beating so hard he thought it would burst through his chest. When she nuzzled her face into his groin he actually groaned. Roan pulled Lara to her feet and kissed her passionately. Her mouth opened easily beneath his. Their tongues sparred lustfully back and forth. She caught his, and briefly sucked on it. But then Lara broke off the embrace, and stepped back to frankly survey him.

"It is true," she said thoughtfully.

"What is true?" he managed to ask her in return.

"You are hung as well as your own stallion, my lord Roan. I had heard it said, but so often such rumors have no place in truth." She ran her fingernails very lightly down his length then wrapped her hand about his thickness, squeezing gently. "Ah yes, I believe we will give each other great pleasures," Lara told him.

He was beginning to regain his equilibrium. Her boldness was very exciting, but it was not in the natural order of things. He needed to regain control of their situation. Pushing her firmly to her knees, he rubbed the tip of his manhood against her ripe lips, watching through slitted eyes as she opened her mouth and took him in. "Very good, my beauty," he told her. "Now please me, woman, as you were meant to do."

A single hand began to knead at her head, his thick fingers digging into her scalp as she tugged and sucked at the large manhood. She could sense its life force as it began to throb. She could taste his excitement. Lara teased the manhood within her mouth, drawing it deeper into her throat. He groaned again.

"Cease your torture, faerie woman! I can bear no more," he admitted to her.

Lara rose long enough to collapse upon the mattress, her legs open and hanging over it. "Come, my lord, and take what you have so long yearned for," she invited him.

He knelt down. "First, faerie woman, you must suffer as you have made me suffer," he told her. His tongue licked swiftly up the inside of one thigh and down the other. It flickered down her shadowed slit, pushing between her nether lips, seeking out her sensitive spot. Her whimper told him when he had found it. His mouth tugged on the little nub of flesh until she was writhing upon the mattress. Satisfied at last he stood, and, sliding his hands beneath her hips, Roan drew Lara to him, sheathing her slowly until he was deep. Then he began to pump her.

Lara's entire body relaxed as he filled her and began to work his great manhood back and forth. As he moved faster and deeper, her head began to spin with the pleasure that began to arise from deep within her. "Do not stop," she cried out to him. "Use this mare as long as you can, my great stallion! Deeper! Aah, that is it! Yes!"

Her words seemed to excite him further, and Lara could have sworn that his manhood became thicker and harder within her. She wrapped her legs about his torso, and, well mounted now, he released his hold upon her hips, reaching out instead to grasp her full breasts, squeezing them hard, and leaning forward so he might suckle her, and bite her tempting nipples while his great manhood pistoned her until Lara was moaning with the pleasure he was giving her. Finally unable to bear any more of this delight, she released her juices, screaming softly as she did.

At the sound of her voice raised in pleasured agony the Horse Lord spilled his own juices, and roared with his open pleasure. It was difficult to stop pumping her, for his lust was hot and highly engaged. At last he managed to withdraw from her, and collapsed next to her upon the mattress. When he found his voice again he said, "You are even more magnificent than I imagined, my beauty. You were well worth the wait."

"And you, my lord Roan, are to be complimented for your tender vigor," Lara told him. Rolling over, she nipped at his shoulder. "I want more of you."

"You are the boldest female I have ever known," he said.

"I am an honest woman, my lord Roan," she responded. "The night is new, and I have many pleasures to share with you before the dawn comes. Do you think a woman is only to be taken upon her back?" And Lara laughed at the look of surprise upon his rough, handsome face. "You are more than well equipped to play stallion to my mare. I am not surprised you have eight wives, and I will wager none pleases you as I have pleased you in these last few minutes."

"My women are gentle and complaisant," he replied. "A man likes a woman who knows her place."

"Was not the pleasure you just had with me better than any you have previously known?" Lara demanded to know. "It was, and you lie if you say otherwise!"

He roared with his laughter, admitting, "Aye, I have never known pleasures such as we have just shared. Why is that?"

"Because I am as you have proclaimed, bold. I am your equal, Roan. Indeed I am your superior! You do not know what to expect of me. I am not ordinary. We could not be wed to one another, my lord, but we will be grand lovers if you will trust me, and follow my lead. Do you think you can, Horse Lord?"

She was the most exciting woman he had ever know. "Aye," he said. "Lead on!"

Lara jumped up. Following her, he climbed through the narrow window, and out into a moonlit field where she knelt in the sweet grass. He mounted her as a stallion would a mare, thrusting deep, biting her neck, roaring with pleasure as she squealed and bucked beneath him. She was pure magic, and more than well worth his long wait.

CHAPTER EIGHT

ALFRIGG, CHANCELLOR TO the imprisoned Twilight Lord, Kol, was troubled. Of late he had heard rumors that someone outside the Dark Lands sought for his master's twin sons. But he could not determine for certain if the whispers on the wind were true. Or, if the rumors were truth, then who was it looking for Kolbein and Kolgrim? And why were they seeking them out? Alfrigg's brown eyes were thoughtful. His gnarled fingers clasped and unclasped as he considered what to do.

Rising from the dais step where he had been seated, the old dwarf began to pace about the chamber with its silver-veined black marble walls. The tall silver censers that had once lined the room were dark but for one, which burned with a feeble flame. This was the throne room of his master, silent now but for the sound of his booted footsteps. Reaching the tarnished silver double doors, he turned, and began to pace back toward the gray and silver throne upon its matching dais. The purple-and-silver-striped silk canopy over the throne was faded, the deteriorating fabric hanging in shreds. Beyond the black marble colonnade to his left the darkened skies thundered with an impending storm.

How he wished his master were here. But no one knew what had happened to Kol, or where he was. Yet Alfrigg had pretended that he did, and had run his master's kingdom ever since the Twilight Lord's disappearance. No one had dared to question the dwarf, for their fear of Kol was greater than their curiosity. The twin princes had been sent away in their infancy to be fostered. Kolbein going to a family of Wolfyn and Kolgrim to a family of giants. Alfrigg was the only one who knew where they were. And now an unknown someone sought them.

Could it be the faerie woman who had given them life? He would not know unless he asked. Did he dare approach Lara? But why would she want to know the whereabouts of her sons unless it was to destroy them? Perhaps Kol was dead, and if she killed his heirs did she believe her victory over the Dark Lands would be complete?

There was another possibility he hated to even consider. Kol's daughters. But why would they search out their half brothers? He had seen that three of the four of his master's daughters who survived infancy and childhood were married off to those who could be of use to Kol one day. Only one, the Darkling Ciarda, remained unwed. He smiled a small smile. Ciarda was so much like her father. She had been born several years before Kol took the faerie woman for his mate. And her mother had been fortunate in not retaining Kol's favor, for several of the women who did were killed when he had mated with Lara to produce a male heir. Alfrigg had to admit to himself that he had always had a grandfatherly weakness for Ciarda. He would speak with her before he made any decisions.

The chancellor sent for Kol's daughter, and marveled at her beauty when she came to stand before him. She was as pale as moonlight with her father's ebony hair, and silver-gray eyes that changed color with her moods. He tried to recall what her mother had been like, but he could not. Ciarda stood before his chair, which was set upon a lower step on the throne's dais. She waited patiently for him to speak.

"There are rumors," Alfrigg's reedy voice began, "of someone seeking out your brothers, my lady Ciarda. Is it you? Or would you know who would look for the twins?"

"It is not I, my lord Alfrigg," she answered him, eyes lowered properly as they should be. "Why, I wonder, would someone seek out my brothers?"

"Perhaps to destroy Kol's male heirs," the chancellor said, not really meaning to discuss serious matters with a mere female. Still, Ciarda was wiser than most women.

"Oooh! That is terrible, my lord! We must protect my brothers for my father's sake," Ciarda said to him. Then she blushed. "Forgive me, my lord Alfrigg. You will have already thought of that. I should not have been so bold. Punish me if you will." She hung her dark head in shame.

Alfrigg immediately felt a burst of compassion. The

girl had meant no harm. She merely wanted to help. "Nay, my child, you need no punishment. You are but anxious to be of assistance." Reaching out, he took her hand, and patted it before dropping it again.

"Oh, thank you, my lord," Ciarda gushed. *Old fool,* she thought. *When the Dark Lands are mine to rule I will twist your head off myself. Creatures like you can never accept that women are capable of ruling, and I shall rule!*

"Then if it is not you searching for the princes it has be someone from outside our lands. Certainly they mean Kol's sons harm, else they would come to me," he muttered as if speaking to himself. And then remembering the girl he said, "I thank you for coming, my lady Ciarda. I will give your father your loving regards. He had begun to consider a suitable husband for you, my dear."

"I want no husband," Ciarda said in a suddenly hard voice that caused Alfrigg to look at her more closely.

"Lady, you must have a man to guide you. You are female," Alfrigg reminded her. He noted her eyes had engaged his briefly, and were dark with her displeasure. For a brief moment Alfrigg was reminded strongly of the Twilight Lord himself, and was rendered speechless. She was Kol in female form, he thought uncomfortably. But then before he might remonstrate with her Ciarda curtsied politely to him.

"I will go now, my lord Alfrigg," she said and, turning, went through the tarnished silver doors of the throne room.

The dwarf hummed beneath his breath thoughtfully for a long moment. As fond as he was of Kol's daughter he was no fool. He never had been, which was why he had managed to retain his position as the Twilight Lord's chancellor. His keen instincts had been the key to his survival. He would set a watch upon Ciarda. He had seen a ruthlessness in her today that both surprised and worried him. He had known women in his day who were ambitious. He shuddered. They were unnatural creatures.

It was time, he realized, to decide which of Kol's sons would have the kingdom of the Dark Lands. Wherever his master was, if he was even alive, it was obvious he was not returning to rule. Kol had offended those with far greater powers than his, and by failing to gain the faerie woman's powers he had rendered himself virtually helpless. Kolbein and Kolgrim would be fifteen now. He would choose one of them, remain with him long enough to guide him properly, choose his successor and retire to his home atop a mountain peak far from this castle. But which boy? And how to choose? He knew the families in which they had been raised would champion their fosterlings. He must first learn all he could about those families.

Kolbein had been put with a Wolfyn lord and his mates. Kolgrim had gone to one of the few Forest Giants who had not defected from Kol's allies before the battle of The City. He had placed them with these families, and never set eyes on either of them since. He had received no reports, made no visits to Kol's twin sons. In this manner he had protected their whereabouts. Now, however, he would make a visit to each family to see how these two boys had grown up. Then he would make his decision.

Neither boy knew about the other. Neither knew of his heritage. Alfrigg had gained an oath from each of the foster families in this matter that they would not tell. It was important because the laws of the Dark Lands forbade the killing of a male from the ruling family. For centuries this had not proved a problem as only one male was born in each generation. But Kol's chosen mate had birthed identical twin sons, and only one could rule. Alfrigg would choose between them, and the other would never know he might have been a great ruler.

Alfrigg departed the deserted throne room and found his way to his own small chamber. There upon a little table was his supper of oat porridge, black bread and a wedge of hard cheese. There was a goblet of bloodred wine. He ate the food and drank the wine. Then locking his chamber door and, setting a heavy iron bar across it, he climbed into bed to fall instantly asleep as was his custom.

When he was deep in slumber, his snores rattling the small window, in the wall a wraithlike Munin appeared. He stared long and hard at the Twilight Lord's chancellor. Then with slender gray fingers the Munin reached into Alfrigg's head to draw out a gnarled gold thread. He studied the thread thoughtfully, unraveling it, reading it carefully. Then, replacing the thread, the Munin disappeared into the shadows of the chamber to reappear in Prince Kaliq's palace of Shunnar. The Munin shivered. The Prince's desert kingdom was too warm for him. The Munin far preferred a more temperate climate. He would deliver his information, and depart as quickly as he could. Making his way to the prince's privy chamber he entered.

"Were you able to obtain what I seek?" Kaliq of the Shadows asked the Munin.

"He had obviously been thinking of them, for the memory was on top, not buried deep in his subconscious," the Munin said. "The one called Kolbein was placed with the Wolfyn. His twin, Kolgrim, is with a Forest Giant. I also found new memories of the Darkling Ciarda. She came to see him, and roused his suspicions. He has put a watch on her, for although he is fond of her he does not trust her," the Munin reported.

"Were you able to obtain the name of either the Wolfyn or the Forest Giant?" Prince Kaliq asked the Munin.

"He has buried those memories much too deep, my lord. He is an ancient dwarf, and I feared to harm him if I probed any harder. Alfrigg is a careful fellow. I suspect he has actually almost forgotten the names of the Wolfyn and the giant in order to protect his charges. I did my best for you," the Munin said.

"I know that you did," Prince Kaliq said. He tossed the Munin a bag of gemstones. "As you requested, half of them are Transmutes from the Emerald Mountains mine. Give your lord my felicitations. You gained me enough information so that I will more easily be able to seek out the names that I need. Thank you."

"Thank you, my lord Prince," the Munin said, and then, clutching the chamois bag containing his fee, he faded away.

A Wolfyn and a Forest Giant, Kaliq considered carefully. Skrymir, Lord of the Forest Giants, would know who had remained behind in the Dark Lands before the battle of The City. There had been one or two, but given the opportunity to escape the Twilight Lord's kingdom the remaining Forest Giants had gone with Skrymir to the forested hill country of Terah. Kolgrim should be easy to find. Kolbein would be more difficult because the Wolfyn were yet numerous despite their defeat at the battle of The City.

Their mates always bore litters of several pups who grew to adulthood within two years, and so their numbers, while diminished by the battle of The City, still remained high.

"Skrymir, Skrymir, heed my call. Come to me from out yon wall," Kaliq said aloud, and then watched as the wall seemed to melt away, and the Lord of the Forest Giants stepped through into the Shadow Prince's privy chamber.

"What is it you want of me, Kaliq of the Shadows?"

Skrymir asked, and he shook himself. "This magic of yours is too compelling." He was so tall his head was close to touching the high ceilings of the chamber.

"Let us go outside," the prince invited, attempting to make his reluctant guest a bit more comfortable. "My garden is lovely." He ushered the giant into the outdoors.

"Ah, yes, that is better," Skrymir agreed, stretching. He held out his hand. "Step into my palm, Kaliq of the Shadows, so we may speak face-to-face."

The Shadow Prince might have made himself larger, but he sensed that the giant was intimidated enough, and so he graciously stepped into the offered palm, which Skrymir raised so they might speak more comfortably. "The darkness is threatening to rise again," Kaliq began. "Kol has a daughter, a Darkling called Ciarda, who is stirring the pot. Because of her, Alfrigg believes it is time for one of Kol's twin sons to take over the Dark Lands and begin to rule."

"Will not Kol return, my lord?" the giant asked Kaliq.

"Anything is possible," the prince answered, "but it is unlikely Kol will return. Alfrigg has been keeping up a pretense in order to maintain a peace of sorts within his master's kingdom. Now he believes the time is right for a new ruler. The twins have been hidden most of their lives. One of them has been fostered by one of your own, Skrymir. Who remained behind in the Dark Lands when you brought your people out?"

"Arild and Gnup," Skrymir replied. "Arild is my kin, but he once attempted to supplant me with our people.

They would not have him, and it angered him greatly. Gnup is his toady. He is a vicious fellow, but he is useful to Arild, for he will do whatever is asked of him. His loyalty to my kin is his only virtue."

"Which one of them would take Kol's son and raise him?" Kaliq asked.

"Gnup would not have the means as he was always a hanger-on. It would be Arild. He had two wives, both Mountain Giants, a comfortable home and he would do whatever he had to do to gain the Twilight Lord's favor," Skrymir replied.

Kaliq nodded thoughtfully. "Despite the different choices you made those many years ago have you remained in contact with this Arild?"

"Alas, my lord, no," Skrymir said. "He called me traitor, and was so certain that Kol would win he ceased speaking to me. And then of course when we were given our new home Arild would not come. And because he would not, Gnup would not."

"It is likely that one of the twins has been fostered by your kinsman," the Shadow Prince said. "Do you know where within the Dark Lands Arild makes his home?"

"Before we departed his home was located on a mountainside near the valley of the Penumbras. I see no reason for him to have relocated. His lands were wide, his house spacious. And he was well isolated," Skrymir said. "If the Twilight Lord wished to hide one of his sons with Arild, the boy would be well hidden, and well protected."

"Then I shall seek him there," Kaliq said. "Now I shall return you back to your own home. I apologize if I took you from something important."

"Just my bed." Skrymir chuckled. "I hope my wife did not awaken and find me gone. She will be sure I am visiting a certain pretty giantess." Then, lowering his big palm, he set Kaliq back down on the gravel path next to the fishpond.

The Shadow Prince laughed, and, raising his hand, he said, *"Return Skrymir from whence you came. Come back when once I call again."* And the giant was gone from the garden. Kaliq sat down on the marble bench next to the pond and considered what should be done next.

He'd virtually found Kolgrim, but Kolbein's Wolfyn protector would prove a slightly more difficult creature to locate. While the Wolfyn were more numerous now there were only but half a dozen or more dominant families where Kolbein could be safely fostered. Kaliq called a servant to him, instructing him to send to his brothers inviting them to a feast on the morrow. He would tell them of what was transpiring, and then ask for volunteers to go into the Dark Lands and seek out Kolbein. Once both boys were located Lara would observe them and make a decision as to which would rule in place of his father.

That decided, Kaliq took himself to the Hall of Arild. It was early evening, and servants moved about the large hall setting the High Board for the meal. In a corner by the great hearth two women sat talking while they sewed. At their feet three small children, all girls, played. Clothed in shadows, Kaliq listened to their chatter, for women's chatter was often quite informative.

"Kolgrim grows more determined to learn who his parents are," one of the women said. "Arild does not know what to do. He has sent to Chancellor Alfrigg for instructions. We should hear within the month."

"Do you know who Kolgrim's parents are, Broska?" the younger woman asked.

"Nay, I do not for certain, but I have my suspicions, Guri," came the reply.

"Oh, tell me!" Guri whispered excitedly.

"I think he may be the son of the Twilight Lord himself," Broska whispered back, and then she placed a quick hand over Guri's mouth. "You can say nothing!" Then she nodded her head toward the little girls. "Little pitchers have big ears, sister."

Guri pulled the hand over her lips away. "Why do you think that?" she wondered.

"You know the tale that is told of how he got his son on a faerie woman. They say she was very beautiful and very powerful. He wanted her, and he wanted her powers. After Lord Kol's son was born she died, or ran away, I do not really know. But the child would have needed fostering since Lord Kol disappeared from the Dark Lands, wouldn't he? And if Kolgrim isn't the Twilight Lord's son why would Chancellor Alfrigg be involved? Arild knows, but he won't say anything about it even though I've asked him," Broska said. "But I am certain that I am right, Guri."

"Then should not Kolgrim be his father's heir? And if that is so will we not be among the highest in the land, for we have raised him? He even sucked at your teat, Broska. You fed him and your own son, Evert, together."

"They are like brothers," Broska exulted proudly. "And if I am right will not my son be among Kolgrim's closest advisors?"

"You have always been so fortunate," Guri said. "All I can give Arild are daughters although hopefully this child in my belly will be a son. It is far more active than they were. I am certain it is a giant and not a giantess this time."

"You are so pretty," Broska said, "that he will forgive you anything, Guri. Even another daughter." And Broska laughed. "I may have given our husband two sons, but our elder, Vili, is useless. He does not fight. He will not kill. All he wants to do is stick his nose in books. Praise Krell for our Evert!"

Kaliq had heard enough. Kolgrim was here. Although he had not seen the boy himself there would be time enough for that. He returned to his privy chamber where, using the silent language of magic folk, he called to Lara to come to him. She did not come immediately, but he knew she had heard him and would come as quickly as she could. How difficult this would be for her. But Lara would do what had to be done. She had never been a creature to shirk away from duty.

And then she appeared in a puff of pale green smoke. "My lord, you have news for me," Lara said. "I am sorry I could not come immediately, but I was with my lover, and I needed to see he slept before I left him."

"You have taken a lover?" He swallowed his jealousy.

"Why are you surprised, Kaliq?" Lara said. "You know my faerie nature."

"Who is it?" he demanded, unable to help himself.

She laughed. "Oh, Kaliq, do not look so fierce. It is Roan of the Aghy. He has lusted after me for years. He is vigorous, and offers rough pleasures, but he will never engage my heart in any way. You need not be jealous. Am I jealous when you take lovers of pretty mortals? Nay, I am not." But Lara lied, for she had always been jealous when he took other females to his bed. She never understood why, but she was.

"He is not worthy of you," Kaliq replied stiffly.

"Nay, he is not, but his curiosity is now satisfied. No woman ever satisfied him before me nor will any do so after me. But I could hardly take a lover from among the Fiacre clan, and I certainly could not take one who was not of noble blood," Lara said casually.

"Faerie witch!" the Shadow Prince swore softly at her.

And Lara smiled at him wickedly in return. "Now, my lord," she said, "what have you to tell me that you have summoned me here in the middle of the Terahn night?"

"It is still late afternoon here," he remarked. "I have found Kolgrim."

"Have you indeed?" she replied. "What is he like?"

"I have not seen him, but I have visited his home, and his foster mother positively dotes upon him. She suckled him along with her own son. He was out hunting with his foster father and brother."

"Who are these people who fostered the boy?" Lara asked, unable to restrain her curiosity. "Most in the Dark Lands would not have had the means to take Kol's sons."

"Kolgrim is with a Forest Giant and his family. They are kin to Og's father, but refused to leave the Dark Lands, and remained loyal to Kol. The giant is called Arild. He has two wives, five children, an enormous hall even considering his size and a large, isolated holding. The boy does not know who his parents are, but has recently become curious, and demands answers Arild dare not give him. The wives do not know the boy's parentage, either, but the elder of them has guessed though she says nothing. Because of Kolgrim's curiosity they have sent to Alfrigg for answers. Consequently we do not have a great deal of time in which to act. Better you choose than Kol's chancellor."

"Where is the other?" Lara asked him.

"All we know right now is that he is with a Wolfyn family. I have invited my brothers to a feast tonight, and will ask for their help in this matter. Will you remain and join us, Lara?" Kaliq asked her.

"Yes," she said, "I will. Now if that is all you have to

say to me I shall go to my chamber and sleep for a few hours. Send a serving woman to me, my lord."

"What of Roan of the Aghy? He will awaken to find you gone," Kaliq said.

"We share pleasures, my Prince, nothing more. If I am gone he will go. He will not question, for Roan knows he has no right to answers from me," Lara said. Leaning over, she arose from the bench next to him, kissed his cheek and found her way to the chamber that was always kept ready for her. She smiled to see a serving woman waiting for her. Kaliq was so marvelously sensitive to her needs.

"How may I serve you, Domina?" the servant said.

"I will attend tonight's feast. Waken me an hour before the guests will arrive. I will want to bathe. Tell the bath mistress to use oil of freesia."

"Of course, Domina, but may I suggest you awaken an hour and a half before the feasting begins. You will have time for a massage then," the servant said.

"Aye, 'tis better. Thank you," Lara replied.

The serving woman bowed from the waist, and left her master's guest alone. Lara immediately lay down upon her bed, and was quickly asleep. She did not dream but awakend naturally just before the servant returned to rouse her and escort her to the bathing chamber. When she arrived her sleeping garment was taken from her, and she was scrubbed with a rough cloth to remove dead skin and dirt. A stream of warm water rinsed her. Next she was gently washed with a soft sea sponge and fragrant soap redolent with the scent of freesia. Her long pale gold hair was washed, too. Another rinse followed, and Lara immediately went to sit for a few minutes in the bathing pool, her long hair spread over the marble edge to be toweled, then brushed damp dry and pinned with a silver pin atop her head.

After a short time had passed the bath mistress came to help her out of the perfumed water. "The masseur is awaiting you, my lady Domina," she said as she led Lara from the bathing room into a small square room lit only by a single light.

Lara climbed onto the high marble table with its soft feather mattress. "You may begin," she told the masseur, and, lying facedown, closed her eyes.

"The prince says I am to massage *everything,* my lady Domina," the masseur said.

"I will permit it," Lara responded, "but you would do it anyway, for he has commanded it." Then she laughed softly. "Begin!" she repeated.

The masseur's hands were skilled. They began with her shoulders and neck, digging lightly, then more strongly as they moved down her torso. He kneaded the silken oil of freesia into her shapely buttocks, pulling the twin halves apart to fully attend to them. A single digit rubbed oil about the opening to her second passage, then the thick finger pushed slowly into her, sheathing itself to the knuckle. He worked the finger inside her carefully. Then, satisfied, withdrew it, washing his hands before continuing on down her lush body. The masseur released the tension in her thighs and calves, finally reaching her small, narrow feet. His large thumbs pressed into her heel, the arch of her foot, the pads of her feet before gently massaging each toe. Then he paid the same careful attention to her other leg.

"If the Domina will turn herself over now," he said politely.

Lara rolled over with a sigh, and the masseur began anew with her neck and shoulders. Next he moved on to her breasts, massaging each one in turn, drawing the nipples out and pinching them gently to stimulate them. Her torso and belly were then attended to before he reached her silky, smooth female mound. Pulling her legs apart, he massaged the mound, drawing her nether lips apart to rub a goodly amount of oil into them. He ceased but a moment to reach into a small open jar, taking a bit of white powder upon the tip of his finger. Then he carefully inserted the finger into her main female passage, spreading the soft powder into the walls of her sheath.

"What is it?" Lara asked him.

"Alum to tighten you," the masseur told her, rubbing gently.

"What else?" Lara said.

"I would not know, Domina," the masseur answered.

"Did your master give it to you?" she queried him.

"Aye, he did," the masseur replied, withdrawing his finger, washing his hands again and then continuing on to complete the massage.

Lara closed her eyes again and smiled. If she knew Kaliq he had mixed something with the alum to make certain her arousal was complete this night, for Lara knew before the banquet was over she would share pleasures with several of the Shadow Princes, for that was the custom at these feasts. She had not attended such an event in many years, but she remembered the last one as an incredibly pleasurable experience. The Shadow Princes were sensual and skilled lovers of women.

"I am finished now, Domina," the masseur announced.

"Thank you for your attention," she said to him. "Your fingers are most skilled."

The masseur bowed in response, and departed the room even as the bath mistress reentered it to escort Lara back to her chamber where the serving woman awaited to help her dress. The gown she held out for Lara's inspection was of the finest silk and as sheer as a cobweb. It was midnight-blue in hue, but she would not don it until her hair was done. But first Lara sat while the servant painted her nipples a carmine-red.

The color was made from a sweet fruit that came from Umbra trees, which were native to the Desert Kingdom's gardens. It was, along with the horses raised by the Shadow Princes, highly prized by the people of Hetar, but so rare that it was available to only those magnates and a few Pleasure Mistresses who could afford to purchase it. Lara sat quietly while the serving woman blew the dye dry.

Next the servant dressed Lara's beautiful long hair, brushing it and then braiding two narrow plaits intertwined with slender chains of jewels on either side of her head while leaving a long swath of golden hair to stream down her back. Then she slipped the gossamer gown onto the faerie woman's form. A loose-fitting thin gold chain was fitted about her waist as a final adornment. "You are ready, Domina," the serving woman said. "Shall I escort you to the banqueting hall?"

"Nay," Lara responded. "I know the way. Thank you for your service." Then she left the smiling servant, walking across Kaliq's private garden to the main corridor of his palace. She looked over the marble balcony that opened out to the Valley of the Horses below. The herds of the Shadow Princes, sleek and beautiful as ever, grazed in the early-evening sunlight. Lara sighed. What memories she had of that valley, of traveling across it with Noss, and through its magical cliffs into the Outlands once populated by the clan families. Now, of course, it was all changed because of Hetar's insatiable greed.

"You will be late for the banquet," a familiar voice murmured in her ear.

"Lothair!" Lara turned to greet her old sword master.

"How is Andraste?" he asked as he escorted her down the wide corridor to the banquet hall.

"Cranky, for there has been nothing for her to do in these last years," Lara said.

"That will all change soon," Lothair said dryly.

"What do you know?" Lara was immediately curious.

"What you will eventually know," he teased her. "You are Kaliq's protégée, not mine, beautiful faerie woman, and he is jealous where you are concerned, as you know." He led her to where Kaliq was seated and greeting his guests. "Brother, I bring you Lara," Lothair said, seating her next to his fellow prince. "Now I must leave you, for there are two delightful little beauties eagerly awaiting me." He bowed and walked away.

"Where did you find him?" Kaliq asked her.

"He came upon me in the main corridor as I looked down into the valley, and was assailed by memories," Lara told him. "Sometimes my memories seem like just yesterday, and at other times they seem so long ago. Why are you doing this feast, Kaliq?" Reaching out, she put a hand upon his silk-clad arm.

"We will need my brothers' aid to find Kolbein," he said. He was wearing a loose-fitting white silk robe trimmed in gold thread and tiny sapphires that matched his eyes. He took the hand she had laid upon his arm, kissing both its back and palm.

His eyes met hers, and Lara smiled. "Why is it I am always happy here in Shunnar?" she said.

"Because you belong here," he told her quietly.

Do not break his heart with a hard word, child, Lara heard her guardian spirit say.

"Will your brothers involve themselves in this matter?" she instead asked him.

A quick, brief smile touched his lips as she avoided

his passion. "Some will. Others will not," he told her. Then, looking about his banquet hall, he saw that all his guests had arrived, and signaled with his hand to his majordomo for the feasting to begin.

Kaliq's efficient serving staff came forth with bowls of oysters, prawns and other crustaceans, offering crocks of mustard and dill sauces along with the sea-food. The guests all reclined upon couches as they ate. Each Shadow Prince was accompanied by one or more beautiful women gowned in sensual garments all meant to entice. They were of every skin hue with beautiful long hair in all colors. Some fed their male companions, some were fed by them.

Platters of poultry, ham, beef and game followed as a second course along with green salad, hot fresh breads, butter and cheeses. Lara ate sparingly, for she knew she would take pleasures soon with Kaliq and some of his brothers. She feasted upon two fat prawns, some capon, ham and salad. She nibbled a few bites of bread and cheese. And when a servant offered her a platter of fresh fruits she picked an apricot and some cherries. Her silver cup of wine was never empty it seemed. When a servant brought a small bowl of scented water and a towel, she washed the remnants of her meal from her hands and face.

Kaliq stood up then to speak. "The darkness threatens to rise again, my brothers," he began, looking about the banqueting hall.

"There must always be a balance of good and evil,

Kaliq," one of his brothers said. "You know that better than any."

"The Dark Lands grow restless, and need a ruler once again," Kaliq said.

"Has Chancellor Alfrigg grown too weak, then, to control it?" came the query.

"He grows old, and is tired of the responsibility. He had maintained a charade no one believes, but no one has dared question until now. Kol's daughter, the Darkling Ciarda, is about to challenge the natural order of things. One of Kol's sons must take his place as the Twilight Lord before she does so, my brothers."

"Would not a female strong enough to gain the Twilight Throne be an advantage to us all?" a Shadow Prince asked. "A civil war to unseat her would be more to our advantage than one of Kol's sons would be."

"The Darkling means to complete her father's plan of conquest, my brothers," Kaliq said quietly.

"She has not the power to disturb us," someone said.

"Nay, she does not," Kaliq agreed, "but should Hetar and then Terah fall into her hands, my brothers, the darkness would rule our world."

"What do you want us to do?" Lothair asked.

"We have already located one of Kol's sons. And we know the region in which the other dwells. Alfrigg has been clever. Neither of the twins knows his heritage. It will be up to Lara to choose which one shall rule in his father's place. As for the other, he will never learn of his heritage and war will be avoided. If Kol's son comes forward the Darkling will be defeated."

"Will he not be a danger to us, too?"

"Each of these boys has been raised as the children of their foster parents. They have no idea how to rule. Alfrigg will have to teach them to be royal. It will take time. We will see that they are corrupted by the sudden power, the wealth and the women who will be available to them. The Dark Lands will always accept a male heir over a female one. If the Darkling Ciarda tries to take over it will cause civil strife, which would also be to our advantage, my brothers, but she is more dangerous."

"Then what do you want of us, Kaliq?" Lothair asked.

"There are only a few families where the twin, Kolbein, may be hidden. I need to know which family has fostered him. It is a simple enough task, but time is of the essence, and so I come to you, my brothers, for help."

There was a murmur of discussion among the Shadow Princes in the hall. Finally one of them, Eskil by name, said, "You seem to involve yourself much in the affairs of these mortals. Can they not evolve on their own?"

"Did we?" Kaliq asked in return.

"Blasphemy!" came the brief cry, but he who spoke the word was shouted down by the others.

"It is written that the fates of those of us in the magical worlds are inexorably intertwined with the mortal races," Prince Nasim reminded the others. "It has always been our duty to guide, but some of you have forgotten that. You prefer to live comfortably in your palaces with the women who attract you, raising horses and existing in utter idleness. Many of you will not even take your turn on the Hetarian High Council, leaving that duty to just a few of us."

"The darkness cannot be allowed to prevail over the light," Kaliq reminded his guests. "We need to keep these forces of evil off balance. I will seek among the Wolfyn for Kol's son Kolbein. Who will join me?"

Nasim, Eskil and Lothair called out that they would come. Kaliq's stern gaze swept the banqueting hall until two other of his brothers, Gaszi and Terriss, volunteered to help seek for Kolbein, as well.

"We will go on the morrow," Kaliq announced. "Now, however, my brothers, it is time for us to partake of the pleasures we all enjoy so very much." He clapped his hands thrice and at once all the guests were rendered naked. Good-natured laughter followed and the servants began bringing in sweets and making certain the wine cups were well filled. Within a very few minutes the princes and their women began partaking of passion.

Lara lay back, her golden head in Kaliq's lap. She smiled up at him lovingly. Two of the princes availed themselves of her breasts. They began to suck upon them eagerly. The sweet juice of the Umbra tree that had been painted upon her nipples had upon contact with her flesh become a powerful aphrodisiac. Lara could feel their male rods lengthening and growing hard against her thighs, which were spread wide, allowing another of the princes to suckle upon her love bud. She closed her eyes, and sank into the depth of the passion that was beginning to overwhelm her.

"Is it good, my love?" Kaliq asked her, licking at her ear, and then kissing it.

"Aye, my lord, it is good," Lara murmured.

"They will want you all at once," he told her.

Lara smiled softly. "I know," she said.

Then one of the princes lay flat upon his back, and, lifting Lara up, impaled her upon his love rod while pulling her forward so his brother might avail himself of her rear passage. That prince oiled his rod, and Lara's opening. Then, holding her hips in a firm grip, he pushed into that tight passage. Now the prince who had suckled upon that tender bit of her flesh stood before her, lifting her head up to put himself into her mouth. Then the three Shadow Princes began to move in perfect rhythm together. The quartet swam in deepest pleasures, releasing their juices at the exact same moment, sending Lara into a deep swoon of delight. When she came to her senses once again she was lying in Kaliq's arms while around her the sounds of the taking of pleasures arose. There were moans of contentment, and soft cries of fulfillment as the princes and the women enjoyed each other's bodies. A handsome prince that Lara did not remember seeing before came and stood before her.

May I? he asked in the silent language.

Kaliq? Lara said.

I am content to wait, as you will be mine for the re-

mainder of the night, my love, Kaliq told her. *His name is Coilin.*

Lara held out her arms to the handsome prince, and he came into them. His lips touched hers, and she was afire with restored lust. A new lover was always exciting. Lying in Kaliq's arms, Lara's hands slipped beneath her breasts, and she offered them up to Coilin. With a smile he lay on his side, and, taking one of her breasts, fondled it, caressing it with light touches, finally closing his lips over the nipple. The sweetness of the Umbras juice quickly roused him, but he continued to suckle her as he pressed two fingers into Lara's sheath, moving them back and forth until she was writhing and eager for him. She whimpered her need.

Roll over, and kneel to me, he ordered her.

Lara complied, and sighed with pleasure as he thrust deep into her female passage. He continued to thrust until she had peaked twice, and her juices were flowing copiously. Only then did he release his own juices. Withdrawing from her, he thanked her for the pleasures she had given him and left.

Now it is our time to be together, my love, Kaliq said. *There is no need for you to share yourself any further.* He arose from the couch where they had been sprawled together. *Come!*

Where? Lara wanted to know.

Kaliq smiled, and took his long white cloak from the servant who had suddenly appeared with it. Wrapping it about them, he said aloud, "The Oasis of Zeroun, my love."

Lara felt the faint rush of their transport, and then Kaliq threw back the silk cloak, and they were there. A wave of his hand and her pavilion appeared. "Oh, my lord Kaliq," she said softly. Above them the moons of Hetar in their various phases beamed down upon them. "I would bathe," she told him. "I do not want the scent of other men upon me when we take pleasures tonight."

He led her into the water of the pool, and it was warm against her flesh. They swam together, and then Lara stood beneath the little waterfall for a few minutes before diving back into the water to join him. Kaliq took her into his arms, and kissed her a deep kiss that seemed to go on and on and on. Lara sighed, slipping her arms about his neck as he lifted her up, her body molding itself to his. Breast to chest. Belly to belly as they kissed again in the moonlight.

He carried her from the little pool, across a carpet of warm sand and into his tent. He dried their skin with a thick towel and brushed her long golden hair, which had long since come loose, shedding the filigreed jeweled chains plaited earlier into it. Taking a lock of her hair between two of his fingers, he kissed it. And when his sapphire eyes met Lara's emerald ones a new understanding bloomed suddenly between them.

What is happening, my lord Kaliq? Lara asked him silently.

Even I am not certain, Lara, my love, he replied.

The Celestial Actuary plays with us, I believe. Do not be afraid. We will follow our instincts. Putting the hairbrush down, he wrapped himself about her, kissing her shoulder first, the side of her neck and finally her ear, which he tongued teasingly, and then nipped the lobe.

Lara leaned back against him. His arms felt strong and comforting. She did not have to be strong with Kaliq. She could be merely female. Turning her head, her lips met his in another passionate kiss. The tip of his tongue encircled her lips. She followed his lead then surprised him by pushing her tongue into his mouth to find his and play with it. Their mouths were fused as he turned her so they were facing each other.

His hands fondled her breasts, tracing their shape with his fingers, tickling the nipples, which were now free of Umbra juice. Laying her back, his mouth closed over one of those tempting nipples, encircling its pointed nub with his tongue, then biting down gently upon it. Her fingers kneaded his neck as he did, her nails pressing into the flesh as his teeth scored her. "Faerie witch!" he groaned, taking her head between his hands, his fingers deep in her golden hair as he kissed her again.

Lara's hands ran down his body. She petted him with skillful fingers until she felt him shudder with delight at her touch. Her hand stroked his love rod, moving gently up and down its length, slipping beneath it to cup his love sac in her warm palm. She fondled it, fingers playing with the two large seeds within. The sharp intake of his breath was audible. She tweaked the sac a final time, and returned to caressing his length once more. Then Lara lay back upon the pillows of the large bed, and spread herself open for him. "I have waited for you all this long night, Kaliq, for no one gives me pleasures as you have always done."

"And I have waited for you, my love. Tonight for the first time I regretted our code of hospitality that requires me to share you with my brothers."

"It was most pleasurable, but I could be content with only you, my lord Kaliq," Lara told him. "Your brothers are skilled, but it is you I always want."

"Do you?" he surprised her by asking.

"Aye, I should not say it were it not so," Lara swore to him. "That bit of mortal blood that flows in my veins prevents me from being duplicitous with you, Kaliq. Certainly you knew that. I am not Ilona."

His answer was to lean forward so he might run his tongue along her shadowed slit. Feeling her quiver beneath him, he pressed his tongue between her nether lips. Finding her love bud, he teased it unmercifully until she was writhing, and her juices were beginning to flow for him. Seeing it, tasting her, Kaliq mounted Lara and thrust deep. Her immediate cry of pleasure encouraged him to his best efforts. Her legs wrapped about his torso. Her sharp nails dug into his shoulders. As he drove deeper, rode her harder, her nails raked down his long back.

"Please don't stop!" Lara begged him. "It is too delicious!"

"I cannot promise," he groaned. His lust was high, and his genuine desire for this woman was great. "These pleasures may come quickly, but we have the night together, Lara, my love," Kaliq told her as he pistoned her until she was crying out with the pleasures he was giving her, and he cried out with the pleasures she was giving him as the muscles of her sheath tightened about his thick rod. Finally he could restrain himself no more. Her body had quivered for him again and again, and her juices had flowed for him thrice. Now as they began a fourth journey he released his own juices into her with a shout of pleasure fulfilled.

He let her sleep then for she had partaken of pleasures much this evening, but when the morning came he was awakened by her mouth upon his rod encouraging it to new delights. Happily, Kaliq complied, driving her passions to heated heights until Lara laughingly cried her surrender. "No one," he told her afterward as they kissed and cuddled together, "can rouse me as you do, my love. And no one has ever actually tired me out as you do. Had you not given over now I should have had to," Kaliq admitted.

Reaching up, she caressed his handsome face with a gentle hand. "Be careful today, my lord, when you travel the Dark Lands. Bring word to me when you return."

"Will you remain at Shunnar?" he asked as he reclothed them with a snap of his fingers.

"No. I must return to the New Outlands else they worry. Ever since that summer the Twilight Lord kidnapped me they fret if I am gone more than a day or two," Lara explained to him. "Put me back in my chamber in Liam's house in New Camdene."

"With the Horse Lord?" Kaliq said dryly.

Lara laughed. "Stop being jealous, but if it will satisfy you I am through with Roan. He was beginning to become possessive of me. If he is still in Liam's hall I will send him back to his own hall and his eight wives."

"I will admit that that would please me, my love," Kaliq said.

Lara laughed softly. "Oh, Kaliq, you must not let me be your weakness," she told him. "Remember I have a cold faerie heart, my lord."

"Then I appeal to that bit of mortal within you," he teased her. "Now I must send you back, my love, before I give in to my desire to take pleasures with you again."

"You must return to your own hall, and meet up with your brothers," she reminded him. Then she quickly kissed his lips. "Until later, my lord," she said, and disappeared in a puff of green haze.

He laughed. She had taken herself off before he might send her back. Sometimes her beauty caused him to forget that she had powerful magic, too. Not as powerful as his, but her powers were great. With a swirl of his cloak he returned himself to his own privy chamber. The sun was rising over the Desert Kingdom, and it was time to go into the Dark Lands to find Kolbein, son of Kol, before the Darkling Ciarda could cause any serious damage to their worlds.

CHAPTER NINE

THE DARKLING KNOWN as Ciarda had made her home in a stone castle her father had erected long ago in the Valley of the Penumbras. It was small, for those for whom he had brought this castle into existence didn't need a great deal of space. It was cold, but that suited Ciarda's icy nature although her two servants were always whining about it. She had finally given them permission to keep a hot fire in the kitchen where they slept. The fires that burned above the stairs in her hall and elsewhere were cold fire, and gave off no heat and but dim light.

The Darkling sat at her High Board staring out into her hall and considering her next move. She must set her twin half brothers against one another. Whichever of them survived she would take as a mate. She would force him to give her his male heir, for, having been raised with no knowledge of his heritage, he would know no better. Then she would encourage him to a thoroughly debauched life that would soon kill him.

And when he was dead she would take power in the name of her son. As for that son, she would see he was encouraged from the moment of his birth to indulge himself in every way. Nothing would ever be denied

him, and, used to having his own way, he would find
ruling a tedious bore, and leave it to his dear mother,
who would do whatever necessary to keep her boy
happy. Ciarda laughed at the picture she was painting.
She would complete her father's dream to conquer Hetar
and even Terah when the power was all hers. Patience,
however, had never been her strong suit.

Irritable now, she called to her Wolfyn lover, who lay
by the fire in his animal form. Springing up, he took
on a more human appearance, and walked over to the
High Board where she now sat. "Pleasure me," she said
in a cold, hard voice.

From the shadows where he stood Kaliq watched,
amused for a brief moment, and then he returned to his
privy chamber where he found Gaszi and Eskil already
awaiting him. "No luck?" he said to them.

"None," Eskil replied. "Their manner of living is
disgusting, by the way."

Gaszi nodded in agreement. "To put a child with
creatures like that," he said, shaking his head. "The
Wolfyn clan you visited?"

"The boy was not there, either. I did check on Ciarda,
and listened to her thoughts. She is quite devious and
clever. She means to set her brothers against one another for starters, marry the survivor, mother his heir
and kill her mate off. Kol would be very proud of her,"
Kaliq remarked dryly. "She is ruthless, dangerous and
completely without mercy. But she is also extraordinarily beautiful and has a vast appetite for pleasures.

Her Wolfyn lover was doing his best to sate her when I left. His youth and his endurance are his only advantages. I actually felt sorry for him."

Lothair, Terriss and Nasim suddenly materialized within the privy chamber.

"I believe I have found him, brothers," Terriss said excitedly.

"Did you see him?" Kaliq demanded to know.

"Nay. He was with his foster father and brothers in the forest. But the women of the household spoke of Chancellor Alfrigg's impending visit," Terriss responded. "I could only surmise that meant the boy was a member of the household."

"That would seem a reasonable assumption," Kaliq said. "Did they say when the chancellor was expected?"

"Nay, but it seemed as if it would be very soon as the women in the household were busy cleaning and scouring," Terriss replied.

"Their hundred-year cleaning undoubtedly," Eskil murmured. "There were bones all over the floor of the house I visited." He shuddered.

"We will set a watch on Alfrigg, and on the Darkling Ciarda," Kaliq said. "And Lara must now begin to observe the sons she bore Kol." He looked to Terriss. "Did you leave the crystal where it would not be found as you were instructed?"

"I did," his brother replied. "You will be able to observe Kolbein wherever he is now. Shall we see if the token is working?"

Kaliq nodded, and, going to a cabinet, opened it to take out a beautiful crystal bowl, oblong in shape. Setting it upon a table, Kaliq raised his upturned palm slowly over the bowl, and it filled with a clear liquid. "Show me Kolbein," he said. Immediately the liquid darkened then cleared. The Shadow Princes gathered around the bowl saw the Wolfyn's hall. Uproarious laughter came to their ears and they saw the males of the Wolfyn pack gathered about a table where a female was bent over, her bare buttocks being whipped by a tall boy. They could hear the woman's cries of distress.

Finally the boy threw aside the dog whip he had been plying. From his baggy trousers he pulled forth a manhood larger than any mortal his age would possess. Grasping the woman's hips, his fingers digging into her soft flesh, the boy thrust himself into her, and then began to pump her hard. The woman screamed, which sent the men surrounding her into further bursts of hilarity.

"That's it, Kolbein lad," an older man encouraged the boy. "Stuff her full. Make the wench give you her pleasures. Go deeper, lad, and harder!"

"She isn't a virgin," the boy complained. "You promised me a virgin, Father Thorolf. The wench has a sheath that is wide as the open road and slack, too." He pulled out of the female and pushed her away. "Go back to the kitchens," he ordered her.

"But, my lord," the woman said, clutching at his arm,

"I did not give you pleasures." She looked up anxiously at him.

"A creature like you could not give me pleasures," the boy said sulkily. "Be gone!" His gray eyes were darkening with his irritation.

"Go!" Thorolf told the woman, and thrust her away. "Before he loses his temper and throttles you."

"I want a virgin," Kolbein said. "I want a virgin whose sheath is tight, and who will weep and beg me not to take her precious virtue away from her. I want a virgin I can thoroughly despoil, Father Thorolf. You found virgins for Wulfgar and Wulfram. Why will you not find one for me?"

"Your foster brothers found their own virgins, Kolbein. They hunted them down in their wolf forms. A Wolfyn can scent a virgin, but you are not Wolfyn, Kolbein. You were given to us to foster."

"Who gave me to you?" the boy demanded to know.

Thorolf shook his head. "I am forbidden from telling you that until he comes himself to tell you. And that will be soon, I promise you."

"Your promises are worthless." The boy sneered. "You promised me a virgin, and then gave me a kitchen wench that every male in this house has futtered. Bah!" And the boy stormed from the hall angrily.

The liquid in the bowl darkened again before reverting to its original form.

"A lovely boy," Kaliq murmured. "If it were my choice I would kill him where he stood right now."

"It is amazing to realize that Lara birthed him," Lothair said. "Can we have a look at Kolgrim now?"

"Show us Kolgrim," Kaliq said, and the bowl clouded darkly, then cleared to reveal the hall of the Forest Giant. Arild sat at his High Board with his wives to his left, and three boys on his right. The boy on the end, while tall for a man, was small in comparison with the giants, but his hair was golden-blond and he was extremely handsome. "Kolgrim," Kaliq murmured. "He can be no other."

His companions nodded in agreement.

"The giants keep a better hall than the Wolfyn," Eskil noted.

"Let us watch and see if this son of Kol is as vicious as his brother," Terriss said.

But Kolgrim was pleasant and had good manners. He spoke respectfully to his foster parents and their elder son, the scholarly Vili. He joshed with the foster brother closest in age to him, Evert, as any normal mortal boy would do with a sibling.

"Wait," Kaliq said. Then, looking into the bowl, he said, "Show me Kolgrim in his bed," and the bowl clouded and cleared to reveal the boy with two buxom mortal servant girls. An insatiable and skillful lover, Kolgrim used both women until they were exhausted and begging for mercy.

"I am not satisfied yet," he told them. "Neither of you has succeeded in pleasuring me. Until you do you will have no rest." When one girl was foolish enough to protest he slapped her several times, bringing tears to her eyes. "Aah, I am beginning to be aroused by you," he told her, slapping her face and then her breasts. "Yes, you are starting to amuse me." He turned the girl over onto his lap, and smacked her plump bottom again and again until she was begging him to cease.

"Interesting," Nasim observed. "They both seem to have large appetites for pleasures, but both require pain to obtain it."

"Both parents have great appetites," Kaliq said quietly. "Passion doubled is a difficult burden to bear. Bowl clear!"

"Lara will have to observe more than we have in order to make a decision," Lothair said. "Kolbein looks like his father as does Kolgrim but for the golden hair."

"When will she begin her observations?" Gaszi asked. "Is she still here in Shunnar? Was she not magnificent last night? Such beauty! Such passion! Such perfect trust in us not to harm her." He sighed gustily. "When her lips closed about my rod I felt like a boy experiencing that pleasure for the very first time."

"Mind yourself, Geszi," Lothair teased. "You know how Kaliq feels about her."

"I love her," Kaliq said quietly.

There was a shocked silence.

"We do not give our hearts, brother," Eskil said sympathetically.

"Nay, I have never given my heart before in all the millennia that we have walked this world, but she is meant to be mine, brothers," Kaliq told them. "Not yet, but one day." He smiled at them. "Do not look so concerned, brothers."

"Indeed it is rare that we love for eternity," Nasim said, "but it has happened before, and will happen again as long as we exist upon this world. Kaliq will never allow his love for the faerie woman to keep him from his duties. I wish him good fortune!"

"And I," Lothair said, and the others echoed their best wishes. Then the Shadow Princes left Kaliq. They had done their duty this day.

For a moment he sat quietly enjoying the silence. The bowl with its clear liquid looked innocent enough now. Lara would not be pleased to see the twin sons she had borne the Twilight Lord Kol those many years ago, but she would not be particularly surprised that despite the lack of their natural father they had become quite like him. He called out to her in the silent language. *Domina, hear my plea. Cease all else and come to me.*

She appeared in an instant. "What have you learned?" she asked him.

"Come, and see for yourself. We have found Kolbein in the family of a Wolfyn lord called Thorolf. He has your golden hair, but looks exactly like his twin otherwise."

"They both had dark hair when they were born," Lara noted. "Have they any redeeming qualities, or are they totally Kol's get?"

"Their sire would be proud of them," Kaliq said

dryly, "although Kolgrim does have beautiful manners. Both of them seem to enjoy painful passions."

Lara walked to the table containing the bowl. "Show me Kolgrim," she said. Then she peered into the crystal as the liquid darkened, then cleared. The boy who slept amid the tangle of bedclothing, the two young women curled next to him, was beautiful, but he did have his father's features despite his golden hair. "Show me Kolbein," Lara said, and then she shuddered. This boy who also slept with two women was, with his ebony hair, Kol's image. He lay upon his back, his manhood flaccid now, the second manhood hidden beneath the dominant one. His mouth had a spoiled twist to it, and Lara saw one of the young women slept with a dildo still embedded within her. That alone bespoke his cruelty. "I can make no judgments now," Lara said.

Kaliq put a comforting arm about her. "Nay, you cannot. You need to see far more than you have seen, my love. But the Darkling Ciarda has plans for her half brothers. We have set a watch upon her so she does not trump us."

"Will the bowl let me see her?" Lara asked.

He nodded. "Show us Ciarda," Kaliq said.

The liquid revealed a beautiful young woman with long ebony hair that fell to her hips. She sat before a mirror brushing her long tresses. The face was Kol's in female form. It was intelligent, and when she stared deeply into the glass Lara saw that she had black eyes just like her father. Suddenly the girl looked directly into her mirror, and smiled a small, knowing smile.

"She knows she is being observed. Bowl clear!" Lara said. "Her magic is strong, Kaliq. Let us hope she does not know who it was who watched her just now."

"You did not linger, but left her quickly enough," Kaliq said. "She will think it was her imagination, a momentary sensation. She is a highly excitable creature. We will be more careful next time and use a shielding spell."

"How long do I have to make my decision?" Lara asked him.

"Until Alfrigg visits each family. He believes he but goes to observe the twins, and make a decision as to which will serve the Dark Lands best. But both of the boys have recently become curious about their heritage, and have asked their foster parents to reveal their true heritage. The Wolfyn lord and his giant counterpart have told their fosterling almost the same thing. That when the chancellor visits he will reveal the truth to them about their parentage."

"If he does it will cause civil strife in the Dark Lands, which usually would be to our advantage, but not now," Lara replied.

"He has no intention of telling them until he chooses Kol's successor," Kaliq said. "One boy was to learn who his parents were. The other would be lied to by the chancellor, and given a false parentage so that he be satisfied, and the plot could move forward. Ciarda, however, has become an ingredient that this stew did not need."

"Have you learned what she means to do?" Lara was frankly curious.

"She means to reveal the truth to the twins, and set them against one another. She plans to mate with the victor, have the son he must create and then do away with him."

"And she will rule for her son even as I rule for mine," Lara said. "What an interesting juxtaposition of fate. But the twins are her blood, Kaliq."

"It is unusual, but not unheard of for half siblings to mate," he replied.

"I can but imagine the child of such a mating," Lara said with a shudder. "Give me your bowl, Kaliq. I must go home. I will observe the twins for the next few days, and see if I can make a decision in this matter."

"You will not stay?" He looked disappointed.

"I have a kingdom to rule, my lord," Lara told him softly.

With a reluctant sigh the Shadow Prince put his hand, palm down, over the oblong bowl and said, "Bowl empty." Then he handed the vessel to her with one hand while drawing her to him for a kiss with the other.

His lips on hers were both tender and passionate. Lara kissed him back. Then before he might say another word she evaporated from his arms, and was gone. She reappeared in a small windowless room within her castle where she came to work on spells and other magical pursuits. Carefully she set the bowl upon a shelf. It would not be disturbed for the door to her chamber always locked behind her, and would open to no hand but hers. As she walked toward her own apartments she could see the sun had already set, and she was glad. It had been an exhausting few days.

Taj was waiting for her. "Where have you been, Mother? I was worried," he said.

"I had business to discuss with Prince Kaliq," she answered.

"You are always with him," the young Dominus replied, and she heard the jealousy in his voice.

"Kaliq is my mentor, and has been for many years," Lara said quietly.

"What business did you discuss?" he demanded to know.

"Magical business, my son, of which you are unfamiliar," Lara replied. "And of which you will remain unfamiliar. I may have birthed you, Taj, but you are pure mortal as was your father. I am glad of it. Being magical is a great burden to bear."

"I hate being alone," Taj told her, and they sat together. "I miss my sisters!"

"You always complained about your sisters," Lara said with a small smile. "You said Anoush was too dreamy, Zagiri too vain and Marzina too magical."

"They were!" Taj insisted. "But they were here, Mother. If my head hurt Anoush always had a remedy for it. And Zagiri always helped me when my lessons were too hard. And my twin sister could make me laugh with her magic when she would turn a servant into some creature, and then turn it back again. The creatures always looked like the person, too, Mother. I miss her."

"I know, Taj. The castle seems empty to me, too, now, but Anoush wanted to remain with her father's people for she is happiest with them. And Zagiri ran away from us, and it was time for Marzina to go to your grandmother Ilona. It was necessary she learn the strict discipline that someone with great magical powers needs. It is those magical beings who have not that discipline who fall into the darkness," Lara told him.

"We will go to The Gathering this year, won't we, Mother? And my sisters will be there, won't they?"

Lara ruffled her son's dark gold hair. "Anoush will be there, and I know your grandmother will send Marzina to be with us. As for Zagiri, Taj, I do not know when you will see her again," Lara said.

"Could I not send a message to the Lord High Ruler of Hetar demanding that he send my sister to The Gathering?" Taj asked. "I am, after all, Dominus of Terah."

"And Jonah is Lord High Ruler of Hetar, Taj," Lara replied. "He believes his status is equal to yours, my son."

"My lands are vaster, and richer," Taj bragged.

"Which is why Hetar covets Terah," Lara pointed out. "You must learn not to be boastful, Taj. Envious people will stop at nothing. You should remember that.

A wise leader is gracious, and has no need to vaunt himself above others."

"You should remain home, Mother," Taj said. "I learn much from you."

Lara laughed. "You sound like your father," she teased him. Then she grew serious. "Your father knew I had a destiny, Taj, which is why he never held me too closely. You will have to learn that lesson, too, my darling. It is part of your growing up." Then she kissed his brow. "Go to bed, Taj. I can already see Belmair glowing brightly in the night sky. I will be here in the morning when you awaken, I promise."

He returned her kiss, and then went off to his own chamber. What a difference, Lara thought, between Kolbein, Kolgrim and her son Taj.

The other two are your sons, too, Ethne reminded her.

Lara's hand went to the crystal star resting above her heart that was now glowing. *How can I think of them as mine?* she said. *They are Kol's, not mine. He forced his seed on me, Ethne. Only in having my memory restored was I able to thwart him by dividing that seedling into two. But I did not want them!*

And Marzina? Ethne asked. *She is Kol's child yet you love her with all your heart, Lara.*

I have never considered Marzina his. *She is Magnus's daughter, and Taj's twin!*

Who came from the Twilight Lord's seed as did Kolbein and Kolgrim, Ethne said. *Now you are being asked to choose one over the other, my child. It will not be easy.*

You must help me, Lara responded.

I am always here for you, Ethne replied. And then the magical spirit's flickering flame dimmed as it always did when she had said what she must.

For the next few days Lara would go to her little privy chamber to view the twin sons she had borne the Twilight Lord. She kept the bowl filled with the clear liquid so she might quickly view them. As Kaliq had said, they were Kol's get without a doubt. Selfish and cruel, ignorant, libidinous and vicious. She could find few redeeming qualities in either of them. Kolbein and Kolgrim lived for themselves. Though they were not quite two and a half years older than Taj, their maturity was far greater than the young Terahn Dominus. And then word came that Chancellor Alfrigg had left the Twilight Lord's castle and taken to the road leading to the home of the renegade Forest Giant, Arild.

Lara watched both, repelled and yet amused as the golden-haired Kolgrim charmed the old dwarf with his exquisite manners and pleasant demeanor. Kolgrim could not know that the Twilight Lord's chancellor was at first quite taken aback by him. But then Alfrigg saw the boy viciously punish a servant who had spilled a drop of soup on his hand, and he was reassured. He remembered that Kol had had beautiful manners when it pleased him, too. But the golden hair continued to trouble him.

Alfrigg left the Forest Giant's house promising to return, and next traveled to the Wolfyn Thorolf to see Kolbein. The dwarf was actually shocked by Kolbein's behavior. The boy was rude. He was crude. There was a question in Alfrigg's mind of whether he could be retrained so that he ate like a great lord, and not an animal. But the boy did have his father's penchant for cruelty, and his lust was truly awe-inspiring, the old dwarf concluded as he watched Kolbein amuse himself with three serving women in a corner of the hall. It could be a difficult decision. And then Kolbein forced the chancellor's hand.

"Thorolf tells me that you know who my parents are," the boy said. He showed no respect for the dwarf's position as chancellor to the Twilight Lord.

"Thorolf says what he should not," Alfrigg responded. He glared at the Wolfyn.

"Who are they, then, little man?" Kolbein demanded to know.

The Wolfyn females gasped at the boy's bold demand, the one who had mothered him chiding gently with a low warning growl.

The boy turned and struck her a fierce blow. "Be silent! This is not the business of females, nor should you dare to reprimand a male of the pack." Turning back to Alfrigg he snarled, "Well? What answer do you have for me?"

Alfrigg looked coldly at the boy. "Your parents were in service to the Twilight Lord. When they died shortly after you were born he put you out to be fostered in hopes that one day you might be of service to him as they were. However, I see no future for you, boy."

As the scene unfolded Lara watched it all happen in the oblong bowl. Alfrigg had solved her problem, she thought relieved. But then a burst of laughter erupted, and the Darkling Ciarda appeared in a flash of bright scarlet flames.

"Tell him the truth, my lord Alfrigg. I see much promise in the boy," she said.

Kolbein's mouth dropped open in surprise. Never had he seen such a lovely maiden, and his lust was almost instantly engaged. But her words had also penetrated his brain. *"What truth?"* he asked in a hard voice.

The old dwarf drew himself up. "Darkling!" he thundered at her. "You do not know what you do. Stay out of this matter, or be punished."

"You have not the power to punish me," Ciarda said. Then she turned to the boy. "You are not the spawn of servants, boy. You are my half brother, and our father is the Twilight Lord himself."

A look of pure evil lit Kolbein's handsome face briefly. He swiveled to look down at the chancellor. "If I am the Twilight Lord's son then I am his heir," he said softly. "And when my father learns you have lied to me, old man, it is you who will be punished. Perhaps he will even let me do the deed. It will be a slow and painful death I can assure you, and I will enjoy every minute of the process."

The Darkling laughed. "What a lad he is!" she crowed. "Our father would be proud of him." Ciarda moved next to Kolbein and he stared boldly at her full breasts. "There are ways of prolonging agony that I can teach you, *little brother,*" she purred at him. "Alfrigg is old, and you wouldn't want him to die quickly and cheat yourself of your fun." She laughed again. "But you would do better to keep him alive for he has served our sire for eons, and is most useful." She whirled about again to face the chancellor. "Tell him the rest of it, my lord."

"What rest of it?" Kolbein wanted to know.

"You have begun the tale, lady," Alfrigg said quietly. "You tell him."

"You are a twin!" Ciarda said. "You have a brother."

"He must be killed," Kolbein declared without sentiment or hesitation.

"Yes, darling lad, he must be. But not yet," Ciarda replied. "Not at least until we have met him. That would not be polite at all, little brother."

"Where is he?" Kolbein demanded to know.

Now Alfrigg spoke up. "We will go tomorrow," he said.

"My magic could take us now," the Darkling replied.

"Tomorrow," the chancellor repeated in a firm voice.

"Oh very well," Ciarda acquiesced prettily. Reaching out, she took Kolbein's hand in hers. "Shall we get to know one another better, little brother?" she asked him.

"Aye!" he said. "Come!" And he led her from the hall.

"We have been responsible for raising Lord Kol's son," Thorolf finally spoke in a hushed tone. "We shall be in great favor when Kolbein becomes the Twilight Lord!" Then he raised his head up and howled. The cry was taken up by all in the hall.

"You might have at least seen he had better table manners," Alfrigg grumbled when the sound had finally ceased. "His father would not be pleased at all."

"You say *would?*" Thorolf said slyly.

"Would! Will!" Alfrigg snapped. "What difference does it make to you?"

"Would is the past, will the present, my lord Chancellor," Thorolf replied.

"Very well, Lord Wolfyn. His father will not at all be pleased. Does that satisfy you?" The chancellor was very angry. He had planned an orderly transfer of power, and now thanks to the Darkling all had become chaos.

Lara watched it all. She heard Alfrigg's thoughts, and briefly felt sorry for him. But he was right about Ciarda. She had brought discord into what should have been an easy process. *Prince Kaliq, hear my call. Come to me from out yon wall.*

A golden light appeared in the center of the blank stone wall of the chamber. It quickly revealed a tunnel and Kaliq hurried through it into Lara's little privy chamber. It closed behind him. "What is it, my love? What has happened?"

Lara quickly explained what she had just heard and witnessed in the oblong bowl.

"We must go to Arild's hall," Kaliq said. "There is no help for it. We cannot be certain that Alfrigg will be allowed to live long enough to tell Kolgrim the truth."

"I cannot," Lara said. "I cannot face those two nightmares. I am brave, but this I cannot do. You ask too much of me, Kaliq."

"There is no other choice," he responded.

"Why can you not go alone, my lord? I bore them, for that was a part of my destiny, you said. You put me in Kol's hands. Allowed him to steal my memories and impregnate me. Now you will have me decide their fate? I bore them. Was that not enough? Nay! It is not fair! I cannot!" Tears filled her emerald eyes.

"Kolgrim and Kolbein are a part of your destiny, Lara. And you are a part of theirs," Kaliq told her. "This task is a part of what you must do." He put an arm about her. "I will be by your side. If your strength falters I will give you mine."

She stood silent for several long moments before she said, "Very well. Let us go and attempt to put an end to this disaster." *Andraste, to me!* Lara called to her sword, and the scabbard and sword were suddenly upon her back. "I am ready," she told the Shadow Prince. She felt his kiss atop her head, and then he enfolded them both in his long white silk cloak. The cloak smelled of sandalwood, and Lara breathed deeply of it, taking in his essence, calming her nerves. When Kaliq flung back the fabric they stood in a stone hall.

With a roar Arild leaped from his High Board towering above the strangers. "Why do you invade my hall uninvited, Shadow Prince?" His hand was on his sword.

Lara stepped from the protection of Kaliq's cape. With a slow, deliberate motion, she drew Andraste from the scabbard, and planted it before her. The sword hummed softly, menacingly. "I am Lara, Domina of Terah, Arild, kin to Skrymir, Lord of the Forest Giants, kin to my friend, Og. I come to you in peace, but if you do not remove your hand from the hilt of your weapon I will remove your hand." She looked up at him boldly. "Where is your fosterling? I have business with him."

Kaliq stood silent, a small smile playing at the corners of his mouth as he watched Lara take charge of the situation. He was pleased to see her years in Terah as a wife and a mother had done nothing to take away her ability to command a difficult situation.

"What business have you with Kolgrim?" the giant demanded. "He was given to us by the Twilight Lord's chancellor as a little one." He took his hand from his sword.

"Hear me well, Arild. Kol is where he will never again do anyone harm. His chancellor, Lord Alfrigg, has kept his kingdom together since the day Kol was incarcerated for his crimes. He did this so Kol's sons would have time to grow and to mature. That time now grows short, and one of Kol's daughters, the Darkling Ciarda, seeks to steal the Dark Lands from her half brothers after she has set them against one another so that only one will triumph."

"How can you know this, Domina of Terah?" Arild asked.

"Indeed, lady, how do you know?" Kolgrim stepped from the dais, and came to stand before Lara. "It is the first time I have ever seen anyone of my proportions," he noted. Then he took her hand and kissed it, his black eyes meeting her green ones.

"It does not matter how I know these things," Lara began, but he cut her off.

"You are my mother, aren't you? I certainly did not gain my golden hair from my father. I have a brother? Which of us was born first?" Kolgrim asked, coming directly to the point.

"You have a twin brother," Lara said. She had grown very pale at the sight of the boy. "The serving women helping as you were birthed were so surprised to see a second son born they put you both in your cradle without marking which of you came first. As you were identical at birth they could not tell us which of you was the elder."

"Why did you desert us then?" Kolgrim asked her bluntly.

"Your father stole me from my husband and children to force his seed upon me," Lara said simply. He did not need to know all of it. "After you were born, as soon as I was able, I fled back to my own family. I am of the light, Kolgrim. You belong to the dark. You belong to your sire."

"Yet now you have come to help me, haven't you?"

Lara sighed. "Nay, I have come to keep the light shining over our worlds. Your half sister and your twin brother are ready to murder you. Even now they are coming with your father's chancellor, Lord Alfrigg. Which of you is meant to rule here in the Dark Lands I do not know. Fate decided that long ago. It is not up to Ciarda to manipulate the situation. She does it for her own advantage not yours. Do not trust her."

"Listen to her, my son," Broska cried. "The wisdom of the faerie woman is legend. If she stands behind you you will rule the Dark Lands!"

"Are you she who fostered Kolgrim?" Lara asked.

Broska hurried down from the High Board and knelt before Lara. "I am she, Domina. It was an honor. He is a good lad. Mannerly and well spoken. He excelled at his lessons. I hope he pleases you."

Kolgrim looked amused by this declaration of devotion spoken by his foster mother. Broska was like an amiable milk cow. Biddable and loyal.

"You remind me of your father," Lara said softly. "He could hide his evil behind his charm, too, as you now do. Make no mistake about it. I have not come to champion you, Kolgrim, son of Kol. I have come to warn you so you may be on your guard against your half sister. Darklings have magic. Some more than others. She will use that magic against you if she decides you are not worthy of her plans. And your brother has already bedded her you may be sure. Like you, he enjoys pain with his pleasures."

Kolgrim flushed, but then he laughed. "Have you been spying on me, *Mother?*" he taunted her. His gray eyes darkened and danced wickedly.

Lara paled again. "I am not your mother," she said coldly. "I am only she who bore you, Kolgrim, son of Kol."

"Tell me of my twin," he said. "Give me some small advantage as he has an advantage with our sister."

"His dark hair makes him look like your father, but facially you are the same, Kol's get," Lara said. "He is ignorant, vicious and cruel. He lacks manners, and has no loyalty at all. He enjoys punishing his women. His name is Kolbein and everything you see of him is exactly what he is. He does not hide his wickedness as you do."

Kolgrim nodded. "Thank you," he said to her.

The Forest Giant Arild suddenly knelt before Lara. "Help us, faerie woman. Return when the chancellor and his party come."

Before Lara might speak Kaliq did. "Call us and we will come," he said. Then, wrapping his cloak about them, he took them back to Lara's small privy chamber.

She pulled away from him angrily. "Why did you tell them we would return?" she demanded to know. "Have I not done as you asked, my lord?"

"Our task is not yet complete. You cannot leave Ciarda to manipulate the situation with Kol's sons, Lara. We must be there to preserve the balance between light and dark. Arild is stubborn, and only remained in the

Dark Lands because his fellow Forest Giants rejected his attempt to supplant Skrymir. He is not a bad fellow, and while Kolgrim is his father's son he is less of a threat than Kolbein would be. At least Arild and his wives managed to instill a public civility into Kolgrim for all the boy's private vices. And I did not see the Forest Giant's toady, Gnup, in the hall. This could very well mean that Ciarda has already subverted him. If she has he could easily become an assassin to be used against Kolgrim, Arild and his whole family."

"I hate this whole matter," Lara cried.

"Then help to correct it!" he almost shouted at her.

Lara looked directly at him. Her lips were pressed together tightly, and she was silent for several long minutes. He waited for her to compose herself, to consider the situation now unfolding, to make the right decision.

"You know what you have to do, and only you can do it, Lara. We must be there when Alfrigg arrives with Ciarda and Kolbein," the Shadow Prince said.

"I know," Lara replied reluctantly. "I know, Kaliq."

He reached out to take her into his arms. She stood silent against him, her head on his chest while he stroked her hair soothingly. He said nothing for no words were necessary between them.

Finally Lara spoke. "It is getting harder," she said, sighing again.

"I will be with you, my love," he replied.

"In the shadows of Arild's hall only, Kaliq. I will not allow this Darkling to pretend her powers are stron-

ger than mine. They are not, and everyone in that hall
must know it. I will appear alone so it cannot be said
that it was your powers not mine that corrected this
situation. Kol's sons are young, untrained and have no
idea what magic they could possess. They will be dangerous enough without it. The Darkling cannot be allowed to aid them further. I will banish her from their
lives. Whatever happens in the Dark Lands after that
will be between Kolgrim and Kolbein. And hopefully
they will be so busy trying to outrule each other they
will not have time for Hetar and Terah."

Kaliq smiled but Lara did not see that smile, for she
still nestled against his chest.

Two nights later Lara awakened suddenly, and heard
the voice of the Forest Giant Arild calling to her. "Come
quickly, faerie woman, for the chancellor approaches
my hall!" Lara knew Kaliq heard Arild's voice, too, for
a moment later he appeared in her bedchamber just as
her feet touched the floor. With a wave of his hand he
dressed her in a sapphire-blue gown, a narrow golden
circlet with a sapphire in its center about her head and
golden slippers on her feet. The crystal star holding
Lara's guardian, Ethne, hung about her neck. Wrapping
his all-enveloping cloak about them, Kaliq transported
them instantly to the hall of the Forest Giant Arild.

Kaliq loosened his robe and Lara walked forth into
the large chamber.

"Greetings, *Mother,*" Kolgrim said, coming forward

with a smile and kissing her hand gallantly. "Where is the Shadow Prince? Is he not with you?"

"This is my affair as you will soon see," Lara replied tartly. She turned to Arild, looking up at him. "How near are they?"

"They should pass through my gates in just a few more minutes," the Forest Giant said. "I have sent my women and children from the hall for safety's sake."

"Bring them back," Lara told him. "I will protect them. Where is Gnup?"

"I have not seen him in several days," Arild admitted.

"Then he has betrayed you. Take care of the matter as quickly as you can find him, and do not believe the lies he will tell you to save his miserable hide. Arild, you and your family are welcome in Terah among your own people should you wish to return to them. Skrymir will forgive you, and I will put your hall in their forest. Your sons and your daughters will need mates one day. Some sooner than others. Who will you wed them to if you are not among your own? You have done your duty by Kol, but he will not return to the Dark Kingdom ever again."

"Is he dead then, faerie woman?" the giant asked hesitantly.

"Worse," she said, "but ask no more. Now quickly send for your family."

Arild's family came into the hall, and Lara set a protection spell about them. They would be safe from any magic flung about the chamber this day. A servant ran into the hall to tell his master that their guests were even now entering the hall. Lara took a deep breath, exhaling slowly. She was ready now.

Kol's chancellor hobbled into the chamber, leaning heavily upon his staff of office. Behind him the beautiful Darkling Ciarda followed, walking beside Kolbein. Lara almost gasped seeing Kolgrim's twin, for with his dark hair he was the image of his father. The Darkling's eyes widened in surprise as she saw Lara. Kolbein, however, let his black eyes roam insultingly over Lara, as he licked his lips in apparent anticipation. But then, seeing Kolgrim, his eyes widened in complete surprise.

"Welcome to my house, my lord Chancellor," Arild said, bowing. He ushered the dwarf, careful not to step on him, to a comfortable chair by the enormous hearth.

Before he sat Alfrigg acknowledged Lara. "My lady," he said, and there was distinct relief in his voice as he spoke.

Lara immediately realized that Kol's chancellor had no real part in this situation, and was therefore no threat.

"Who is *she?*" Ciarda demanded to know. "And why is she here?"

"Why should I not be here?" Lara replied. "It is you who are unwelcome, for deciding the fate of Kol's sons is not in your purview. In the absence of their father it is my authority that decides their fate."

"And who are you?" Ciarda demanded to know.

"I am she who bore them," Lara replied.

"She's our mother," Kolgrim said cheerfully to Kolbein as he came to offer his hand to his twin brother. "But for some reason she cannot bear to say the word."

Brother love will stronger be than anything that comes from thee, Lara said in the silent magic language as she looked directly at the Darkling.

Ciarda shrieked with fury for of course she had heard the spell as Lara pronounced it. The others in the hall including Kolgrim and Kolbein had not heard. Horrified, Ciarda watched as the twins embraced one another. Exclaiming over their identical features, Kolbein touching his brother's golden hair, and then glanced toward Lara. They would never be enemies now. Rivals, yes, but not foes.

"You have ruined all my plans!" Ciarda snarled at her opponent, realizing exactly what Lara had done. "But I will have my revenge upon you, Domina of Terah! Wait and see if I do not. We will meet again, and next time I will have the advantage, I promise you!" Then the Darkling disappeared in a thunderous flash of fiery flame.

All in the hall but Lara shrank back in fear, but with a wave of her hand Lara banished the stench of burning, replacing it with the smell of sweet lavender. "She is gone now, and will not be back," she told her companions. Then she looked to the chancellor. "Well, Alfrigg, I have made my decision. Let them rule together even as they came into this world. And you must be their guide for the next five years."

"Lady, I am old and tired," Alfrigg said piteously, rising from his chair.

"Loyalty should not be punished, and your loyalty to your master is commendable, my lord," Lara told him. Then she set her hands upon the dwarf's shoulders, and said, *"Let the years drop away. For ten years and a day. Unchained from pain limbs be free. Bright eyes be clear all to see. Ears be sharp, and memory sound. From your years you're now unbound."* And Lara smiled at the surprise that dawned on the old dwarf's face as he heard her words, and experienced the result of them.

"My pains are gone," he marveled. Then he said, "But you said I must only serve them five years. You have freed me from aging for ten years and a day."

"Your loyalty to Kol is rewarded," Lara told him. "You were always his voice of reason, and whether you meant to or not you have helped us keep the darkness at bay. Serve his sons, as well, although I do not imagine they will be any easier than he was. In fact they will be twice the trouble. Still, Alfrigg, you should be able to manage them as you did their father, particularly given your newfound youth."

"We are to rule the Dark Lands? Why, *Mother dear,* how generous of you," Kolgrim said with a wicked smile.

"You are the most beautiful creature I have ever seen," Kolbein said admiringly.

"I am not a *creature,*" Lara said coldly. "I am a faerie woman."

"Why did you desert us?" Kolbein wanted to know.

"Don't ask her. I'll tell you everything, brother dear,"

Kolgrim said. "She doesn't like us because she didn't like our father."

"Which one of us was born first? It is the firstborn who should rule alone," Kolbein said angrily.

"I'll tell you all about that, too," Kolgrim replied. "No one knows which one of us came first." He chuckled. "It was really quite careless of them."

"Why is it you know more than I do?" Kolbein asked irritably. Then he held up his hand as his twin was about to speak. "I know! I know! You'll tell me that, too."

"Can you send us back to the castle of the Twilight Lord?" Alfrigg asked Lara.

"I can," Lara told him. Then she looked to Arild. "Will you return to the light, Forest Giant? Or will you remain here? Remember your children when your pride reaches up to bite at you."

"You are certain Skrymir will forgive me? Welcome us back into our family?" Arild asked her, trying not to sound too anxious.

"I am certain you will all be welcomed," Lara promised him.

Arild looked to his family. "I have decided we will return to our own people," he told them.

"What of Gnup?" Lara wanted to know.

"I told you we had not seen him in several days. If I find him I will kill him," Arild told her.

Lara nodded, satisfied, then turned back to Kolbein and Kolgrim. "Go and stand next to your chancellor," she told them. "Kolgrim, make your goodbyes to your foster family quickly."

Broska and Guri ran forward sobbing. Broska picked Kolgrim up in her hand and squeezed gently as she kissed the top of his head. Guri kissed his head, too. Then they set him back on the ground, and, sobbing harder, returned to where their own children stood.

Evert, Kolgrim's foster brother, offered him a finger to shake before Kolgrim returned to stand next to Kolbein and Alfrigg. But as Lara raised her hand to transport them to the castle of the Twilight Lord he called out to her, "Farewell, *Mother dear.*" And she heard his laughter and that of Kolbein as they faded away.

"My lord Kaliq, hear my plea. Cease all else and come to me," Lara called, pretending so the giants would not know he had been there all along.

The Shadow Prince immediately stepped from the shadows in a corner of the hall.

"Will you help me transport this hall to the realm of the Forest Giants in Terah?" she asked him prettily.

"It is done even as you spoke the words, Domina," Kaliq said. "Go and open the door to your hall, Arild."

And when the Forest Giant did so he was amazed to find his house in a sunny clearing in the midst of a lush green forest. And down the road that led from the house he saw his cousin Skrymir, Lord of the Forest Giants, hurrying forward to meet him, a smile of welcome upon his face. Brushing away his tears, Arild went forth, his hands outstretched to greet him.

Lara looked to Kaliq.

"While you were straightening out everything else I sought out Skrymir," he told her.

"Thank you," Lara said, smiling as the two giants embraced each other after their many years of separation.

CHAPTER TEN

THE DARKLING CIARDA paced angrily back and forth within her hall. Ruined! All her plans had been ruined. How had she been found out? And she had certainly never expected the faerie woman who had birthed her half brothers to become involved in their fate. The bitch had deserted them, deserted her father, who had actually loved that golden creature. Ciarda would have never guessed that Lara's magic was that strong. She had so wanted to complete her father's plans for the conquest of Hetar and Terah. To draw the darkness over this entire world would have been a magnificent accomplishment. To be the first female to rule from the Twilight Throne. Ciarda seethed with her fury.

Then suddenly her ire began to lessen slowly. Perhaps all was not lost. She just had to rearrange her plans, and attack the problem from another direction. The Hierarch she had been creating to govern Hetar for her was still waiting in the wings. If she could bring him to the forefront sooner than she had planned it would cause chaos for the Lord High Ruler Jonah and his minions, who would hardly appreciate being replaced. The Hierarch would draw them to his side efficiently, isolating

Jonah. Her Darkling's magic would guarantee that the Hierarch would triumph over his opposition.

And once Hetar was firmly under her control she would set her half brothers against one another. The faerie woman's spell could certainly be broken, Ciarda considered, if she just thought about it. It was a simple spell, after all, wasn't it? And she would leave Terah in peace until they could be lulled into a false sense of security. Why would the faerie woman care what happened to Hetar, or to the Dark Lands? Ciarda believed that Lara had only interfered out of a sense of maternal duty toward her sons. Kol, her father, had appreciated that kind of loyalty, and for his sake Ciarda decided she would leave Lara and her kingdom in peace for the interim. After all, ruling an entire world was a great undertaking. Better she gather that world to her little by little. She didn't have to be so greedy. She didn't need it in her grasp so quickly. She had been foolish in her eagerness. She would not be foolish again.

She considered Lara. She had never until today seen the faerie woman, although she had heard of her beauty from the other women in her father's harem. Her father had wanted Lara's magic, and Ciarda had never understood why until today. Ciarda possessed certain magic from her father, but she hadn't ever known a woman could possess such strong magic as Lara did. Or was it all her magic? She had seen the Shadow Prince standing in the dusky corner of the giant's hall although she knew no mortal eye could have detected him. Perhaps Lara's magic wasn't all that strong. Perhaps it had been the Shadow Prince's magic. Of course it was! Women did not have that kind of strength. But one day she would, Ciarda vowed. *One day.*

She turned her thoughts now to the one she had chosen to be the Hierarch. She had sought for a young man whose background would fit the legend. The Hierarch, it was said, would come from a far place. He would be a simple man of the people whose natural charisma and handsome face would draw Hetarians of all ranks to him. And no one would question his sudden appearance among them because her magic would make him a wondrous figure to behold. But his heart was as black as hers was, Ciarda knew.

IN THE FIELDS of the New Outlands the cattle of the Fiacre grazed peacefully in the sunlight of a late summer's afternoon. Anoush, daughter of Vartan the Heroic, walked slowly through the meadow gathering the daisylike flowers and leaves of the chamomile plant. She carried a woven willow basket, rectangular in shape, that was divided into individual sections. Carefully she tucked her harvest into one of the sections.

"Hello, Anoush!" she heard a male voice greet her.

"Hello," she answered. She didn't know who the tall and muscular young man was, but she had to admit to herself that he was very handsome with his curly black hair and light blue eyes. And when he had smiled at her her heart had fluttered.

"You do not recognize me, do you?" he said.

"Nay, I do not," Anoush admitted shyly and made to move on.

He did not stop her, saying instead, "Well, perhaps you will remember me eventually. Will you be at The Gathering?"

"Yes," Anoush said as she walked away.

"We will meet again then," he called after her.

Arriving back at her fine stone house, Anoush said to her servant, Gadara, "There was a herdsman in my fields today whom I did not recognize. Do you know who it might have been? He was very handsome."

"Two of Sholeh's men came to speak with Lord Liam today," Gadara said, "but I did not see them, mistress."

Anoush cudgeled her memory, but she could not recall ever having seen the young man who had addressed her. If he was one of Sholeh's men she probably wouldn't see him again until The Gathering. But if she did she would ask him who he was. Anoush smiled to herself. He really had been very handsome to behold. She was so happy to be back among her father's people. It was where she belonged.

Lara noticed a sparkle in her eldest daughter's eye, and wondered what had put it there. Anoush was usually quiet, and more circumspect than her siblings.

"She met a lad while out gathering her plants yesterday," Noss said. "She didn't recognize him as one of our village. Gadara said she thought it might be one of the herders from Rivalen who came to speak with Liam."

"He was bold to speak with Anoush if he did not know her," Lara said.

"Ask your daughter about the incident," Noss replied. "I am only telling you what Gadara told me. She is very protective of Anoush. Once she had a mate and a daughter, but they died one Icy Season from some malady of the chest and throat. Anoush would be about her daughter's age, and Gadara has grown quite fond of her."

"I will speak with my daughter," Lara said, and went off to find her. Anoush was in her apothecary carefully spreading the leaves and flowers of the chamomile plants she had harvested the preceding day onto a flat surface so they would dry. She greeted her mother with a warm smile.

"Do not dry the flowers and leaves on the same slate," Lara said. "They have different properties, and you don't want them mixing."

Anoush nodded, and carefully spread the leaves onto another cool slate.

"Noss says a young man spoke to you yesterday in the meadow," Lara remarked.

"Aye," Anoush answered her mother. "He addressed me by name. He was very handsome, Mother. He said he would see me at The Gathering."

"You did not know him?" Lara spoke casually.

Anoush shook her head. "But he seemed to know me. He addressed me by name, and asked if I did not recognize him. I didn't. But he was very fair to look upon,

Mother. Why do you ask? Do you think he might be a suitor for my hand?"

"I have never before heard you speak of marriage for yourself," Lara said.

"There was no one in Terah for me, Mother, so why would I bother to speak of it?" Anoush responded in a practical tone.

"He was a herder? You are certain?" Lara wanted to know.

"Aye, he wore herder's clothing. Why are you so interested in this young man, Mother? Is it so hard to think a young man might be interested in me?"

"Nay, darling girl," Lara told her child. "But you are now a woman of property. You have your own house, some land and a fine herd of cattle. And you are the daughter of a great hero of the Fiacre, of all the clan families. You are extremely eligible. But as your mother I would wish to know the name of those courting you, Anoush."

Anoush chuckled. Then she stopped what she was doing and hugged Lara. "Oh, Mother, I do love you. And I love that you would worry about a young man from another village who would pay a bit of attention to me. He is gone now, whoever he was, and unless I see him at The Gathering it is unlikely I will ever see him again. There is no harm done to me, or threat implied by this lad. It is nothing more than it was."

"You may not be at the castle with me any longer,

Anoush, but I still worry about you," Lara told her daughter. "Especially given Zagiri's impetuous behavior."

"She is very happy," Anoush told Lara. "She sends me missives via faerie post several times a month. Does she not communicate with you?"

"Nay," Lara said tersely.

"You must forgive her, Mother," Anoush said quietly.

"Your sister disobeyed me, and by doing so has put herself in a terrible position although she is too foolish to realize it," Lara said. "Jonah of Hetar thinks Terah will come to his aid if he needs us because he is wed to the sister of the Dominus. But that is not necessarily so, Anoush. I will do what is best for Terah first. Hetar is neither my province nor my responsibility, Anoush. Zagiri is young and romantic. She has no idea of what is involved in keeping these worlds of ours safe from the darkness. I will wager I know what she writes about. The luxuries of Hetar that arc now all hers. Of the servants who serve her and grant her every wish and whim. Of her husband with whom she enjoys pleasures and who would appear to adore her."

"Well, yes," Anoush said slowly.

"Does she speak of the poverty afflicting Hetar? Or the corruption of its magnates and Merchants Guild? Does she ever venture outside of the Golden District in which she lives to see the filth in the streets? Has she seen the Mercenaries who are idle, and wander the streets ill, hungry or drunk on Razi? Has she visited the Garden District to meet with her grandfather's wife, and her uncles now living in the genteel poverty of the Crusader Knights' faded glory? You must answer nay to all of these things for even if she were curious, and she is not, Jonah would not allow her to see the truth of what Hetar has become, Anoush. The beautiful daughter that I bore Magnus Hauk has become the prized trophy for a corrupt man," Lara concluded bitterly. "You want me to forgive her, but how can I? She has veered from the path of light."

"But she has not gone into the dark, Mother," Anoush said earnestly. "And she will not. What she has done has a purpose. I know it! I don't know what that purpose is, Mother, but there is one."

"I hope you are right," Lara said bleakly. Zagiri's defection to Hetar had hurt her more than anything any of her children had ever done. She was puzzled by it, and she didn't like feeling helpless. Feeling helpless was a mortal trait.

The summer finally came to an end. The time for The Gathering, a yearly event held by the clan families, drew near. When it was over Lara and Taj would return to the castle on the Dominus's Fjord. They traveled with the Fiacre clan families to The Gathering Place where tents were set up, campfires started and the eight clans of the New Outlands came together. Each had brought something for the several days of feasting and trading. The Fiacre brought beef. The Felan brought lamb. The Blathma and the Gitta were growers of produce, which they brought to add to the feast. The Aghy were ready to trade and sell horses. The Piaras and the Tormod had gold, silver and jewelry for sale. The Devyn were the Memory Keepers and Bards of the clan families. Their contribution to The Gathering each year was to sing the history of the clans. Each evening they would entertain around a large central fire. The Gathering would conclude with a meeting of the New Outlands Council headed by Rendor, Lord of the Felan.

Lara loved this time of the year for it allowed her to meet with old friends. Her years among the clan families had been happy ones. Now she noticed that many of those whom she knew were growing older while she appeared to have changed not at all. While Lara was revered by all of the clan families, she found the younger members of these families looked upon her either with suspicion or indifference. She supposed it was natural that to them Vartan the Heroic was a legend. Nothing more. The fact that he had been married to a faerie woman was but part of the legend for them. When they looked at Lara they saw a beautiful, young and desirable woman, not the widow of a legendary hero.

But Anoush was another matter. There was nothing magical about her. She was a healer with *the Sight,* which they both respected and admired. Once this had not been so, but as they had come to know Anoush it was accepted that she was just a lovely maiden with rare talents. And the fact that she had no husband and was propertied made her a magnet for men seeking a wife. She was never without her admirers this particular Gathering. But Anoush's soft blue eyes searched the crowds about her seeking one man.

And then late one afternoon he appeared before her. "Hello, Anoush," he said with a smile. "Have you remembered who I am?" He towered over her, and Anoush felt suddenly small and fragile.

"Nay," she said. "I do not remember you. Who are you, sir?"

"You do not remember a Gathering long ago when we played together by the water?" he said, low. "I wanted to kiss you then, Anoush, but your brother prevented it."

And a picture suddenly bloomed in her memory of a sulky boy who put his hand beneath her gown, and stroked her leg with knowledgeable fingers. She had been but a little child then, and it had been very wicked of him. Anoush blushed, remembering. "You are Cam," she said. "You are my cousin Cam."

"I am," he admitted. "We have both grown up some since those carefree days, Anoush," he said with a charming smile. Then he kissed her cheek.

"You were our grandmother Bera's favorite," Anoush recalled.

"Only because my parents were dead, and she felt sorry for me," he said. "It is fortunate when Lord Liam realized how spoiled I was becoming he sent me to our kinswoman Sholeh," Cam said. "I was not spoiled in the village of Rivalen." Cam chuckled. "I was taught how to become the man I am today. Now, my pretty cousin, take me to your mother. I should greet her, and obtain her permission to court you."

Remembering now the wicked and devious boy Cam had been, Anoush was not certain her mother would give her permission, but certainly Cam had changed. Lara must be made to see that. "Come along, then," she said, offering Cam her small hand, which he took in his large one. Then together they sought out Lara. They found her laughing with Roan of the Aghy, Rendor of the Felan and Rendor's wife, Rahil, who raised an eyebrow at the sight of Anoush and Cam.

"Mother, this is the young man I told you about, and I have remembered who he is," Anoush said excitedly.

Lara turned, smiling, but, seeing the young man with her daughter, her smile faded. "Cam, son of Adon the Curst and his wife, Elin," she said. "I would never forget you."

Cam dropped to his knees before Lara. "Lady, I was but a child when the terrible deed was done. Do not, I beg you, hold me responsible for my parents' crimes. But for my own childish wickednesses I do beg your forgiveness." He looked up at her hopefully. "I have admired Anoush since we were children, and would ask your permission to pay her my court."

"He has made himself invaluable to Sholeh," Roan spoke up. "He is one of her finest herders, Lara."

"Bad boys can grow into good men," Rendor added.

"This man's father killed your father," Lara said to

her daughter. "Knowing that, can you allow him your company?"

"His father was the one at fault, not Cam," Anoush responded. "But I am not Zagiri. If you forbid it then I will send him away, Mother."

Lara looked at Cam as she debated what to do. Perhaps he had changed, and Anoush liked him. If she forbade them each other her daughter would do her best to obey, but forbidden fruit was always sweetest. Eventually Anoush would be unable to keep her promise to her mother, especially if the young man begged and begged. Better she not forbid them. If Cam misbehaved in the slightest Anoush would chase him away. Anoush had been sheltered, it was true, but she was past twenty. It was time for Lara to let her eldest daughter fly. She sighed. "Very well," she told them. "You have my permission to pay Anoush court, Cam of Rivalen. Anoush, you have my permission to receive this suitor but only in public, or if Gadara or some other suitable woman is with you. Do you both understand me? Remember, Anoush, remain with Cam for two nights, and you will be considered wed among the clan families. Do not do it. If this association progresses to a point where you both wish to wed let us do it properly."

"I swear it will be so, my lady Lara!" Cam said, and then he stood up, grinning.

Anoush was wearing the same silly look on her face as Cam.

You did the right thing, Ethne said. *He is her first*

suitor. She should tire of him soon enough. But I will admit he is handsome.

His beauty is almost ethereal, Lara said. *I am not easy with this, but how could I forbid her? I do not want another incident like Zagiri.*

Zagiri's fate is a different one from Anoush's. Remember she is Vartan's child, Ethne said. *This place is her world. You have seen how happy she is here.*

I know, Lara replied, looking at her daughter, who was now in animated conversation with Cam.

"That would be an interesting match," Roan of the Aghy said.

"They are cousins," Lara responded.

"Cousins marry," Roan noted. "But would Vartan approve, I wonder."

"Vartan had a large heart," Rendor of the Felan said. "He would not have held the lad responsible for his parents' evil."

"I remember him as a boy. He was wicked," Lara recalled. "Dillon disliked him intensely, and felt he had designs on Anoush that he should not."

"Of course he was wicked. Everyone expected it of him because of Adon and Elin. And old Bera was never right in her head after Adon murdered his brother. She clutched at Cam, and spoiled him terribly. Taking him away from her was the best thing Liam could have done. It's made a man of him. Ask Sholeh if you are concerned," Rendor told Lara. "She will tell you the truth of the matter."

"I will ask Sholeh," Lara said, and, leaving the two clan lords, she went off to find Vartan's kin, who was head woman of Rivalen village.

Sholeh was aging, as were the rest of them, Lara thought as she greeted her. The long auburn hair was streaked with silver-gray. The two women embraced, and Sholeh said before Lara might speak, "Cam came to me to ask my permission to speak with you about Anoush. Has he come to you yet?"

"I am not comfortable with his interest in my daughter," Lara said candidly.

"He is not the boy who came to me," Sholeh said. "We have made him a Fiacre to be proud of despite his grandmother and his parents. You cannot hold Adon's behavior against his son."

"Nay," Lara agreed, "I cannot, but I remember him as a young boy. He was wickedness incarnate. Yet now he seems to have become a fine young man."

"He is!" Sholeh replied. "And he is an excellent herder, Lara. If one day he became a husband for Anoush it would not be the worst thing that could happen. And such a union would help to put an end to his parents' memory."

"It should never be forgotten that Adon killed his own brother, Vartan, Lord of the Fiacre, or that he was encouraged by his wife, Elin, to commit the deed," Lara said in a hard voice. "And it was done out of jealousy, malice and envy."

"Aye," Sholeh responded, "they should be forgotten

along with the terrible murder they committed. They should be forgotten entirely. Only the memory of my kinsman Vartan the Heroic should remain bright among the history of our people, and of how his wife, the faerie woman Lara, took her singing sword, Andraste, and slew the murderers of her husband, Vartan, taking vengeance for herself and her children as was her right. But Cam should not have to suffer for his parents' crime."

"I can see you have come to love the boy, Sholeh," Lara said quietly. "Very well then, but I will hold you responsible for his behavior. If he should hurt my daughter in any way he will suffer the same fate as his parents."

"You are harsh," Sholeh said. "Will you never forgive Adon and Elin? Has your life then been so difficult since Vartan's death?"

"It is not up to me to forgive those two. That is the province of the Celestial Actuary, but I will never forget what they did. My life has been what it was meant to be, but I never thought that Vartan's life should have to be sacrificed."

"Yet you could not have wed Magnus Hauk had Vartan not been gone," Sholeh pointed out.

"My marriage to Vartan was not meant to be forever. I am faerie, and I love whom I choose," Lara replied.

"You have changed from the girl you once were though you look exactly the same as you did when we first met. I envy you that," Sholeh told Lara with a grimace.

"Because I am young in my own race's time I have never had to watch the friends of my early years age,"

Lara said. "I have to admit that I do not like it. That drop of mortal blood that runs through my veins has made me sensitive to the passage of the years. My mother says if I did not have that bit of mortal blood in me that I should not notice time at all."

"I suppose there are disadvantages to every race," Sholeh said.

The High Council met on the last day of The Gathering. Lara took her seat among the clan families' representatives. She brought Taj with her, and introduced the young Dominus formally to all the lords of the New Outlands clans. Taj promised to honor all of the promises his late father had made to the people of the clan families. They in return swore their fealty to Taj, and paid their yearly tribute. The clan leaders were impressed with young Taj's manner and air of assurance. And comforted that Lara was his mother.

"He will be a fine man one day," Rendor of the Felan, the council head, said to Lara. "Magnus would be proud of him."

"He was," Lara answered him.

"How long will *you* rule?" Rendor asked candidly.

"At least five more years," Lara told him. "I have appointed Taj's uncles as his little council, which satisfies the Terahns, and allows them to believe that Taj is truly their Dominus. Marzina calls me a Shadow Queen." She smiled at her old friend.

"We missed Marzina and her tricks this year," Rendor said with a smile.

"She is with Ilona, and very happy. It is safer for her in my mother's forest right now," Lara told him. "Especially after what Zagiri did."

"There is one thing I have learned from Prince Kaliq," Rendor said. "Everything happens for a purpose, Lara. You may not comprehend that purpose, but it is there. The Celestial Actuary, or Great Creator as the Terahns call him, does not make mistakes."

"You know how I dislike the *mysteries* in life, Rendor," Lara reminded him.

Rendor laughed. "I know," he said. "You would see everything immediately, and understand it all, but life even for a faerie woman does not work that way."

Lara nodded, and she bid her old friend farewell. Then she went with her son to each of the clan lords and said their goodbyes. After, her magic returned them all home quickly as it did each year. Coming to The Gathering usually took several days.

Back in Liam's village of Camdene the Dominus had a request of his parent. "Mother," Taj said, "could Gare and Sinon come back to the castle with me? They have some learning, but would have more. And I would like to have my two friends to study with me this year. With my sisters gone now the castle is lonely."

"If their parents will allow it I see no reason for them not to come," Lara told him.

"Let us find them now, then," Taj said excitedly.

The parents of both Gare and Sinon were at first reluctant to allow their sons to go, but the enthusiasm of the three boys convinced them that this would be a great advantage for their sons.

And Liam, Lord of the Fiacre, spoke in favor of such an arrangement. "Retaining the friendship of the young Dominus is a good thing," he said. "It is to the clan families' advantage for a new generation to be part of Terah. It is not like the old days when we were content to remain isolated in the Outlands. These are the New Outlands, and our survival requires a new tactic. Send your sons with the Dominus. You may be certain that Lara will watch over them herself. They will be safe."

The permissions granted, Lara sought out Dasras, and told her stallion that she would ride home alone. "I have told the boys I will send for them in two days."

"It will be like the old days, mistress," Dasras said as she mounted him. Then he began to race down the long meadow, his snowy-white wings unfolding as he ran. They ascended upward into the blue skies heading across the fertile plains beneath and toward the Emerald Mountains. Lara could see as they traveled over the hills that the autumn was coming. Here and there she spied spots of red and gold as the trees began to color. Briefly she was overcome with sadness. She and Magnus had returned home together at this same time last year. Dasras had carried them both, and they had all laughed and talked, recalling their summer idyll. The stallion always had wonderful stories to relate as most people overlooked the fact that the magical beast was intelligent and so they ignored him, speaking freely.

"What did you do when Roan asked you to leave his meadows?" Lara asked the great horse as he flew.

"Why, I went to another meadow, mistress, taking a dozen delightful mares including my own beloved Sakira with me. Roan's young stallion blustered and bristled. I spoke with him and offered to fight him, but I warned him if I did I should win because I have magic. I would overcome him, and then I would geld him myself. Oddly he did not annoy me after that. He is a beautiful creature, mistress, but a complete fraud. He gallops about the meadow tossing his head, flinging his mane back and flaring his nostrils as he snorts. And as he basked beneath the light of the full moon, admiring himself in the meadow pond, I jumped the hedge separating us, and spent the next several hours impregnating every mare I could catch and mount. Roan will have a bumper crop of colts next spring I can guarantee, and most of them will be silver-white." Dasras chuckled wickedly.

Lara laughed heartily at her stallion's recital. "Roan, of course, will know what you have done," she said.

"That youngster he's pinning his hopes on would be better off gelded," Dasras replied dryly. "He will only produce ordinary offspring, but Roan is no fool. He will see that sooner than later. Now, mistress, tell me what troubles you, for I can see you are disturbed. Is it that you will miss your Aghy lover?"

"Nay, I kept him for pleasures just a short while. I am sad because for the first time I have noticed those

I love growing older," Lara said. "And when they are gone with whom will I share my history? With whom will I talk?"

"We will share our history, and we will talk, mistress," Dasras said.

"But your time is certainly limited, too, Dasras," Lara replied.

"I was created to live as long as my mistress," the horse told her. "I will be with you as long as you exist in this world."

"Oh, I am glad!" Lara said. "When Magnus died so suddenly and unexpectedly last spring I began to realize the true frailty of mortals, Dasras. It saddens me."

"Do not waste your time bemoaning that which you cannot change," Dasras advised Lara. "Enjoy what you have, and the time you have with those who give you happiness, mistress. It is true you will outlive three of your children, but the other two will be here for you. You will get to see a grandson, a great-grandson and other descendants rule Terah after your son. And Anoush and her descendants will keep you connected with the clan families even after Liam, Rendor, Roan and the others are gone."

Lara's sadness evaporated, and she leaned forward to pat Dasras's neck. "Thank you," she told him. "I had begun to wallow in self-pity. My mortals still have many years ahead of them. Oh, Dasras! What would I do without you?"

"You would do very well, mistress. Not as well as you do with me, of course," Dasras told her drolly.

Lara laughed, feeling lighter now that she had gotten her foolish fears off of her chest. "Look!" she said, pointing below. "It is Sapphire Lake. We are halfway home."

Dasras galloped on through the blue sky. They finally crossed the Emerald range of mountains. Below she could see the small villages and farms of Terah. Eventually the coastline came into sight, the Sea of Sagitta beyond. From her vantage point Lara could see at least four of the fjords, and then she saw the castle of the Dominus looming up from the green cliffs. She had always thought it beautiful with its towers and turrets, with its terraced gardens that hung out over the fjord.

Dasras began to decrease his altitude. He cleared the far cliff and sailed out over the waters of the dark blue fjord. Then, circling, he dropped down into his stable yard, coming to a gentle landing. It was always more difficult for him to land than it was for him to take off. Jason, his personal attendant, came racing from the stables to greet him.

Lara slid from the saddle. "Thank you, Dasras," she said, and, rubbing his muzzle affectionately, she hurried into the castle.

"We didn't know you were coming home today, mistress," her servant, Mila, said as she came forward to welcome her home. "Where is the young Dominus?"

"I will bring him back in two days' time," Lara told

Mila. "Two of his friends are coming with him. They will live in the castle and study with Taj. Tomorrow we must see that suitable quarters are made ready for them. I am tired, Mila. Fetch me something to eat. I am going to the baths to rid myself of the stink of my travels."

"At once, mistress. I know just what you need for you look tired. All that feasting and playing at your Gathering." She bustled off.

Lara entered her private bath. The attendants were waiting, having been notified by another servant that the Domina had returned. She stood silently as they soaped her and scrubbed her. The smell of the rough encampment of The Gathering and several hours on Dasras's broad back was rinsed away. With a smile of thanks she walked to the marble soaking tub, immersing herself in the perfumed water so she might relax.

It had been an incredibly eventful few weeks. Seeing the twins she had borne to Kol—she still had difficulty thinking of them as her sons—had been quite a revelation. She had begun to wonder what they would have been like had she brought them into the light to be raised. She should not have allowed Kaliq and the others to make her leave them behind to Kol's mercy. Certainly not after Kol was punished for his assault of her on the Dream Plain. Would not the Dark Lands, without heirs or their Twilight Lord, have been just as confused and conflicted? But it was too late to second-guess what had been done.

Kolgrim and Kolbein were their father's sons. Kolbein was, of course, the worst of the two, having been raised by the Wolfyn. But Arild and his family had not been bad giants. And Kolgrim certainly had his father's charm. And though she disliked admitting it, she had been amused by his sense of humor. *I could almost like him,* Lara thought, surprised. He and Kolbein would quarrel, of course, over everything having to do with ruling the Dark Lands. Alfrigg would have his hands full, but it was no longer her concern, especially as she had prevented the Darkling from interfering.

But it was Ciarda who concerned Lara the most. She had just enough magic to be troublesome, but not enough to accomplish all she sought to do. Unfortunately Ciarda did not realize that. Having no idea what she would do next, they would have to watch her carefully. Lara stepped from her soaking pool into a thick towel held by one of the bath attendants. "Nothing more tonight," she said, waving the servants away as, wrapped in her long towel, she made for her bedchamber. The castle, she noted, was very quiet. She had never known it to be that quiet. Too quiet. She was glad she had let Taj bring his two best friends back with him. Three noisy boys would bring the old castle back to life again. She remembered Dillon's youthful adventures when he lived here.

"I've brought you a nice poached breast of capon," Mila said, coming into the room with a tray. She placed it on the table that was set in the wide bay window. "Fresh bread, a salad and a piece of that delicious sponge cake that your brother's mate so loves." She placed a fresh white napkin in Lara's lap when she sat. Then Mila poured her mistress a goblet of pale golden wine. "Do you want company while you eat?" she asked. "Who are these boys who will return with the Dominus?"

Lara realized that Mila was not, despite her query, going to leave her to herself. "They are his two best friends, sons of Fiacre clansmen. They have played together since they were children." She ate some of the capon and buttered her bread. "He had no sooner arrived than he was off with them." She smiled and chewed her food slowly.

"I wonder that their presence might not offend some of the more important Terahn families," Mila said slowly. "Why should these two foreigners be allowed to live and study with our Dominus? Are there not Terahn boys who are good enough? These are questions that will be asked, Domina."

"Asked by the narrow of mind, and the insular," Lara said, irritated, but Mila did make a point. "And please do not call folk from the Terahn province of the New Outlands foreigners. They had Terahn citizenship granted to them by Magnus Hauk, and all he gave them our son promised to continue. Taj has lived an isolated life here at the castle as most Terahn children do in their own homes. If he attended a Terahn school he would be deferred to, and nothing would be natural. You know how formal Terahns can be toward their Dominus. You live here at the castle, Mila, and you know us as people.

The average citizen does not. I suppose I shall have to ask two Terahn boys to join Taj and his friends, but when those boys bow and scrape to my son, Gare and Sinon will certainly be put off by such behavior. And so will Taj."

"You could offend those you do not ask," Mila pointed out.

"Then I shall ask none at all. It will be announced that the Dominus has requested two friends from the New Outlands join him this year so he may learn more about these people, and integrate them better into Terahn life," Lara told Mila with a grin.

Mila could not help but chuckle. "You are too clever for us, mistress," she said. "There will be talk nonetheless, but if the Dominus has said it, the wealthy will swallow their pride and let it be. However, the Dominus's aunts and grandmother will be certain to involve themselves in the matter."

"Taj will silence them, you may be certain," Lara replied as she finished her meal.

"You did not eat your cake," Mila noted.

"I will eat it later," Lara said. "Leave it, and take the tray away. I will not need you again tonight, Mila."

The serving woman picked up the tray, and with a bow left her mistress. Lara unwrapped the towel she had been wearing and slipped a pale blue silk night garment over her head. Then, sitting, she brushed out her long hair and replaited it into a thick braid. Walking out into her garden, Lara looked out over the fjord and the cliffs around her. Terah was surely the fairest place in any world. To her right a moon rose. A night bird sang from some hidden perch.

"You don't really want to be alone, my love, do you?" Kaliq asked her softly. He stood behind her, slipping an arm about her waist, kissing the side of her neck.

"I thought I did, but I don't," Lara answered, leaning back against him. "The castle is so quiet, my lord. I will be glad to have my son and his friends home."

"This is the time for a respite, my love. We have put a watch on Ciarda. She considers what mischief she will next create."

Lara rested her head against his shoulder. "She will be cautious, for she must certainly consider that we will be monitoring her."

"Like most Darklings she is reckless," Kaliq said. His free hand slipped beneath the sheer blue silk to cup a breast. His thumb rubbed the nipple slowly.

Lara sighed and relaxed against him. "I am so tired," she said. "These last days overseeing Kol's sons, thwarting the Darkling, have been busy."

"Shall I go?" he asked her, and his fingers closed about her breast, squeezing it gently. "I will go if you wish, my love."

"Nay," Lara responded. "Do not go, Kaliq, but then curse you, you knew I would not want you to go. Why do you pretend the choice is mine when you know full well that it is not?" She turned in his arms, taking his handsome face between her two hands. "The passion

you hold for me strengthens me, Kaliq. We both know it.
But does it weaken you, my lord? I would not harm the
great spirit you are in the slightest." Her eyes searched
his face for the truth, but then if he had lied to her she
would not have known it for he was skilled at conceal-
ing his emotions.

He kissed her. His sensual mouth closed over her
mouth as he drew her to him. The magic between
them melted their garments away. They stood as the
kiss deepened, their lips fusing together as their souls
blended them briefly into a single entity before they finally broke apart, both breathless.

Kaliq's hands fitted themselves about Lara's waist.
Slowly he lifted her up, his renewed kisses touching her
neck, her chest, her breasts and belly. Restoring her to
her feet, he took her by the hand, leading her to the bed
where they collapsed together, limbs intertwined, belly
to belly, her breasts flattening against his smooth, broad
chest. He began to kiss her again and her lips parted to
receive his tongue.

Lara felt as if her bones were melting away. Pleasures with Kaliq were like no other pleasures. His mouth
left hers, and now fastened over one breast. He suckled upon the nipple. He played with it, drawing it out
as far as the skin would stretch, mashing the tip of it
between his two lips until she sighed with the delight
it gave her. Releasing the nipple, he took the breast in
his hand, squeezing it, kissing it as he traced its shape

with his tongue. She sighed a long sigh, and he heard the happiness in that sigh.

His lips now began to travel across and down her torso. He used his tongue, his teeth and his mouth upon her as he traversed the length of her lush body. The chamber was silent but for the sounds of their love-making. Reaching her mons, he ran his tongue along the shadowed slash separating her nether lips. Eagerly he pushed his tongue between those fleshy folds seeking, seeking, and then finding precisely what he sought.

Lara gasped sharply as his tongue began to play with the sensitive core of her sex. He fastened his lips about it and began to suck upon it, causing her to cry out, but he knew he was not causing her any pain. He tugged fiercely upon that nubbin of flesh, and was rewarded when her juices began to flow. "I need you inside me, my lord," Lara whispered into his ear as she licked at it.

He covered her body with his as their fingers laced and unlaced together. She felt his manhood pressing into her, and wrapped her legs about his torso. He thrust hard and deep, and she cried out as he continued the rhythm moving back and forth, back and forth, back and forth. Lara began to claw at him as he fiercely pleasured them, and now it was he who cried out as she tightened herself about him, increasing his delight.

Kaliq knew he could have kept up his passion for her for quite some time, but after an hour he brought Lara to complete and total fulfillment, taking his own release at the same time. The purple shadows beneath her eyes told him that she really did need her rest. There would be other times, other nights in which they would revel in each other. For now, however, she needed sleep.

Lying next to him, she snuggled into the curve of his arm. "You always know just what I need, and when I need it," she told him. "Why is that, Kaliq?"

"You are a part of me, my love," he told her. "Now sleep, Lara. The days ahead will be busy. Our impatient Darkling will not wait long to make her next move."

"And I must be ready," Lara said sleepily. "But not tonight, Kaliq. And not tomorrow. Stay with me, my lord. I do not want to be alone."

"Meet me tomorrow at the Oasis of Zeroun," he told her. "You must remember that you are the Domina, and as such have a reputation to uphold."

"I am beginning to see the advantage in being pure faerie," Lara murmured. "If I were I should not care what anyone else thought."

"Magnus is gone but six months, my love," he reminded her. "I will not allow you to let anyone have an advantage over you. You and you alone must guide Taj until he is old enough and wise enough to reign for himself. This is important, Lara, and while you may not understand why yet, you will eventually. Until tomorrow, my love." And he kissed the top of her head.

She did not have to open her eyes. He was gone. His scent lingered, but the weight of him next to her on the bed had vanished. With a deep sigh of regret, Lara rolled over and went to sleep. To her amazement she did not waken until midday. "Why did you not call me?" she asked Mila.

"Because you needed the rest," Mila said.

"But I have much to do, and I wanted to get away briefly today," Lara grumbled.

"What is there for you to do, mistress? I have seen to the apartment that the Dominus's young friends will share. I have notified the tutors, and the schoolroom is prepared for three instead of one. Dasras is content. The day is yours, and you needed your sleep," Mila repeated.

"You take good care of me, Mila," Lara complimented her serving woman. "Send to the stables, and tell Dasras I would ride out today. Then fetch me something to eat. I find that I am suddenly starving."

"At once, Domina," Mila said with a broad smile, and she hurried off to do Lara's bidding.

Lara went off to her bath and bathed quickly. Then she dressed in her riding breeches and a white silk shirt, pulling her boots on over her stockinged feet. Mila returned with a tray, and Lara ate heartily of eggs poached in a cream sauce flavored with celery seed, a thick slice of ham and fresh bread, butter and cheese. Then she was off to the stables where Dasras awaited her saddled and ready to go. "Take his saddle off, Jason," she told her horse's stable man. "I intend riding him bareback today." Jason obeyed the Domina but thought it odd. Still, when he saw her mount easily, grasping the stallion's heavy, thick mane, he realized she knew what she was doing.

"We are going to the far meadow overlooking the

sea," she told Dasras. "You will wait for me there until I come again."

"And you will be where, mistress?" the horse asked her.

"I go to Zeroun to meet the prince," Lara told him.

"And as you value your reputation you wish this meeting to be private," Dasras said. "That is very wise, and good advice the Shadow Prince gives you."

"Can I not make a sound judgment without the prince?" Lara said.

"Indeed, mistress," Dasras answered her, "but in this case I believe you have been well advised."

Lara laughed. "You are right, of course. How did you know?"

"Sometimes your faerie nature overcomes your common sense," the horse answered her. "Prince Kaliq is a prudent man."

Dasras had trotted from the stable, and moved into a loping canter, and finally a long gallop. They arrived at the small meadow overlooking the sea. The grass was still lush enough to graze upon despite the fact is was midautumn. And there was a stand of trees for Dasras to escape the sun should he wish it, along with a little brook. Lara slid easily off his back.

"Wait for me. I shall return by nightfall," Lara told her horse.

"Come before sunset, mistress, or they will be out looking for you," he warned.

Zeroun, Zeroun, is where I would be. Transport me

now across the sea! And Lara was gone in a puff of green smoke to reappear upon the sands of the oasis. The tent was there awaiting her, and Kaliq was standing in its entrance. Lara ran to him.

CHAPTER ELEVEN

"You took your time in answering my call," Ciarda said to the young man before her. "Remember your fate is in my hands. I control you."

Cam of the Fiacre looked at the beautiful Darkling and smiled his charming smile. "It is you who should remember that without me you cannot continue on with your plans, Ciarda," he told her bluntly.

"Where were you?" she demanded to know.

"With Anoush," he replied, knowing the answer made her jealous.

"That vapid girl? Really, Cam, can you do no better than that weak Halfling?" Ciarda's color was high as she imagined his time with Anoush.

"You tell me I am the Hierarch," Cam answered her. "Whether that is true or not I do not know, but I do know that your magic will make it appear so. But we will need more than that, Ciarda, to convince the people of Hetar to accept me. Remember I am an Outlander. We will not be able to hide that fact, and Outlanders are still scorned and believed savage by Hetarians. The Lord High Ruler is wed to the daughter of Magnus Hauk. Her mother is my aunt Lara, the faerie woman. Should not my wife be one of Lara's other daughters? I have known Anoush since childhood. She is perfect for me."

"What of the other of Magnus Hauk's daughters?" Ciarda wanted to know. "The twin of the young Dominus. Would she not be more suitable? I am told she has magic, which could be to our advantage, Cam."

"She is too young, and besides, Anoush tells me she is with her grandmother Ilona now. You are forbidden from Ilona's kingdom, Darkling," he taunted her. "No, I want Anoush. She has *the Sight,* which could be valuable to me, and she is a healer."

Ciarda hissed angrily with her frustration, but she knew she had no choice. She needed this mortal man if her plans were to succeed. The origins of the legend of the Hierarch had vanished in the mists of time. When she had lost the opportunity to manipulate her twin half brothers she decided to use that legend to her own advantage. Times were hard in Hetar, and the rumors among the poor had already begun of a savior who would rescue them all from their misery, and restore Hetar to its glory.

What fools these mortals were! Did they not realize they alone were responsible for their own miseries? And only they could overcome them? Mortals were odd creatures, for they always hoped for a better tomorrow. Well, she would give it to them, if only briefly. The Hierarch was central to her plans. And Cam of the Fiacre was the perfect mortal to play the role. He was beautiful, charismatic and had incredible charm. The people would flock to him. She knew she already had him half-convinced that he was what she proposed he be.

She had found him quite by chance. Her plans were blooming and ripening within her mind's eye, but she had yet to consider the unfortunate mortal she would use to bring these plans to a conclusion. And then one evening as she lurked unseen in the hall of the head-woman Sholeh, Ciarda had seen him. At first he appeared to her to be just a beautiful young man whom she might seduce. But then as she watched she had seen him charming Sholeh. The headwoman was known for her practical nature and no-nonsense attitude, yet Cam had her eating out of his palm. Ciarda was impressed.

Over the next few days she watched Cam, and the more she saw of him the more Ciarda realized that fate had put the Hierarch into her hands. His way with the people around him was quite amazing. His smile was infectious. His public manner patient. He was quick to reach out to others when help was needed. He was really quite perfect. And yet he was perhaps too perfect, which meant that he certainly had a dark side.

Ciarda revealed herself to Cam one afternoon as he sat beneath a tree watching one of the herds belonging to Sholeh. To her complete amazement he did not seem shocked by her dramatic appearance in a burst of fiery flames. Indeed, he smiled at her. Ciarda struggled to maintain her composure. Mortals facing her were usually frightened. This man was not taken aback in the least by her. "I am the Darkling known as Ciarda," she announced to him, tossing her head so that her ebony hair swirled about her.

"Your coming was foretold to me," Cam said.

"Who told you such a thing?" Ciarda said, surprised.

"The shade of my mother," he said. "Before her spirit was taken into Limbo she reached out to the little child I was. She said someone would come to me one day, and that I should be a great man."

"Indeed," Ciarda replied. "Well, I know nothing of your mother's shade, Cam of the Fiacre, but it is my duty to see you reach greatness. You are the Hierarch of legend, and you will return Hetar to its former glory."

"Indeed," Cam said. And then he burst out laughing. "Darkling," he said to her, "you would use me for your own purposes. I am no simpleton to believe what you tell me. But I will help you if you will help me. I would take my revenge against she who slew my parents. I have waited many years to do so. Your power will aid me, and in return I will help you to gain whatever it is you desire. Do we have a bargain?"

"Upon whom do you seek revenge?" Ciarda asked him.

"The faerie woman Lara," he replied.

"What form will your vengeance take?" she wanted to know.

"I will take something from her that she holds dearest," Cam answered. "And that is all I will tell you, Darkling."

Ciarda nodded. Revenge that black she understood,

and she didn't care what he did to the faerie woman as long as she gained her goals, her father's goal of uniting the worlds in darkness. "We have a bargain," she agreed, "but we must seal it by exchanging tokens. Take pleasures with me now, and I will keep your seed in pledge of our covenant. In return I will give you the ability to go where you want by simply asking to be there."

He stood up from beneath the tree where he had been lounging. Reaching out, he grasped her by her long black hair, and pulled her to him. "I will have you here and now," he said, loosening his garments and turning her about and pushing her up against the wide trunk of the tree.

Ciarda was astounded by his boldness. She magicked her garments away, but her nakedness neither shocked nor surprised him. His hands slid beneath her buttocks. The brief glimpse she gained of his manhood delighted her. He was large and he was thick. She moaned as he rammed himself into her. She gasped as he used her roughly until she was whimpering with her great need. Need such as she had certainly never known. And he satisfied her again, and again, and yet again. This mortal was the finest lover she had ever had. She clawed at him, pushing him even further until they were both groaning with the pleasures they were gaining from one another, and wet with their exertions. Finally he flooded her with his juices, which were so copious that they overflowed her womb, and ran down the insides of her thighs.

"You are magnificent!" Ciarda gasped as her legs fell away from his torso, and she clung to him because she could not quite stand on her own right now.

"Your sheath is narrow and tight," he told her. "I quite enjoyed it. Now give me the small power you promised me."

"You had it the moment you gave me your seed," Ciarda told him.

"Let's see if it works," Cam said. *"Take me to Ciarda's bedchamber!"* And he suddenly found himself in an exotic room with a large round bed covered in red silk. And there in the middle of the bed Ciarda lounged temptingly. He looked at her. "You are tempting, but I cannot shirk my duty as Sholeh's herder. *Take me back to the meadow,"* he said.

"Come back tonight!" Ciarda called to him.

"Perhaps," his fading voice answered her.

But he had not come back that night. She waited for several nights for him, and to her annoyance he did not come. She expected him to be surprised when he found her in his rustic bed several nights later, but he was not. He complained that it had taken her long enough to come to him. Then, mounting her, he rode her hard the night long, sleeping briefly and leaving her without a word in the first minutes of dawn to attend to his duties. Ciarda didn't know whether to be furious or not.

In the end, however, she decided not to be angry. There was no mortal sentiment in Cam, and that was a good thing. In the weeks that followed she discovered

into battle the Hetarians had been warned. His mistake was in not taking The City first. If you control The City, you can control all of Hetar. But he let his forces march across the land and The City was warned. Then the faerie woman took her revenge on him, marshaling her allies to defeat my father. You speak casually of the Domina of Terah. But you do not really know her, Cam. She is dangerous."

"She is a faerie woman, and all women can be manipulated," Cam replied. "Do I not manipulate you? And my sweet Anoush?"

"When you speak of Vartan's daughter you sound as if you truly care for her," Ciarda said jealously. "Do you?"

"In my own way, aye, I do. As a child she was my friend when no others were," he recalled. "But then her cursed brother interfered. Still she tried to remain loyal, but her mother took her away to Terah. I was sent to Rivalen, and into Sholeh's care. At first it was just for the summer, but then I was not allowed to return to Camdene. When that happened I realized I must pretend to change my ways. I did. Even Sholeh, wise as she is, believes I am what I appear to be," Cam said. "You are envious of my feelings for her, Darkling, but be warned. Should she be harmed in any way I will hold you responsible, and you will lose my help."

"I will not harm her," Ciarda said. *Not yet,* she

...arda could not believe what was happening. He was controlling her, and to her shock she found it more exciting than anything she had previously experienced. She was a Darkling. She was magic, and yet this mortal man was forcing her to his will, and for all her protests she was enjoying it even as he withheld pleasures from her. She ached with her need. Her desires were running hot. She needed pleasures. *She needed them!* "Yes, my lord!" she gasped out, and then screamed with joy as he met her needs more than satisfactorily, groaning as his own lusts were fully sated.

Afterward as Ciarda lay in his arms she told him, "If you were not so necessary to my plans, Cam of the Fiacre, I should kill you without hesitation."

"And if you were not so necessary to *my* plans, Darkling, I should have not accepted your bargain," he responded. "We need each other. I need you so I am finally able to gain my revenge, and you need me so you may complete your father's plans. I am curious though, Darkling. Why do you attempt to accomplish what he could not? You have not his great powers."

"His powers were great, it is true," Ciarda said, "but he felt he needed the faerie woman's magic. It was a mistake. He could have done without her, but it was foretold that she would birth his son. But he did not need her for more than that. A well-coordinated and

his insatiable need for power. He would be ruthless with his enemies, and that was a good thing. Ruthlessness inspired fear in the masses, and fear gave one the ability to control.

As Hierarch Cam would rule Hetar for her with an iron fist. And for now she would give him the girl he desired for a wife because in the end when she controlled it all, the faerie woman's daughters would be taken from the men who cherished them, and given to the Wolfyn for playthings. She expected Magnus Hauk's daughter to last longer.

"You are smiling," Cam said to her.

"I am thinking of our future," Ciarda answered him.

Cam laughed. "You are so deliciously vile, Darkling," he told her. "Let us hope your powers are strong enough to do all you seek to do. If my aunt decides you are an annoyance she will quite happily destroy you as she did your father," he told her cruelly.

"Hateful mortal," she snarled at him. "If my father had succeeded in his plans you would now reside beneath his boot, and not in my bed."

"I enjoy your bed," he said, grasping one of her large, round breasts. "Slaking my fierce and unquenchable lusts on your body allows me to play the gentle suitor with Anoush. She is falling in love with me, Darkling." He squeezed her breast hard, and she was unable to restrain a whimper of pain. "In the spring I will make her my wife." His mouth took Ciarda's in a hard kiss. "And eventually you will both come to my bed together, and we will take pleasures. Anoush is a gentle maiden, but she will have her mother's appetite for passion, I am certain. I will have you lick her secret treasures while I plunge myself into you over and over and over again. Will that please you, Ciarda?"

He forced the Darkling onto her back and pushed his fingers into her sheath, moving them back and forth until she was begging him for release. "Or perhaps I shall mount her while you kiss her lips until they are bruised. Would you like that, Darkling?" He was atop her now, entering her body, driving deep, relishing her cries. He cared not if they were of pain or pleasure.

"Yes!" she sobbed to him. "Yes! I should like it, Cam. I would!" She writhed beneath him in a frenzy of lust unsatisfied.

"You must learn to call me *my lord,* Darkling, for I am the Hierarch, and to be respected." He caught her thrashing head between his two hands. His fingers dug into her scalp. "Say it, Darkling. Say, *yes, my lord.*" The blue eyes blazed down at her. His great manhood was suddenly still within her.

"Mortal, you forget yourself!" Ciarda cried. "It is I who command you."

The sound of his laughter actually sent a chill through her. "Darkling, without me you can do naught. We are equals. *For now.* Now humor me, and do as I have asked you, my pretty Darkling. Say, *yes, my lord.*"

"I could turn you into a beetle to crush beneath my foot," she told him.

He laughed, and began to ride her again. "There will be no pleasures for you until you have obeyed me, Darkling."

Ciarda could not believe what was happening. He was controlling her, and to her shock she found it more exciting than anything she had previously experienced. She was a Darkling. She was magic, and yet this mortal man was forcing her to his will, and for all her protests she was enjoying it even as he withheld pleasures from her. She ached with her need. Her desires were running hot. She needed pleasures. *She needed them!* "Yes, my lord!" she gasped out, and then screamed with joy as he met her needs more than satisfactorily, groaning as his own lusts were fully sated.

Afterward as Ciarda lay in his arms she told him, "If you were not so necessary to my plans, Cam of the Fiacre, I should kill you without hesitation."

"And if you were not so necessary to *my* plans, Darkling, I should have not accepted your bargain," he responded. "We need each other. I need you so I am finally able to gain my revenge, and you need me so you may complete your father's plans. I am curious though, Darkling. Why do you attempt to accomplish what he could not? You have not his great powers."

"His powers were great, it is true," Ciarda said, "but he felt he needed the faerie woman's magic. It was a mistake. He could have done without her, but it was foretold that she would birth his son. But he did not need her for more than that. A well-coordinated and unexpected attack on Hetar should have given him the victory he sought. But by the time he sent his armies into battle the Hetarians had been warned. His mistake was in not taking The City first. If you control The City, you can control all of Hetar. But he let his forces march across the land and The City was warned. Then the faerie woman took her revenge on him, marshaling her allies to defeat my father. You speak casually of the Domina of Terah. But you do not really know her, Cam. She is dangerous."

"She is a faerie woman, and all women can be manipulated," Cam replied. "Do I not manipulate you? And my sweet Anoush?"

"When you speak of Vartan's daughter you sound as if you truly care for her," Ciarda said jealously. "Do you?"

"In my own way, aye, I do. As a child she was my friend when no others were," he recalled. "But then her cursed brother interfered. Still she tried to remain loyal, but her mother took her away to Terah. I was sent to Rivalen, and into Sholeh's care. At first it was just for the summer, but then I was not allowed to return to Camdene. When that happened I realized I must pretend to change my ways. I did. Even Sholeh, wise as she is, believes I am what I appear to be," Cam said. "You are envious of my feelings for her, Darkling, but be warned. Should she be harmed in any way I will hold you responsible, and you will lose my help."

"I will not harm her," Ciarda said. *Not yet,* she

thought to herself. "If the little mortal female means that much to you keep her. And then one day we will sport together as you have previously said we would, my lord Hierarch."

"You are clever, Darkling," he replied. "We will do well together. Now tell me. When am I to be revealed as Hetar's great hope?" He laughed softly.

"You will appear first in the Coastal Kingdom, where you will perform several wonders that will be reported to the Lord High Ruler. I want Jonah to be afraid of what is to come. You will disappear from the Coastal Kingdom mysteriously only to reappear in the Midlands, where your miracles will be even more amazing. The gossip will race forth into The City, where eventually you will make a grand entrance. Once there we will go about winning over the magnates and others of importance. That is all you need know for now," she told him.

"When will this all begin?" he asked.

"Toward the end of the Icy Season when the populace will have endured another bitter few months. Food will be scarce. The cold will be numbing. Sickness will run rampant as the spring rains begin. And then the Hierarch will come promising to end the want, the plagues, the general unhappiness of the population. You will promise to return Hetar to the days of her glory. You will point out that all these changes that have been made have not bettered Hetar, but ruined it. That by flouting the great traditions of Hetar, Hetar has been almost destroyed."

"And will I be able to return Hetar to its former grandeur?" Cam asked the Darkling. "Will my promises be good? Or will they be worthless?"

"There are enough of those who wish to return to the old days to help us do just that," Ciarda said. "The Crusader Knights and the Mercenaries are both unhappy. The magnates are not pleased that certain Pleasure Women now own their own houses, cutting the magnates out of what had been a most lucrative business. There is enough discontent among the wealthy and formerly powerful to work to our advantage, my lord Hierarch."

"And when the Hetarians are convinced the good old days have returned?" Cam asked her. "What then, Darkling?"

"Then you will rule in Hetar, my lord Hierarch. I will give you several cohorts of Wolfyn to keep the peace. And the darkness will fall over the land even as my father desired it," Ciarda said with a smile. "He will be so proud of me."

"If he lives," Cam told her. "But why would the Twilight Lord be pleased to see a slip of a female succeed where he had failed? You fool yourself, Darkling, when you say you do this for your father. You do it for yourself, for you are an ambitious woman. You will see the women of Hetar subjugated once again while you overcome all odds to take power for yourself. You are wickedly clever."

"And you are too clever," she responded. "What

makes you think I will not dispense with your services once I gain what I want?"

Cam laughed. "Darkling, you need me, for no other lover has ever satisfied you as I do, and your appetite for pleasures is as great as mine."

Ciarda looked irritably at him, but then she said, "You are right, my lord Hierarch. Not even the Wolfyn have your talent for pleasures. Perhaps when I have accomplished all I desire I will take you for my consort."

Cam laughed again. "My aunt will defeat you, Darkling. But as long as I rule Hetar and Anoush is by my side, she will not care."

"You are nothing without me, Outlander!" she cried. *"Nothing!"*

"I will not argue the point with you, Darkling. I am but an ordinary man without your magic. But you will continue to give me that magic because I suit your convenience. You will find no other to play the part who can lead the people of Hetar into your web, Ciarda. I know my own worth. Do you?"

He was right, of course, but the truth rankled her. A stupid man would not be able to convince Hetar that he was who he said he was. Cam was everything the legend said the Hierarch was. His appearance was like a sunrise, sudden and unexpected in its beauty. His charm could make every person who heard him speak believe that he was speaking directly to them. "We must not quarrel," Ciarda said. "Our goal is Hetar, and you will rule it as my govenor, my lord Hierarch. We must be united."

"Agreed," he said. "Now leave me be until you absolutely need me, Darkling. I would court Anoush, and it is difficult enough without your interference."

"Very well." She pouted. "But you must give me pleasures before you leave me."

He granted her wish, and when he finally left her Ciarda lay but half-conscious and in a weakened state. He did not even glance back at her as, using her magic, he returned himself to his own bed. In the morning he arose early, and, going to a nearby hot spring, washed his body free of the stink of their lust. It would not do to go to Anoush smelling of another woman. He wanted to rid himself of every memory of the Darkling for now. He wanted to simply be Cam, a herder from Rivalen, who wanted to court Anoush, a maiden of Camdene.

In the hall that morning he went to Sholeh, the headwoman, who had acted as his foster mother these past few years. She smiled warmly at him as he approached her.

"Good morrow, Cam," Sholeh greeted him.

He took her hands up in his, and kissed them respectfully. Then he knelt before her. "I would beg a boon of you, my lady. If you can grant it my heart will be happy."

Sholeh reached out and ruffled his curly dark hair. "What do you want, Cam? If it is within my power I will give it to you."

"Invite my cousin Anoush to visit with you, lady," he

asked her softly. "I cannot shirk my duties to the herd, which makes it impossible to know Anoush again. If she were here with you we could sit together in the evenings by the fire and talk. Perhaps she would bring a basket out to the meadow in the noonday so we might eat together."

"Ah," Sholeh said, "to be young and in love again." She smiled fondly at him. "Of course I will ask my kinswoman Anoush to come and visit with me, Cam. I will send a message to her today via faerie post."

His handsome face lit with pleasure, and he kissed both her hands again. "Thank you, my lady! Thank you!" Then he rose to his feet.

Sholeh laughed. "Are you so eager for a wife, Cam?" she asked him.

"Until now, nay, but now that I have seen Anoush again, aye!"

"Do not hurry the maid, Cam. Anoush is a careful girl. Take time to reacquaint yourselves again. If she cares for you none will dissuade her. You have time," Sholeh advised him. "I believe you can rekindle the feelings Anoush had for you as a child."

"I hope so!" he said earnestly.

There was a boyishness about him that touched Sholeh's heart. Cam saw it and was satisfied that Sholeh would do whatever she had to to help him. The Lord High Ruler of Hetar had been clever in taking a princess of Terah as his wife. But he had made a mistake in angering her mother by stealing the girl. When Anoush agreed to be his wife he would go to her mother and plead for her permission to make her his bride.

He knew that when Hetar had been taken by the forces of the Darkling, and he was given the power to rule it, he could take his revenge on Lara. He would see that both of her daughters were turned over to a new Pleasure House he would create especially for the rapacious Wolfyn soldiers. Within a few months both of the young women would be dead, but those last months would be spent in an agony of unending pleasures as they were used over and over and over again. Thus would he destroy the faerie woman who had murdered his mother and father. She would never forget how her two daughters had ended their lives, nor that she had been unable to prevent it, for the Darkling would put a spell around that Pleasure House that could not be broken.

Cam smiled. He suspected that Ciarda had planned to just give the two sisters to the Wolfyn despite her vow not to harm them. But his way was a far more refined torture, and he knew when he told her the Darkling would appreciate the subtlety of his plan. Multiple rape by the Wolfyn would kill Anoush too easily. Zagiri would last longer, but she, too, would succumb quickly enough. Setting the sisters in a Pleasure House to endure the slow attentions of their cruel Wolfyn lovers was a far more satisfactory revenge.

He would be sorry to lose Anoush for he did have feelings for her. But the knowledge of what he must do would make their time together all the sweeter for him. In the end, however, she would have to be sacrificed, for he must have his revenge against her mother. And he was being quite generous. He was taking only two lives for the two taken. The laws of revenge did allow him more, but he was not a greedy man.

True to her word Sholeh sent an invitation to Anoush to come and visit. Several days later Anoush rode into Rivalen on a small golden mare, one of Dasras's daughters. And that same evening she walked hand in hand with Cam beneath the autumn stars. It was the beginning of their romance, and as that romance deepened word spread among the Fiacre clan families that the daughter of Vartan was being courted by the son of her father's killers. Anoush's other suitors were outraged.

But when the respected headwoman, Sholeh, kin to Vartan, defended the lovers, pointing out what a fine man Cam had become beneath her tutelage, opinions began to change. Especially when Anoush and Cam were seen together, and they were so obviously in love. Winterfest came, and Cam was ready to solicit Lara's permission to ask Anoush to be his wife. Forewarned of this by Noss, Lara chose instead to go to Shunnar. She did not often join the Fiacre except for those weeks late in the summer, so it would hardly be thought odd.

Seated at supper with Kaliq, Lara said, "Noss still does not like Cam despite what everyone else seems to think. Our friendship goes back so far that I trust her instincts as much as I would trust mine."

"And what do you think?" Kaliq asked.

"He seems changed, and yet…" Lara paused. "There is little light surrounding him. He says all the right things, but beneath his smiles and fine words I sense something else although I have not been with him enough to put my finger on it."

"You don't want to be with him, do you?" the prince said as he reached for a small bunch of grapes.

"Nay, I do not," Lara admitted. She took a golden apricot, split it with her two thumbs and ate one half of it. "Every time I look at him I see his parents. I do not care what others may think of him. Yet Anoush is in love with him. She does not remember her father for she was a baby when he was killed. All she knows of Vartan is his legend. Yet Cam has managed to revive those feelings she had for him as a little girl before Dillon warned me of his wickedness. Anoush's letters to me are so sweet, Kaliq. So filled with the joy and wonder of first love. How can I who have known such great love in my own life deny my child love? I thought others would court Anoush, that she would come to consider Cam as her kinsman only. It has not happened, and now he would wed her. If I allow him to ask me for her what can I reply feeling as I do? I do not want this man as my son-in-law. I do not want grandchildren from his black blood. If I refuse him will my daughter turn against me as Zagiri did?"

Reaching out, he took the other half of the apricot from her hand, sucking the juice from her fingers before he ate it. He did not release her hand. "I am pleased to see your instincts are as sharp as ever despite these last months, my love. I told you that we had set a watch upon Ciarda. We have discovered some very interesting things about her. Cam is her lover, and the skill of his passions has enslaved the Darkling. We have not dared to come too close to her for we are not yet certain ourselves how attuned her senses are. Remember, she seemed to know she was being observed when you first sought her out. As soon as we can determine the proper cloaking we must use to hide our presence from her we will know more. But for now you understand that if Cam is Ciarda's lover there is some wickedness afoot between them. Your daughter must not be involved further with him. If necessary we can bring Anoush to Shunnar for her own safety."

"Nay, Kaliq, that would but alert Cam that we suspected something of him. Let me put Anoush into a deep sleep from which she cannot be awakened by mortal hand. I will surround her with a protective barrier so that the Darkling cannot harm her. Cam dares not ask me for my daughter's hand when she lies in an unconscious state from which no one can arouse her. And when I am called to her side I will deny all knowledge of what has befallen my child. You and I both know that to forbid Anoush the man she believes she loves would be fatal, for then she would be even more determined to have him. In that she and her sister are alike."

"In that all females are alike." Kaliq chuckled. Then

he grew serious. "There is one more gate that must be closed to prevent your mare from escaping. We must bar the Dream Plain to Anoush. Her sleep must be one without even the remotest chance of a dream where something evil might approach or attack her. If there is some reason why Cam needs to wed Anoush he will use the Darkling to reach out to her and force her awake so his purposes may be realized. I would come with you when you set the spell, Lara. Not because I do not believe you are capable, but because you will need all the help that can be given to you."

"I will not argue that, Kaliq," Lara replied. "My primary concern is that Anoush be kept safe from any and all harm. Now that you have told me of Cam's involvement with the Darkling I cannot believe his feelings for my daughter are genuine."

"There is indeed something wicked afoot, my love," he said. "I had hoped when we imprisoned Kol for a thousand years there would be peace. This Darkling is an ambitious female, something that is very rare among denizens of the Dark Lands. I wonder who her mother was. One day I will satisfy my curiosity to that. For now we must contain the evil she would perpetrate."

"Sometimes I grow tired of this constant battle," Lara said candidly. "Sometimes I wish we might just go to Zeroun, and never return. But then I know I have a destiny, and a purpose in life. I feel the strength filling me again."

"And that is as it should be," Kaliq told her. "Even

those of us in the magical realms feel despair now and again. I suspect we should feel that way even if we only dealt with our own kind." He chuckled. "But the Celestial Actuary has given us the task of monitoring the mortal races, and they are not easy creatures under normal circumstances. But when the darker among our numbers seek to encourage them mayhem is certain to ensue, my love. This is a never-ending battle between the light and the dark."

"Will one side ever triumph over the other for good and all?" Lara asked him.

The Shadow Prince shook his head. "Even I do not know the answer to that question, my love. But I do know we must do everything in our power to prevent the darkness from overwhelming us. It is my belief, and that of many others in both the magical worlds and the mortal worlds, that the light must prevail at all costs."

"Then we should get on our way, my lord Prince. It will be night in the New Outlands, and Anoush should be sleeping in her own bed, in her own house. I dare not wait any longer, for I must face Cam sooner than later."

"Then we go, my love," the prince told her. Stepping next to her, he enveloped Lara in his long white cloak. When a moment later he threw back the edge of the garment, they were both standing next to Anoush's bed. *She can neither see nor hear us,* Kaliq said to Lara. He stepped away from her, and looked about the chamber. Then he nodded, satisfied. *Whatever mischief was planned involving Anoush, there is no magic in this place right now but you and I,* he told Lara. *Weave your spell, my love.*

Is she not beautiful, Kaliq? Lara said. *When I look at her I can see Vartan, although her hair is more the shade of mahogany while his was black as the night. Such is the nature of evil that it would reach out to take the fairest.* Lara sighed sadly. Then she said, *"The natural world you now forsake. Sleep until I bid you wake. No dream or call will break your rest. Though some will put it to the test. Your mother's love protects you well. None can break your mother's spell. Sleep, Anoush. Sleep sound and deep. Your spirit now I shall well keep."* Bending, she kissed her child upon her cheek. And as she spoke in the silent language of the magical worlds Lara's hands, raised just slightly above her daughter's body, moved from Anoush's dark head to the very tips of her toes and back again. When she had finished she looked to the Shadow Prince.

Kaliq put his two hands together, and then, slowly opening them, he ran them from the head of Anoush's bed to its foot. *She is now sealed effectively in a protective spell,* he told Lara. *No one will be able to touch her or disturb her.*

Seal the room, as well, Lara said.

Nay. If no one can enter it becomes too obvious what has happened, and suspicion will fall upon you. It will be said you did this to prevent a marriage between Anoush and Cam. The Fiacre like the idea of a union between Vartan's daughter and Adon's son. They see it as an end to the terrible memories. What I will do, however, is seal the windows against evil, but even if it comes through the door nothing will awaken Anoush, or be able to touch her. Not even you, Lara. Not until this is settled, and this new evil, whatever it may be, is found out and defeated.

I bow to your wisdom, my lord, Lara answered him.

He chuckled, and gave her a wry grin. *We should go, and decide what our next move is to be.*

A moment, she said. Lara looked down at her oldest daughter. Anoush looked so peaceful as she slept. How long would she have to remain like this? *My beautiful, gentle child,* Lara thought sadly. *I am ready,* she told Kaliq.

The prince threw his cloak over her, his arm about her shoulders, and a moment later they were back in his garden in Shunnar.

Lara felt the heat of the late-morning sun warming her shoulders, and it felt good after the chill of Anoush's bedchamber. "Today," she said, "I shall go to Camdene to speak with Liam and Noss. I shall be told of Anoush's condition, and proclaim no knowledge of what has happened to her. But I will reassure them that she appears fine otherwise. Cam shall be told of Anoush's condition. I shall ask him if he has had anything to do with her condition. Of course he will deny it."

"He will believe his jealous lover, the Darkling, is involved," Kaliq remarked. "And she will deny it, of course."

"I will see he does not believe her, for I will assure him Anoush's condition is certainly magic." Lara chuckled. "It may very well spoil whatever alliance the Darkling has with Cam."

"Nay," Kaliq said. "It will sour it, but Cam is an ambitious man or he would not be treating with the Darkling at all. He will continue on with their plans. Anoush, I believe, was somehow involved with those plans, but the enchantment about her will not deter the Darkling or Cam. We need to know exactly what mischief they are up to, Lara."

"Have any of the princes been able to get closer to her?" she asked him.

"Nay. Her powers of instinct seem to have grown stronger. It is as if she is tapping into some source of power. Another mystery about Ciarda we must unravel," Kaliq told his companion.

Lara sat down upon the marble bench by the pool. "I love it here," she said, watching the fat goldfish darting among the pale yellow water lilies and lavender water hyacinths. "Don't ever forbid me from this place, Kaliq."

"Never!" he exclaimed, sitting next to her. His fingers tipped her face up to his, and he kissed her slowly, deeply. Her lips were like rose petals beneath his mouth. Her sigh of delight at the kiss gave him simple pleasure. Wherever their paths in life would take them, he realized, they would always belong together.

"I must go," Lara said, reluctantly breaking off their embrace.

"To Camdene?" he asked.

"Nay, back to my castle to get a little bit of sleep before I must be on my way again. Thank goodness Gare and Sinon are with Taj now. He does not resent my absences so much. This past year has been a hard one for him. A few months ago he had two parents and three sisters living with him. Then suddenly he was alone except when I was there. He is much like Magnus, and did not like it at all. Now with his two friends by his side he is content. His whole world is Terah, Kaliq. He understands little beyond it, but in time he will. For now, however, he is still a boy. I am grateful Terah is a simple land with few problems, unlike the complexities of Hetar."

"Go, then," Kaliq told her as they stood up.

With a quick smile at him she was gone in a puff of green mist.

The night was half-gone as she appeared in her own bedchamber. Lara did not bother to undress. She lay down upon her bed and fell asleep. Mila found her there when she came to awaken her mistress as she did each morning. The serving woman never knew if she would find Lara in her bed or not these days. But seeing her this morning, she went to give orders to the bath mistress to be ready. Mila saw that Lara had fallen asleep in her gown, and knew she would bathe upon waking.

The young Dominus came to his mother's apartments. "Is she back?" he asked.

"Aye, my lord," Mila said, "but still sleeping."

Lara heard her son's voice, and called sleepily, "Taj, come and see me."

He entered his mother's bedchamber, and at her invitation sat on the edge of the bed. "Good morning," he greeted her. "I see you returned late." And he grinned mischievously. "Where were you?"

"Hiding in Shunnar," she told him. "But you must not tell anyone that, Taj."

"I will keep your secret, Mother. I suppose you do not wish to face the problem of my oldest sister and her suitor," he remarked.

"I do not," Lara admitted. "But today I must. I cannot run away forever."

"What have you decided?" Taj wanted to know.

"I haven't. Yet," she said to him. Taj would not know what she and Kaliq had done. It was better that way. Her son, like his father, was not a good liar. "I suppose I will say I want them to know each other a little better before I give my permission."

"Clever," he noted. "You do not say yes, but neither do you forbid them. There is so much I can learn from you, Mother. I wish you were here more."

For his own safety she had to say something. "Taj," Lara began, "it has come to the attention of the Shadow Princes that some evil has again begun to rear its head. When this happens the magical beings of the light must band together to stop the darkness, and sooner rather than later. That is why I have been away of late. But this is another something you must keep to yourself. Discretion is an important part of ruling, my son."

"If there is danger should not you be here protecting Terah?" he asked candidly.

Lara sighed. "There is no danger to Terah right now, and if we can stop this thing before too much longer there will be no danger. Rest assured that if I am needed to watch over Terah that I will be here, Andraste in my hand. You must learn to trust me as your father learned to trust me, Taj."

"Do you love Prince Kaliq?" Taj surprised her by asking.

Lara answered honestly. "I do. I have always loved Kaliq."

"But you loved my father," Taj replied, puzzled.

"I did, Taj. I do. And before Magnus Hauk I loved Vartan of the Fiacre. The heart, my son, knows no boundaries. I may love another mortal man in my day, and his time to die will come eventually. But like me Kaliq is magic. He will never leave me. The mortals I have loved do leave me. They have no choice in the matter. And the most difficult part of being who I am is that while you and your siblings will age, grow old and die, I will remain as I am for many centuries. I will die perhaps a bit earlier than most of my faerie kin for I do have that drop of mortal blood in my veins. However, it is likely that I will see my grandchildren, my great-grandchild and so on into the next several generations, my son. I shall not leave you, Taj. It is you who will leave me one day. So do not be jealous of Kaliq, or of the time I am gone from you." She leaned over and kissed his cheek. "One day when you are a man grown you will fall in love. You may fall in and out of love a dozen times before the girl you will wed comes into your life. You will understand a little better then," Lara assured him with a smile.

"You always explain things so that I can understand them," Taj said. "Well, if you must go today then you must go."

"Not right away. Tell me if you are enjoying having Gare and Sinon with you?"

"Aye, Mother, I am! Thank you for bringing them with us. Like me they enjoy their studies. They are not like Zagiri, who was always looking to escape our schoolroom, or Marzina, who wanted knowledge of naught but magic. We are studying the history of the Middle Centuries of Terah, but our tutor has asked Gare and Sinon to tell him of those same years in the Outlands. We are learning so much about each other!"

"That is very good," Lara praised her son. "The more you know of other times, other peoples, other cultures, the better for Terah. I am pleased Master Vadin is so open-minded. Master Bashkar chose him carefully when he needed help."

"Master Bashkar is very old now, Mother. He sleeps in our classroom while Master Vadin teaches," Taj told her.

"Master Bashkar has earned his rest," Lara said.

"Perhaps we shall let him go home to Shunnar. He always loved the heat of the desert. Now, my darling, run along. I must bathe and dress, and magick myself to Camdene before their evening begins."

Taj jumped up from his place on her bed. Giving her a kiss upon her cheek, he dashed off. He had taken her little lecture on life span rather well, Lara thought. He had certainly surprised her by asking if she loved Kaliq. And she had surprised herself with her answer. She did love the Shadow Prince, and she had since girlhood. But he had been so insistent that it was naught but a fancy. Of course now she knew he had said it so that she would move on to experience life, to learn from it, to become what she must to meet her destiny. But wasn't all of her life her destiny? The men she had loved. The problems she had faced and solved. Her children. And the unknown. It was all her destiny. And now once again she was being called upon to thwart the darkness.

With a small sigh of resignation, Lara transported herself into the hall of Liam, Lord of the Fiacre clan families. Beyond the open door she could see the leafless limbs of the trees black against the red-orange sky. The servants were quietly going about their evening duties, laying the tables, bringing in pitchers of Frine and beer. Noss was seated at her loom showing her daughter, Mildri, how to do a particular stitch.

Seeing Lara's arrival, she jumped up and ran to her. "Oh, Lara, thank the Celestial Actuary that you are here. I wanted to call you earlier, but Liam would not let me."

Lara immediately took her friend's hands in hers. "What has happened, Noss? What has distressed you so greatly?"

"It's Anoush!" Noss said, and she began to sob.

"*Anoush?* Noss! What has happened to my daughter? You must tell me!" She squeezed the two hands in hers hard, and felt guilt for deceiving Noss, but the truth was Anoush was safer as long as no one knew the truth.

"She cannot be awakened. This morning Gadara went to wake her, but she could not. And, odder still, she was unable to touch Anoush. It was as if there were some invisible barrier surrounding her. What can be the matter? What can have happened?"

"I must go to my child!" Lara said. "Who can have done this to her?" She hurried from Liam's hall and through the village of Camdene until she reached her daughter's fine stone house. Gadara saw her coming and opened the door, following Lara upstairs into Anoush's bedchamber where Lara stood at the girl's bedside looking down on her daughter. Anoush lay quietly, not moving at all.

Lara looked to Gadara. "Tell me how this has happened."

"Domina, I do not know," Gadara wept. "I came, bringing her her cup of dandelion tea. She likes to sip a cup each morning before arising. I saw her sleeping, which is unusual, for my mistress generally awakens with the dawn. Reaching out, I tried to shake her, but I was prevented from touching her."

Lara reached out to put a hand on Anoush, but Kaliq's invisible barrier blocked her. She sprang back as if she had touched something hot. "This is not my magic," she said as if speaking to herself, "but it is powerful magic." She turned to the servant. "Gadara, you will remain with your mistress. I must find a way to awaken her. I will be in Liam's hall if there is any change in my daughter's condition."

"Yes, Domina," Gadara whispered.

"Let no one but Noss in to see her," Lara instructed further.

"Yes, Domina."

Lara hurried back to the hall where Liam had now joined Noss. "My daughter has been touched by magic," Lara told them. "The barrier that surrounds her is not my magic. Has Cam been here of late?" she asked them.

"Nay, he has not," Noss said. Then her voice dropped to a whisper. "Do you think he had something to do with Anoush's condition, Lara?"

"The lad has no magic in him," Liam said. "And he hasn't been here in several days, Lara. You must look elsewhere for the guilty party."

"I had come to speak with my daughter and her suitor," Lara told them. "I know that they have wanted me to come, but I was at Shunnar with Kaliq."

"They were going to ask your permisison to wed," Liam said. "Would you have given it to them, Lara?"

"Liam!" Noss shook her head admonishingly.

"Not yet," Lara said candidly. "I would have wanted

them to become even better acquainted before I gave my permission. Besides, I always envisioned an autumn wedding for Anoush. Has anyone sent for Cam to come?"

"We didn't want to do anything until we had spoken with you, Lara," Noss told her best friend. "Besides, we were not certain that Anoush wouldn't wake up."

"The spell woven about my child is an unbreakable one," Lara told them. "She will not awaken until whoever put it there unlocks it. You must send for Cam to come and see what has befallen Anoush. Send a faerie post to him at Rivalen on the morrow. I mean to return home now, and speak with my mother. I will return in two days' time, Liam. See that Cam is here so I may speak with him then."

"Yes, Domina," the leader of the Fiacre replied to her.

And without another word to them Lara was gone from them in a puff of green smoke.

CHAPTER TWELVE

LARA RETURNED AS she had promised two days later. Arriving in Liam's hall, she looked about to find Cam staring in surprise at her entrance. Lara restrained a smile. She had caught him off guard, and that was a good thing.

Noss hurried forward. "There is no change," she told Lara. "She sleeps. She does not appear to be in any kind of pain or distress."

"There is a blessing there," Lara answered her. Then she turned to Cam. "Do you have anything to do with my daughter's condition, Nephew? Do not even consider lying to me for I shall find you out."

"I have no magic about me," he said. "How could I be responsible?"

He lies, Lara thought to herself, surprised. *He has been given some sort of magic. It is not great, but it is there. The Darkling, of course.* "Forgive me if I misjudge you, Cam, but whatever barrier contains Anoush it is not my magic. I came two days ago to speak with you and my daughter only to find her in this unwakeable sleep," Lara said. "I do not even know why this was done to her. *Do you?*" There! Let her put a hint into his head that his Darkling lover might have done this out of jealousy. Lara almost laughed aloud at the sudden look upon his handsome face that was as quickly gone as it had come.

"Did you mean to give us your permission to wed, my lady aunt?" he asked her.

"Nay, not yet. I wanted you to know each other better before I made that decision, Cam, but your concern for Anoush's well-being warms my heart." She gave him a smile.

"Can you not awaken her?" Cam asked. "It is said of you that your magic is great, and grows stronger every year."

"If I knew the type of spell that was used I might be able to unravel it and reverse it," Lara said. "But I have yet to decipher it. Some spells like this one are quite unique, and meant only for the person who has been enchanted. You are a handsome young man now, Cam. Is there some lass you have disappointed who might have been jealous of Anoush, and sought out someone to magick her? Think carefully, I beg you."

A thoughtful look touched Cam's face, but then he shook his head. "I can think of no one who might have misunderstood my attentions toward her. Ask the lady Sholeh if you would confirm my words. Besides, I spend more time with the cattle than I do in society, Aunt."

"Then all I can do is try to discover what sort of spell this is so I may lift it from my daughter," Lara said.

"When she is herself once more we will speak on what you would both desire."

He bowed to her politely. "I can only await your success, but be assured that I love Anoush with all my heart, and she loves me."

"It pleases me to hear your words, Cam, and I am touched by your sentiments regarding yourself, but as for Anoush I must hear her declare her love for you from her own lips," Lara told him. Dismissing him with a small smile, she turned again to Noss. "Continue to watch over my child, and send to me if there is any change." Then Lara was gone from Liam's hall in a burst of her pale green smoke.

"I must return to Rivalen," Cam said to Noss and Liam. "There is no reason for me to remain here. If Anoush wakes up will you let me know?"

"Of course, lad," Liam said sympathetically.

Noss nodded. She had not liked Cam as a child, and she didn't like him now, but she had concealed her dislike from all but Lara.

Cam hurried from the hall, going to the stables to fetch his mount. He would ride far enough from the village not to be seen, and then he would transport himself to Ciarda's dwelling. Lara did not know about Ciarda, of course, and so her remarks had been but innocent ones. But it had set Cam to considering if his Darkling lover had put an enchantment upon Anoush so he might not wed her. Ciarda was inclined to jealousy.

He rode from Liam's stable and out into the cold late

morning. He could smell snow in the air as his horse plodded along. Finally, when he saw by the landscape about him that he was halfway between Camdene and Rivalen, he drew his horse to a halt. He tied the animal to a tree, and said aloud, "Take me to Ciarda." And instantly he was there within her bedchamber.

Ciarda was with her Wolfyn lover. She was kneeling as he pumped himself within her. Cam watched them dispassionately until the Wolfyn howled with his attainment, but he could see Ciarda was not satisfied. He almost laughed as she rounded on her lover, beating him on his long snout with her fists.

"Pig! Do you dare to take your pleasures before giving them to me? Get out! And never return!" Her eyes lit on Cam. "This mortal knows well how to pleasure me, don't you, Cam? Come, and show this fool of a selfish Wolfyn how easily I can be pleasured if one but tries. You will remain and watch us."

Without a word Cam loosened his manhood from his breeches. A few quick strokes of his hand, and he was ready. Ciarda knelt upon the bed, her bottom toward him. Cam grasped her hips, and drove himself hard and deep. At once Ciarda moaned.

"You see, Wolfyn," Cam explained, "she requires a great deal of slow preparation to ready her. Then a quick thrust to impale her firmly so she feels all of your length and thickness." Reaching beneath the Darkling, he used one hand to squeeze her full breast, pinching the nipple hard before he released it. "Her breasts are particularly sensitive. Come, and slide your head beneath her so you may suckle and fondle her. She will like that, won't you, Ciarda?"

"Yes!" Ciarda said breathlessly as the young Wolfyn did as Cam bid him, his mouth closing over the sensitive tip of her breast. "Oh, yes!"

"She is a greedy bitch where pleasures are concerned," Cam continued on in a pleasant tone. "Since you have disappointed and angered her you must work twice as hard now to pleasure her. Suck her! And while you do I will begin to stoke her lust." He began to move himself in and out of Ciarda, slowly at first, then with increasing vigor and speed. He could sense her grasping for completion, but he deliberately kept her just short of it, explaining as he did so that it would drive her wilder, and give her far greater pleasures to be denied for a time, and then finally satisfied.

The young Wolfyn crawled from beneath Ciarda's breasts, which he had sucked until they were swollen and sore. Now he forced his manhood between her lips, growling at her to suck him until he bid her cease. The Darkling attained great pleasures as Cam's juices burst into her as her sheath spasmed and tightened about his manhood even as the Wolfyn's juices spurted down her throat, and he howled again with delight before collapsing onto the bed.

Cam withdrew his now-satisfied manhood from Ciarda's hot dripping sheath, rearranging his garments into a semblance of order. He smacked the Darkling's plump bottom a stinging blow. Then, grasping her by her ebony hair, he yanked her head up, looking down into her face. "Did you dare to lay an enchantment upon Anoush, you bitch?" he snarled at her.

Ciarda scrambled to her feet. She was naked, and very beautiful. "Get out!" she said to the Wolfyn, and, scrambling to his feet, he fled her. "What are you talking about?" she demanded of Cam as she picked up a scarlet silk robe and wrapped it about her. "What has happened to your precious mortal lover? Nothing serious, I hope."

"She lies in a deep sleep unable to awaken," Cam said.

"Her mother has done this, you fool," Ciarda said, tossing her black hair at him.

"Nay! There is even an invisible shield about her. Lara says it is not her doing."

"And you believe her? She has done this to prevent you from wedding her child," Ciarda said. "She has not given you her permission, has she? But the girl is in love with you. She will defy her mother and wed you. The faerie woman knows this, and so she has woven an enchantment about the girl."

"Nay, if Lara says she is not responsible then she is not," he defended her. "She is not known to lie. And I believe she will allow me to wed Anoush if Anoush wants it. And she does, Ciarda! You are jealous, Darkling! Remove the enchantment you have put upon Anoush, or you shall never know pleasures with me again."

"How prideful you are, mortal." The Darkling sneered. "There are other lovers I can take to my bed. You are not the only manhood available to me to ride."

"I saw what you rode but minutes ago, and he did not satisfy you, Ciarda. Only I can do that, and you know it."

"I swear to you that I have not laid any enchantment upon your beloved," the Darkling said. "You will tire of the girl sooner than later, Cam. As you are the only one to satisfy my lusts, I know that I am the only one who can satisfy your lust. You have not taken pleasures with Anoush, have you?"

"She was not ready," Cam said.

The Darkling laughed scornfully. "You were afraid to touch her lest she flee you," she said. "Does she not like pleasures?"

"She is shy, but once she is mine I will cure her of that affliction," Cam boasted. Then he said, "If you did not place that spell upon Anoush, and Lara did not, then we must at least find someone who can remove it."

"Only whoever placed the spell can remove it," Ciarda told him. "You must forget the girl at least temporarily. Soon you will make your first appearance as the Hierarch, Cam. You can think of nothing else."

"Is she safe?" Cam asked Ciarda.

"Who? Oh, you mean your little mortal girl. If she has not been harmed other than being put into a slumber then aye, she is safe. If someone had meant her harm she would have suffered. She does not. She only sleeps. I still think it is her mother's doing, but if not then someone close to her."

"I tell you her mother is too distraught to have done it," Cam said.

"If that is indeed so then the faerie woman has another enemy," the Darkling said, and she smiled. "I wonder who it is, but then it has naught to do with us. Leave me now, Cam. I will call you in a few days, and begin your tutelage for your appearance in Hetar as the Hierarch. I vow, mortal, you have quite exhausted me with your vigorous lust."

Using the small magic she had given him, Cam took himself back to where his horse stood waiting. It had begun to snow. The first snows of the Icy Season. He hurried the beast along, eager for the warmth of Sholeh's hall and a cup of hot mulled cider. The horse beneath him was as anxious for his stable. Anoush's state still disturbed Cam. Someone was lying, but he trusted neither Lara nor the Darkling enough to be able to discern which of them it was. Both had a reason to keep Anoush from him.

Finally the roofs of his village began to be distinguished amidst the falling snows. The day was ending in a blue-gray light. Reaching the headwoman's hall, he stabled his horse, instructing the stable boy to see to its comfort. Then he hurried into the hall where the evening meal was just being served. Sholeh waved him to her High Board, pointing to a place to her left.

"Tell me what has happened," she said. "Has Lara

given you her permission to marry with her daughter?" Sholeh pushed a cup of cider into Cam's hand, nodding to the servant with the tureen to fill Cam's trencher with hot stew.

Cam drank deep of the mulled cider. Then he told Sholeh what had happened.

The headwoman listened quietly. When he had concluded his tale she said, "I am sorry, Cam. It is obvious some enemy of Lara's has attempted to strike at her through her beloved daughter. She will learn their identity, and Anoush will then be restored to you."

"She did not say she would give us her permission to wed," Cam said.

"But she did not refuse you, either," Sholeh noted with a small smile. "Lara is a careful woman, and this is Vartan's daughter you ask for, my lad. When Anoush awakens her mother will ask her what she wants. And if it is you, Cam, then knowing Lara as I do she will, no matter her own reluctance, allow you to marry her child."

Sholeh was right, of course, Cam thought as he lay in his bed afterward. Lara did not like him. He could sense it even as he sensed her busybody friend, Noss, Liam's wife, did not like him. But Anoush loved him, and that was all that mattered. But what if she didn't awaken by the time he must reveal himself as the Hierarch? She was an integral part of the plan to get Hetar to accept him. If the Lord High Ruler Jonah had Lara's daughter Zagiri for his wife, then the Hierarch must have another

of Lara's daughters. Jonah must have no advantage over
the Hierarch. And with her two older daughters wed to
the husbands they would have, the faerie woman could
not, would not, interfere. She would never show partial-
ity. Anoush must awaken!

HETAR WAS SUFFERING through one of the worst winters
in its history. The Forest and the Midlands were blan-
keted in snow. In The City the snows seemed to fall
more heavily. The streets were blocked, a narrow passage being opened down the center of the main avenues.
The ground floors of many houses were blocked by the
white. The Pleasure Houses, however, were available to
the wealthiest of their clients, who somehow managed
to reach them. Their lights glittered through the nights
as the sound of music and laughter echoed through the
unusual quiet of The City. And many of the Razi kiosks
remained open, the narcotic drink being the escape of
the poor from their cold, their hunger and the dead bodies lying frozen in the streets. The more humane among
the magnates tried to feed the poor with what was left in
their warehouses. The less humane among them called
the charitable fools, and said that with fewer mouths to
feed what was left would go further.

The Lord High Ruler of Hetar was becoming more
and more concerned by the situation. Especially when
his young wife was accosted by beggars on her way
to visit her relations in the Garden District, and saw
the truth of the situation. Zagiri had known only love

and comfort in her life. To have skinny fingers clawing at her fur-lined cloak while rasping, whining voices begged her for a coin or two had been a revelation to her. She had emptied her purse as her litter bearers struggled to get her into the safety of the district populated by the Crusader Knights.

"The poor are always among us," Jonah told her when Zagiri had related her adventures to him. "I'll hire a troop of mercenaries next time you wish to visit your uncles and grandmother," he said.

"Poverty like this is not known in Terah," Zagiri said. "Hetar is wealthy. There should be no poverty here at all. And Susanna is not my grandmother. She was my mother's stepmother, and disowned Mother after she went to Terah. As for my uncles, other than Mikhail, I find them too rough-natured. It is not likely I will visit them again."

"But if you do leave the Golden District it will be in the company of armed men, my golden girl," Jonah told her. "I will allow nothing to happen to you."

"I want to go home to visit my mother," Zagiri said.

"Such a journey would prove far too difficult," Jonah told her.

"Why can I not return as I came?" Zagiri asked him bluntly.

"You were brought to me by means of magic," Jonah said. "It was not my magic, but that of my late wife's. You would have to travel overland to the Coastal Kings, and then take passage upon one of their vessels, which would meet a Terahn ship in the middle of the Sea of Sagitta. It is a dangerous journey, Zagiri."

"If I went to one of the Shadow Princes who is currently on the council he would take me to Terah," Zagiri said to her husband. "There would be no danger."

"I do not want you leaving me right now," Jonah told her. "I have given you everything for which you asked me, my golden girl. Now I ask that you remain by my side for the interim." He tipped her face up to his. "I need you, Zagiri. I do not believe I could go on without you right now." Then he kissed her lips lightly.

Zagiri sighed. "Very well," she said. "But come the spring I want to visit Terah."

"We shall see," Jonah answered her. He put an arm about her. "It is a cold night, and I am in the mood to take pleasures with you. Let us call your two sex slaves to our bedchamber, and we shall play together. I very much enjoy watching Doran and Casnar as the three of you give and take pleasures." He kissed her cheek. "Your appetite for passion is unequaled, my beautiful golden girl. It is quite astonishing." His hand began to fondle her breasts. "I want all three of your orifices filled tonight over and over again."

Zagiri turned and, slipping her arms about his neck, ran her tongue over his lips. "And when you fill me with your fine cock, my lord, we shall move together in perfect rhythm and the pleasures will roll over us until we are weak and replete."

Her sensual and suggestive words excited him. He

could feel his male member hardening beneath his robe. "Yes!" his voice grated in her ear. *"Yes!"*

Zagiri laughed. "Oh, Jonah, I am so glad to be your wife. I could want no better husband for you know well how to please me." She kissed him until they were both dizzy with their rising excitement. And Zagiri forgot entirely that she had wanted to go home to Terah to see Lara. Instead she walked with her husband to their apartments, and sent for the two sex slaves. From midnight until the early hours of the dawn the three men and Zagiri amused each other until even the *First Lady of Hetar* admitted to exhaustion, and dismissed her slaves so that she and her husband might sleep.

The Icy Season began to wane. The snows melted, the rains came, and with them flooding that filled the streets with dirty water as the sewers overflowed. There was much sickness now, and the council ordered carts to traverse the streets on a regular basis, taking up the dead, who were buried in mass graves outside of The City's walls. The fields in the Midlands were flooded, and crops could not be planted. In the Outlands there was drought, and great whirlwinds that turned the plains into dust. The vineyards of the magnates were desperate for water, and when none was forthcoming the vines shriveled and died.

In The City there were food riots as the populace demanded the warehouses be opened to feed them. The magnates resisted, for there was no profit in giving grain away. Dogs, cats and rats disappeared from the streets

as they were used for food. The markets were empty
for the most part. There was nothing to sell, and the
luxury goods from the Coastal Kings began to fill up
the warehouses, jockeying for space with the bags of
rice and grain that were being hoarded by the magnates.
By late spring the rains had finally stopped, but so had
all trade. There was no work to be had, no food to be
sold in the markets, no coin to buy food had there been
any. Several smaller warehouses were broken into and
robbed. Grain or rice could be had for exorbitant prices
if one could find those who were selling.

The City was suddenly quiet during the day for there
was no commerce to be done. It was deathly quiet once
the sun set for no one dared to venture forth from whatever shelter was theirs. Finally the High Council was
called into session in order to discuss the many difficulties facing Hetar. Jonah had resisted this meeting but
Lionel, his body servant who was his confidant, had told
him bluntly there was no escaping Hetar's problems.

"They will not improve on their own, my lord," Lionel had said several months ago.

And they had not. The newly elected Master of the
Merchants, Jonah's late wife Vilia's uncle, Cuthbert
Ahasferus, had told the Lord High Ruler quite frankly
that if he did not call a meeting of the High Council and
correct the situation he would be overthrown, and in all
likelihood executed for someone had to be held responsible for what had happened to Hetar.

"Now that my dear niece is no longer with us," Cuthbert Ahasferus said pointedly, "I find it difficult to defend you, Jonah. After all, *we* have no blood tie."

"You have a blood tie with my son," Jonah replied in a hard voice.

"And of course Egon could be protected from your mistakes," the Master of the Merchants said in a cool tone.

"Remember who my mother-in-law is, Ahasferus," Jonah snarled.

"The faerie woman's only interest in Hetar is her daughter, whom you stole to wed when my poor niece died," Cuthbert Ahasferus snapped at the Lord High Ruler.

"It was Vilia who chose her!" Jonah almost shouted.

"So you say," Cuthbert Ahasferus replied. "But this is of no matter, Jonah. You must call a meeting of the High Council. We cannot avoid this disaster any longer."

"It would have been less of a disaster if your merchants had opened their warehouses and distributed some of their grain," Jonah responded.

"Forgo a profit?" Cuthbert Ahasferus looked appalled at the thought.

"You cannot make a profit if no one can buy the grain because there is no coin to buy it because there is no employment to earn the coin," Jonah pointed out. "But, aye, you are right. We need a council meeting. I will call one."

"You had better, and quickly," the Master of the Merchants told him.

Jonah was not surprised on the day of the meeting to find that the council chamber was filled to capacity. Larger than it had been in past years when the High Council was made up of two representatives from each of Hetar's provinces, it now contained as well representatives from the Crusader Knights, the Mercenaries, the Merchants Guild, the Guild of Pleasure Women, the Guild of Pleasure Mistresses and two elected members from The City's General Population. The women of Hetar had lobbied hard to gain a larger council where they might be better represented, but with the death of the Lady Vilia, who had been their most influential member, they had lost a strong voice. The Lord High Ruler's new wife had been importuned to join with those working for women's rights in Hetar, but she had declined for she was very young, and seemed only to be interested in pleasures and the acquisition of pretty things.

"I cannot believe she is the Domina Lara's daughter," Maeve Scarlet, a famed Pleasure Mistress, said disapprovingly. "I thought the women of Terah modest in their desires and their needs. This girl is more Hetarian than any born here."

"And it is said that Lady Farah is quite jealous of her for our *First Lady of Hetar* has far greater influence over the Lord High Ruler than does his mother," Lady Gillian, retired head of the Guild of Pleasure Mistresses, said.

"Of course," Maeve Scarlet said. "She is her mother's

daughter there, and knows well how to give pleasures to her husband."

"I have heard she keeps two sex slaves, and performs with them for her husband's amusement," Lady Gillian said. "Then he joins them and they all take pleasures together quite enthusiastically, I am told."

"What a Pleasure Woman the girl would have made," Maeve Scarlet replied admiringly. "Can you imagine the fortune you could gain from a girl like that?" She sighed. "What a waste! No wonder Jonah doesn't want to face up to our troubles."

Lady Gillian and Maeve Scarlet represented the Guild of Pleasure Mistresses, to the annoyance of the Guild's Headmistress, the Lord High Ruler's mother, Lady Farah. But she managed to attend the council meeting with her daughter-in-law, seated in a gallery above the council chamber. Zagiri had brought her servant, Alka, who she knew would answer her questions directly, unlike her mother-in-law.

"Do you know who the other council members are?" Zagiri asked Alka.

"Around the main table are the representatives from the original provinces," Alka explained. "The Shadow Princes are represented by Prince Lothair and Prince Coilin. The one called Lothair has been here before, but Coilin is new to the council. From the Midlands is Squire Darah, and his son-in-law, Rupert. The two Coastal kings are Pelias and Delphinus, who are familiar faces on the council. The Forest Lords, those two rough-looking men, are Enda, who is known as the Head Forester, and his companion, Adal."

"And the others who sit in the second circle?" Zagiri asked. "I recognize my mother's half brother Mikhail son of Swiftsword. Does he represent the Crusader Knights?"

"Nay, he is one of the elected representatives of the General Population from The Quarter," Alka said. "Master Mikhail is much respected, and even loved by the people. The other is a woman, Clothilde, who has a large stall in the main market selling perfumes and soaps. She can be very influential, and her vote is sought by all sides for she is honest and fair. The other women on the council come from the Pleasure Guild, and the Pleasure Mistresses. Cuthbert Ahasferus, who was kin to the Lady Vilia, stands for the Merchants Guild. The other is Aubin Prospero, who was Lady Vilia's son by the late Emperor Gaius Prospero. The Crusader Knights' two members of the council are Sir Philip Bowman and Sir Anatol Boldspear. The Mercenaries have elected Peter Swiftfoot and Burley Goodman to serve them."

Zagiri nodded. "What are they meeting for today?" she asked.

"They must decide how to help Hetar recover from the problems besetting it," Alka said.

"You mean the disturbances I met with last Icy Season have not been solved yet?" Zagiri asked, sounding surprised. "My lord Jonah said he would take care of it, and I should not be concerned."

Alka hesitated, then she said in a voice so low Zagiri could only just hear her, "My lady, the troubles besetting Hetar are very great, and no one has, until today, sought to seek a solution for them. Please do not say I said such a thing, but it is true. There is terrible illness everywhere, starvation and general misery. You will hear it all, for no one will remain silent this day."

Zagiri nodded, and fixed her eyes below upon the double-ringed council table. She was disturbed by what Alka had told her, for her heart was not a hard one. Jonah had said nothing of this. She had let herself be swept up in his love for her, and had thought of nothing else except for how happy she was. Happier than she had ever been in all her life, which seemed odd as her childhood in Terah had been a happy one until last year. Everything had changed when her father had died. *Everything!* The pounding of a golden gavel caught her attention as the council meeting began.

The Lord High Ruler of Hetar looked out over the council chamber from his throne. "This gathering will come to order. We are met here today to discuss the difficulties now facing our glorious Hetar," Jonah pronounced.

"Glorious no more!" shouted Adal of the Forest Lords. "Do you know what we have been reduced to in our Forests? At least those you have left to us. We ground acorns in order to bake bread this winter past.

Had it not been for the game we would have all starved! And there is much sickness among our folk. Tell me, my Lord High Ruler, what are you going to do about it? Why are the Taubyl traders not traveling the land with their goods, or bringing us the items we cannot make or grow ourselves?"

"And why will the magnates not open their warehouses to the people of The City?" demanded Peter Swiftfoot of the Mercenaries. "There is virtually no work for us. Our guild cannot repair the hovels because we have run out of coin. There is sickness in The Quarter, too, while you take pleasures in your palace, Lord Jonah, with your new wife."

"Be silent, all of you!" Jonah roared. He did not as a rule speak loudly, but he needed their attention. Surprised, they looked to him. "Hetar has suffered hard times before, my lords, good masters and ladies. It is the Celestial Actuary who is responsible for too much rain or not enough of it, and decides if our harvest will be good or bad no matter the work we do. Our fates are in the hands of the Celestial Actuary."

"Who is obviously quite angry at us," Squire Darah said.

"Aye!" came a chorus of assent at his words.

He heard the words coming from his mouth even as he knew he should not ask them. "And why," Jonah said, "do you believe the Celestial Actuary is angry with us?"

They all began shouting at once until the Lord High

Ruler signaled his guard to beat the council members
into silence. Then he pointed an elegant finger.

"King Pelias, what say you?" Jonah asked the Coastal
King.

"I believe we have disappointed the Celestial Actuary by moving away from our old traditions," came the
answer. "Recently in our Coastal Kingdom we were visited by a beautiful young man who chided us gently for
turning from the old ways of Hetar. He said if we would
turn back to them Hetar would prosper once again."

"A simpleton's answer to complex problems," Cuthbert Ahasferus snapped.

"Perhaps," King Pelias replied, "but for months there
have been few fish to be caught in the Sagitta or for sale
in the markplaces. Like the rest of Hetar our people
have been starving. This young man took us down to
the seashore. He bid our fishermen step out waist-deep
into the water, and cast their nets. They did, and their
nets were so full of fish it took half a dozen men on each
net to haul the nets in, my lords. Then the young man
told us that if we would accept our old traditions back
our prosperity would return."

"A coincidence," sneered the Master of the Merchants.

"Nay, 'tis not! We have begun restoring the lands
that Gaius Prospero and his cronies took from us. We
are building our living vessels once again to trade with
Terah. This spring while The City and the Midlands
were flooded with rains we had just enough rain to

grow our grain, and the garden crops our people favor for themselves. The Coastal Kingdom is blooming and returning to its old self, for we have accepted the words this young man brought to us."

"Who is he?" Aubin Prospero asked, thinking as he did that he had inherited quite a bit of property in the Coastal Kingdom. He now supposed it lost.

"I believe he is the Hierarch come to us as was foretold," King Pelias said.

"Where is he now?" Jonah wanted to know.

"We do not know. He left us with his blessing, and we have not seen him since," came the answer.

"It sounds like the same young man who came to the Midlands," Squire Darah said slowly. "He is tall with curly black hair, and eyes as blue as the sky above our fields. He brought an end to the rains for us. He dried our fields with a wave of his hand, making them perfect for plowing. He opened the doors of our empty granaries, and with another wave of his hand bags of good planting seed appeared. He blessed it, and the green shoots already can be seen row upon row in our fields. Our orchards have flowered like trees at their peak. It is a miracle. Our people have hope again."

"And did he suggest you return to the old ways?" Jonah asked.

"Aye, he did! And we have! We will not stray from them again," Squire Darah said firmly.

"And do you think this young man is the Hierarch?" Prince Lothair asked.

"We do! Has he not visited your Desert Kingdom, Prince?" Squire Darah inquired. "You will be so blessed if he does!"

"We have never given up our *old* ways," the prince answered.

"Why has the Hierarch not come to The City?" Mistress Clothilde wondered.

"The City has become a cesspit!" the Head Forester Enda said.

"Has this young man come into your province yet?" Jonah asked.

"Nay, but if he does we will welcome him!" Enda said.

"How can you go back to the old ways when you no longer can claim to have any pure bloods among the Forest families?" Master Rupert said in an almost pitying tone.

"The Hierarch will guide us," Enda replied. "He will tell us what to do, and we will do it! I pray he comes to us soon."

"This is all quite interesting," Master Mikhail said quietly, "but none of it addresses our problem, or a solution to our problems. Is not that what we have come here today to do, my lords, good masters and ladies?"

"Swiftsword's son is correct," Maeve Scarlet spoke out. "The Hierarch is a legend, but if he isn't we cannot wait for him to come to The City and perform his miracles. The City is the heart of Hetar, and if we cannot bring it back to its former prosperity and greatness then Hetar will fall as a kingdom."

A murmur of assent broke out among the council.

"Then the magnates will have to open their warehouses to the people, and forgo their profit," Jonah said. "What else is there for us to do?"

"Can the council at least promise to see that we are reimbursed for our goods eventually?" Aubin Prospero asked them.

"It is the greed of the magnates that has caused much of this in the first place," Sir Philip Bowman said angrily. "They have put profit before the people."

"That profit has kept you and your Knights comfortable for many years," Cuthbert Ahasferus snapped.

"We have protected the kingdom," Sir Philip said. "We were entitled to whatever we got, and none of us has a great deal of coin."

"But you live quite well in your Garden District while we Mercenaries must be satisfied to live in our small hovels in The Quarter," Burley Goodman said loudly.

"My lords, good masters and ladies," Mikhail, son of Swiftsword, said. "We are straying once again from the problem. I am certain that the council can offer the magnates and the Merchants Guild something in return for their generosity, but the people must be fed or the populace will die. Many good people have been lost already."

"Form a committee," Aubin Prospero said. "The committee can decide what is fair and just. When they do we will vote upon it, and if their recommendation passes then we will open the granaries."

"We must open them before then," Mikhail said quietly. "You know as well as I do that a committee will go on and on for weeks until all parties are satisfied. We cannot let our folk starve while we talk. If we can at least agree that the magnates and the Merchants Guild will be paid then we must feed the people today and every day after."

"My uncle is very wise, isn't he?" Zagiri said softly, and Alka nodded.

"But what if we do not like what the committee decides, and the council approves?" Cuthbert Ahasferus wanted to know. "We must not be cheated!"

"If you wait any longer," Prince Lothair remarked dryly, "it will be a moot point, for there will be no mouths to feed at all, and you will get nothing for your trouble."

"The prince is right," Master Rupert said. "Let us vote now!"

"Very well," the Lord High Ruler said. "All in favor of opening the granaries today raise your hands." The hands went up, and Jonah saw all but the two agents from the Merchants Guild in favor. "The motion is passed. All in favor of forming a committee to decide what will be paid the magnates and merchants raise your hand." All the hands were raised. "The motion is passed," Jonah said again. "If there is nothing further to discuss, my lords, good masters and ladies, we will adjourn this meeting."

"Wait!" Mikhail, son of Swiftsword, said. "We must pass a motion that those who attempt to profit from the grain to be given the populace will be punished. Would Sir Philip and Sir Anatol like to suggest a punishment?"

"Twenty lashes in the main public square for the first offense," Sir Philip said. "Male or female."

"Beheading for the second," Sir Anatol replied. "Male or female."

The council agreed unanimously.

"Notices will be posted to that effect," the Lord High Ruler said. "Are we adjourned now, my lords, good masters and ladies?"

There was a murmur of assent.

"That was quite wonderful," Zagiri said. "We have nothing like this in Terah, although I will say my mother has tried. Terahn women don't want to be involved in the business of government. My grandmother says it is not seemly."

"I would think the Queen of the Forest Faeries would approve considering she rules her own kingdom," Lady Farah said.

"Nay, not her," Zagiri said. "My father's mother, the Lady Persis. My grandmother Ilona paid very little attention to me once it became apparent that I had no magic in me." Zagiri laughed. "She adores my little sister, Marzina, who has much magic at her fingertips. Marzina is with her now learning as much as she can."

"Well, I probably would like this Lady Persis," Lady Farah said. "A woman should always know her place. You certainly do, my dear. My son is obviously very happy with you. You will give him children soon, I hope."

"We have Egon," Zagiri replied. "I am not ready yet to be a real mother."

"You are almost eighteen!" Lady Farah said, shocked.

Zagiri laughed. "If my belly grew big I could not take pleasures with my husband and our sex slaves, my lady. We are considering adding a female sex slave to our household. Jonah has so much fun watching me with Doran and Casnar, and we both enjoy watching them together, but I should like to see them, and my husband, with another girl. Do you have any suggestions for us?"

Lady Farah sighed. "There is a special slave market we could visit together, I suppose, if you are determined to follow this course," she said. "Your appetite for pleasures is amazing, my child. You may not have your mother's magic, but you have her lust for life."

"Let us go to your slave market this afternoon," Zagiri said. "Poor Jonah will need to be distracted after today's council meeting. All this talk of the Hierarch will have upset him, I am certain. Do you think such a person really exists, Farah?"

"I do not know," Lady Farah admitted. "But whoever he is I hope he does not come into The City before we can get the populace calmed. It would only cause more troubles for my son, and the council."

Her hopes were not to be realized because despite the council's promise to pay the magnates for their grain, the magnates refused to open their warehouses so that the food might be distributed. Word had spread throughout The City that there would be food, and when there wasn't, several small riots broke out, which had to be put down by the Mercenaries. Jonah was fit to be tied. He called Cuthbert Ahasferus and Aubin Prospero to him. They would not come, for they feared the wrath of the people. And then it happened as crowds gathered outside one of the largest warehouses and granaries in The City.

As the hungry citizens led by Mikhail, son of Swiftsword, demanded in the name of the council that the warehouses be opened, there was a sudden burst of bright light. And there before the warehouse stood a tall young man who thrust out his hand toward the warehouse door, which immediately burst open. The crowd surged forward, but the young man again held up his hand.

"My children, there is food for all here, and I know you are starving, but the distribution must be done in an orderly manner. Everyone will be fed, I promise you. Your own elected councilman, Mikhail, son of Swiftsword, will guide you. Do as he says, and all will be well."

"It is the Hierarch!" a voice in the crowd cried out.

The people surged forward again, but this time it was to touch the hem of the Hierarch's dark blue robe.

Some began to weep. Others cried out for his blessing, and the Hierarch obliged them, touching their heads, clasping their hands, offering a kind and gentle word of encouragement.

Councilman Mikhail ordered the workers in the warehouse to prepare to feed the people who stood behind him. Frightened for their lives, they hesitated.

The Hierarch came forward, and spoke to them in low and soothing tones. "My children, you must feed your brothers and sisters. It is my wish you do it."

"My lord," the foreman of the workers said, "we do not know you, and our masters will punish us if we allow their goods to be stolen."

"I am the Hierarch," Cam said, "and I have come to lead Hetar back to its glory. You have strayed, my children, from the path of noble tradition. You must restore the old ways, and I will help you. Your masters will hear me, and they will follow my ways. But first we must feed the citizens of this great city. They will need their strength if we are to rebuild Hetar. Help us now, brothers, to distribute the grain."

It was as if the foreman and the workers had been touched by magic, for, nodding, they began immediately to gather the people outside the warehouse into orderly lines, and the grain and rice began to be passed out. Hearing of this, several of the magnates came to the warehouse to protest, but the Hierarch approached them, assuring them that they would be paid for their goods.

"Did not your own council promise it?" he asked them.

"Aye, they did, but then they formed a committee to decide how much we will get," one plump magnate said. "Do you have any idea how long it takes a council committee to make a decision? They will argue over the smallest point for weeks. It will be months, if not years, before we see a single coin."

The Hierarch smiled. "The monies you will get from the grain in these warehouses is nothing to what you will gain if you will but listen to me. I know how difficult it has been these last years for you, but Hetar is to return to its old ways. A time when each citizen had a purpose, and a place. When all were fed well, and housed, and sickness was rare. A time when profits were as fat as a Winterfest goose. I have come to lead you back into your righteous ways. Has my coming not been foretold to you?"

"It was thought by most that the Hierarch was legend," one of the magnates said.

"Legend begins in truth and fact. Then as the centuries pass it becomes blurred until it is believed nothing more than fantasy. But I am real, my lords. And if you will follow me we will together return Hetar to its former glory, and your vaults to their former wealth." He smiled a brilliant smile, and to their surprise the magnates gathered at the warehouse felt their own lips turning up in an answering smile.

The distribution now under way, Mikhail, son of Swiftsword, quietly departed the warehouse, making his way to the Golden District where the Lord High

Ruler lived. Easily recognized by the guards at the gates to this district, he was passed through, and made his way through the beautiful parkland whose flowering trees were now coming into bloom. There were beautiful homes scattered throughout the woodlands, and Mikhail frankly enjoyed the walk, almost feeling regret as he reached the palace, where he was admitted immediately.

Once the home of Gaius Prospero, it had been enlarged when its former owner had managed to make himself emperor of Hetar briefly. It would not have been considered a large palace in other kingdoms, but it sat upon the largest and finest piece of property in the Golden District, and commanded a fine view.

"Tell the Lord High Ruler that Councilman Mikhail, son of Swiftsword, awaits him," Mikhail told the majordomo who had come to greet him.

"At once, my lord," the majordomo said, bowing obsequiously. "At once!"

"Thank you," Mikhail replied, amused. It was hardly his position on the council that gained him such courtesy. It was because he was his father's son.

John Swiftsword held the distinction of having been the greatest swordsman in the Kingdom of Hetar. He had been the greatest Hetarian hero to fight in the battle of The City, losing his life, but helping to gain the victory. And, more infamously, he was the father of the faerie woman Lara, Domina of Terah, a legend in herself. Mikhail smiled to himself. It had been some time since he had seen his half sister. His mother was jealous of Lara, and had hidden her existence from her younger brothers for many years. But Mikhail remembered the lovely girl who had played with him, because his father had quietly seen that he remembered. And then when they were both grown they had met again, and the rapport had been immediate between them.

The majordomo returned. "The Lord High Ruler bids you to await him in the library. He will be with you as soon as he can." The servant led Mikhail to a beautiful book-lined room. "I will bring you refreshment, my lord Mikhail."

"It is just Master Mikhail," the councilman said, and sat down to await Jonah.

The majordomo left, and when he returned he was accompanied by a serving woman who carried a small tray, which was set on a nearby table. "If you need anything else, Master Mikhail, you have but to call out. The servant will await outside the library door." Then he lowered his voice. "Refresh yourself. It will be a while before my master can come to you." Then the two servants bowed themselves from the library.

Mikhail poured himself a goblet of strawberry Frine. He set it and a small plate of crisp cheese wafers next to his chair. Then, choosing a book from the library shelves, he sat down to await the Lord High Ruler, immersing himself in a rather interesting small history while nibbling upon the wafers and sipping from his goblet. He did not often have the opportunity to read in quiet with such delightful refreshment. He lived with his mother and brothers. His siblings were all Crusader Knights, each striving to match their father's reputation, and none coming even close to it. He himself was a scholar. His father had been a fine man, but Mikhail had discovered young that he had no talent for weapons.

He did not know how long he sat reading. The plate with the wafers was empty, as was his goblet, when the Lord High Ruler finally entered the room. Jonah was garbed in a house robe. His hair was tousled and he looked tired. The councilman rose to his feet, and bowed to Hetar's sovereign. "My lord."

"What do you have to tell me that is so important?" Jonah demanded.

"There are two things I thought you would want to know, my lord," Mikhail said.

"And they are?" Jonah asked.

"The distribution of the grain has begun at long last, my lord."

"And?"

"The Hierarch has come, my lord."

"What?" Jonah look surprised.

"The Hierarch has come, my lord," the councilman repeated. "It is he who managed to get the warehouses opened when even the council's orders could not."

Jonah grew pale. His worst fears were being realized, but he swallowed his fears, saying to Mikhail, son of Swiftsword, "I must meet the Hierarch. Can you arrange it, Councilman?"

"I can try, my lord," Mikhail replied.

"Then do it," Jonah said. And, turning, left his library. He sensed his throne was in danger. Best to meet the enemy before planning how to survive him.

CHAPTER THIRTEEN

THE WORD BEGAN to spread swiftly throughout Hetar. The Hierarch had come. Come to bring them back to the glory that was Hetar. A Hetar where everyone had a place, where tradition was honored. And in Terah word of the Hierarch reached Lara when one of the Terahn trading vessels brought this news to the young Dominus.

"What is a Hierarch?" Taj asked his mother.

"It is nothing but a legend," Lara said, "but someone is using that legend to their own advantage."

"But what is this Hierarch supposed to do?" Taj persisted.

"Make Hetar all glorious and powerful once again," Lara responded.

"Then Hetar and its Hierarch could be a threat to us once more," Taj said thoughtfully, surprising his mother with a new astuteness.

"Perhaps," Lara told him. "Perhaps not. But now are you not late to your lessons? Do not keep Sinon and Gare waiting, my son."

The boy hurried off, and Lara raced to the little windowless room she kept for her magic. She had a library of old volumes on several shelves, and now she began to look through them for an early history of Hetar. Finding it, she took it from the shelf and began to thumb through it. Finally she came upon what she sought.

At the end of her days the Lady Ulla was suddenly blessed with the gift of Sight. *She saw a great future for her adopted land, but she also saw a time when Hetar would become bloated with its own importance, when false leaders would lead the kingdom astray, taking them from the traditions that had made them great. It was then that Hetar would fall upon terrible times. There would be starvation, and plague, and many deaths. But just when all was considered lost a savior would appear. He would be called the Hierarch, and if the people of Hetar would heed his words, and obey his dictates, Hetar would be returned to the great and prosperous kingdom that it had once been. He would come suddenly, his origins lost in the mists of time. No one but the Hierarch could save Hetar. And before he came a direct descendant of the Lady Ulla would sacrifice her own life to save that of her son. A son who would eventually become the most faithful of the Hierarch's adherents. There would be those in Hetar, powerful persons, who would attempt to deter the Hierarch, but he would prevail against them, for he was Hetar's only hope. This was the last prediction made by the Lady Ulla, and as all her previous prophecies had proved true, the foretelling of the Hierarch was to be taken seriously.*

Lara closed the small book from which she had been

reading. She was suddenly both amazed and admiring of the sorcerer Usi, whom she had defeated back when she had first come to Terah. Like all with magic, he had never expected his own end. But he had prepared for it nonetheless. His two concubines had borne his children in secret. A son whose descendants ruled the Dark Lands. A daughter from among whose descendants the forerunner of the Hierarch, the Lady Vilia, came. And it all led but to one end. The darkness that would envelop Hetar, and then Terah.

The Hierarch was no savior. Oh, she was certain that he would appear so in the beginning. But once Hetar was back to where it had begun the darkness was certain to fall. A people who believed that they were superior to all other peoples, who believed that they could do no wrong and justified their evil with their own righteousness, were a dangerous people. And a dangerous enemy. Terah would have a difficult time standing against such an enemy. But who was controlling the Hierarch? Kol was imprisoned and helpless. Was it his sons? It was something she needed to learn quickly. She chanted:

Kolgrim, Kolbein, come to me
Though you would rather hidden be
This faerie woman calls you her way
And you cannot help but obey.

And the twins, identical looks upon their startled faces, were immediately before her.

Kolgrim smiled warmly. "Why, Mother, how nice of you to invite us to visit."

Kolbein reached for the dagger in his belt, but with a snap of her fingers Lara turned it into a thorny rose. Kolbein yelped as his fingers were sorely pricked.

"You should emulate your brother's manners," she told him. "Sit down, both of you!" And Lara pointed to two stools as she settled herself in the chamber's single chair. "I have some questions for you, my lords. What do you know of the Hierarch?"

"A Hetarian legend," Kolgrim said.

"Never heard of it," Kolbein snarled, but he did not look at her.

"Do not lie to me, Kolbein," Lara said sharply. "You were your half sister's lover, and I am certain she is behind this alleged Hierarch now making himself known in Hetar. Ciarda has great plans, and I will wager they do not include sharing the throne of the Dark Lands with her little brothers, or the spoils of Hetar."

"Why, brother dear," Kolgrim purred, "you lay with the bitch? More fool you to give her your essence. If she makes a child it will be more powerful than either you or I. Did you not consider such a thing as you rutted on her? But no, you would not have. Your only interest would have been in satisfying your need for pleasures. I cannot believe that we shared our mother's womb, for you are surely a fool!"

Kolbein's hand went again to where his dagger had been, but he remembered in time the thorns, and pulled his fingers back. "You are just envious that she wanted me for her lover," he growled.

Kolgrim laughed. "I should sooner bed a pandorian spider, dear boy," he said. Then he turned to Lara. "The Hierarch has announced his presence in Hetar?"

She nodded. "And has performed enough small miracles to gain the adoration of the populace, and the attention of Hetar's Lord High Ruler and the magnates."

"You believe Ciarda is behind it?" Kolgrim asked.

He was so like his father in thought, and gesture, Lara thought, fighting back a shudder of distaste. But it was obvious he was the cleverer twin, whereas Kolbein was a rough brute with little intellect. "I do believe Ciarda is pulling the strings of her puppet," Lara told him. "She would complete the conquest that your father could not."

"Where is your proof?" Kolbein demanded to know.

"Do you deny that she spoke to you of the Hierarch? Do you deny that she planned to murder your twin, leaving you to control the Dark Lands?"

Kolbein flushed, said nothing, but shuffled his feet uncomfortably.

"You fool!" Kolgrim burst out. "She meant to rule our kingdom through the son you would give her, or have you already given her a son? And you would have been disposed of at her convenience in some manner that suggested a normal death. How could you be so stupid, Kolbein? Thank Krell that our sire is not here to see you destroying everything our ancestors so carefully built." Now he turned to Lara. "Thank you for warning me of this viper you birthed."

"I did not bring you here to help either of you. If my actions to prevent the darkness from escaping your kingdom has accomplished that it was not my original purpose. But perhaps it is good that you both know what is going on outside the Dark Lands. I imagine you have both been so busy attempting to supplant each other it did not occur to you that it is not all about the pair of you."

"You sound like Chancellor Alfrigg." Kolgrim chuckled.

Suddenly there was the sound of tinkling bells, a puff of bright pink smoke and a young girl appeared in Lara's magic chamber. "Mother!"

"Marzina!" Lara gasped, horrified.

"Well, well, who have we here, Mother dear?" Kolgrim asked, a toothy smile lighting his handsome face.

"Return, Dark Lords, from whence you come! I'll call if you must come again," Lara said quickly, and the twins were immediately gone.

"Mother, who were those young men?" Marzina wanted to know. "Do you like what Grandmother's taught me? I wrote the spell myself."

"You should have warned me that you were coming, Marzina," Lara said, taking a long, slow breath to calm her beating heart. "And you should never transport yourself into this chamber. You know it is for my magic."

"But who were those two men?" Marzina repeated. "Their faces were the same, but one had golden hair like you while the other was dark haired."

"Prince Kaliq sent them to me to answer some questions," Lara lied. "There are problems in Hetar of late."

"The Hierarch, I know," Marzina said. "It's all over the Forest Kingdom. Our people have overheard the Forest Lords talking and complaining of late. The Head Forester says that his province is always the last to be considered, but then the Hierarch came, and with a wave of his hand restored the forests that had been previously cut down by the Midland farmers in their quest for new land."

"I'm sure that pleased Squire Darah," Lara said dryly.

"Nay!" Marzina gossiped on. "The Midlands are suddenly as fertile, if not more fertile, than they ever were. Squire Darah is very happy. He says it is just like olden times. But I am forgetting my purpose in coming. Grandmother says she wishes to see you as soon as you can come. I think she actually means now, Mother."

Lara had to laugh. "You have come to understand Ilona well, Marzina. Tell your grandmother I will come tomorrow at the moonrise."

Marzina threw her arms about Lara and kissed her cheek as she hugged her hard. "I have missed you, Mother. When will it be safe for me to come home for a real visit?"

"I do not know," Lara said softly, "but sooner than later I hope, my darling. Do you have time to go and see Taj?"

"Nay, but I will come to him soon. Grandmother is expecting me back quickly," Marzina said. "Goodbye,

Mother!" And she was gone with the sound of tinkling bells, and in a puff of pink smoke.

Lara let out a gusty sigh. What a near thing it had been. While Marzina had briefly seen Kolgrim and Kolbein, Lara had managed to get them sent back to the Dark Lands before they had a chance to speak to one another. Had Marzina heard Kolgrim address her as *Mother?* She hadn't said anything about it so Lara was hoping her youngest daughter had not heard his mocking address. She had not quite finished with the twins when she had been forced to remove them from her chamber. Now she must speak with their keeper, and she knew the old dwarf had enough magic to heed her command.

Chancellor Alfrigg, heed my call. Come to me from out yon wall!

And the stone wall suddenly opened showing the golden tunnel through which the Dark Lands' ancient chancellor now hurried on his short little legs.

"Far too bright! Far too bright!" he complained as he entered her room. "I am almost blinded by your light, Domina. What do you want?"

Lara told him of the twins' visit, explaining why she had brought them to her, and why she had quickly returned them. "My other children know nothing of that lost year," she said. "Nor do I choose to share that time with them."

"What do you want of me then, Domina?" Alfrigg asked her.

"I believe Kolbein is dangerous. Far more so than

Kolgrim, who is much like his father. His evil is elegant and subtle. Kolbein is an ignorant brute, and the Darkling is using him for her own purposes. I believe that one way or another she means to rule the Dark Lands herself. If you would, protect Kolgrim, and make certain that Kolbein understands that the shedding of blood between brothers is forbidden by tradition within their family."

"I will not ask where you gained your information," Alfrigg said. "How odd that we have become allies of a sort, Domina. My lord Kol would be pleased to see you looking out for the interests of your children."

"They are his, not mine. I do not claim them. My only interest is in keeping the darkness from leaving the Dark Lands, and spreading over our worlds," Lara said.

"I have been suspicious of the Darkling, although I will admit a fondness for her. She is much like her dear father. Is he still alive, Domina?" Alfrigg inquired curiously.

"I do not know. I do not want to know. His fate was the province of the Shadow Princes." Of course she did know, but Lara felt ignorance was the better path in this case. Alfrigg had been Kol's chancellor for several hundred years, and he was devoted to him.

The old dwarf nodded. "I have held the kingdom together since his disappearance. I have monitored the progress of his sons. Now I must guide them."

"Keep them in their place, and beware Kolbein and

Ciarda," Lara warned him. "You are a reasonable man, Alfrigg, and reason must prevail."

"Thank you, Domina. Now, if you would open the tunnel for me, I will return."

Lara raised her hand, and the tunnel appeared in the stone wall. Without another word the chancellor of the Dark Lands turned and hurried through the passageway. She watched him go, the opening closing behind him until the wall was wall once again. Lara sat back down again, and considered the past few hours. She had not heard from Kaliq, or any of the Shadow Princes, in several days.

Prince Kaliq, heed my plea. Cease all else and come to me, she called out in the silent language. But he did not answer her call, and instead Lara felt herself drawn into a golden tunnel, which ended at the Oasis of Zeroun. The desert moon shone down with its copper light dappling the pool and its waterfall. A light flickered from the tented pavilion. Lara walked toward it, and was suddenly greeted by Kaliq, who appeared before her in a loose white robe.

"I called to you," she said. "And you did not come, my lord."

"I decided that you needed a respite from your problems," he said with a smile. Holding out his hand to her, he drew Lara into his arms and they were suddenly both naked. "'Tis not subtle, I will admit, but your son will expect you to emerge from your privy chamber in a few hours. I have missed you, my love." His hands caught her head, holding it still as he kissed her, a deep and passionate kiss.

Lara slipped her arms about his neck, her fingers caressing his nape, setting the little dark hairs upon it to bristling beneath her touch. "Aah, Kaliq, this is wickedly perfect," she murmured against his mouth. "My day so far has been difficult."

"Tell me," he said.

"Nay, not yet. I want to take pleasures with you first, my lord," Lara said.

He swept her up in his arms, carrying her to the silken mattress upon the dais. Laying her down, his lips met hers again. Her mouth opened beneath his, and their tongues entwined slowly. They breathed each other's essence, sighing. He lay upon his back and set her astride him, feeling the firm flesh of her bottom against his thighs. Reaching up, Kaliq took her breasts in his hands, fondling them, squeezing them individually, pressing them together. He suckled upon each of her nipples, nibbling teasingly, drawing hard so that she gasped aloud.

Lara reached out and caressed the length of his love rod. The very sight of it excited her, for she knew how well he could wield it. It grew in length and breadth beneath her touch. He laid her upon her back, straddling her, and when she pressed her two breasts together he pushed his rod back and forth between the soft flesh. Lara raised her head and leaned forward so she might lick the tip of him, laughing softly when he gasped.

Finally he turned himself about upon her so she might take him into her mouth while he began to play with the soft folds of her nether lips. He licked along her slit, pushing his tongue between the flesh to find the sensitive core of her. He licked at it first, but then he sucked and nibbled upon her even as he pushed two fingers into her tight sheath, moving them slowly back and forth.

"Ooh, Kaliq!" Lara exclaimed. And her juices bedewed his fingers and hand. He continued the love torture until her juices flowed again, this time more copiously. Then, turning his body back once again, he slowly drove himself as deep as he could into her eager body again and again, bringing her to the brink of pleasure, then withholding it. She wrapped her legs about his torso and his long, thick rod sank deeper as he pistoned her until she was crying with delight.

He could feel himself throbbing with his need, but he wanted more of her. Still deep inside her, he stopped to unfasten her slender legs from his body, and push them back until they were over her shoulders. Then, kneeling, his rod once again began to work her, deeper than he had ever gone, and Lara cried his name over and over and over again until the sheath in which his rod was so tightly encased began to tighten about him, and quiver with its need as she reached her peak. Her love juices flowed heavily as she attained pleasures such as she had never found before. She screamed softly with delight as her body spasmed over and over and over again.

"Kaliq!" Lara cried as she felt him stiffen, groan, and then his manly juices poured into her. *"Ooh, Kaliq!"*

He held her tightly, his kisses covering her heart-shaped face, her throat, her chest. *It matters not to me the lovers you take, Lara. You are mine and mine alone. No man, mortal or magic, can give you the pleasures that I do. No female, mortal or magic, can pleasure me as you do, my darling,* he said to her in the silent language. *The fates and all destiny help me, for I love you.*

Oh, Kaliq, Lara murmured back to him in the same language, *I love you, too. I have always loved you from the first. I loved Vartan, and I loved Magnus, as well. But not as I love you, my dear lord.*

He said nothing more but held her in his arms until he knew that they had both recovered from the tremendous passion that had overwhelmed them. His hand stroked her golden hair as he enjoyed these moments of perfect peace with her. When finally he sensed her heart had calmed itself he said, "Tell me about your day."

And Lara told him how she had brought the dark twins to her, of what had been said, of how she had quickly returned them to their own kingdom when Marzina had intruded upon them. "It is so like my mother to have taught her a spell like that," Lara said. "It was thoughtless with no balances and checks. What if she had appeared a few moments ago as we labored together?"

"I suspect," Kaliq said, "that her education would have been quite furthered, at least in the areas of pleasures." The prince chuckled. "What did you tell her about Kolgrim and Kolbein?"

"I said you had sent them to me for questioning in the matter of the Hierarch," Lara told him. "It was all I could think of to say. And of course, Kolgrim, with his usual vile humor, called me *Mother*. But I don't think Marzina heard him."

"Nay, it would not have been very good if she did," Kaliq agreed. "It will be better if Marzina never knows who sired her, my love."

But Marzina had heard Kolgrim call Lara *Mother,* and, returning to her grandmother's castle, she told Ilona of the two young men with the same face who had been with Lara when she arrived. "Why did the one with golden hair call her *Mother?*" she asked the Queen of the Forest Faeries.

"I have absolutely no idea," Ilona replied, pretending puzzlement. "If Kaliq had sent them to your mother for questioning perhaps the young man was being sarcastic. Did you not say you greeted your mother properly? He heard you call her mother, saw your mother's surprise at your arrival. He was taunting her, Marzina. And did she not send them immediately from her presence?"

Marzina nodded. "She addressed them as Dark Lords," the girl said.

"And they probably were," Ilona responded. "Your mother and the Shadow Princes are seeking those behind the Hierarch. They are certain to come from the Dark Lands, Marzina. Your mother has been known to obtain information when others could not. This is a serious and dangerous business. A powerful Darkling is involved."

"What exactly is a Darkling, Grandmother? Is it faerie?"

"Aye and nay," Ilona said. "This one is a particularly beautiful female. She will have magic in her veins, and her mother or a grandmother was probably faerie, but from the dark side. She uses her beauty among her other skills to seduce men in order to gain power and wealth. But particularly power. We are not all light, my child."

"Could I not help my mother in this endeavor, Grandmother?" Marzina asked.

"One day you will be strong enough, and you will be skilled enough to help your mother should she require your aid, but you are still too young, Marzina," Ilona said.

"Did my mother not begin her adventures when she was about my age?" Marzina responded pertly.

"Your mother was sent into the world by her father not understanding the heritage she possessed. She had no magic then and was helpless. It was her brave spirit that helped her to survive to reach the Shadow Princes, who, learning she was my daughter, Maeve's granddaughter, trained her in the ways of magic. Once they unlocked the barrier she bloomed even as you bloom under my tutelage, Marzina." Ilona stroked her granddaughter's dark hair affectionately. "I know how much you love your mother, and that you want to help her. But right now your presence would weaken her at a time she must have and use all of her strength."

"Why?"

"Because she loves you, my child. Because as long as you are safe with me your mother does not have to fear. Anoush is safe with her father's family in the New Outlands. Taj is safe in his castle. Both are surrounded by spells your mother and Prince Kaliq have woven to protect them. Only your foolish sister Zagiri in Hetar is in danger from the chaos about to descend upon that unfortunate kingdom. Lara will do whatever she has to to safeguard Zagiri. She cannot have you to worry about, as well, Marzina. Once she has taken Zagiri from harm's way her entire concentration must be upon exposing this mortal who dares to pretend he is Hetar's savior. If he is not removed then Hetar will be taken into the darkness. Escaping the darkness is never an easy thing, my child. Do you understand now?"

"Aye, Grandmother, I do. But it still will not prevent me from wishing I could help my mother," Marzina said.

Ilona smiled. "I know," she said, completely understanding her granddaughter's desire. Then she grew serious. "You must promise me you will remain here with me until this matter is cleared up, or until your mother sends for you herself. And no more surprise visits, Marzina. What if you had intruded upon your mother in an intimate moment? She would have been very distressed by it."

Marzina giggled. "Prince Kaliq is her lover," she

said. "He is so handsome and kind, Grandmother. I hope I have a lover like that someday."

Ilona made a very un-faerielike sound, quite like a snort. "I have no doubt you will have many lovers, Marzina. The women in our family quite enjoy taking pleasures. One day you will, too, but not until you have grown up a little more. You have centuries ahead of you, my dear child. Centuries!"

"I am only half-faerie, Grandmother. My father was quite mortal, and of the three children my mother bore him I am the only one with magic," Marzina said.

"Which is exactly why you will survive far longer than your mortal siblings," Ilona pointed out.

Marzina, of course, was incorrect. She was almost pure magic. Her mother had been newly pregnant with Taj when Lara was attacked upon the Dream Plain by Kol, the Twilight Lord, and impregnated by him for a second time. Marzina's natural father was Kol. Lara had become his weakness, and to his misfortune he loved her.

That first time she had been stolen from Magnus Hauk, and her memories taken. It had all been part of a plan by the powers of light to stop the Twilight Lord from bringing his darkness into the mortal worlds of Hetar and Terah. When she was pregnant with Kol's child, Lara's memories were returned to her, and she divided the child in her womb into two sons, not one, thus causing chaos in the Dark Lands, for each Twilight Lord had by tradition the ability to produce but one son.

Ilona had been present at the birth of the twin children believed to be Magnus Hauk's offspring. No one had been more surprised than Lara when having birthed her husband's longed-for son and heir, she then birthed a beautiful little girl who looked nothing like her blond mother and father. The Queen of the Forest Faeries had loudly proclaimed that Marzina looked like a distant relation, a Nix, and nothing more had been thought about it. Magnus Hauk never knew his littlest daughter was not his natural child, and Marzina never knew, either.

When she showed a talent and ability for magic naturally at a very early age neither Lara nor Ilona had been surprised. Given that his two other children were as mortal as could be, Magnus Hauk was amazed by Marzina's talents, but accepted them. And the few months that Marzina had spent with her grandmother had already proved successful. Marzina was already writing her own spells, one or two of them quite advanced, especially for a faerie girl of her age. She was more than proficient at casting spells and mixing potions. She had learned much about herbs from her oldest sister.

"She has a knack for sorcery," Ilona said to her consort, Thanos.

Lara came to visit her mother at moonrise as she had promised.

"You have been with Kaliq," Ilona noted. "I smell his sandalwood."

"Hours ago," Lara murmured, but she felt her cheeks warm.

"Tell me what is happening, and why were Kol's sons with you, Lara?"

"I needed to know what they knew of Ciarda's recent actions. Kolgrim knows little or nothing. Kolbein is another matter. I have managed to expose his duplicity to his brother, which should keep them at each other's throats. It has become obvious that Ciarda is behind the Hierarch. We will observe and then destroy him. Now, I have not told you of Anoush." And Lara went on to explain to her mother how she had put her daughter into a deep sleep to protect her from Cam because of his association with the Darkling.

"Why would Ciarda be bothered with someone like Cam?" Ilona said. "He is a common Fiacre cattle herder. Of course, these rough brutes all seem to have large and talented manhoods. The Darkling would appreciate that. Or is it something else?"

"What else could it be?" Lara said, and then her hand went to her mouth to stifle the cry of sudden realization. "Cam! She has made Cam the Hierarch! He is a perfect cat's paw for her to use. And if indeed she has chosen Cam she has made a fatal mistake by doing so, Mother! She is so eager for power, foolish Darkling!"

"What mistake?" Ilona wanted to know.

"You know how the Hetarians have always despised the Outlanders? They consider them savages and barbarians. Do you believe that Hetar can accept a Hierarch who is Outlander born and raised? I do not think they can. If they learn that their savior is one of the despised they will reject him."

"And what then?" Ilona said. "It is true we must keep

Hetar from being swallowed by the darkness, but will not exposing their Hierarch send them tumbling into the void even faster? Their Hierarch has brought them hope."

"He is turning them back to what they were. Over-proud and greedy. A Hetar where men rule, and women are little more than objects for pleasure, bearing children or hard work. I helped the women of Hetar to find their voice, Mother. I cannot allow that voice to be stilled."

"It does not have to be, Lara. What if we, the faerie kingdoms, and the Shadow Princes help the Hierarch to see the Darkling's evil? What if we make Cam believe that he really is the Hierarch? We will give him powers greater than Ciarda's. Temporary, of course, but enough to convince him, and possibly to convince her. We can keep her from bringing the darkness to Hetar by making her cat's paw ours. We will help him to re-interpret Hetar's old laws and traditions for the better not the worse. We will see that he gives the women of Hetar even greater autonomy."

"Mother, it is a brilliant plan!" Lara cried. "And if I can manipulate Kol's sons a tiny bit more we can close the Dark Lands to her, as well."

"You are both extremely clever," Prince Kaliq said, stepping from the shadows of Ilona's privy chamber where the two women were sitting.

"We cannot let Hetar retreat into its past," Lara said. "But the misery there now is terrible. If the population of The City should rise up against those who live in the Golden District, innocents could suffer."

"You think of Zagiri," Ilona said.

"Aye, I do," Lara admitted. "Zagiri is Terahn. She should not have to suffer because she has been foolish enough to marry a Hetarian against my will."

"We have not been able to get close enough to the Darkling," Kaliq said, "but we know her basic plan. I will send my brothers among the people of Hetar to learn more about the Hierarch."

"And I will approach Cam, for he is an ambitious man, and when he learns my powers are stronger than the Darkling's powers I will be able to win him over," Lara said.

"Will you keep Anoush sleeping for the interim?" Ilona asked.

Lara nodded. "I will. In matters like this she is an innocent. And I do not want Cam to have any advantage over me, or believe he has an advantage."

"I will speak with the King of the Mountain Faeries, the Empress of the Meadow Faeries and the King of the Water Faeries to see if they will help," Ilona said.

"And if they will not?" Kaliq asked her.

"If they choose not to aid us they will at least keep silent," Lara said.

"Agreed!" Ilona replied. "Know, my daughter, that each of these monarchs owes me a favor. I will not force their compliance, but their silence is another matter."

The trio dispersed. The Shadow Prince to Shunnar

to speak with his brothers and bring them up to date. Lothair and Coilin joined them to tell them how things were progressing in Hetar

"There is talk," Lothair, the elder of the two, said, "of taking ownership of the Pleasure Houses back from the Pleasure Mistresses, and putting them once again into the hands of male owners."

"And of closing the new male Pleasures Houses that have been opened for women clients," Coilin added.

"That will not bring prosperity back to Hetar," Kaliq said. "The Pleasure Houses have flourished twice as well since the females took them over. And opening houses with male Pleasure Slaves for the women was a brilliant idea."

"I know," Coilin agreed. "Many young women are now celebrating their fourteenth birthday by taking pleasures for the first time in them. There is even one that caters to such birthdays. It has an excellent group of male sex slaves who specialize in the uninitiated. It is considered quite fashionable to say that you first took pleasures with one of these sex slaves."

"We must work with those who are reasonable, and would modernize Hetar's traditions without scorning them," Kaliq said, and his brothers nodded in agreement.

"What is Queen Ilona doing to help in this matter?" Prince Eskil asked.

"See for yourself," Kaliq said, offering Eskil a round crystal ball.

Taking it up, Eskil gazed into the sphere.

Ilona had chosen to visit Gwener, Empress of the Meadow Faeries, first. Every bit as beautiful as Ilona, Gwener had long red hair and dark green eyes. She had a smaller kingdom than the other faerie rulers, and had a tendency to be overproud and difficult. Ilona had sent ahead requesting an audience with Gwener, saying it was a most urgent matter. The empress sent back a message that she knew Ilona was involving herself in non-faerie matters, and that she was not interested in speaking with the Queen of the Forest Faeries. Ilona, however, persisted. She invited Gwener to visit her, saying that Annan of the Water Faeries and Laszlo of the Mountain Faeries would be there. Not wishing to be left out, Gwener came.

Ilona explained the situation to her fellow monarchs, concluding, "We must help these foolish mortals straighten out the chaos they have made of their lives, and protect them from the darkness."

"You are certain the darkness threatens?" Laszlo of the Mountain Faeries asked.

"This Hierarch is currently being controlled by a Darkling called Ciarda," Ilona answered. "She is one of Kol's daughters, and she wishes to complete what he could not. She has already seduced one of her half brothers, and her very existence threatens the other one who, though it pains me to say it, is the better half."

"They are your daughter's children, are they not?" Gwener said cruelly.

"Not by choice!" Ilona snapped. "The Twilight Lord stole Lara from her family, gave her memories to the Munin to keep and impregnated her. You know well it was planned for this to happen. Lara's memories restored, she turned the one child into two to cause chaos in the Dark Lands as we wanted. But now the darkness threatens to rise again, and all of us are needed to help stop it. How dare you criticize Lara!"

Gwener shrugged. "I was only refreshing the memories of our two fellow rulers," she murmured.

"Nay, you were being a bitch, Gwener," King Annan of the Water Faeries said. "You have always been jealous of Ilona, but this is not the time for your pettiness. Ilona is right. We have a serious problem."

"Agreed," King Laszlo said. "How can we help, Ilona?"

"We must all be vigilant and we must work together to enclose each of our kingdoms in a protective spell that will keep the darkness from us. Because it is our practice not to consort with mortals except now and again for pleasures, we are considered vulnerable. The darkness will attack us first, for we surround the mortal worlds. But if our own kingdoms are protected from the darkness it will give Lara and the Shadow Princes more time to turn the Hierarch from his Darkling mistress. If we foil her then she will return to her own lands. Let her brothers have to fight with her."

The two kings nodded their heads in agreement.

"I must be protected first if you expect me to help you," Gwener said.

"Of course," Ilona answered her. "Your beautiful meadows would die if they were sunk in the darkness. Would you not agree, my lords?"

"Indeed," King Annan replied.

"Yes, of course," King Laszlo responded.

"Let us not delay, then," Ilona said.

Prince Eskil set the crystal globe aside. "Ilona has gathered her fellow monarchs, and they are doing what they need to do. Now we must infiltrate The City and learn all we can about what the Hierarch is doing, and what he proposes to do. Then we must turn the people's hearts to what is right."

The other princes nodded.

"And Lara?" Prince Nasim asked.

"She will have the most difficult task of all," Prince Kaliq said. "She must convince Cam that he really is the Hierarch, and that his purpose is for good not evil."

"Given his bloodline that will not be an easy job," Lothair noted. "But if anyone can do this, Lara can. And, Kaliq, remember, you must allow her to do this on her own. We all know that you love her, but do not interfere with her destiny, my brother."

Kaliq nodded slowly.

"Love is painful, isn't it?" Lothair said. "It skews the judgment."

"I am not a youth that I lack judgment or self-discipline," Kaliq snapped irritably.

The other princes laughed aloud, and Kaliq flushed, but then he laughed, for he knew they were right. His love for the faerie woman was both bitter and sweet. But he had never really loved any female as he loved her, and he knew he would never again love another as he loved her.

"She will be fine," Prince Nasim said.

If Lara had heard his words she might not have agreed, for suddenly she was faced with having to deal with her instinctive feelings of dislike and distrust for Cam, the son of her first husband's murderers. Was it possible to overcome these intense feelings? And as for Cam, she knew he hated her. How could he not hold her responsible for the deaths of his parents? She had taken up her sword, Andraste, and slain them within moments of Vartan's murder. It had been her right to do so. But in doing so she had orphaned Cam. He had grown up with a grandmother who had been in the hall that terrible day, and had been driven mad by what she saw.

The Lady Bera had been unable to face all that she had seen. Her younger son had murdered her older son in cold blood. All she could recall of that hour was that Lara had cried out to her sword, Andraste, which had flown into her hand from its place above the hearth. The sword was already singing in its deep and deadly voice as Lara grasped its hilt in both of her small hands, and then took revenge for herself and her children by decapitating both Adon and his wife, Elin. Elin, it was later learned, had been bribed by Hetar, and had in turn encouraged her husband to murder. But from the look on Elin's face that day, and her screams of encouragement to her husband, Lara had known that she was equally responsible.

But Cam had lost both of his parents that day, and then been put in the care of a madwoman who did nothing but rail against her surviving daughter-in-law. It was then that a terrible darkness came over the child. It took hold of him, driving him to wickedness against other children, including Lara's son and daughter, Dillon and Anoush. Finally Cam had been removed from his grandmother's care, and sent to the headwoman Sholeh of Rivalen village. A widow had been put into the Lady Bera's house to watch over her, and several years later she died a peaceful death, the names of her sons the last words upon her lips.

Sholeh had taken charge of raising Cam, the son of her kinsman. And he had seemed to change outwardly. But Lara had also sensed that darkness still possessed Cam's heart and soul. How was she going to be able to appeal to him? His weaknesses, of course, were his hunger for wealth and power. Could she use those weaknesses to exorcise the evil in him? And did he really love Anoush, or was Lara's daughter just a means to an end? Had he attempted to use Anoush as Jonah was using the besotted Zagiri?

These were all things Lara needed to know. And there was only one way to find out. She had to deal with Cam face-to-face, which meant she would have

to go to Hetar. But first she must speak with her son
Taj. He needed to understand what was happening. He
was young, but he was also very intelligent. She found
him in the castle hall playing a game of Herder with his
friend Gare. She watched them for a while, but then,
seeing the game would take a while, she put a hand on
Taj's shoulder.

The young Dominus looked up, smiling at her.

"When you are finished with your game come and
speak with me," Lara said.

"It may be a while," Taj told her. "Gare has gotten
very good at this game."

"I was always very good at it," Gare said, grinning.
"That you realize you are having difficulty beating me
indicates you have improved your skills at Herder. I
used to be able to beat you before you even realized
what was happening."

Lara laughed. Gare and Sinon's companionship had
kept Taj from losing touch with reality. It would have
been easy for the fourteen-year-old Dominus, ruler of
a kingdom and catered to by all, to forget that he was
just a growing boy. If they would remain with him for
the next few years she would be grateful. Terahn boys
would have treated Taj far differently because he was
the Dominus, which would, of course, defeat the whole
purpose. Lara patted her son's shoulder, and left him
to his game.

Taj came to his mother's apartments an hour later.
Lara greeted him with a kiss upon his cheek, and then

drew him down to sit next to her on the cushioned couch. "I am going to have to go away for a time," she began, "and I want you to understand why. Terah must be protected and kept safe from the darkness, as must Hetar."

"Are you going to Hetar?" he asked her.

Lara nodded.

"For Zagiri's sake?"

"Nay, for Terah's sake. You have youth, courage and honesty with which to fight against the darkness, my son, but it is not enough. Especially when other mortals, in their quest for power and wealth, give themselves over to evil in exchange."

"You speak of the one known as the Hierarch, do you not, Mother?"

"The man claiming that title is the son of those who slew Vartan of the Fiacre, Taj. Anoush's father. He is manipulated by a beautiful Darkling who uses his hate for her own purposes. The Darkling's father is the Twilight Lord, Kol. She desires, like her sire, to bring darkness to our worlds. And she uses Cam, for that is his name, to help her accomplish this."

"Why do you go to Hetar, then, Mother?" Taj asked her.

"I must know if Cam can be turned back into the light," Lara said. "If he can then we can use him for the good, and defeat the darkness, send the Darkling Ciarda back to the Dark Lands where she belongs, and where the darkness is held and thrives."

"Will it be dangerous for you to go to Hetar?" Taj wanted to know.

"Aye and nay. I have many friends there, and a half brother I can trust to shelter me should I need shelter," Lara told him.

"You must go to my sister," Taj said. "Zagiri must know you are there."

"Nay, Taj, I do not want Zagiri or her husband knowing I am in Hetar," Lara said. "Jonah stole your sister and wed her because he believed that in times of trouble Terah would aid Hetar because we were bound by blood. It wasn't enough for him that our kingdoms had an alliance, and that Terah would keep its word. As for Zagiri, she was told she was not to marry the Lord High Ruler of Hetar, but she schemed with Jonah to do so. She must live with the choices she has made, but I will tell you that I am told she is very happy as *First Lady of Hetar.* I will only interfere in Zagiri's life should I believe that life is in danger, Taj."

He nodded his understanding now that she had explained. "Who else aids in this endeavour?" Taj asked.

"The faerie kingdoms and the Shadow Princes," Lara said.

"I think you should ask Aunt Nidhug to come from Belmair and scorch the Darkling and the Dark Lands into ash," he told her.

"Nay, Taj. There must always be a balance between good and evil. Light and dark. If there were not who knows what would happen to all the kingdoms of all the worlds both magic and mortal," Lara explained.

"There is so much to learn," Taj complained. "Will I ever know all that I must to be a good Dominus, Mother?"

"Nay, you will not," Lara said. "And the older you get you will find there are many more questions than there are answers, Taj." She ruffled his golden head.

"Some days growing up is very difficult, Mother. And other days it is wonderful, and I cannot get to where I am going quick enough," Taj told her.

Lara laughed. "It is the same for me, my darling. Remember I am still considered a child in the faerie world."

"A clever child," he replied with a grin.

"I do not know if your grandmother would agree," Lara said.

"Grandmother Ilona is very proud of you," Taj answered her. "Oh, she probably will not say it, but she is. I see how she looks at you, Mother. It is more than love in her eyes. It is pride in you."

"That is very observant of you," Lara noted, feeling a rush of pleasure at the boy's words. Sometimes the very young saw what older eyes did not.

"How long will you be gone?" he asked.

"I cannot say," Lara responded.

"It is almost time for my coronation, Mother. And you must be here. It cannot be postponed, as you know," Taj reminded her.

Lara swore softly under her breath. He was right. If he was not formally crowned on the first anniversary of the day of Magnus Hauk's death then there was a window of opportunity for any male within the Hauk clan to claim the throne. She had become so involved in the problems assailing them that she had completely forgotten the time. "I will be here," she said, "and I will help you plan the coronation, as well. Your uncles will also aid you as part of their duties as your council." She leaned over and kissed Taj's cheek. Gracious! Did she feel a bit of beard erupting on his face? "Go to bed, my darling," she told him. "I will be here in the morning, I promise you."

He arose and returned her kiss, then left Lara to her troubled thoughts.

CHAPTER FOURTEEN

THE DOMINA CALLED the Dominus's Council to her the following day. "The time draws near for the Dominus to be officially crowned," she reminded them. "Unless, of course, one of you would like to take over." And she laughed at the look of dismay on their three faces. "In less than a month's time the first anniversary of my husband's death is due, and on that day Taj must be crowned. I need your aid, Corrado, Tostig and Armen. There is trouble coming outside of Terah, but if it is not stopped it will spread to Terah. I am among those who must stop it, and so I must learn from you what is involved in Taj's coronation now. I will then give instructions, and trust that you will carry those instructions out while I am gone."

"Like our marriage ceremony," Corrado said, "the coronation is a simple affair. There will be three days of festivities sponsored by the family for any and all who would come to the castle. A stipend will be awarded to each village in Terah for local celebrations. This will include the New Outlands. On the first day the memory of Magnus Hauk will be celebrated. On the second day the crowning of the new Dominus will be solemnized.

On the third day we observe the blessings bestowed on Terah by the Great Creator in providing us with a new Dominus."

"I see," Lara replied, considering that it would be easy to arrange everything for her son's crowning, and still do what must be done. "What of the ceremony itself?"

"It, too, is simple," Armen answered her. "Only the family and a single representative from each fjord is permitted to observe it."

"You cannot offend the people of the New Outlands," Lara reminded him.

"Of course not," Armen replied. "This will be the first time they participate in such an affair. We will accept your guidance in this matter, Domina."

"Since each fjord sends a single person I think the New Outlanders are entitled to only one representative. Let it be Rendor, the head of their High Council."

"Agreed," the Dominus's three uncles said.

"What of Hetar?" Corrado asked. "With the Dominus's sister married to its Lord High Ruler, and that same man having once served his government as an ambassador to Terah, I think we have no choice but to ask him."

The council members looked to Lara.

"I must go to Hetar shortly," she told them. "I will ask Lord Jonah, and if he would come then I will bring him by means of my magic, and return him the same way. It is not wise for him to leave The City right now so I will transport him to Terah for only the second day, and see that he is sent back immediately afterward. His absence when it is known will be an afterthought and nothing more. It will help his cause, however, that he was here for the official ceremony."

"What is happening in Hetar, Domina?" Tostig asked her. "Can you tell us?"

"Hetar, for all its braggadocio, has fallen upon hard times. Its laws have not been followed, and there is a great deal of corruption, starvation, general poverty and plague. There is a legend in Hetar of a man called the Hierarch who will come when Hetar is facing its darkest hour, and return the kingdom to its glory. Unfortunately the legend is probably just that. Legend. But the powers of darkness have taken a mortal unknown in Hetar, and put him forth as the Hierarch. They are using what small magic they possess to make it seem as if he is making miracles. Their aim, of course, is to drag Hetar into the darkness, and if they accomplish this goal they will look to Terah. We have banded together, the Shadow Princes, four faerie kingdoms and myself, to prevent this from happening."

"How does the Hierarch manage to gain the people's trust?" Corrado wondered.

"By promising to return Hetar to its old ways and traditions, which have been ignored in the past years," Lara said. "Every country must have checks and balances within its governing body. Unfortunately the greedy have managed to bypass the laws, and have caused a collapse of Hetar's civilization. But the forces of light can help the Lord High Ruler return Hetar to where it should be without dragging the kingdom into the darkness. The faerie kings have aligned with the Shadow Princes to help in this matter. It is my task to deal with both the Lord High Ruler and with the Hierarch to bring about a resolution to Hetar's problems and to save them from the darkness."

"Jonah is a greedy man," Corrado noted.

"But he is also ambitious," Lara returned. "He schemed for years so that he might rule Hetar. Given the choice of losing his high place or future sources of wealth he will, I know, do everything in his power to protect his throne."

"So marrying our princess did in the end gain him Terah's help," Armen remarked dryly. He cocked a questioning eyebrow in Lara's direction.

"I do not do this for Zagiri," Lara replied sharply. "She has made her bed. But if we do not stop the darkness from enveloping Hetar, it will next devour Terah. You are no fool, my lord Armen. You know this to be so."

"I do," he admitted, nodding.

"How long must I live in Terah before you will stop anticipating and interpreting my motives?" Lara asked him.

Armen flushed. "Forgive me, Domina," he said humbly.

"When must you go to Hetar?" Corrado asked, attempting to defuse the situation.

"We will plan Taj's coronation first. I will visit Hetar briefly, and then return for my son's crowning," Lara told him. "I will entrust you with the first day, Corrado, as you were Magnus's best friend. My lord Armen, you will do the second day, and you, my lord Tostig, will be responsible for the third and final day. I shall see the monies distributed to the villages, and the invitations written and sent to those who are meant to be here. Are we agreed, my lords?"

"We are agreed," they chorused.

Lara dismissed them, and sent to her son's chief secretary, the former head scribe, Ampyx. "I will need your help," she told him. "The Dominus's coronation is near. Invitations must be sent to the headman or headwoman of every fjord, and to Rendor, head of the High Council of the New Outlands, as well as family members, and the High Priest and High Priestess. I will also carry to Hetar with me an invitation to their Lord High Ruler, Jonah. A blanket invitation is to be offered to all in Terah who come to the castle during those three days of festivities. And monies must be distributed to every village in Terah and the New Outlands so they may hold their own celebrations. The invitations must go out within the next few days."

"Of course, Domina," Ampyx replied, not looking in the least ruffled. "Is there anything else?"

"Is that not enough?" Lara teased him with a smile.

"Indeed, Domina, it is," Ampyx returned. Then he bowed and left her.

Lara left the council chamber, and walked out into one of the castle's many gardens. Like most of them it hung over the fjord below. Putting her hands flat on the top of the wall, she looked out over the green cliffs, and breathed deep. *I am doing my best, Magnus,* Lara said silently. *Soon it will be a year since that terrible accident. Taj will be formally instated as Dominus on the anniversary of that first day. I miss you, Magnus, but if you were here I know you would be arguing with me about what is happening.*

Lara smiled at that thought. She would have had to take time and energy explaining it all to him, and then he would have argued some more to make certain she understood that the decision was his alone to make. He had come a great distance in his thinking after she had married him, but hopefully their son would see things with a broader eye, understanding that Terah was no longer an isolated kingdom that could hide from evil. Having two companions who were not Terahn but New Outlanders was a good start. And sooner than later he would have to learn the true nature of Hetar. Jonah's son, Egon, was just about Taj's age. Perhaps when this was all over she would invite the boy to live in Terah for a year. Now that Taj was Dominus he could hardly leave Terah to spend time in Hetar. *I am doing my best, Magnus,* Lara repeated. A single tear slipped down her cheek. He had been a good husband.

Several days later Lady Persis appeared at the castle. She was, Lara noted, becoming frailer by the day, but her mind was still sharp. "Have you invited Zagiri to come to her brother's coronation?" she wanted to know.

"I doubt her husband will allow her to come," Lara answered, "but she has been included in the invitation I will personally carry to Hetar."

Persis nodded, satisfied. "My grandson's coronation robes?" she queried.

"No one has spoken to me about them," Lara replied, and then she added, "Would you help me with them, Persis?"

Magnus Hauk's mother smiled. "It will be my privilege, Domina. These garments, like the ceremony, are simple. He will wear a brocaded all-white silk robe. Nothing more. I have the robe his father wore those many years ago. It can be altered to fit Taj. Would you consider that suitable? Or would you prefer something new?"

"Nay! How wonderful that you kept Magnus's coronation clothing. Taj will be so proud, Persis," Lara exclaimed, and impulsively she hugged her mother-in-law.

The old lady's eyes filled with tears, which she brushed away. "I will do the alterations myself," she said. "My eyes are still good."

"And Magnus will, in a sense, be with his son on that day," Lara remarked. "Thank you, Persis. Thank you! Let me send for your grandson that you may tell him yourself." And then in her head she heard Kaliq calling to her. She hurried from the chamber, and, seeing a serving woman, sent her to bring the Dominus to his grandmother. Then Lara went to her privy chamber to find the prince awaiting her.

"The situation grows worse in Hetar," Kaliq said.

"My son's coronation is in another ten days," Lara replied. "But I will go tonight when all here are sleeping. It will be morning in Hetar. Tell me now what is happening."

"There have been riots in the streets," Kaliq began.

Lara gasped. It was not like Hetarians to riot. Once in the days of the Emperor Gaius Prospero the women of Hetar had gathered before his palace protesting for their individual rights, but it had not been violent.

"The Lord High Ruler was so astounded by what happened he could not make a decision what to do," Kaliq continued. "A group of magnates hired several large groups of Mercenaries, who attacked the crowds. There were deaths."

"Why would the people become so violent? Have they not been fed by the Hierarch?" Lara asked.

"It is rumored that the Hierarch is directing chosen minions among the people to help bring the government down. Under normal circumstances I might agree, but not at this time. Not while the Darkling controls Cam."

"Is my daughter safe?" Lara asked.

"I have instructed Lothair to remove her immediately if this intrudes into the Golden District. He will take her to Shunnar for safety's sake," Kaliq said. "Lara, our time is growing short. You must go to Hetar."

She nodded. "The Dominus and his council know I

must leave, but I must be here when Taj is coronated. It would seem extremely odd if I were not here."

"Aye," Kaliq agreed. "We cannot allow *anyone,* particulary Ciarda, to wonder about your absence from this important day."

"Let me tell Taj I am going. I don't want to just disappear," Lara said.

"I will wait for you," Kaliq replied.

Lara hurried back to her own apartments, where she found her son sitting with his grandmother. She smiled at them both, saying, "Taj, remember that short journey I said I must make in conjunction with your coronation? I think I shall go today."

"What is this?" Lady Persis wanted to know.

Lara laughed gaily. "Now, Persis, it is a surprise for Taj, and you know how bad you are at keeping secrets from your grandchildren. They can always manage to wheedle them from you. But Taj does need to know that I will be away for a few days." She smiled at the pair seated together on the pillowed couch.

"Of course, Mother," the boy said, smiling back at her with a look of complete understanding in his turquoise-blue eyes. "I cannot wait to learn what it is you have done. It will be wonderful, I have not a doubt." He chuckled.

"Obey your tutors, and do try not to get into too much trouble with Gare and Sinon," Lara responded indulgently. She turned to her mother-in-law. "You know how boys are, Persis. But since I must go, let me return you to your own hall now. I am so glad that you came, and I know Taj is, too. You did thank your grandmother, didn't you, my son? It is a wonderful thing she is doing for you."

Taj stood up, drawing his grandmother up with him. He kissed the old woman on both of her withered cheeks. "You are the best grandmother any boy could have," he told her. "And I do thank you once again for your thoughtfulness."

And before Lady Persis could offer to remain with her grandson, or ask more questions that could not be answered, Lara kissed her and, silently invoking the return spell, sent her mother-in-law back to her own home, which was several miles distant from the castle. Then she turned to Taj. "I must go. Kaliq has come, and brings word that the situation in Hetar grows worse by the minute. I will be back in time for your coronation."

"Bring Zagiri with you, Mother," Taj said. "I command it of you."

"Do you, my lord Dominus?" Lara responded. Then she smiled at him. "If it is possible I will bring her," she heard herself promise. She kissed her son's cheek, and hurried from her apartments back through the castle halls to her little privy chamber.

"Are you ready?" Kaliq asked.

"But a moment," Lara said, opening a drawer in a table and drawing out the official invitation to the Terahn coronation. "For the Lord High Ruler and his wife," she told Kaliq. "Now I am ready."

He enveloped them in his white cloak, murmuring as he did so, *We will be invisible when I uncloak us. I thought it wiser until we see with our own eyes what is happening, my love.* He opened his cape now.

Where are we? Lara asked him. Then, looking about more carefully, she said, *This was once Gaius Prospero's privy chamber.*

It is now Jonah's, Kaliq answered her. *But wait, someone comes.*

The door to the room opened and a man stepped inside. He was tall and slender with a long, scholarly face that was neither young nor old. His close-cropped dark hair was lightly sprinkled with silver. He was not a handsome man, but neither would he be considered homely.

Reveal me to him, Kaliq. You will know when I wish to not be seen again.

The prince touched Lara's shoulder, and she became visible to the Lord High Ruler of Hetar, who was now seated at his desk.

Jonah blinked once, then again as if trying to clear his sight.

"You are not imagining it, my lord Jonah," Lara said. "I am here." She drew the elegant vellum invitation from her robe and handed it to him. "You are invited to the formal coronation of my son Taj, Dominus of Terah, in eight days' time. You may bring your wife if you choose."

"You did not come to just deliver an invitation,"

Jonah responded. "You know what is happening here. Your kind know everything."

Lara smiled a wicked smile. "Aye, my lord, we do. Do not think you have gotten an advantage over me, over Terah, by stealing Zagiri and marrying her. You have not. If you wish to save your worthless hide, *my lord,* you will have to do as we say. And it will pain you greatly, I am certain."

"You can defeat and destroy the Hierarch?" Jonah leaned across the large table that served him as a desk. "*How?* He preaches to the people about returning Hetar to its days of glory, but he does not say how he will do it."

"Nay, he does not," Lara replied. "Because no kingdom flourishes by returning to the past. You can only flourish by moving forward, my lord Jonah. This man who calls himself the Hierarch is being controlled by a Darkling named Ciarda. Aye! I see from the look upon your face that you know of whom I speak. It was she who aided you in stealing my daughter from Terah. And since then you have had no contact with her, have you?"

Jonah looked abashed.

"Ciarda is a daughter of Kol, the Twilight Lord. She loves her father, and wishes to complete his plans to bring the darkness to our worlds."

"But we defeated him!" Jonah said.

"Aye, we did, but one defeat cannot keep the darkness from attempting to encompass us again. You are no fool. You know that. This is a never-ending battle,"

Lara said. "Your late wife descended from a powerful sorcerer named Usi. Her ancestress, Ulla, was his concubine, and bore him a daughter here in Hetar. His other concubine, Jorunn, bore him a son who became the Twilight Lord, and from whom all subsequent Twilight Lords descend. In each generation of Ulla's descendants there is but one female able to touch the darkness should it be necessary. The Lady Vilia was the one in her generation, which is why Ciarda could reach out to her.

"It was the Darkling who put your son's life in danger, and then bargained with Vilia for his life. It was the Darkling who convinced her to choose Zagiri for your next wife. The darkness does not just want Hetar. It wants Terah, too. By attempting to set us against one another she weakens us both."

"But would Terah not have aided us in our time of troubles?" Jonah asked.

"Terah wishes no congress with Hetar, and never has. I am beginning to realize, however, that perhaps that can no longer be possible. Even if you had not married Zagiri against my will. It seems our worlds are becoming bound together, my lord Jonah."

His black eyes narrowed a moment, and Lara almost laughed to see him considering the possibilities in her words.

"Whatever is to be, my lord, it cannot be. Our only goal together at this time is to defeat the powers of darkness once again. To this end the magic world will aid you," Lara told him. "But in exchange for our help you must alter your ways."

"What do you want of us?" he asked her.

"Hetar does need to return to its traditions, but not in the same way as this Hierarch suggests. He would have you go back to the past. Your traditions need to be made more modern to suit the time in which you live. Hetar always gave those who worked hard the opportunity to improve themselves. Yet today your people have no such opportunities. You have become a society of the wealthy magnates and the poor. Everything has stood still in Hetar. This must change," Lara told him.

"The Hierarch wants women to take a more traditional and subservient position in society again," Jonah said. "He wants them off the High Council."

"Ah, of course. He would tempt the magnates with the offer of more wealth, he would present the women as a scapegoat for those who seek someone to blame, but you cannot allow that to happen, my lord. You have always been a man of action, Jonah of Hetar, yet suddenly you demur to make decisions for fear of offending one voting block or another, of losing your position," Lara said. "You must show Hetar that you are a strong leader again if you are to prevail."

"He has the masses in the palm of his hand, Domina," Jonah said.

"And many of those people are female," Lara pointed out. "Refuse to disenfranchise the women. Say Hetar needs their aid to return to its greatness. Be they wives or Pleasure Women, Hetar needs their best efforts, and if females are considered unequal then why would they give their best? Say Hetarian women are entitled to help fashion the future of Hetar every bit as much as the men are. Men have ruled Hetar for centuries, and look where it has gotten you. There are other things you can do that I know will go against your need for profit, but for now profit must be sacrificed if you are to save Hetar. You must see laws passed preventing profiteering from all this misery. You must fix prices of staples such as wheat, rice, bread. You must keep your promise to repair the hovels in The Quarter. Put your Mercenaries to work doing that, and to rebuilding the roads and bridges leading to the other provinces. In exchange for their services see that their hovels are given to them, to their families to own. And it is past time the Crusader Knights rebuilt their own Garden District. Zagiri wrote her sister that it is very shabby. And announce that in a year's time they will again hold a tournament to pick new candidates for their ranks. Retire the eldest of them and send them to good homes in the Outlands. Hetar needs hope. It has become stagnant."

"And the magic kingdoms will stand behind me in these efforts?" Jonah asked her. "What you are suggesting will cost a small fortune."

"You and the magnates have the coin to spare. And what of the taxes you have collected? I will assume the government has its monies in a safe place. As for the magic world, my lord Jonah, you cannot say we are behind you lest you alert the Darkling and her minions," Lara told him. "She must not know that you are fighting her efforts."

"Do you know who the Hierarch is, Domina?" Jonah asked her.

"We know," she said, "but until the Darkling is defeated no one would believe you if you told them. We will marshall our efforts against the darkness. You must gird your loins, and fight for Hetar's survival. If you do not, prepare to die, and my daughter with you, Jonah of Hetar."

"You must keep Zagiri safe!" he said, and Lara suddenly saw the fear in his face for his young wife.

Her tone toward him softened. "I had heard it said that you love her."

Jonah's normally cold black eyes were suddenly warm. He said nothing, but he nodded.

"Then do what you must to prevent the darkness from spreading, my lord," she told him. "My daughter linked her fate with yours, and so it shall be to the end." And then she disappeared before his very eyes.

"Domina!" he cried after whirling about as if he might see her in another part of the room, but Lara was gone from his sight.

'Twas well done, my love, Kaliq said.

If he has the courage to act. I have never really known if he was cowardly or brave. Clever, aye! Diabolically so. He outplayed Gaius Prospero and claimed his throne, but has he the fortitude to go against the magnates? Does he have the nerve to stand up to the Hierarch? He will need allies. Let us go and see the Lady Gillian, my lord Kaliq. If she knows we are helping she will gather the strongest of her kind, and they will marshal the women of Hetar, most of whom will not want to return to the good old days.

Prince Kaliq wrapped them once again in the folds of his cloak, and when he threw back the white silk they found themselves in the privy chamber of the former Headmistress of the Pleasure Guilds.

Lady Gillian looked up, surprised, from a tapestry she was weaving. "Lara!" She smiled a welcoming smile, and then her eyes went to Prince Kaliq. Rising, she performed a deep curtsey. "My lord, and welcome to my home."

Kaliq took both of Gillian's hands in his own, kissing them respectfully. "I thank you, lady. To my delight the stories of your beauty have hardly done you justice."

Lady Gillian laughed softly, and bowed her head in acknowledgment. "And you, my lord Prince."

It was rare that Kaliq conversed with mortals, but Lara was always amazed by the ease he displayed when he did. She coughed softly. "We are going to need your aid, my lady Gillian," she said.

"Of course," Gillian answered, and with a graceful gesture invited them to sit. "May I call for refreshment?" she asked.

"Best not to," Kaliq answered. "We prefer that our presence in Hetar be discreet."

"How may I help you, then?" Gillian queried them.

"This Hierarch is more than likely a fraud," Kaliq began. "He is being controlled by a Darkling who wishes to bring Hetar into the darkness as did her father, Kol. I will let Lara explain the particulars to you."

Lara began to speak, explaining the history behind Ciarda, her desire to complete what her father had not, how she had apparently chosen this young mortal man to be her cat's paw. "He has no powers to create these miracles he is believed to perform. Invisible beside him, it is she who makes the magic the people see," Lara explained. "If he is allowed to overthrow the Lord High Ruler this Hierarch will bring the darkness upon Hetar. As much as I despise Jonah and his ilk, the Hierarch must not be allowed to do this, Gillian."

Then Lara went on to explain her visit to Jonah and the reforms she had suggested he would have to make if he was to hold on to his throne. "We will soon learn if his ambition or his greed is the greater," she said. "Wealth is easier to recoup than power, however, and I think Jonah understands that."

Lady Gillian nodded her agreement. "What can I do?" she said.

"You will have to gather the important women together quickly so they may each speak with other women in The City. When Jonah says that he will defend the rights of women to be heard and participate we need a vocal majority to back him. This will throw off the Darkling, who expects the women to capitulate easily. Why should the Pleasure Houses be returned to the ownership of men only? Or the new houses that cater to women be closed down? The Pleasure Guild pays a great deal of taxes, and that is due to the women who own the houses and those who work in them. You do not cheat the council as the men used to do when they owned these lucrative businesses."

"But the taxes have not been used as they should have been," Gillian pointed out.

"I suspect they will be in the future," Lara said dryly.

"How can you be certain of this?" Gillian wanted to know.

"Because the women on the council are going to see to it," Lara told her. "The council is made up of twenty members, with the Lord High Ruler voting only to break a tie. Only five are women. And men like the Forest Lords and the Midlanders are unlikely to ever see women as anything but subservient. But they are only four. There are eleven other votes you can work to sway. You won't get them all, of course, but you need only six. My half brother is a reasonable man. Make a point of speaking with the wives of the representatives from the Mercenaries and the Crusader Knights. These women can influence their husbands on matters that concern their families and their children. And my daughter can sway her husband."

"Hetar's *First Lady* is interested only in her own enjoyments," Gillian said candidly. "Her lust for pleasures is said to be prodigious and inexhaustible. They say it is her faerie blood run wild. Jonah is the envy of his companions, and is so jealous of her that he will only share her with their household sex slaves. They possess three. Two males and a female. Once I would not permit you to be sold into one of The City's Pleasure Houses because your beauty would have destroyed us all. It is fortunate that your daughter is not a Pleasure Woman, though there are some who wish she could be."

"Unlike other girls in Terah who at fourteen are permitted to take lovers, Zagiri never wanted a lover," Lara said. "When her pent-up desires are fulfilled she will be less aggressive in her needs. Speak to her, Gillian. Ask her to use her influence with her husband for the betterment of Hetar."

"Why will you not speak with her?" the retired Pleasure Mistress asked.

"My own anger at what happened has still not cooled," Lara admitted frankly.

"Yet you spoke to Jonah," Lady Gillian observed.

"I had no choice in that matter," Lara said. "I do where Zagiri is concerned. If I speak with her, and she angers me as she can so easily do, then the breach between us widens. I don't want that. In time I will overcome my reluctance, and my repulsion."

"You are repelled? Why?" Lady Gillian asked.

"Because of her choice of a husband. My beautiful young daughter has shackled herself to a man who could be her father. He will be old when she is still young!" Lara cried. "As a faerie woman I know the pain you can suffer watching your mortal lover grow older. That is why faeries never linger long with their mortal partners. Yet my mortal daughter has picked an all-too-mortal man to love who is many years her senior."

"I cannot convince Lara that this is Zagiri's fate," Prince Kaliq said softly.

"What kind of a fate is that for my beautiful child?" Lara said angrily.

"Her fate," Kaliq said in a stern voice. "Not what you would wish for her, my love, for rarely does what you desire for your children come to pass. Each mortal born has its own fate to follow."

"I will speak with your daughter, Lara," Lady Gillian said sympathetically. She understood, although she had never borne a child herself. But she had mothered many of the young women in her Pleasure House, nurtured them, taught them, wept with them and been proud of their accomplishments and good fortune when it had occurred.

"Thank you," Lara replied. She was unhappy with how she felt regarding Zagiri. It was a more mortal feeling than a faerie one. Perhaps because Zagiri had been born of the love she and Magnus Hauk had shared, and Magnus was now dead. Had he lived, would this union between Zagiri and Jonah have taken place?

"We are through here," Kaliq said quietly.

Lara and Lady Gillian embraced.

"Call to me if you need me," Lara told her. "You know that I will come."

"I will," Gillian said, smiling as the two magic folk disappeared before her eyes.

Where are we going now? Lara asked Kaliq as she pressed against him for warmth. She was suddenly feeling chilled.

Into the streets of The City, but we shall not be visible to any, he answered. *I think we need to know the mood of the people.*

And, flinging back his cloak, they were in the main market square of The City. Lara was appalled by how shabby it had become. There were few goods, and what was there was expensive. Once the main market had had a large table beneath an awning where day-old goods were placed for the poor to come and take. It was, Lara noted, no longer there. Her eye went to a small boy who was creeping up unnoticed upon a baker's kiosk. She watched as he waited patiently for the baker to be occupied elsewhere, and then, with lightning speed, the boy grabbed a loaf of bread just as the baker turned to see him. The baker's face grew red with his fury.

"Thief!" he shouted. "Thief! Catch him! Thief! Thief!"

The boy dodged in and out of the few shoppers, evading grasping hands that reached out to stop him. Lara raised a hand, pointed her finger and suddenly a clear path opened up. The boy dashed from the main market and disappeared into the side streets that surrounded it.

Come! Lara called to Kaliq. *You wanted to gauge*

the mood of the people? Let us see where our little thief goes.

They moved quickly after the boy, noting that once he was certain the chase had been given up, he moved with sure steps, obviously knowing exactly where he was going. They followed, and Lara suddenly realized where the boy's steps were leading them.

He is headed for The Quarter, where I was raised, she told Kaliq.

And sure enough the boy went past the guard-house entrance where, Lara noticed, no guard sat any longer. They moved through several narrow streets until finally the boy came to a small hovel and slipped in. The magic couple followed him silently. Inside, they could see the thatched roof was damaged; there was no fire in the hearth. Two children even smaller than the little thief huddled in a bed where a woman lay nursing an infant. And then Lara's eye was drawn to a corner by the cold hearth where a man lay supine. Walking over, she bent, sniffed and shook her head.

He is drunk on Razi, Lara said quietly to Kaliq. *No fire in the hearth to keep his wife and children warm, but he finds the coin for Razi.*

They watched now as the young thief placed the bread upon a table, and, fetching up a knife, cut four small slices. He then wrapped the remainder of the loaf in a piece of cloth, and put it in the hearth oven for safe-keeping from the rats. Then he handed his mother and siblings their bread while finally sitting down on a stool to slowly eat his.

"You stole it," the woman said wearily.

The boy nodded. "What else could I do? He's been drunk for two days, and we need to eat. You cannot feed the infant without food yourself."

"What if you had been caught?" the woman said despairingly. "There is no mercy for thieves, my son."

"I wasn't caught," he answered her stubbornly.

"But you might have been!" the mother cried. "What would I do without you?"

"Well, we have bread for a few days," the boy said. "I won't have to steal again for a little while."

"You must have faith in the Hierarch," the woman said.

"What can the Hierarch do for folk like us?" the boy demanded.

"He will make it all right again if we but have faith," she told him.

"We will starve before that happens," the boy said dryly.

"Has he not opened the warehouses for us?" she said.

"And each of us was given a small share of grain, which is now gone, but the bakers seem to have enough wheat to make bread to sell at an exorbitant price. Why does the Hierarch not prevent them from profiteering while we starve?"

"He will! He will!" the mother insisted. "Did the prophecy not tell us that in our time of trial the Hierarch would come and save us? He is in The City now, my son. Soon he will bring Hetar back to the way it once was, and all will be well for us."

"In the meantime we must eat," the boy said, "so I must steal, and you must pray to the Celestial Actuary that I not be caught."

We have heard enough, Lara said. She stood next to the boy at his seat and placed her hand just above his head. *Steal only when you must. Your speed will leave all in the dust.* Lara wove the small protection spell about the boy.

Your heart is so good, Kaliq told her.

He is not a thief by nature. He will be a fine man one day. He cannot be any older than nine or ten, yet he accepts the responsibility of his mother and siblings. As you can see, the father is lost to Razi because there is no work for him. Lara sighed.

The mother despite all believes in the Hierarch, Kaliq noted as they walked back out into the streets of The Quarter again. *Let us look farther, and see what we can hear, and learn, from these poor souls.*

They walked about listening, hearing the same thing over and over again. The Hierarch would make it all right again for them. They waited eagerly for the miracle, and blamed the magnates and the government for their troubles. Yet amid all the talk neither Lara nor Kaliq heard any in The Quarter suggest a solution to their problems or say how the Hierarch would bring about change. The Hetar that had once been had always supplied the answers, and the people expected it to be that way again. They had all had a place, and knew that place. Now no one knew where they belonged, or what to do.

I never before realized that few Hetarians think for themselves. They want everything supplied for them. Tell them what to do, where their place in life is, and they thrive. Take away their place, and they collapse, Lara said.

Hetar was an orderly society, and now that the order has been disturbed it has caused chaos, Kaliq said to her. *There are those who think, my love.*

But not enough!

Kaliq laughed, replying, *In every society there are those who do not consider beyond the end of their nose, but you are correct. Too many in Hetar have come to accept things as they have always been. And now the Hierarch would bring them back to that, and it appears to many to be the answer to their problems.*

But it isn't, Kaliq! Hetar needs to move forward.

It won't until its problems are solved, but this time they must be solved in a different way while meeting the needs of its citizens. It will not be an easy transition, my love. We will have to struggle mightily to make these mortals see the light, and protect them from the darkness that will encompass them in their desperation.

Then I must befriend Cam. If he has not been totally lost to Ciarda, perhaps I can help him to return into the light. I realize now that the darkness has sur-

rounded him since his childhood. His parents were so filled with envy and wickedness he was probably tainted in his mother's womb. He claims to love Anoush, Kaliq. If he truly does then perhaps that love will help him to escape the clutches of the Darkling.

Be careful, Lara, Kaliq warned her. *Ciarda is very determined.*

Aye, she is, Lara agreed with him, *but you and I both know that love is stronger than any other force in any of the worlds.* She stood on her toes and kissed his cheek. Then she was gone from his side.

The Shadow Prince smiled his enigmatic smile. Lara was a force to be reckoned with. As dangerous as Ciarda was, she had no idea of how powerful his beautiful faerie woman was. Kaliq chuckled, and returned himself to his desert palace even as Lara, having observed Cam in his simple quarters and seeing him alone, appeared before the startled young man's eyes.

"Aunt!" he exclaimed, startled, his blue eyes wary.

"Why?" Lara asked him quietly.

"Why? I do not understand you, Aunt."

"Why do you allow the Darkling to control you? You are an Outlander, and the Hetarians will never accept an Outlander as their Hierarch. If indeed there really is a Hierarch, Cam. Do you truly wish to have power over Hetar? But of course, you really wouldn't have any power but that which she allows you to have," Lara taunted him gently, and then she smiled at him. "Your parents were ambitious, but until your father made the error in judgment of listening to your mother, who, by the way, was in the pay of Hetar, I never thought Adon stupid."

"Do you not consider it justice that an Outlander is called Hetar's Hierarch? How long have they scorned us? And we would still be in our ancient homeland had they not invaded it and sought to enslave us," Cam said bitterly.

"But the clan families were saved by the Shadow Princes, and by me," Lara reminded him. "We who stand in the light brought you to safety in a beautiful new land, Cam. Forgive me, Nephew! Forgive me for my anger toward an innocent child. You belong in the light, not in the darkness."

He looked very surprised by her request for his forgiveness. *"Forgive you?"* he said slowly. "You did me no real harm, Aunt. Taking me from my grandmother probably saved me. Sholeh was good to me. Aye, you are forgiven." Amazing, he thought. The faerie woman had a mortal conscience. Now what could he gain from her? He was no fool, and he knew that Ciarda was using him, but the temptation to play the great man had been too much for him to resist. Now, however, Cam was beginning to realize that it was a dangerous game he played. Disappoint Ciarda, and he could find his life at an end. Still, the power she had put into his hands was too delicious to relinquish. Yet if the faerie woman who was his aunt could offer him something better, would he not take it? Of course he would. Cam smiled. "There is always a battle between the light and the dark, Aunt," he said.

"But there must always be balance," Lara responded. "If one overwhelms the other, Cam, then chaos follows."

"Ciarda enjoys chaos," Cam murmured, "and I find it exciting, too, Aunt."

"Ciarda will ultimately fail. How great the cost to mortal Hetar is what we are now discussing," Lara said softly. "She has taken you as her lover, hasn't she? And before you she took one of the Twilight Lord's twin sons as a lover. Her own half brother, Cam. She wants everything her father wanted. The Dark Lands, Hetar and finally Terah. She will be stopped, and all who follow her will fall victim to her greed and her ambition."

"What can you offer me that she cannot?" he asked bluntly.

"Your life. A life with Anoush among your own Fiacre clan family," Lara said. "If you truly love my daughter that is the life you will choose, Cam."

"Does she still sleep?" he asked, and his cold blue eyes had suddenly warmed and become tender with emotion.

"She sleeps," Lara said, "and only when you return to the light, Cam, will she awaken. Anoush will never be part of *this*. And you are a fool to believe that your lover, Ciarda, will allow you to take a wife that you actually love. Mind you, she does not want your love, for she does not know how to love herself, but she does not want you giving it to anyone else," Lara told him. "You are her possession, and she does not share her possessions."

"Can you protect me from her wrath if I heed your pleas, Aunt?" he asked her.

"You can be protected," Lara told him.

"What would you have me do then?"

"Instead of seeking to overthrow the Lord High Ruler, become his wise counsel, and stand by his side to help him reform the system that has brought Hetar to its knees," Lara said to Cam. "Like you, Jonah is an ambitious man."

"And when Hetar stands strong again?" Cam asked her.

"You disappear even as you appeared," Lara told him. "You will, of course, return to the New Outlands to pick up your old life."

"Anoush will awaken, and you will give us your blessing and permit us to marry?" he asked.

Lara nodded.

"My wife has a house, and she has land and cattle. I must have a house in Rivalen, land and cattle, too," Cam said. "I have my pride, Aunt, and will not be just Anoush's husband. I would be my own man."

"Of course," Lara said. "It should be no other way."

"I must think on it," Cam said. "I must weigh and balance what is being offered to me by both you and by the Darkling."

"The Darkling cannot win, nor can she offer you

Anoush," Lara told him. "If you love her what is to think about, Nephew?"

"I must determine if I love her enough," he said, slowly, "to give up all this glory that the Darkling offers me. I think I do, but I would be certain. I should not like to have any regrets in the years to come, nor should I wish to harm Anoush in any way."

Lara felt her anger swelling. "If you must consider it, Cam, then you cannot love my daughter enough. That is unfortunate for you, and for Hetar. Farewell, Nephew! You have sealed your own fate, and chosen poorly!" And Lara disappeared in a cloud of dark green mist followed by a clap of thunder.

A minute later Ciarda entered the chamber in a cloud of red smoke. She sniffed, and sniffed again. "Who has been here?" she demanded of him.

Cam laughed. "My aunt," he said.

"What did she want?" Ciarda demanded.

"Perhaps I shall tell you, and perhaps I shall not," Cam said. "Now come to me, my Darkling. My lover's rod needs to sheath itself in your heat." He quickly pushed her against a wall of the chamber, and before she might refuse or protest, Cam had his way with her, driving deep and making her cry out with surprise as he took her pleasures from her. And all the while he used her Cam kept thinking, *She is not Anoush. She is not Anoush.* But he would eventually have Anoush. The Darkling would give her to him because she needed him, and Anoush would make him happy. If his aunt's magic was as strong as all said it was she surely would not have come to him for help. No, the Darkling had the power, and he had the Darkling.

CHAPTER FIFTEEN

ALFRIGG, CHANCELLOR OF the Dark Lands, was beside himself with frustration. He could get nothing accomplished, for his young masters quarreled constantly over everything. Women in particular. This was what the powers of light had wanted, of course, and they had certainly succeeded in causing confusion and disorder in the kingdom. If Kolgrim said aye, Kolbein said nay. The chancellor despaired, and when their half sister appeared to stir the pot, he found himself for the first time in his very long life close to committing violence. He always knew when she was about to appear, for the heavy scent of night-blooming lilies filled the air just prior to the cloud of scarlet mist in which Ciarda transported herself into his privy chamber.

"Alfrigg, dearest friend and Chancellor of the Dark Lands," she greeted him, smiling her beautiful, wicked smile. "Where are my brothers? I have need of them."

The old dwarf drew himself up, ignoring the pain in his back and shoulders. The heavy black and gold brocade robe he wore chafed at his bare legs above his old leather boots. His seal of office with its weighty chain felt heavy upon his chest. He glared at the Darkling as if she had interrupted something momentous. "Is it so important that I must disturb the Twilight Lords?" he asked her haughtily.

Ciarda shuddered. "How can you bear the plural on your tongue, my Chancellor?"

"I bear it because it is the reality," he replied irritably.

"If there were but one," she murmured. "Kolbein, perhaps?"

"If there were but one I would hope for Kolgrim," he told her bluntly. "Your lover is too hot-tempered and ignorant, Darkling. Think not that I do not know what you are about, for I do. Remember, it is forbidden by the Book of Rule that any citizen of this kingdom raise their hand in violence against a member of the royal family. Do you suggest disposing of one of your half brothers, Ciarda? And to what purpose? So you might rule through the other? Foolish female! Put such nonsense from your head."

"I can succeed where my father failed," Ciarda said heatedly.

Alfrigg laughed scornfully. "Lord Kol was the greatest of the Twilight Lords, and you are a mere Darkling girl. Do not dare to be so presumptuous in your boasting."

"You will see what I can do, old one. It is why I allow you to live, so that one day you will kneel at my feet to praise my accomplishments and beg my forgiveness," Ciarda said half-angrily. "If the tone of your apology is sincere I may permit you to live an even longer life than you already have. If it is not I will kill you myself. Now send for my half brothers, and have them meet me in the throne room." Whirling about, she stalked from his privy chamber.

If only she had been a male, the old chancellor thought to himself. She had strength and determination, and though she was only female, she was intelligent, he was forced to admit. If he could convince her to mate with Kolgrim, who was equally strong and intelligent, they would produce a son unlike any born into the lineage of the Twilight Lords. There had been matings between half siblings in the family before. But if Kolbein gave her a son it could be disastrous. The chancellor called a servant to him, and said, "Go and find both of the Twilight Lords. Tell them I request they join their half sister in the throne room where she awaits them."

The servant bowed and hurried off. Chancellor Alfrigg pressed a panel in the wall of his privy chamber. Stepping into the narrow corridor he made his way to the throne room, where he exited directly behind the throne. Ciarda was only now entering the chamber. He watched her as she paced back and forth waiting for her siblings. When they entered, Kolbein attempting to push ahead of Kolgrim, and failing, she went forward to greet them.

"Brothers!" She smiled at them.

"What do you need *him* for?" Kolbein demanded, glaring at Kolgrim.

"Half sister, you are as lovely as ever," Kolgrim

greeted Ciarda. "Forgive my brother's wretched manners. He had the misfortune to be raised by Wolfyn."

"You think your traitorous giants better?" Kolbein demanded. "Given the opportunity they bolted for Terah."

"But not until after they had done their duty by our father," Kolgrim said.

"Brothers," the Darkling said, "I need your help."

"I can do whatever you want done," Kolbein insisted. "Send him away!"

"How may we be of service to you, half sister?" Kolgrim asked.

"I need a place to hide the faerie woman's daughter. This castle is perfect, for it is unlikely she will consider the girl is here," Ciarda said.

"I thought that Lara's daughter was put into a deep sleep, and surrounded by a protection spell fashioned by the Shadow Prince. There is no way we could overcome that," Kolgrim said sensibly.

"The protection spell is no longer there," Ciarda said excitedly.

"How would you know that?" Kolgrim asked. He was fascinated by her.

"I have gone each night to stand by the girl's bedside. To see what I could do to unravel Prince Kaliq's spell. But I could not decipher it. I do not like to admit defeat and so I kept returning to that little chamber where the girl lay sleeping. And then today I went, and the spell was gone! It had vanished. I reached out to touch the girl, and my hand met with the fabric of her garment."

"If the spell is gone then why do you need us?" Kolgrim asked Ciarda.

"I would take this girl, and hide her here. She is the leverage I need against the Hierarch. If he knows I have her he will obey me again without question. But I need the power of our blood, and the power of three to make a spell strong enough to transport this girl from her chamber in that Fiacre village."

"We are only learning the magic that is ours," Kolbein said. "We can't help you."

"Aye, you can," Ciarda insisted. "I will weave the spell, brothers. The power lying dormant in you will, when we join hands, make the spell work."

"You are certain of that?" Kolgrim asked her.

"I am," Ciarda assured him.

"Your lover will not be pleased," Kolgrim said softly. "And he may not believe you, half sister."

"I will bring him here to prove to him that I hold his beloved as my captive," the Darkling replied.

"*Our* captive, half sister," Kolgrim said, and he smiled a toothy smile at her.

Ciarda nodded in agreement.

"When shall we do this thing?" Kolgrim asked her.

"Now! I do not know why that protection spell is gone, but if anyone else learns of it, rest assured the girl will be protected again, and quickly," the Darkling replied. "Where will you put her?"

Kolgrim laughed. "I think the chamber in which her mother resided once will serve."

"Which chamber is that?" Kolbein wanted to know.

"Why, the one in which we were conceived and born," Kolgrim said, and the trio laughed together. It was a sound that sent a chill down the chancellor's spine as he watched and listened from his hiding place behind the throne of the Twilight Lord.

IN THE KINGDOM of the Forest Faeries Ilona was at a loss, for her granddaughter had been hiding from her. "What is the matter with the girl?" the queen asked her consort.

"She is either being naughty and willful, a most faerielike trait," Thanos said wisely, "or she has done something she doesn't want us to know about."

"It is more than likely the latter," Ilona replied. "I cannot handle her, my lord. She is very intelligent, and very impatient to learn all there is to know about our kingdom, our ways, our magic. Whatever I teach her, or try to teach her, is never enough for Marzina. She wants more, and she wants it now. But my instincts tell me that we must find her sooner than later, and learn what it is she has done."

"Call our son, Cirillo, for she adores him. He will be able to lure her out of hiding if anyone can," Thanos advised his wife.

Cirillo was called from Belmair, where he now spent much of his time with his dragon lover, Nidhug. Knowing his parents were now resigned to his choice of a mate, he assumed it was some emergency that forced them to ask him to return to the Forest Kingdom. Ilona explained the difficulty of the missing Marzina, and Cirillo agreed to find his talented niece and learn what was troubling her.

Encasing himself in an invisibility spell, he began to search the forest. It took him several days, but then, deep within the woodlands by a small, still pool, he found Marzina. She was weeping bitterly. Uncloaking himself, he knelt and gathered the distraught girl into his arms. "Little one, little one, what is it that troubles you so greatly? Your grandparents are very worried over your absence."

Marzina looked up at him. Her eyes were red with much weeping. "Oh, Uncle! I have done a terrible thing. I will never be forgiven! *Never!*"

Cirillo struggled not to laugh. She was fourteen. She lived with her grandparents. What could she have done that was so awful? "Tell me," he said, not knowing what to expect, but assuming whatever trifle she confessed to could be quickly corrected.

"I have undone someone else's spell!" Marzina cried.

Cirillo was surprised. This was perhaps a bit more serious than he had anticipated. His faerie green eyes were curious. "Whose spell did you undo, Niece?"

"Prince Kaliq's!" Marzina wailed, and burst into fresh tears.

Cirillo was astounded. "You undid a spell that Kaliq

fashioned, Marzina? Are you quite certain? You put it back, of course."

"I couldn't!" Marzina howled louder. "I tried and I tried, but I just couldn't reweave his spell, Uncle! And now Anoush is gone, and it is all my fault!"

"What do you mean Anoush is gone?" Cirillo had been on Belmair for months and did not know the situation unfolding in Hetar.

Marzina explained the situation to him between sobs and gulps, concluding, "It was a protection spell, Uncle. By removing it I left my sister vulnerable to the forces of darkness, and now she is gone. Mother will never forgive me. I can't forgive me!"

"We must return to the castle at once," Cirillo said. He took the girl by the hand, and she tried to pull away. "Marzina!" His tone was sharp. "Aye, you have done a dreadful thing, Niece, but it cannot be corrected if we do not call your mother and Prince Kaliq to us at once. Perhaps it is not as bad as you think. They may have found the spell gone, and removed Anoush to a safer place. Come! Quickly! Unfold your wings, and let us hurry, for I suspect time is of the essence in this matter."

Wings Marzina had never known she possessed until she entered her grandmother's kingdom unfolded from her shoulder blades. They were lacy in texture, and gilt in color. Her uncle's were identical. Together the two quickly made their way through the summer green trees to reach the castle of the queen and her consort. Ilona hugged her granddaughter to her breast, relieved the girl was all right. But when she learned of what Marzina had done she was at first astounded, and then furious.

"You dared to meddle with another's spell?" Ilona demanded in a hard voice such as Marzina had never heard her use. It was the queen's voice.

"I just wanted to see how it was made, and if I could do it, too," Marzina muttered.

"What in the name of all the faerie worlds made you think you could replicate a spell fashioned by a Shadow Prince? You are a child, Marzina! A mere child, and you have shown me a great lack of courtesy by sneaking off to that Fiacre village and tampering with Prince Kaliq's spell. But worse, you say your sister is now gone? If she has been taken into the darkness you will have endangered her very life!"

Marzina began to weep again.

"My dear," Thanos said, but Ilona cut him off.

"Nay, my lord, there is no softening this misadventure. We must call Lara and the prince to us immediately!" And she did.

Prince Kaliq appeared first, followed by Lara.

Seeing the look on her mother's face, and noting that her youngest child was verging on hysteria, Lara demanded to know, "What has happened, Mother?"

"Your overly precocious daughter may have put Anoush's life in danger," Ilona said. And she glared angrily at Marzina.

"She did not mean to, my dear," Thanos said quickly,

"but the damage is done, I fear, and now you two must correct it."

"What has happened?" Prince Kaliq asked.

"The brat undid your protection spell," Ilona said. "And, of course, she could not reweave it back. When she went back to try to correct the damage she had done Anoush was gone. So what did this child do? She hid from us in the forest. I had to call Cirillo from Belmair to find her. Only then did she confess her misdeeds."

"Marzina!" Lara gasped, shocked.

The Shadow Prince's eyebrow had cocked with surprise when he learned what the young girl had done. "You undid my spell?" he said to the tearful Marzina.

She nodded. "I thought it easy until I tried to put it back together again, my lord," the girl confessed, shamefaced.

Kaliq laughed aloud. "Aye, it is complex in its fashioning, Marzina."

"I cannot have her with me any longer," Ilona said. "You must take her back to Terah, Lara. I am unable to control her. The wickedness is in her blood, I fear."

"Nonsense," the Shadow Prince quickly said. "She is no more naughty than Lara was at that age."

"At that age," Ilona began, and then she closed her mouth at a look from Lara.

"Of course I will take Marzina home, Mother. As much as she desires to study faerie magic she is obviously not mature enough yet to do so," Lara said quietly. "We will find Anoush and bring her home safely. I suspect whoever has her will not harm her. But, of course, it is imperative that we find her quickly."

"We will go to Shunnar," Kaliq said. "She should not go back to Terah quite yet, my love. Under the circumstances she is safer with us there."

"Thank you, Mother, for all you have done. And you as well, my lord Thanos," Lara said quietly. "Cirillo, come and see me soon." Then, taking her daughter's hand, she stepped beneath the Shadow Prince's cloak, and when he threw it back with a flourish they were in his desert palace.

The prince quickly called for refreshments to be brought to his garden escorting Lara and her daughter there. Sweet apricot Frine was brought, along with cheese and rounds of crisp flatbread. Kaliq poured a small goblet of Frine for Marzina, handing it to her along with a circle of flatbread and cheese. Lara helped herself, struggling to keep calm. If she frightened Marzina any further she might forget something important.

"Now, child," the prince said quietly, "tell me everything that happened when you returned to the chamber where Anoush had been sleeping."

"She was gone," Marzina said. "The bed upon which she lay, too, my lord."

"Did you notice anything else about the chamber?" he asked her.

Marzina's brow wrinkled as she tried to remember. "It was cold, my lord. Colder than it should have been." She paused. "And there was a smell."

"What kind of a smell?" he pressed her gently.

"Flowers," Marzina told him. "The scent was heavy and sweet like—" she thought "—like lilies. Night-blooming lilies!"

"The Darkling!" Lara exclaimed. "That is the fragrance that always surrounds her, Kaliq. How did she know that the spell was broken? She must have been trying to undo it herself, and kept coming to Anoush's bedside. I can but imagine her surprise when she discovered my daughter was hers for the taking. But where will she have secreted Anoush?"

"I want to help!" Marzina cried.

Lara turned a fierce eye on her youngest child. "Nay," she said. "You have not the skills and your interference in something you did not understand has put your sister in danger. You lack self-discipline, Marzina. You are so eager you will not take the time to learn, nor do you have the patience you need to learn properly. You have been given a gift, and when this is over you will be taught how to use it properly. But until then I forbid you from attempting magic of any kind."

Marzina's violet eyes grew stormy with rebellion. "You are just jealous," she said. "My powers will one day be greater than yours."

"Possibly they will," Lara answered. "But not unless you learn how to channel them properly."

"You will remain here at Shunnar for the interim," Prince Kaliq said in a quiet voice, "for you are in danger, too, my child. When this is over I will teach you

myself as I did your brother Dillon. You have the ability
to be a great sorceress, Marzina. But if you would learn
from my brothers and from me you must swear to me
you will obey your mother's dictates and eschew magic
for the time being." The Shadow Prince looked into the
young girl's face. "Can you promise me that, Marzina?"

"Oh, yes, my lord!" Marzina cried. "To learn from
you would be an honor!"

"Then when this battle is done you will return to
Terah for one year," the prince told the girl. "You will
live in the Temple of the Daughters of the Great Creator learning self-discipline from the High Priestess Kemina. If at the end of that time she can assure me that
you have learned your lessons well then I will take you
as a student, Marzina. But your return to Shunnar will
depend upon your learning patience and composure. If
there is no peace in your heart and soul then I cannot
teach you, for you will be unable to learn from me as
your mother once did."

"A whole year?" Marzina said. "Could it not be half
a year, my lord?"

"It will be a full year unless you arc unable to absorb
the lessons of the High Priestess. Then it will be longer,"
Prince Kaliq said firmly in a stern voice.

"I will learn, my lord," Marzina said.

"Excellent! Now, do I have your word that you will
practice no magic until you are once more allowed to
do so?" he asked her. "And it is I, not your mother, who
will make that decision, my child."

Marzina sighed a deep sigh. "You have my word, my lord," she promised him.

He smiled warmly at her. "Good." Then he clapped his hands, and a serving woman came into the garden. "Take the princess to her bedchamber, Cressida. You will care for her while she is here in Shunnar."

"Yes, my lord." The servant bowed. Then she turned to Marzina. "If you will come with me, my princess."

"Good night, Marzina," Prince Kaliq said.

"Good night, my lord. Good night, Mother," the girl said, and followed Cressida from the prince's private garden.

"It was good of you to offer to teach her," Lara said.

"Her skills are far beyond her grandmother's abilities, and those of the Forest Faeries," he answered. "That she managed to unravel my protection spell is quite amazing. Her blood is yours, and Kol's. She must learn how to control her great skills lest she become destructive. My brothers and I will teach Marzina, but a year with Kemina will help her, I think you will agree. I will keep her here until this new war is won. Now, however, we need to find out where Ciarda had taken Anoush."

"I will go to Cam. If the Darkling means to use my daughter to control him I will learn it. He may even know where Anoush is," Lara said.

"As we are certain it is Ciarda who has Anoush, I believe we can also be certain that she will keep your daughter safe. She would not have stolen her without reason, and her reason is to control her puppet, the Hierarch," the Shadow Prince said. "We will begin again on the morrow, my love."

"Nay, I must go now," Lara insisted.

"You need your rest," he scolded her.

"I need to ascertain my child is safe," Lara said.

"You need sleep first," Kaliq told her firmly, and, raising his hand, he put a sleep spell upon her even as, seeing it coming, she protested. He caught her up in his arms as she collapsed, and, carrying her through his garden, he brought her to her own chamber, laying her upon the bed. Kissing her brow, he whispered, "Sleep well, my love." Then he left her.

When Lara awoke it was just before dawn. Rising, she went to her bath, bathed and put on fresh clothing. A servant brought her yogurt, fresh fruit and hot tea made from the baby leaves of the Umbra trees, those same trees whose fruit produced red dye. The liquid she drank was a pale red-gold, and had its own faint sweetness to it. Lara sat quietly in the private garden off her bedchamber that separated her quarters from the prince's. The air around her was yet cool as the peach and gold clouds in the blue skies above her began to fade away with the rising sun. Kaliq, she had to admit, had been right. She had very much needed the sleep he had given her. Refreshed now, she was ready to face not just the day, but whatever else she needed to face.

When she had finished her meal Lara descended from the prince's palace into the great meadow of horses nestled between the cliffs where she knew she would find her friend the giant Og, who was the prince's horse-master. "Og," she called. "Where are you?" And then at the far end of the meadow she saw his red head. *"Og!"* she called as loudly as she was able to, and she waved to him.

He was not a large giant, but Og quickly covered the mile separating them in several great strides. "Lara!" He set his palm down, and she stepped into it. Og raised her up so they might converse face-to-face.

Leaning forward, Lara planted a kiss on Og's ruddy cheek.

He beamed at her, his light blue eyes crinkling with delight. "It is good to see you, Lara. How goes the battle between the light and the dark?"

"As always," she said, and then she brought him up to date. "My youngest daughter will be at Shunnar for a while. Will you befriend her?"

"I thought she was with your mother," Og said.

"She was until she did the unthinkable." And Lara explained what had happened.

"She undid the prince's spell?" He was amazed.

"Undoing it was the easy part for her. She got into difficulties because she could not reweave it back together," Lara replied.

Og could not help but chuckle. "What a minx the lass is," he said. "Reminds me of a certain someone not so long ago."

"I certainly never did anything like *that*," Lara said.

"She had no right to do what she did, and now I must begin again with the Hierarch because Anoush is gone."

"I will befriend the lass," Og promised. "It would appear she is amazingly talented as Dillon was. She will make you proud one day."

"She is so eager, Og. But she has been forbidden the use of magic until she gains self-discipline. Marzina is so anxious to be grown. Perhaps because she is the youngest of my children she feels a need to be taken seriously. But for now she needs to be diverted. Will you help her to find a horse?"

"Aye," he promised. "Some wild little thing that needs training. That will keep her busy while she is here. Especially if she can't use magic."

"Thank you, my old friend," Lara said. "Now I must be going, but you need not put me down. I'll just transport myself from your hand." And her words hadn't even died when she was gone.

Lara reappeared in Cam's privy chamber. He had fallen asleep as he sat at his worktable, his head upon his arms. She touched him gently. "Awaken, Nephew," she said softly, but as he tensed beneath her hand Lara knew he was now awake.

Cam raised his head. "What do you want?" he asked her.

"The Darkling has stolen Anoush away. Do you know where she is?" Her faerie green eyes looked directly at him.

"Nay," he answered. "She would not tell me. All she

would say was that she had Anoush now, and if I ever expected to make the faerie woman's daughter my bride I would obey her every command."

"Do you see now, Nephew, the evil of this creature? Or are you still not certain if your ambition is greater than your love for Anoush?" Lara said.

"Why can I not have the power and the woman I love?" he wanted to know.

"Because you are not worthy of both," Lara said candidly. "You are a mere mortal, Cam, for all of Ciarda's plans. Had she not chosen you to be her cat's paw you would be herding Sholeh's cattle in the summer meadows of the New Outlands now."

"And would Anoush be my wife?" he asked her.

"Perhaps," Lara said.

"And perhaps not," he responded.

"I have not lied to you," Lara told him.

"Nor I to you," Cam replied. "I am torn, yet whatever choice I make I would like it to be my choice and not one that is forced from me for expediency's sake."

"I find the fact you struggle with the choices before you oddly encouraging," Lara said to him. "In anger I said I should not return to your side, Nephew, but it would be easy for me to leave you to the darkness. However, I cannot do that. I have made a hard choice. Now you must make one."

"I love her," Cam admitted. "But I love the feeling that power gives me, too."

"Use this masquerade to help the people of Hetar,

Nephew," Lara encouraged him. "Go to the Lord High Ruler Jonah, and stand by his side. I will make the magic that you need if you do. And when this battle is over I will do as I previously promised you. The Darkling underestimates my powers, for she is young, ambitious and foolish."

"She will kill Anoush if I betray her, Aunt," Cam said, and his eyes were fearful.

"Think, Nephew! What did she say when she told you she had Anoush in her power? She had to have said something," Lara prompted him.

His brow furrowed as he sought to remember the conversation with Ciarda. Then Cam said, "She told me she had hidden your daughter in the one place you would never consider looking. She was almost gleeful as she told me."

"I will find Anoush," Lara said firmly. "For now, Cam, do nothing. If she gives you a task, do it so slowly that it takes forever to get it done."

He nodded. "But I cannot deny her forever, Aunt. The Darkling is no fool. If I demur too greatly she will suspect something."

"Then do what all men do when they seek to avoid an issue," Lara instructed him.

He cocked his head questioningly.

"Give her pleasures, Cam," Lara told him with a small smile, and then she was gone from him in her green mist, and it seemed he heard her tinkling laughter faintly in the air as she vanished.

He considered her words. Was it possible that she could find Anoush and retrieve her, bringing her to safety once more? He had been surprised that Ciarda had managed to gain possession of his love, especially given that she was protected by not only her mother, but a powerful Shadow Prince. He should have asked Lara about it.

He would ask Ciarda about it, although he suspected she would lie to him or evade his questions. If his aunt could aid him with her magic bolstering his persona as the Hierarch, and he actually helped Hetar's ruler, could he, having tasted power, be content to disappear into anonymity and return to the New Outlands? Could he be happy being just a propertied member of the Fiacre clan family? A man with a wife he loved, and children? Again there was no easy answer to his questions, and no help for him. It was he who must make the decision. Cam didn't know if he wasn't ready to make it, or if he simply couldn't make it.

When Ciarda appeared a short time afterward needing to take pleasures with him, he made certain that they were both well satisfied before the pillow talk that invariably followed their passions. The Darkling was never truly at ease, as if she feared to show a vulnerable side to her nature. Cam knew she relaxed a little if he brushed her long black hair, and so, taking up a brush, he began to do so.

"Anoush is safe?" he asked. "You are certain of it?"

"Of course she is safe," Ciarda said impatiently.

"I am amazed that you were able to destroy the spell put about her," Cam murmured.

Ciarda giggled. "It was not just my magic," she admitted to him. "And my half brothers aided me in spiriting her away. They now possess the Twilight Throne that was once our father's. In the Book of Rule, which contains our history, past, present and sometimes future, there are spells to be had. None of us individually has the real power. We are too young. We used the power of three to gain your Anoush. Together we are powerful."

"Powerful enough to break a spell cast by a Shadow Prince?" he queried her.

The Darkling cocked an eyebrow but neither confirmed nor denied his question. She just smiled mysteriously.

Cam could not help but wonder whether the power of three was stronger than the power of a Shadow Prince. It wasn't something with which he had a familiarity. When his aunt came again, and he was certain she would, he would ask her. He had to be very careful of the path he chose lest he be destroyed, for he stood haplessly between two forces of magic, and he wasn't certain which held the real power.

Lara had returned to her privy chamber in the Dominus's castle. The windowless chamber was quiet, and she was able to think without distraction. She considered carefully what Cam had told her. The Darkling had told her nephew that Anoush was hidden in the one place that Lara would not consider looking. Where was it? Where would she not consider looking? And then it came to her in a burst of certain clarity.

"No!" She heard herself say the word aloud.

You must go, Ethne, her crystal spirit guardian, said.

I cannot! Lara answered her in the same silent magic.

Would you leave your daughter in that *dark place?*

I barely escaped with my sanity and my soul last time, Lara cried. *Perhaps she is not there. I am surely mistaken.*

You cannot know for certain unless you go there yourself, Ethne said.

The Dark Lands. The castle of the Twilight Lord. Lara had spent many months a prisoner in that terrifying place. Memories of Kol assailed her, and she struggled to push them back. Kol had been handsome and he had been seductive. His rapacious appetite for pleasures had been legendary. He had stolen her memories and stolen her to be his mate. Lara shuddered. She remembered every moment of the time she had spent with him, even those minutes when she had no memory of who she was, and he had fabricated lies to make up for the loss.

And then Kaliq had gotten her memories restored, and Lara learned that everything that had happened had been carefully planned by those in the magic realm of light, including Kaliq and her own mother. Planned so that she would birth twin sons, causing chaos in a line of rulers who traditionally only birthed one male a generation. And it had all come about as they had planned it.

She was pregnant with her husband's son when the Twilight Lord had caught her upon the Dream Plain. He had taken the powers of a succubus, and he had violated Lara, planting his seed in her to grow along with Magnus Hauk's son so that when her time came, she birthed that boy, and she had birthed a daughter, Marzina. No one knew Marzina's true sire but Kaliq, Lara and Ilona. Kol had been imprisoned in a hidden place for a thousand years. And her life had once again moved in a straight line. *Until now.*

She couldn't go back. *She couldn't!* But if Anoush was imprisoned in the castle of the Twilight Lord as she once had been, Lara knew she would have to go back. She couldn't leave her oldest daughter helpless to... to... Lara gasped. What if they had awakened Anoush? What if Kolgrim and Kolbein had told her who they were? What if despite their blood tie they had violated Anoush? Kolbein thought nothing of taking pleasures with his Darkling half sister, Ciarda.

She had to know if Anoush was in the Dark Lands. And Lara knew that she could trust no one else to learn the truth of the matter but herself. She began to weep, and hated herself for the weakness. When the shock of what she must do had subsided, she bathed her face in a basin of lavender water that she conjured. Then she poured herself a cup of bobble-berry Frine. Finally she stood, and, going to a small cupboard, she drew out fresh clothing, rebraided her hair and stripped off her pale green silk robe.

She would wear the garments in which she had always felt the strongest. She donned an ivory silk shirt, tucking it into the soft cinnamon-colored leather pants she loved best. Next came a pair of silk and wool foot coverings, and the well-worn but comfortable brown leather boots that came to just over her knees. Lara wrapped a dark green sash about her waist. It contained several hidden pockets filled with herbs and special small stones. She tucked an ivory-handled dirk into a leather-lined knife case within the heavy green silk.

Andraste! To me! Lara called, and her famed sword appeared already settled within its leather sheath. Lara buckled the belted sheath about her chest so that Andraste might rest snugly against her back. The sword was already humming softly as Lara drew on her soft dark green leather gloves. It had been some time since she and Andraste had journeyed together.

Fear not, my child, Ethne said to her. *You journey to the Dark Lands, but the light surrounds and is within you. You are protected.*

Lara sat a moment, drawing a small piece of parchment from a drawer in her table. Picking up a quill, she scrawled a quick message to Kaliq. Then, calling a faerie-post messenger to her, she entrusted the tiny faerie with its delivery to Shunnar.

"At once, Domina!" her messenger said, and was gone from Lara's privy chamber in a flash of light.

Lara drew several long, calming breaths. And then she spoke aloud. *"Into the darkness I must go. Keep me*

*safe from harm and woe. Return me back when I would.
And let me do only good."* She felt herself being drawn
into a whirling black vortex where about her the winds
howled and blew icily. Lara bit her lip till she drew
blood to keep from screaming. The spinning slowed,
slowed, and finally stopped. And she was standing in
the throne room of Kol's castle. It was a place she had
never thought to see again. Lara shivered, but then iron
seemed to enter her veins. *I am faerie and I am stronger than anything here,* she thought.

"Why, Mother, how nice of you to pay us a visit."
She heard Kolgrim's familiar mocking voice, and Lara
turned to face him.

"But for the color of your hair you look just like your
father, standing there upon the steps to his throne," she
said to him as she walked toward him.

"Would you like to see my sister?" Kolgrim queried
her pleasantly.

"Where is she?" Lara asked him. Her heart had now
returned to a normal beat.

"We put her in your old room. The place our father
conceived us, and you bore us," Kolgrim said. And he
smiled at her.

"If you have harmed her in any way," Lara began.

Kolgrim held his hand up. "She sleeps," he said. "She
has no idea where she is."

Lara felt a rush of relief.

Seeing it upon her face, he laughed. "Is she so precious to you, then? Unlike us, of course. Did you love her father?"

"Her father is a great hero of his people. Your father was a villian who stole me from my husband, and begat you upon me," Lara responded.

"Yet faeries do not give children to those they hate," Kolgrim said.

"You do not know the whole tale?" She was surprised, but then why would anyone associated with the Dark Lands have told him? "Your father had the Munin steal my memories. He convinced me I was his wife, and had been ill. Kol could be very kind when he chose, and because he needed me to conceive his heir, he was indeed kind to me. Of course, when my memories were restored and I learned what had happened, I did what was required of me. I used my magic to make two of the one, thus bringing chaos to the Dark Lands," Lara told Kolgrim.

He nodded, and his dark gray eyes held an admiring light. "Perhaps it is from you I gained my cleverness," he said to her.

"There is nothing of me in you or your brother!" Lara replied.

"I have your golden hair, *Mother*," he murmured.

"I am taking Anoush back with me," Lara told him.

He shook his head. "I cannot allow you to do that," he said. "I'm afraid it would anger our Darkling sister greatly. Ciarda is particularly nasty when crossed."

"You cannot allow?" Lara burst out laughing. "You

have no real powers yet, and when your powers are eventually realized they will only be half of what they should be because there are two of you."

"We have taken our captive by using the power of three," Kolgrim told her. "There was a spell in the Book of Rule for it."

"There are few spells I cannot overcome," Lara said. "Listen to me, foolish boy. The Darkling uses both you and your brother for her own ends. She means to take the worlds into darkness, and rule it all from this castle. And she favors your brother over you, for she knows she can control him, but she cannot control you. Where is Kolbein now? Do you even know?"

"He is in the House of Women," Kolgrim replied.

"And where is the Darkling? Probably with her mortal lover, whom she will eventually kill when he is no longer of use to her. As she will kill you," Lara told him.

"She cannot kill me," Kolgrim said. "It is forbidden."

"Aye, it is, but why would that stop her?" Lara responded. "In this kingdom women are taught subservience. But Ciarda is not subservient. In this kingdom women do not rule. Yet Ciarda would rule not just the Dark Lands, but all the worlds, as well. And if she would do that, why would you think she would even hesitate to kill both you and your brother?" Lara smiled a wicked smile at him.

"The people of this kingdom would not tolerate a woman attempting to rule them," Kolgrim said.

"The people of Terah do not permit women sovereigns, either," Lara said, "and yet I rule in Terah even as Ciarda will rule in the Dark Lands. She will be a Shadow Queen for her son, and she will see he is too weak to overcome her."

"She has no son! And if she did he would have to be from the direct line of Jorunn and Usi to rule the Dark Lands," Kolgrim said. "I have never lain with her, nor will I ever lie with her."

"For now the Darkling is content to leave things as they are, for she has other matters concerning her," Lara told him bluntly. "But when she is ready it is Kolbein's son she will conceive, and she will have no hesitation in killing you and your brother when she chooses to do so and you are no longer of any use to her. Now take me to Anoush."

Kolgrim had grown oddly silent as he absorbed her words. Then he said, "Come!" and led Lara from the throne room through a familiar corridor to the beautiful apartments that had once been hers. There upon her bed lay Anoush, sleeping soundly and totally unaware of anything about her. "She looks like her sire, doesn't she?" he said, gazing down at the dark-haired girl.

Lara nodded. "Aye, she does."

"And she is my blood through you," he said.

"Aye, she is," Lara admitted.

"Ciarda is my blood, too, through our father," he remarked. "She says it was the power of three that allowed us to bring her here." He looked directly at Lara.

"Yes," Lara said. "The protective spell had already been accidentally broken."

"By whom?" Kolgrim asked, both fascinated and curious.

There was no point in lying or being mysterious, Lara decided. "My youngest daughter, who seems to have been born with a great talent for magic like her mother and eldest brother. She did not mean to do it, became frightened by what she had done and hid herself away. It was several days before she was found, and admitted to her error in judgment. By that time Ciarda had discovered the spell broken, and, using the power of three, was able to bring Anoush here. She could not have done it otherwise, for most of her powers are currently channeled into aiding the Hierarch."

Lara continued as Kolgrim eyed her thoughtfully.

"She needed Anoush, for, you see, the mortal she chose to serve as the Hierarch is in love with my child. As long as Ciarda holds Anoush captive, Kolgrim, the Hierarch will do her bidding. Without Anoush she has been left with little to control him, for the Hierarch is beginning to believe that perhaps he is really who they say he is, and that he actually has the power."

"He doesn't?" Kolgrim said.

Lara shook her head. "No man could be more mortal than Cam of the Fiacre. Without him, however, Ciarda cannot bring Hetar into the darkness, for she has invested much in him now. But why should you care about what this Darkling wants? Should you not be more concerned about your own kingdom? The one you share with your twin? The Dark Lands are but a means to an end for Ciarda. An end in which neither you nor your brother have any place. Will you allow her to steal your heritage, and defile its traditions? If you do then know that Kol would not be proud of you."

"Would he be proud of Ciarda?" Kolgrim asked Lara.

"He would be admiring of her, and amused by her, but he would never permit her to do what she is doing. He would give her to his personal guard for pleasures first," Lara said bluntly. "Then he would have killed her himself, for although she carries his blood she is but a female. It is the direct male line that rules in the Dark Lands."

"What am I to do with Kolbein, Mother? I cannot kill him," Kolgrim said.

"Unfortunately you cannot, according to your own Book of Rule," Lara agreed. "Let him be, for if women and wine are his pleasures, as long as he has as much of them as he wants you can keep him content." She turned away from Kolgrim briefly, and, holding her hands over the sleeping Anoush, she said in the silent language, *Return my child from whence you came. Never come this way again.* And immediately Anoush disappeared.

"I heard you!" Kolgrim cried excitedly.

She couldn't help but smile. "Then the magic is beginning to awaken fully in you, Kolgrim. Tell the Darkling when she returns that I will destroy her should she attempt to harm any of my children again. And warn her that she will not win."

"Would you include my brother and me in that august grouping?" he asked her, mockingly cocking a thick bushy black eyebrow, for though his hair was as golden as hers he had the heavy black eyebrows that his father had possessed.

Lara laughed. She could not help it. Eventually Kolgrim would personify all the darkness in the worlds, but for now he was merely a wicked boy. She considered if he might be saved as she would save Marzina, but then she shrugged in answer to his question. "I must go," she told him.

"If you had to choose, Mother, which one of us would you pick?" he asked her provocatively, and then watched as she disappeared before his eyes, leaving the unanswered question hanging heavily in the air.

CHAPTER SIXTEEN

LARA HAD TRANSPORTED the slumbering Anoush not back to her own house in the New Outlands, but rather to Prince Kaliq's desert palace. No one unwelcome by the Shadow Princes could penetrate into Shunnar. Anoush would be safe. Having seen to her eldest daughter's comfort, she went to find her youngest daughter. Looking out over the open marble porch colonnade down into the horse meadow, Lara saw her with Og. Marzina was sitting upon the giant's shoulder as he walked through the fields allowing the young girl to pick herself a horse. Satisfied, Lara turned away to find Kaliq behind her.

"Remember the first time you looked down into that meadow?" he asked her.

She smiled up at him. "Aye, I do. Your stallion was cutting mares from the herd with which to mate." Then she grew serious again. "I must go to Hetar, and see what I can do to embolden the Lord High Ruler to finally act, and to get our Hierarch to help him. Lady Gillian will have spoken with the women by now."

"Do you want me to come?" he asked her.

"Could I stop you?" She chuckled. "But you must let me be the one to control Cam. He is not yet quite certain that my powers are greater than the Darkling's. She has hinted that without you I would have no powers so you cannot appear by my side, Kaliq."

"Ciarda is young, and very full of herself," the prince said. "Because until now she has not been outside of the Dark Lands, her frame of reference is very small. She has not been educated, and consequently knows nothing of what has gone on before her, but she is dangerous because she is ambitious. What did you learn in the Dark Lands when you went to fetch Anoush?"

"I learned what I already knew. That Kolgrim is the more intelligent twin. That Kolbein spends his days and nights in the House of Women taking pleasures. The Wolfyn certainly raised him as one of their own. He seeks out only what delights him. I expect he will die sooner than later of his excesses. No one will stop him, or protect him from himself, Kaliq, and he is too stupid to see the error of what he does. Unless the Darkling interferes it is Kolgrim who will take his father's throne one day. We must keep her now from being impregnated by Kolbein."

"Among the other things we must keep her from doing," Kaliq teased Lara, and she laughed.

Then she asked him, "Do you know who Ciarda's mother was? Was she magic?"

"Kol's women were ordinary but for you," he replied. "His vanity was such that he wanted only pleasures, their admiration and their complete devotion from them. The only magic the Darkling has comes from her father, and giving her Hierarch the ability to create his miracles is pretty much the extent of her powers, although she might have a trick or two up her sleeve that we do not yet know about. I cannot help but admire her confidence in her abilities, but then as I have previously said she is young, and ignorant of the power of serious magic. Her ability to keep us from getting too close to her, however, still puzzles me, my love."

"Perhaps you should consult with the oldest of the Shadow Princes," Lara suggested.

"You think Cronan may have the answer to that conundrum?" Kaliq was intrigued by Lara's suggestion.

"No one else seems to," Lara gently pointed out. "Does he yet make his home in Belmair, my lord?"

Kaliq nodded. "I will go and visit with him," the Shadow Prince said.

"Then I will go to Hetar while you are gone," Lara said.

They both disappeared from Shunnar in the same minute as they spoke the words.

Kaliq tossed back his cloak to find himself in the tower where Cronan, the most ancient of the Shadow Princes, made his home. It was evening, and Cronan was dozing in a chair by his hearth. Outside, a persistent rain poured down. Kaliq looked at the old one, wondering if he should look like that one day, and if he would survive as long as Cronan. Walking across the small chamber, Kaliq gently shook Cronan awake.

The bright blue eyes opened, and lit with surprise.

"Kaliq!" Cronan sat up. "What brings you to visit me, and so late at night, too?"

"It is not late night in Shunnar," Kaliq reminded Cronan, "but I apologize for not considering the time here. I very much need the benefit of your wisdom." And then he went on to report to the ancient Shadow Prince all the news from Hetar. He concluded by telling Cronan of Ciarda. "She confounds us, for though her personal powers are small she is still able to keep us from getting close to her. She seems to sense when we are near, and is able to block her thoughts from us. We cannot fathom how she can do this."

Cronan did not hesitate. "She is being helped by someone," he said logically.

"But who? Her brothers' powers are only beginning to exhibit themselves, and even using the power of three she could not keep herself from us all the time as she is doing. Who has powers strong enough to aid the Darkling?"

"Her father, of course," Cronan said.

"But we imprisoned Kol, and made it impossible for him to communicate with anyone," Kaliq said. "He is blinded, chained and his vocal cords frozen. He lies in the deepest, darkest part of Kolbyr, his castle, and even the old dwarf who serves as his chancellor does not know where he is, or that he even still exists. How can he have helped his daughter to shield herself from us?"

"Kaliq, Kaliq," the ancient Shadow Prince said. "You

have forgotten the one variable that cannot be overcome by even the strongest magic. Love."

"Love? Kol doesn't know the meaning of the word," Kaliq said angrily.

"But Ciarda does love her father with her entire being," Cronan reminded his companion. "And I am quite certain that that love has managed to allow Kol to aid her in this small way. You have frozen his vocal cords, but not his mind-speak, Kaliq. This is how he has communicated with her, has instructed her what to do, has given her the small shreds of what is left of his power. Even those vestiges are more than she has ever had on her own. He has probably bargained with her to free him when she triumphs."

"I am a fool!" the younger Shadow Prince cried. "I believed I had buried him so deep that no one would ever hear any sound he could make. How could this have happened? And why did he reach out to one of his daughters, and not one of his sons?" He paused. "But of course! His sons might not have helped him. They have virtually no memory of him, and they are too busy squabbling with each other for supremacy of the Dark Lands. But Ciarda was a little girl when we imprisoned Kol. She had strong memories of him. And Kol never had difficulty in cajoling women to his will."

"Exactly!" Cronan said. "He probably remembered Ciarda as being lively and intelligent, recalled how she loved him and decided to use her if he could reach out to her in our silent language."

"Which he obviously could," Kaliq replied, irritated at himself for being taken unawares. He had never considered that there was actually someone who loved the Twilight Lord. Kol used those around him, but his subjects were nothing more than conveniences. Even the devoted and loyal Alfrigg.

"Kol will have brought himself near death with the effort it has taken him to reach out to his daughter, and especially to shield her from our brothers," Cronan said.

"Is he fool enough to kill himself with his effort?" Kaliq wondered aloud.

"I do not think so," Cronan decided. "I suspect he still hopes against hope to regain his full powers. It would be in his nature to believe it."

"Then perhaps we could incite one of his children to dispatch him," Kaliq said. "It will not be Ciarda, for despite her ambition she loves her father. And Kolgrim is too wily to break the law of the land though he wants his father's throne. But the other twin, Kolbein, is a brute, and foolish enough to be tempted to patricide."

"Put such a thought from you, Kaliq," Cronan advised. "We of the Shadows value life too much to sully our spirits by enticing another to murder. To punish is one thing, but to kill is an entirely different matter."

Kaliq sighed deeply. "I know," he said. "Yet when I think of all the evil Kol has sent into our worlds, Cronan..." He sighed again. "But if Kol continues to shield his daughter's thoughts from us he may kill himself."

"Then that will be his decision, his choice that decides his fate, not ours," Cronan said. "But I do not believe he will do it no matter how much she begs him. Have you looked at your prisoner recently?"

"I have not looked at him since I placed him in his prison," Kaliq said. "I despise him. Looking at him reminds me of what Lara had to suffer to accomplish our ends."

"Ah, the beauteous faerie woman. She is your weakness, Kaliq," Cronan warned.

"I love her," Kaliq said. "I know she is my weakness, but there it is, Cronan."

"Shadow Princes can love truly, Kaliq," Cronan told him. "But it is a rare thing. However, you must not allow your love to destroy either of you. Now, hand me the crystal globe on the shelf there. Yes, the large one. Place it here on the table, and let us see what we can see. Show us the imprisoned Kol," he said to the crystal.

The two Shadow Princes stared into the clear ball. It grew cloudy, and then cleared to reveal a small dark stone prison cell. The chamber was square. There was no door, nor window, nor grating visible. There was no candle to light it, or brazier to warm it, but magic gave them the view of the cell and the prisoner. Kol sat cross-legged in the direct center of the little room. He remained perfectly still, his blinded eyes closed. The conditions of his prison were such that nothing about him had changed since the day he had been placed there. He had no beard. His hair remained its same length. His garment remained whole.

"He sits still because he needs to concentrate upon giving her what he can," Cronan said slowly.

"Then he needs to be distracted," Kaliq said. He looked into the crystal, and snapped his fingers once. Immediately a small black fly appeared in Kol's cell, and began to buzz about.

At first Kol did not hear it, but then as it flew near his ear, buzzing, the Twilight Lord became flustered. He flailed about swatting at the insect he could hear, but not see. His concentration was broken, but then he grew still again. The fly buzzed near him, and with unerring aim his hearing, sharpened by his blindness, allowed him to pinpoint and kill the fly. He smiled triumphantly, but then his cell was suddenly filled with not just one fly, but dozens of the pesky creatures. Kol opened his mouth to express his outrage, but no sound could be heard as his vocal cords were frozen. Realizing what was happening, Kol sought to ignore the creatures, but they began to bite at him. He had no choice but to swat at them as they buzzed about him. His attention now diverted, he could no longer help his daughter. When she felt her powers beginning to weaken, she would be in his head quickly enough, demanding his help. Until then he would continue to swat at the flies.

"Nicely done." Cronan chuckled.

"Ciarda will have to get rid of the flies that torment Kol before her father can once again concentrate. She will not find it either easy or simple. Lara will now have time to approach the Hierarch without interference," Kaliq said. "Thank you for your help, Cronan. I am glad you yet live, for you are certainly the wisest of us all. Are you certain that you do not want to return to Shunnar? The desert heat would soothe your old bones."

"For now I am content here in Belmair," Cronan said. "Remain always in the light, Kaliq of the Shadows." His blue eyes closed as he settled back in his chair.

"Then I bid you farewell, great prince," Kaliq said, and, standing, he disappeared from the white-haired old lord's chambers. Returning himself to Shunnar, he looked about for Lara, but she was not there. Of course! She would be in Hetar. But would she be with Cam or with Jonah? Kaliq poured himself a goblet of apricot Frine, and sat down. He would rest briefly and then join her. Wherever the Darkling was she would shortly discover that her powers were almost gone, and would seek to learn the reason why.

Where are you, Lara? Kaliq called out to her. He waited a moment and then she answered him.

I am with Jonah.

Shortly, the Darkling will be gone to learn why her few powers are waning. You will have the freedom to speak with Cam. I will join you soon, but will not be visible to anyone but you.

I await you, my lord, Lara said. Then she turned to Jonah. "I have spoken with the women, and they are ready to stand behind you, my lord. They are not pleased at any attempt to rob them of the few rights they have managed to gain over these past years."

"What of the Hierarch?" Jonah wanted to know.

"It is possible he may stand by your side, but if not in this matter, there will be others, my lord," Lara told him.

"You never ask for your daughter," he suddenly said.

"Hetar's decline and fall and eventual rebirth does not concern my daughter," Lara told him coldly. "I am told she has become the model of a wealthy Hetarian wife."

He laughed. "Aye. Never did I think I would have such a wife."

"And you would not had you respected the wishes of her brother, Dominus Taj," Lara said sharply. "You stole her, corrupted her to your ways, and you wonder why I do not ask for her, my lord?"

"Zagiri was more than ready and eager to be *corrupted,*" he said softly. "But if it makes any difference to you I do love her, Domina."

"Are you actually able to love, my lord? I did not think so. Be careful your lust for my daughter does not turn you into Gaius Prospero and his beloved Shifra," Lara said cruelly. "We all recall how that ended."

"You are cruel, Domina," the Lord High Ruler of Hetar said to Lara.

"I am faerie," she reminded him. "Now if you wish to save your skin, Jonah of Hetar, you had best enter your council chamber, and defend the women of this kingdom."

"Will you be there when I do?" he asked her.

"So the others can think I stand behind you? Perhaps.

Or perhaps not. You will not see me if I come, my lord. You must stand upon your own feet in this matter. You must be a leader now, not a despot. If you do not display strength you will be defeated. There can only be one ruler of Hetar, my lord. Remember that," Lara warned him, and then she was gone from his sight.

Jonah stood up from behind the large table where he usually conducted all of his business. The council chamber would now be preparing to go into session, for he had called for a meeting. He smoothed his hands down the fur-trimmed purple velvet robe he wore. He brushed his dark hair back, and, taking his staff of office, he strode from his library calling his secretary, Lionel, to follow him. Entering the council chamber, he took his seat upon his high throne, and looked about. Every man and woman in the High Council was seated and waiting for him. Jonah thumped the ebony staff with its round gold knob upon the floor. "Let the High Council come into session," he said. "We recognize Cuthbert Ahasferus. Speak, my lord!"

"I have listened to the Hierarch," the head of the Merchants Guild began, "and it would appear to me if Hetar is to return to the days of its glory we must first return to our traditional ways. The greatest change that has come about in Hetar, and which has, in my opinion and the opinion of many others, caused our decline, is our permitting women to involve themselves in matters that they should not. Women are meant for pleasures, for childbirth, for home and hearth, yet we have allowed them to own Pleasure Houses and businesses, which goes against all we have ever known and been taught. For the sake of Hetar, women need to be returned to their rightful place." He sat down.

"I have never heard such nonsense in my life," Ysbail, a representative of the Pleasure Women's Guild, said. "You cannot expect us to give up the power we have fought so hard to win, Cuthbert. We will not do it!"

"Might I remind Master Ahasferus that the profits from the Pleasure Houses have increased at least tenfold since the women were allowed to own them," Maeve Scarlet, a representative from the Guild of Pleasure Mistresses, pointed out. "Certainly you are not so stupid as to believe that was by chance?"

"But such commercial ventures are not a woman's place!" Aubin Prospero said.

"Aye," the two Forest Lords agreed in unison.

"Can you truly believe that asking women to return to the past will solve Hetar's problems?" Mikhail, son of Swiftsword, asked. "I do not believe it will."

"And turning the Pleasure Houses back to male owners could cost you serious profits," Eres, the other representative from the Pleasure Women, said softly.

"Do you dare to threaten us?" Squire Darah demanded to know.

Eres smiled, but did not answer him.

"What think you, my lord Jonah?" Prince Lothair said, and the eyes of all the council fell upon the Lord High Ruler.

Jonah waited in order to give his words even more weight. Finally he spoke, and all within the council chamber leaned forward to better hear him. "Our difficulties do not stem from keeping women subjugated or allowing them the freedom to indulge in business, my lords and ladies. The Pleasure Houses are, quite frankly, the only enterprises still truly profitable in Hetar. And as has been pointed out so succinctly by Maeve Scarlet, their profits have grown tenfold under the control of the women. I think it would be unwise to change management practices, my lords and my ladies."

"What of the women who own shops? What of those who trade?" Aubin Prospero wanted to know. "We have not admitted them to our guild, but they still have the temerity to do business, and often are in conflict with us."

"Perhaps if you admitted these women to your guild, Aubin Prospero, you would have less trouble with them," Jonah murmured.

"Many of these women were widowed by Hetar's foolish wars," Clothilde, representative of the General Population, noted. "They worked with their late husbands, and learned from them. If they did not continue on, who would care for them, Aubin Prospero? Who would feed their children? It is the men who started these wars that helped to bring about our decline. Have Hetar's women and children not suffered enough by your actions? Now you would drive them to beggary in the name of tradition? Be warned, my lords, that should you attempt to force us back into your servitude the

women of Hetar will rise up as one and defeat you!"
Clothilde sat down.

"And the Mercenaries will put you down, lady," Sir
Philip Bowman of the Crusader Knights responded angrily.

"I do not think so, Sir Philip," Peter Swiftfoot of the
Guild of Mercenaries said. He turned to his companion.
"What think you, Burley Goodman?"

"I think that we stand with our womenfolk, my lords
and my ladies," came the terse answer. "Having the
women become involved has been helpful. Especially
now with times so hard. They know better than any
how to earn a coin, or defuse a difficult situation. Those
who enjoy a traditional role are free to do so, but those
who don't are free to seek other ways of being useful
to our society."

There was a murmur of surprise that the two men
representing the Guild of Mercenaries would support
the women.

It was at that point the Lord High Ruler of Hetar realized that the majority of his council favored allowing
the women to keep their hard-won rights. "We will take
a first vote, my lords and my ladies. Those in favor of re-
scinding women's rights will speak now, and raise their
right hands." He looked out as the Merchants Guild, the
Forest Lords, the Crusader Knights and Squire Darah
of the Midlands raised their hands. He counted aloud.
"One, two, three, four, five, six, seven. There are seven
in favor of taking back the women's rights."

"Seven?" Squire Darah shouted. "What do you mean seven? There are eight of us, Lord Jonah!"

"Nay, my lord, there are seven. Your son-in-law has not yet voted."

The Squire turned angrily on Master Rupert. "You will vote with me!" he shouted furiously.

"If I do I won't be able to face your daughter, my wife," Master Rupert said. "Who do you think founded and manages that cheese business that puts so many coins in your pocket? If our women lose their rights that business will founder. I have no time for it, nor do you. We have fields, orchards and livestock to oversee and care for, my lord."

"Your wife can continue to run it, you fool. She will do as she is told to do," Squire Darah blustered, and his son-in-law laughed aloud.

"She will sit at her loom, and tell you that you mustn't break the new laws you have helped to establish. And if she learns I voted for such laws I will have no peace in my house, and certainly no pleasures. No! I do not believe that women are responsible for all our woes, and I will not vote to take away their few rights."

Jonah hid a smile. He wondered if Lara was watching from some corner he could not see. He would not have believed his council would go against the suggestion of the Hierarch. Interesting. "We have not finished with the voting, my lords and ladies," he said. "All those in favor of maintaining women's rights in Hetar, raise your hands now and vote." He counted aloud the thir-

teen hands that shot up. "By a vote of thirteen to seven
women's rights are continued, my lords and my ladies.
Now let us move on to the next order of business we
must address today. There have been rumors of profiteering, my lords and my ladies. I should like to enact
a new law effective immediately to prevent this evil."

"Does that include your own hoard, my Lord Jonah?"
a voice demanded to know, and the Hierarch entered the
room followed by half a dozen of his disciples.

"Aye, Hierarch, it does," Jonah said. "Come, and sit
by my side. Speak your wisdom to my council, and let
us have a discourse." Was he taking a chance? Jonah
wondered. And if he was it was always possible to remove an enemy in such a manner that no guilt would
fall upon him.

Cam was surprised by Jonah's invitation, but he
boldly accepted it, and sat on the bench throne of the
Lord High Ruler of Hetar next to Jonah. "May I speak?"
he asked.

Jonah nodded his head.

"The people have misunderstood my call for a return
to tradition," Cam began. "They believe it to mean stepping back. It is not that at all. Returning to tradition,
my lords and my ladies, simply means honoring those
traditions, and refitting them to the times in which we
live. But first the council must see to feeding the people,
giving them hope. To do that the profiteering must be
stopped. The Merchants Guild works hand in glove with
the magnates, and we all know it. This must cease!"

"And just how do you suggest we stop it?" Cuthbert Ahasferus asked, sneering.

"Surely you do not forbid profit?" Aubin Prospero said nervously.

"You sell your goods to increase your profits, but to what end, my lords?" the Hierarch demanded to know. "You make money, and more money, and more money. What do you do with all those coins, my lords?"

"Why we invest our monies," Cuthbert Ahasferus replied.

"To what end?" asked the Hierarch.

"To make a profit!" Aubin Prospero said. "Is that not clear to you?"

"More profit and to what end? More profit?" the Hierarch said. "Your greed for profit alone has driven Hetar to ruin, my lords. Profit is good when the investment is in the kingdom's folk and infrastructure, not in more and more and more profit. Your coins are nothing more than metal, and useless until those coins are used to help your people."

"Ridiculous!" Aubin Prospero said.

Watching from her corner, Lara thought that the speaker was beginning to resemble his father, the late Emperor Gaius Prospero. He could not see beyond his pile of coins. She was surprised by Cam's words, for she knew at this point the Darkling was not by his side. She knew that when Ciarda had felt most of her powers waning away she had gone to learn why it was happening. And in that moment a Shadow Prince was able to slip next to her and listen to her thoughts.

"We must take our excess profits, and put them into rebuilding Hetar," Lord Jonah told his High Council. "The houses of all the magnates will be searched for hidden wealth. The goldsmiths and the bankers will be called to account for the deposits they hold for the magnates. A percentage will be taken from each of them to fund the rebuilding that must be done to restore Hetar."

"Do we not pay taxes?" Cuthbert Ahasferus shouted.

"Most of the truly wealthy find ways to pay as little as possible. We will assess the truth, and then each of you will pay a quarter of all your wealth, and in future you will pay twenty percent of your yearly profits," the Hierarch said.

"Remain seated, Cuthbert, Aubin!" Lord Jonah told them sharply, for he saw that they were attempting to sneak out of the council chamber to warn their cronies.

"You cannot force us to do this!" Aubin Prospero shouted furiously.

"Obey me or I will set the people upon you. I will see your household sold into slavery, your monies, your house and your goods taken," the Hierarch said in a dark voice. "As for you, son of the traitor and profiteer Gaius Prospero, you will first be whipped fifty lashes in the main public square for your great sin of greed. Then you will be chained to the wheel in a mill house to spend the rest of your days grinding grain."

"Tell him you will show him his fate," Lara whispered in Cam's ear.

"Behold, and see your fate if you disobey me, Aubin Prospero!" And Cam waved his hand in the air.

Immediately everyone in the chamber saw the house of Prospero, the women, children and servants being taken from the house in chains. The picture in the air that surrounded them changed and they saw Aubin Prospero being whipped as the spectators cheered and counted aloud each stroke of the whip. The picture changed again and Aubin Prospero, gaunt and hollow eyed, trod a well-worn circle chained to a wheel that was grinding grain around and around and around the mill house.

Gaius Prospero's son grew pale with genuine terror as he was shown these pictures. He slumped in his chair, and turned his eyes away.

"This *could* happen, Aubin Prospero, if you refuse to cooperate," the Hierarch said. "The decision is yours."

"Tell them you must leave them now," Lara murmured in Cam's ear.

"I leave you, good council members, to discuss this by yourselves," Cam said grandly, and he waved his hand once again only to find himself back in the small room that was now his. Lara was by his side. "Ciarda never allowed me to do anything like that," he said excitedly.

Lara shook her head as if weary. "Your Darkling doesn't have enough power to do what I just did for you, Cam. Oh, I know she gave you the power to come and to go some months ago, but that power no longer works, does it?"

"Nay, it does not. When I asked her about it she said I no longer needed such a small power," Cam told Lara.

"She has few powers of her own, Nephew. And her father has tried to aid her from his prison with the little magic left to him, but the effort he has made has weakened him, and diminished his magic to the point where it is almost gone. He will give her no more, for he wishes to survive to regain his throne," Lara told Cam.

"Ciarda says that will never happen. That the Lord Kol wants her to have his kingdom," Cam said.

"Cam, in the Dark Lands, no woman has ever ruled, nor will ever rule. They are a race of men mostly, and the few women born have their fate decided at birth. It is to produce more of their kind, and nothing more. Ciarda has a little more latitude being the daughter of the Twilight Lord. But it is one of her twin brothers who will eventually rule there. It is the duty of the old dwarf who is chancellor to eventually decide which one."

"But what if those heirs were not there?" Cam asked Lara.

"Then another male in the direct line of Usi and Jorunn would be chosen," Lara told him. "Whatever Ciarda may think, Cam, she will not rule the Dark Lands."

"She will try," he said, surprising Lara. "She means to gain the male seed of the one called Kolbein, and birth a son whom she will rule through even as you rule Terah through your son Taj," Cam told Lara. "Then she will kill them both. She said it."

"If she murdered the heirs she would be killed herself, for it is forbidden to kill any in the direct line of the Twilight Lords," Lara explained to him.

"Oh," Cam answered. Then he said, "I trusted you today, Aunt, and stood by the side of the Lord High Ruler. I aided him, did I not? Now tell me Anoush is safe, and that you found her."

"I found her in the castle of the Twilight Lord and brought her to safety," Lara said. "I do not go back on my word, Nephew."

"And we will wed when this is over?"

"If Anoush wishes it," Lara told him.

"You must protect me from Ciarda, for she is certain to learn what I have done," he said. Cam was beginning to realize it was Lara who had the greater power.

"You will be safe, for as I have told you her magic is little. Her anger is another thing, Cam, but you are clever enough to defuse it, I am certain," Lara murmured.

"If I offer her pleasures she is generally content," he admitted.

"Then do what you must," Lara said. "We battle to keep the darkness from engulfing us all, Nephew. Farewell for now!" And Lara vanished from his sight.

Cam sat down and considered what he had done this day. Ciarda would not be happy, of course, but when he explained that his small act had gained the trust of his aunt she would understand. He didn't believe Lara when she said that Ciarda had only small magic. Had he not seen her magic for himself when she first came to him? Surely that was not small magic. Although his inability now to transport from place to place was suspicious.

Still, Ciarda had promised him that he would rule Hetar. His aunt offered him a bit of land and some cattle. Cam laughed to himself. It mattered little to him if Ciarda was his overlord. He would still control Hetar for her and that was, he had decided, a lot better than being a propertied Fiacre herdsman. As for Anoush, he would have her eventually despite her mother. Had not Jonah gotten Zagiri for himself?

Yet if by chance his aunt were more truthful than Ciarda then his deeds today will have gained him her trust. If he were clever he could, at least for the interim, convince both Ciarda and Lara that he was doing their bidding. He would watch carefully to see which one of them was the real power, and then ally himself with that power. The more he saw of Hetar the more he wanted it. But then, being a propertied man in his own land was not the worst fate he could have. And there again he would have Anoush with her mother's blessing. Cam had never felt more fortunate in his entire life. Whichever way he turned he would win and no one would be the wiser.

No one except the young Shadow Prince called Baram who had been assigned to accompany the unsuspecting Cam wherever he went, now listening to his thoughts. And reporting all he heard to Prince Kaliq. Baram smiled as he listened to the foolish young mortal who thought himself clever enough to play both sides against the middle. Baram saw an unfortunate end for Cam of the Fiacre, and said so as he reported what he had heard before Cam sought sleep.

"He is twisted, for all the Fiacre's attempts to make a good man of him," Kaliq said. "I am sorry, Lara. I know Anoush loves him, and this will cause her pain."

"He is like both of his parents, envious and foolish," Lara replied fatalistically.

"If he chooses our side in the end, will you keep your promise to him?" Kaliq asked.

"Of course," Lara answered him. "He shall have his land and his cattle."

"And Anoush?" the prince queried.

"When Anoush awakens," Lara said, "she will have forgotten that she was enamored of her cousin. And so will the rest of the Fiacre clan family. He may try to woo her, but she will rebuff him. Remember, Kaliq, I said I would give my consent if it was what Anoush wanted. She will no longer want it, however. And there will be several other young men who will seek to court her. Perhaps from among one of them she will find a man she truly loves, the one who will be perfect for her. Cam has always had a dark side, and he will never be completely free of the darkness even if he does turn toward the light. But having heard his duplicitous thoughts, I wonder if that will happen."

"He will never forgive you," Kaliq said.

"He has never forgiven me for slaying his parents despite the rightness of my cause," she answered. "Each time he calls me *Aunt* I hear the scorn in his voice. But enough of this talk of Cam. What of the Darkling? Has she been able to reach out to Kol again, or have we prevented it entirely?"

"Eskil has managed to get next to her. He tells us that she is confused, that she calls out to Kol, and he does not answer her. Of course, he is too busy battling the flies I set upon him. Weakened as he is by his years of imprisonment, he cannot concentrate on more than one thing at a time, and I have distracted him quite nicely. Eventually, of course, Ciarda will find a way to reach out to him, but there is next to nothing left of his magic now. In time it may return, but for now he is nicely defanged."

"So now we continue to keep Hetar on its path to salvation while watching for what Ciarda will do next," Lara said.

Kaliq nodded, but he wondered as he did if they had really stopped Ciarda in her tracks. The Darkling was cleverer than most of her kind. He considered that she might attempt to use the power of three once more in order to reach her father's magic.

"What is it?" Lara asked him. "You look concerned, my lord."

He told her his thoughts. "I cannot help but think we have missed something."

"Does she possess a crystal globe or a magic basin?"

Lara wanted to know. "If she does she can seek out her father."

"That is it!" Kaliq cried. "I forgot to block the cell Kol inhabits from other eyes than ours." He grasped his own crystal. "Show me Ciarda!" he commanded. The sphere darkened, then lightened to show the Darkling bending over a basin of water, then exclaiming, her face both shocked and surprised. "Too late! Too late!" Kaliq said unhappily. "She has seen, and now will act."

"Can we not stop her?" Lara wanted to know.

Kaliq looked back into the crystal. He saw Ciarda's basin still sitting upon a table, but the Darkling was gone. "She's gone," he said.

"Gone where?" Lara wanted to know.

"That is what we must learn," the Shadow Prince said.

"She will have gone for her brothers," Lara told him.

"Aye, but she will have them by now, and will have transported them all to another place that we must locate," Kaliq said wearily.

"Another place where they may attempt to once again use the power of three, but to what end I am not certain," Lara replied. "To help Kol? To give Ciarda powers she would otherwise not have so she may continue to control Cam?"

"We must find her," Kaliq said. "Hopefully Eskil is with her, and can tell us eventually. But if she moved quickly he will have been caught unawares."

"Reach out to him," Lara begged. "We must know what mischief she plots."

AND CIARDA WAS indeed plotting. She had transported herself to the castle of the Twilight Lord to find Kolgrim with old Alfrigg. She did not like it that the chancellor seemed to favor Kolgrim. "Come!" she said to her half brother. "We must go. Where is Kolbein? I will need him, as well."

"My brother is where he always is," Kolgrim said as his eyes swept over her. She did not have his mother's great beauty, but she was pretty enough. He thought her high pointed breasts quite fine. Reaching out, he took her hand. "Take us, then, sister," he said.

"My lord, this is most unorthodox," Alfrigg complained. "I have not finished the lesson, and there is much for you to learn."

"When I return, Alfrigg," Kolgrim promised.

Ciarda managed to transport them with what was left of her few powers to the House of Women, where Kolbein was to be found naked and drunk amid a pile of naked women. Ciarda shrieked in mock outrage. "Are you not supposed to be my lover?" she demanded of him as the women began to scatter away.

"I never see you, bitch," he growled. "You are too busy fucking your little Hierarch to be bothered with me. These women are here for my pleasure, and I will use them as I see fit."

"Our father is in difficulties," Ciarda said. "We need to help him, Kolbein." Aye, she was going to help Kol. She would direct the power of three to set them all in Kol's cell, where they would help him deal with the plague of flies. But when they were finished she would see that only she and Kolbein were transported out. She would leave Kolgrim behind, and he had not the power to free himself. She almost laughed with delight at her own cleverness. With only Kolbein left he would become the true Twilight Lord. She would bear his son, and then... Ciarda smiled. Nothing was going to stop her from gaining her goals, from completing what her father started.

"I have no time for you now, bitch sister. Go away! More Frine!" Kolbein shouted loudly. "More Frine for the Twilight Lord!"

"I do not believe that matter has been quite settled, brother," Kolgrim said, an edge to his voice, but Kolbein just laughed at him.

Ciarda felt her temper rising. Her powers were so weak, and she had used much of herself in transporting them into the House of Women to fetch Kolbein. Now she must render him sober by means of magic. "Get out!" she ordered the few women who remained in the chamber, and when they had fled she put her hand on Kolbein's head. *Mind clear!* The command was not a gentle one.

Kolbein howled as a bolt of pain shot through his head, but when the pain disappeared he was no longer suffering the effects of the massive amounts of Frine he had been drinking. "That hurt, bitch sister," he snarled at her. "I am not sorry that you are jealous of my women."

"We need you, Kolbein," Ciarda said through gritted

teeth. "Join hands now with us so I may summon the power of three. Our father needs our help." She grasped their hands in hers.

Kolbein yanked his hand away from Ciarda and his brother. "*Our father?* That fellow who put me to be raised by Wolfyn, and my brother by giants? I thought he was long dead, bitch sister. Why would I want to help him?"

"Our father was imprisoned by the Shadow Princes and their allies," she answered him. "But he has been transferring his powers to me so I might aid the Hierarch. Recently I have noticed he stopped and when I looked into my reflecting basin I saw he was being distracted by a plague of flies. He is weak, and cannot concentrate on more than one thing at a time. The flies bite at him and buzz at him. He needs us to destroy them so he may return to helping us."

"Why is he transferring his powers to you instead of us?" Kolbein asked her now, totally sober. "Why would he give his powers to a mere woman, bitch sister?"

"Aye, indeed, why?" Kolgrim said. From what he knew of his father, Kol would never willingly give even the smallest of his powers to a female. Ciarda was lying. "I think, sister, that I do not trust you," he murmured. "How have you forced our father into giving you powers you should not have?"

"I merely promised him his freedom when we bring the darkness into the worlds," Ciarda told her two half brothers. "In exchange he is aiding me."

"What a dangerous little Darkling you are, sister," Kolgrim said softly.

"We should kill her!" Kolbein snarled.

"It is against the laws of the Dark Lands for any in this family to kill another of his or her blood," Kolgrim told his brother. "If you spent your time studying with Alfrigg as I have been doing you would know that, brother."

"We should not be arguing," Ciarda said in what she hoped passed for a reasonable tone of voice. "The power of three can bring us to our father, and he will help us, brothers. Please!"

"Our father can rot for all eternity," Kolbein said. "I don't want to see him."

"I, on the other hand, am most curious to see him," Kolgrim admitted.

"Kolbein, please." Ciarda gave her voice a pleading sound.

"I will want something in return," he told her.

"I will give you whatever you desire," Ciarda said.

"I want to watch while my women sexually torture you," Kolbein said. "Then when they are finished I want to whip you first, then fuck you the night long. If you will agree to that then I help you now so we may use the power of three," Kolbein said to her. He grinned evilly at her, his gray eyes more black than gray now.

Kolgrim looked to his twin brother. "I had not realized how creative you are, brother," he said admiringly. "'Tis a delightfully thought-out entertainment."

Kolbein grinned back at his twin. Then he turned to Ciarda. *"Well?"* he said.

Ciarda said, "I agree."

"Good!" Kolbein said. "I will call my women back now."

"Brother, if you could restrain yourself," Kolgrim said in a pleasant tone, "time is very important in this matter. Let us do what must be done, and then you may spend a delightful evening with our dear sister as she is taught her place in our world. And you will not be restrained by time if you wait until later."

Kolbein looked as if he would refuse, but then he said, "You are probably right, brother. I want my women to have all the time they need with her, and then I want my time with our bitch sister to be leisurely and not hurried." He took Ciarda's hand. Kolgrim took her other hand.

"By the power of three I command we be taken to our father's presense," Ciarda said, and there was a crack of thunder as they were transported into Kol's prison. The chamber was fetid, and the swarm of biting black flies was intolerable. Kol now crouched down in a corner in an effort to avoid the flies.

Ciarda waved her hand, unfreezing Kol's vocal chords. "Who is there?" he demanded in a surprisingly strong voice.

"It is I, Father. Ciarda."

"Who is with you?" he asked her. The long chains confining him rattled.

"I am alone," Ciarda said.

"You lie!" Kol said. "I may be blind but my other senses are sharp. There are two others in this room with you, daughter."

Kolgrim stepped forward, and, bending down, he took his father's hand. "I am Kolgrim, my lord," he said. "My brother, Kolbein, is with me."

"You are my son?" Kol said incredulously. "My sons are here with me?"

"Aye, we are," Kolgrim said. The crouching creature was pitiful. He could not believe that this was the great Twilight Lord of legend. He drew back when Kol stood up and looked directly at him. His eyes, which should have been black, were white.

"We have used the power of three to reach you, Father," Ciarda said. "Without you I cannot control the Hierarch. If you do not continue to give me your powers everything I have done so far will be for naught," Ciarda told him.

"My powers have deteriorated," Kol said to her, "and if I could release them to another it would be to my sons. They are the ones who should have my powers."

"But I have worked so hard to complete your dream, my lord father," Ciarda said. She was, to her surprise, near to tears.

"You are female, daughter, and now that I have my sons whatever I have is theirs," Kol told her.

Ciarda was suddenly filled with a burning anger. "Your sons are a joke, my lord father," she shouted at him. "Kolbein is a drunkard and a lecher. All he wants to do is lie about the House of Women drinking Frine and fucking its residents. As for Kolgrim, he finds everything amusing and as far as I can see is useless. I am the only one of your offspring worthy of you, my lord father!"

"She is certainly an ambitious little Darkling, Father," Kolgrim said. "Mother is having quite a time with her."

"You know your mother?" Kol was both surprised and amazed.

"The bitch hates us," Kolbein said irritably.

"He says that because I am her favorite," Kolgrim taunted his sibling.

"Lara favors you, Kolgrim? Then it is you who shall have my throne!" the Twilight Lord said.

"Never!" Kolbein shouted angrily, "It is mine! *Mine!*"

"I have spoken," said the Twilight Lord. "I may be blind, chained and imprisoned, my sons, but I know that if Lara favors one of you then it is he who should be my heir. Ciarda, tell Alfrigg that I have said it."

"Give me what remains of your powers, then, Father," Ciarda said softly.

Kolgrim stepped next to his father again, whispering in the silent language he had recently discovered he could use. *Say nay, Father. Ciarda means to leave me behind and lie to Alfrigg if you give her any powers.*

You want the duplicitous wench? Kol asked.

I will mount her and mate her as soon as we return

to the castle, Father. A son from her body will be evil incarnate. The Dark Lands will need a ruler like that in the future. In the meantime I will rebuild our strength, our forces for that day, Kolgrim said.

Have her killed by another after she has birthed your son, Kol advised. *She is ambitious, and she seeks to rule over the worlds once she has brought them into the darkness.*

I know, Kolgrim replied. *I know Ciarda's heart, Father, and I will keep her under control, I promise you.*

My powers are weak to almost nonexistent, my son. But perhaps back in the Dark Lands they will strengthen, or at least help what is in you to grow strong. Kol took Kolgrim's hand and pressed his hand against it. *There,* he said. *What was mine is now yours, and you alone will reign as the Twilight Lord.*

CHAPTER SEVENTEEN

"NO, FATHER! NO!" Ciarda, who had been able to hear part of the conversation, cried.

Kol looked scornfully at her. "Daughter, do you not understand the way of our world? Females do not rule. What was left of my magic permitted me to reach out to someone who would listen. I knew not what had happened to my sons, but I knew you would still be in the House of Women, and I remembered of all my daughters you loved me best, and were the most dutiful. But you think to be what you cannot be, Ciarda. You have brought my sons to me, and I am grateful. It was careless of the Shadow Princes not to encase me within one of their spells. If they learn that you have used the power of three to reach me they will indeed make changes. I will not see you again, I fear. But I know now my kingdom is safe within Kolgrim's hands, and for that I am grateful to you."

"Not grateful enough," Ciarda said bitterly. "Without my magic the Hierarch will fail. I will never be able to bring Hetar into the darkness. Already the Shadow Princes and the faerie woman plot to destroy me. Without my magic they may succeed."

"You have the magic that you should have, daughter," Kol told her, and then he chuckled. It was a raspy sound. "So Lara still champions the light. Of course she would." His gaunt, handsome face grew almost sad.

"We must go," Kolbein said irritably. "Ciarda! Do what you must."

"Ah, brother, Ciarda no longer has the power. I do," Kolgrim said.

"The power of three! Does not Ciarda control it?" Kolbein asked.

Kolgrim laughed. Taking Ciarda's hand, he said, "Thank you, Father. I will be certain to give Mother your most tender regards. Farewell, brother!" And both he and Ciarda disappeared from the dark cell, leaving his father and brother behind.

For a moment Kolbein did not quite comprehend what had happened, but when he did his face grew bright red with his fury as he realized he had been left behind. "Kolgrim!" he shouted. "Come back for me this instant!"

"He is not returning," Kol said. "There can only be one Twilight Lord, my son, and your brother is he who was meant to be. And by leaving you behind he has not broken our laws for he has not shed your blood. You have no magic of your own, and what little might have been yours is now your brother's. Because of the blood that flows through your veins you will live for centuries here with me. Be grateful you do not carry these long chains that I do."

Kolbein roared his outrage, but the sound bounced off the damp stone walls of the cell to be heard by no one outside of his father and himself. He was trapped even as he had intended trapping Kolgrim. Ciarda would surely help him, wouldn't she?

Ciarda, however, had other problems. Kolgrim had managed to transport them to a chamber in the House of Women. She recognized it immediately. When the Twilight Lord visited his women it was here he came. The walls were stone. The narrow arched windows looked out over the mountains and the gorge below. Furnished with a large bed set upon a dais, it was a room that had but one purpose.

Seeing where she was, Ciarda pulled away from Kolgrim and dashed for the door, but the key in the lock turned, and flew across the chamber into Kolgrim's hand. He caught it, and pocketed it with a nasty smirk. He was already bootless. Then, striding over to the Darkling, he pulled her to him by her long black hair.

"Let me go," Ciarda said in a suddenly shaking voice.

"You are so deliciously evil," he purred at her, caressing her face with his knuckles. "I knew right away you would have to be the one to conceive and bear my son for me, Ciarda." His fingers fastened into the round neck of her gown, ripping it away. His hand reached out to cup one of her high, pointed breasts and squeeze it. Bending his dark head, he bit down on her nipple, causing her to scream. Lifting his head up, he said in a hard voice, "Undress me, Ciarda. It is time we became better acquainted."

"I will not...." she began angrily.

Kolgrim backhanded her ferociously. "Do you not understand, Ciarda?" he said in a cold but calm voice. "I am the Twilight Lord. You are a female. You do not question. *You obey.* I have chosen you to bear my heir. Your wickedness matches mine, and the son you will eventually give me will be great. Today I will seed you thoroughly, but until I wish it that seed will not bloom. But because you will mother my only son I will permit you to sit on a stool at my feet in the throne room so all who come to me may know I hold you in great favor. Now obey my command, Ciarda. My need to fuck you grows greater with each passing moment."

Shocked by what was happening, Ciarda nonetheless hurried to follow his order. Her cheeks were stinging from the blow he had delivered to her. The nipple he had bitten ached. The few powers their father had given him seemed to have grown suddenly. Her fingers fumbled as she undid the laces at the neck of his shirt and slipped it off him. His skin was pale, but tawny gold hair covered his chest. Unable to help herself, Ciarda ran her palms over his muscled torso then bent to lick his nipples with a quick tongue. Kolgrim spoke only one word. "Kneel."

Ciarda knelt down, undoing the belt about his waist. She unbuttoned his breeches and pulled them down so he might step from them, which he did, kicking them away from him. He wore nothing beneath, and his rod lay supine amid a nest of tightly curled golden fur. She felt his fingers digging into her scalp, and knew what he wanted. Ciarda rubbed her cheek against his rod. Then she began to fondle it and to Ciarda's surprise her fingertips brushed over a swelling pocket on the back of his rod. "What is this?" she asked him. "Kolbein did not have this deformity on his rod."

Kolgrim laughed softly. "Then I am indeed the true Twilight Lord," he said to her. "All Twilight Lords possess double rods, Ciarda. That which most men possess is called the dominant. It is not a deformity, it is a wonderment, and you shall be doubly pleasured. Suck me, and see what happens."

His scent was in her nostrils, and Ciarda found it exciting. She reached beneath him to cup his seed sac. She fondled it, her excitement growing. Taking the tip of his rod in her fingers, she slowly licked it up and then down several times. Then she took him into her mouth, and began to draw upon him. Gently at first, but then with harder tugs of her mouth on him until he began to swell. He grew so quickly that his size stretched her lips and almost choked her with his length, which pushed against the back of her throat.

Kolgrim closed his eyes, enjoying the sensation of her lips and tongue on him. He had always been embarrassed by possessing two rods until he learned studying with old Alfrigg that it was a natural attribute of a Twilight Lord. And Kolbein had not possessed it. When he discovered that, Kolgrim knew it was he who must triumph and take the throne of the Dark Lands. The twin rods made him his father's true heir. He moaned as Ciarda's mouth brought him almost to fulfillment. "Cease!" he commanded her. He felt the lesser rod ready to come forth. "Sit back, and see what pleasure awaits you," he said.

Resting upon her haunches, Ciarda stared at Kolgrim's long thick rod. And then her eyes widened as his lesser rod began to slide forth from beneath the dominant. It was far longer, but equally hard, and thin. Its tip was shaped like an arrowhead. "How do you use them both?" she queried him, staring, fascinated, at the two rods.

"You will be required to be placed in a special position to receive both, Ciarda. Are you woman enough to give yourself to me freely?" Kolgrim asked her.

"Will you seed me now?" she asked him. "What if later on you find a woman you prefer to me to bear your son?"

"I am certain over the years to come I will find many women I prefer to you, Darkling, but you are the perfect woman to bear the Twilight Lord's only son. And in answer to your question, aye, I will seed you now, for I do not trust you. Know that without me by your side you will not leave the Dark Lands again. Now get on your back upon the bed, Ciarda, so you may be made ready for me. And from this moment on you will address me as your lord and master." He pulled her torn garment off her.

"Yes, my lord and master," she said to him, and, going to the large bed, she lay directly in its center. She hated him, his arrogance and yet…

Almost at once four chains holding round manacles dropped from the ceiling. They were silver, the manacles lined in silk and lamb's wool. Kolgrim fastened two of the manacles to her wrists above her head. The other two he attached to her ankles, which were pulled wide and drawn back toward her shoulders.

Ciarda was fascinated. She had not known about double rods or restraints, but she frankly found her situation very stimulating. Kolbein had been a rough and crude lover seeking only his own satisfaction. He had been easily manipulated. Kolgrim, however, was not to be led, she now saw. But she realized that he excited her. "How long have you wanted to mate with me?" she asked him softly.

"From the moment I saw you," he admitted to her. "Whether that comes from a genuine lust for you, my wicked Darkling, or because the mating season is upon me I cannot tell you. That was why my brother was so randy these past few weeks." He slipped onto the bed next to her. In his hand appeared a small sable-haired brush dripping some silken substance. Leaning toward her, he spread her nether lips with his thumb and forefinger to stroke the brush back and forth over her love bud.

The sensation Ciarda felt was at first cool and the

brush tickled. But then suddenly an explosion of hot lust hit her so hard she could barely draw a breath. "What have you done to me?" she gasped.

"Does it burn?" he asked her in nonchalant tones.

"Yes! Make it stop, Kolgrim! Make it stop!" The unfulfilled lust consuming her was almost painful.

"Make it stop, *my lord and master,*" he reminded her gently.

"Yes! Yes! Make it stop, my lord and master! Please!"

Leaning over more, he slid his forked tongue from between his lips and began licking her sex. The action but served to rouse her further, and she struggled against her bonds. Kolgrim laughed softly. "You must answer my questions honestly, Ciarda. Will you bear my son with a dark and willing heart?"

She nodded then said, "Aye, I will!" As angry as she was at having been outwitted by him, to bear the next Twilight Lord was an honor to which she had always aspired. What matter that the father she chose was not the man who now prepared to impregnate her with his seed? It didn't matter.

"And will you accept your female inferiority, my naughty Darkling?"

"Aye!" she answered quickly, not daring to hesitate lest he refuse to use her body.

Kolgrim laughed. "You lie, Darkling, but I can control you, and so I will forgive you. I will always know when you lie to me."

"I am not like the others," Ciarda protested to him.

"I have intelligence, and I will pass it on to our son, my lord and master."

He laughed again then he grew serious. "Creation is painful, Darkling. Are you prepared now to be seeded?" Two fingers pushed into her sheath, frigging her wickedly.

"I am no virgin to whimper and whine at a strong manhood," she told him.

She knew nothing really of what was to come, Kolgrim thought, amused. But he had learned much over the last weeks from the old chancellor who tutored him. His hair might be golden like his mother's, but he was Kol's son in every other way. He looked at the girl spread and waiting for him. He gazed at his twin rods, hard and eager. And then without another word he began to press his lesser rod into her rear channel.

Ciarda squealed, surprised, as the pointed tip of the lesser rod began to penetrate her sharply. But the brief pain faded and she felt the slender rod push itself deep into her. When he had filled her she felt the power of it throbbing. Her eyes widened, and it was then Kolgrim drove his dominant rod into her sheath. As he did Ciarda felt little tiny sharp nodules rising up to tear at her tender interior. "What are they?" she cried out to him. "You are giving me pain, my lord and master!"

"The nodules only appear when a son is to be seeded, Ciarda," he told her. Then he began to thrust the two rods in perfect unison. "They will heighten our pleasure."

Oddly he was right, Ciarda realized. The pain of the little nodules drove her excitement to a height she had never before experienced. She screamed with her pleasure, and begged him to release her from her restraints. When he did with a silent command that opened the manacles so that they dropped away from her limbs, Ciarda wrapped her legs about his torso to take him even deeper. Her fingernails clawed his back in a frenzy of lust, drawing blood.

Now he began to thrust rhythmically with both of his rods. He drove harder and deeper into her until Ciarda was screaming with both pain and delight. Kolgrim roared with his own satisfaction as he felt her sheath tightening and releasing about his dominant rod. He felt his juices boiling up. When they exploded furiously into her he shouted with a sound of triumph as she shrieked with her release, and ferocious pleasures overwhelmed them both in a tidal wave of pure hot lust.

"By Krell, Darkling, I have seeded you well this night," Kolgrim declared. "And when I decide it my seed will bloom within you, and you will bring forth my son." Withdrawing both of his rods from her body, he told her, "You may sleep now, Ciarda. You have earned your rest. Tomorrow I will send for you to come to the castle, where you will confirm to Alfrigg what my father said to me." He arose from the bed, and with a wave of his hand reclothed himself. Then he left her.

Ciarda lay, exhausted. She had thought Cam a lover without peer, but now she realized that no mortal could

equal Kolgrim. And now that she held the key to the
future of the Dark Lands within her body, the new Twilight Lord was in her power, although he knew it not.
She was not an inferior female, and one day she would
rule. Ciarda fell asleep with a smile upon her lips even
as, crossing the bridge over the gorge, Kolgrim returned
to the castle.

"Fetch the chancellor to me," he told the first servant
he saw. "Send him to my throne room."

"Yes, master," the servant said with a bow and hurried off.

Kolgrim entered the designated chamber. Walking across the ebony floors, each board separated by
a narrow stripe of pure silver, he mounted the dais,
and sat down upon the gray and silver marble throne.
Smiling, he gazed about the room with its black marble walls veined in silver. His eye went to the black
marble colonnade framing the mountains beyond. The
sky above them was a reddish dun color. The silver
censers that lined the room burned fragrant oils. The
flames from them flickered and made shadows against
the dark walls. Kolgrim leaned back, his eye catching a
glimpse of the new silver-and-purple-striped silk canopy above his head. Then he sighed. It was a sound of
deep contentment.

Alfrigg hurried into the throne room, and, seeing
Kolgrim seated upon the throne, came slowly forward.
"My lord?" he said, the question unspoken but still
needing an answer from Kolgrim.

"The matter of my father's inheritance has now been settled, Alfrigg," Kolgrim said. "On the morrow the Darkling will confirm what I am about to tell you." Then he told the chancellor how Kol had reached out from his prison cell. How Ciarda had answered her father's call. How she had used the power of three to bring them to Kol and what had transpired during the visit.

"Do you know where this prison in which he is kept is located?" the chancellor asked, but he expected even if Kolgrim did he would not reveal it.

"I do not, Alfrigg, nor does Ciarda," Kolgrim answered.

Alfrigg nodded.

"While I want Ciarda to speak with you," Kolgrim said, "I can show you my father and my brother. As I have already said, I did not kill him. No royal blood has been shed by me, I swear it."

"It was most clever of you, my lord, to solve the problem in the way you did," Alfrigg said, and, unable to help himself, he chuckled.

Kolgrim smiled at the sound. "You will continue to serve me for the interim, Alfrigg. In a few years' time we will seek your replacement together, but for now it pleases me to have you by my side. Come now, and I will show you." The new Twilight Lord stepped from the dais and walked to the center of the chamber, where a silver tripod was set. It contained a black onyx bowl filled with crystal-clear water. Kolgrim waved a hand over the bowl. The water roiled, grew dark, and then, clearing, revealed the former Twilight Lord and Kolbein within the tiny stone cell. Kol sat silently, but Kolbein moved restlessly about, seeking a means of escape, but there was none.

Alfrigg peered into the scene within the bowl. He nodded. Then he asked Kolgrim, "If I may be so bold, why did your father choose you over Kolbein, my lord?"

"I told him I was our mother's favorite," Kolgrim said with a small smile.

Alfrigg chuckled again. "Indeed, my lord, I believe that you are," he agreed. "She would, however, be quite distressed to realize that you know it. She was very angry when she learned she had been chosen to bear your father a child. But she has always been a good mother to her children, and loves them well. I know although she would not ever admit to it that it pained her to desert you and your brother. Despite everything that has happened there is a drop of darkness in her even as there is a flicker of light in you."

"You have lived a long while, Alfrigg, haven't you?" Kolgrim said.

"Indeed, my lord, I have. Now might I have your permission, my lord, to discuss what is to be done with the Darkling?" the old dwarf asked his master.

"I have already decided. I have mated with her, and given her my son. When I am ready she will bear him," Kolgrim said.

"My lord!" Alfrigg was shocked.

"She is perfect, Chancellor. She is evil and dark and

has no heart at all," Kolgrim said with a wicked smile. "Is there a more perfect mate for me? We despise each other."

"She is dangerous, my lord!" Alfrigg was very distressed.

"Her powers are weak now, and few," Kolgrim said. "She cannot harm me, and the child will not grow until I decree it grow."

"But after he is born?" Alfrigg fretted.

"Ciarda will not live much past the Completion Ceremony," Kolgrim said softly.

"Of course, my lord," the chancellor replied. "Of course. How foolish of me not to have realized that you have thought this out most carefully."

"I still have much to learn from you," Kolgrim said.

The old dwarf bowed to his master, accepting the compliment.

"Have you seen enough now?" the young Twilight Lord asked Alfrigg.

"I have, my lord. I am sorry for your father, and your brother, but I am relieved to know the Dark Lands are once again in good hands. May I send out a proclamation to that effect tomorrow?"

"You may," Kolgrim said. "Now, Alfrigg, come and sit with me, for I need your good counsel." He sat back upon his throne and indicated a small low stone chair next to it for his chancellor, who quickly sat. "Tell me of Ciarda's plan to bring darkness to the worlds, and if it is practical to continue."

"To bring the darkness we must have a strong army, my lord, and we do not. Our forces were destroyed back in the last battle for Hetar. Your father disappeared shortly afterward, and I had not the authority to rebuild the military. It was not a particularly disciplined army, for your father cobbled together giants, dwarves and Wolfyn to fight. The giants were amenable enough, but before any fighting broke out they were subverted by the Domina and her allies. The dwarves and the Wolfyn did not get on. Though a great battle was fought before the walls of The City, your father's army was defeated, and driven from Hetar. In the years since my people have retreated deep into the mountains, and the Wolfyn have also kept to themselves. We have no army and cannot go to war with anyone. It will take several years to build up an army, my lord. And if it were my decision to make I should create a professional military," Alfrigg concluded.

Kolgrim nodded slowly. "You have thought this over carefully," he noted.

"I have, my lord," the chancellor said.

"Then Ciarda's plan was doomed to failure," Kolgrim decided.

"It was, my lord."

"And the Hierarch, Alfrigg? What of him?"

"Without her aid he is helpless. He will be found a fraud. Hetar will fall deeper into misery, and in a few years they will be a ripe prize for the picking," Alfrigg said. "If there is one thing we have a plethora of, my lord, it is time."

"Will my mother and her allies not help Hetar?" the Twilight Lord asked.

"Your mother is not a friend of the Lord High Ruler, especially after he stole her daughter and married her. But then she was never a friend to Jonah of Hetar. Once she is assured the danger is past she will return to Terah and guide her younger son to manhood so he may be considered a good Dominus."

"How many other children has she had, Alfrigg?" Kolgrim asked.

"Two sons and three daughters, besides yourself and your brother, my lord," the chancellor said.

"Did she raise them, and love them?" Kolgrim asked. The old dwarf nodded.

Kolgrim said nothing more about his siblings. "You have my permission to tell her that the war is over for now, Alfrigg."

"On the morrow, my lord, but would it not be more wicked to say nothing, and let her continue to wonder why we make no attack?" the chancellor queried.

Kolgrim laughed. "For a moment I became foolishly sentimental," he said. "It shall not happen again, Alfrigg. Aye, let her wonder. Let Hetar and its allies scurry about like mice in fear of the cat, waiting, wondering, just when the cat will pounce."

"Oh, very good, my lord! Very good." Alfrigg cackled delightedly. The young man was his father all over again. Alfrigg felt suddenly renewed.

Baram, the Shadow Prince who had finally been able to slip beneath Ciarda's guard, had watched as Kolgrim had taken the Darkling in the violent mating ritual of a Twilight Lord. He heard Ciarda's thoughts as Kolgrim rode her. Some instinct had bade him follow Kolgrim back to the castle rather than remaining with the Darkling. The girl was no longer a danger. He had heard them speaking, but he still did not understand everything that they said. Now he stood in the shadows of the Twilight Lord's throne room listening as Kolgrim spoke with Alfrigg. Shocked by what he heard, Baram had been forced to remain where he was until the two men separated, the dwarf leaving the chamber, the new Twilight Lord seating himself himself back on his throne to think.

Baram drew his cloak tightly about him, thinking of Shunnar, and when he flung it back he was in the open colonnaded hallway of Prince Kaliq's palace. He hurried off to find his brother. He found Kaliq with Marzina. He was teaching her the lesson of patience, and Marzina was having a difficult time of it. Baram thought the girl extraordinarily beautiful, but he could see she had a great deal to learn, for she was very impatient.

"Nay, Marzina," Kaliq said to her. "You are too eager for the end result. A year in the Temple of the Daughters of the Great Creator will be of value to you. Go along now, child."

Dismissed, the Terahn princess ran off.

Kaliq turned to Prince Baram. "You have news, my brother?"

"The Darkling's powers have been almost drained away from her," Baram began, "and Kolgrim rules as the new and undisputed Twilight Lord."

"The other twin?"

"With his father," Baram said.

"What?" Kaliq's face mirrored his astonishment at the words.

"In our own arrogance we did not place a sealing spell around him," Baram said quietly. He then went on to explain all he had seen and heard, for, along with the trio of siblings, he had also stood unseen in Kol's dungeon cell as they had been reunited with their sire. "Kolgrim told his father that Lara favored him. I could see that Kol still loves her, for he immediately transferred the powers of the Twilight Lord to Kolgrim, naming him his successor, and then took back what he had given to Ciarda even as she protested against it. Using his new powers, Kolgrim transported himself and Ciarda back to the House of Women, where he mated with her, giving her a son to be born one day."

Kaliq's crystal globe appeared in his hand. He gazed into it as it darkened and then cleared to reveal Kol and Kolbein together within Kol's cell. *Be sealed, and not be broken unless it is my word that's spoken,* Kaliq said silently. Baram was right. They had been arrogant. Nay! He had been arrogant. He had been so enraged at Kol's conduct toward Lara on the Dream Plain he had not considered clearly all the possible consequences. And now because of him a new dangerous Twilight Lord reigned in the Dark Lands.

Sensing his thoughts, Baram said, "It is not your fault, Kaliq. We are all to blame. Our victory over the darkness made us all careless. And one of the twins was bound to overcome the other one day. If we must have a Twilight Lord, better Kolgrim. Kolbein is a stupid savage, and Ciarda was able to use him. Now she has been relegated to a mere female status by Kolgrim. She will try to maneuver around him, of course, for she is intelligent, and that will keep him busy. He was foolish to seed her with his son, for now he cannot destroy her until the child is safely born one day."

"Removing his brother without shedding his blood was cleverly done," Kaliq observed. "He is like his father."

Baram nodded in agreement. Then he said, "Kolgrim has chosen to desert the Hierarch, and Ciarda no longer has the power to help him, nor will she be permitted to leave the Dark Lands any longer. Our young Twilight Lord has decided to be patient and build an army. A real army, not the ramshackle kind of thing his father gathered together the last time. It will take years, of course, to find and recruit the leaders and the men needed. They will have to be trained, but eventually we will be forced to face them. We have an advantage in that we know they are coming. Their disadvantage is that they do not know we know." Baram chuckled.

Kaliq smiled. "I will speak with Lara about the Hierarch. It will be her decision what is to be done with him."

"It is a decision that will affect us all," Baram said. Then he asked, "Am I to return to the Dark Lands, brother?"

"Nay, there is no need for you to remain there at this point," Kaliq said. "Go now and again so we may be aware if anything of import is happening or about to happen."

"I will," Baram promised, and then he left his superior.

Kaliq sat quietly for several long minutes. He needed to clear away the roiling emotions that were threatening to overcome him. Baram had done well, and his kind words had soothed the Shadow Prince's conscience, but it continued to fret him that he had allowed his love for Lara to make him so careless all those years ago. Yet perhaps it had been for the better that everything played out as it did. The imbalance in the Dark Lands had been reflected throughout the worlds. Now balance was once again restored.

Domina, heed my plea. Cease all else and come to me, he called out to Lara.

"Kaliq, I was just preparing to retire," Lara told him as she appeared before him.

He grinned wickedly at her. "Perhaps we can retire together when I have told you all the news I have for you," he teased her.

Lara laughed. "But I never get any rest when I *retire* with you," she teased back. Then she said, "What has happened, my lord, that you cannot wait to tell me?"

"Kolgrim rules undisputed in the Dark Lands," Kaliq began, and he went on to tell Lara all that had happened.

She listened, and when he had concluded his report, Lara said, "Kolgrim is clever, and I am astounded that Kol still harbors any thought of me. Yet of the two Kolgrim was the better choice if a choice had to be made."

"You like him," Kaliq observed.

Lara thought a long moment. "In an odd way I suppose I do," she agreed. "There is a fascination to such evil, and while I prefer the light, there are those among my race who prefer the dark, as you well know, Kaliq."

"He wants you to love him," Kaliq said. "It may one day be his undoing."

"I know," Lara replied. "But to love him I must accept him, admit to his existence, and how would that affect the other children I have borne? And what of Marzina? If Kol came to know her he would eventually realize the truth. He would use it against me, Kaliq. You know that he would. He would attempt to bring Marzina to the darkness. And how could I ever tell my daughter that Magnus Hauk was not her father? That her father was darkness personified, and her conception was the result of rape?" Lara shook her head. "Nay, I will never acknowledge that Kolgrim is my son. He is Kol's son, but not mine. And I will protect my children from him."

"When we chose you to fulfill our plans for chaos in

the Dark Lands we never anticipated what would happen afterward," Kaliq said.

"How could you?" Lara asked him. "It is my destiny that is being played out, Kaliq, not yours. For years I have wondered just what this destiny I have is. I have waited for some momentous happening to occur, but I have become convinced that there will be no great incident. It is the life I live, the decisions I make that affect not only me but those around me that contributes to my destiny. I am living my destiny, Kaliq." She leaned over and kissed his mouth. "And you, my lord, are a part of my destiny that I very much like. Now, what else is there for us to consider?"

"The Hierarch," he responded. "What are we to do about him?"

"I suppose we could leave him to an unpleasant fate, especially if the Hetarians discover he is an Outlander," Lara said. "But a fragile Hetar is not good for any of us. Hetar needs to recover from its excesses. It will take years, but to expose Cam for the fraud he is would make it far worse. We must help the Hierarch, and then he must disappear. So it is said of the Hierarch's legend, in any case," she said with a smile.

"You will return him to the New Outlands afterward?"

She nodded. "And we shall have the Munin remove his memories of this particular time in his life. As for the clan families, they will believe that Cam's cattle and bit of land have come from his own efforts."

"But you will still prevent Anoush from marrying him," Kaliq said.

"I believe it best, aye. The darkness is in him, Kaliq. You know it. And if it rose to overwhelm him again, if Anoush could not help him, Cam would break her heart. I will not allow that to happen."

He nodded.

"Let me go and rest now, Kaliq," Lara said.

"Remain here," he replied.

"I do not want Taj distressed to find me just gone on the morrow," she told him. "Remember my responsibilities to Terah. I will deal with Cam tomorrow," Lara said. And then she was gone from his side.

Kaliq sighed. She was right, of course, but he would have enjoyed a few hours in her company, in her arms.

WHEN LARA AWOKE the next day she felt as if a great weight had been lifted from her shoulders. She might be faerie, but she wasn't entirely invincible. The knowledge that she would not have to compete with Ciarda for Cam's attention was a great relief. Now her foolish nephew would be forced to do her bidding without question. He could no longer betray her by attempting to make an arrangement with the Darkling more suited to his own nefarious and greedy purposes. She chuckled at the thought of his surprise when he learned that.

She bathed, and then considered what she would wear. A gown would make her seem vulnerable and feminine. She chose instead her leather trousers, a shirt, doeskin jerkin and boots. She sat quietly as Mila brushed out her long golden hair and then braided it neatly into a single, long, thick plait. Then, standing, she called to Andraste, who came to fasten herself onto Lara's back.

"Shall I have Dasras saddled?" Mila asked.

"Nay, I will use magic to travel today. And I would first have breakfast with the young Dominus," Lara answered her serving woman. With a smile at Mila, she hurried off to see her youngest son. She found him with his two companions preparing to break their fast. "I've come to join you," she said, waving them back into their seats, for they had arisen politely at her entrance.

"I have hardly seen you of late, Mother," Taj said, a hint of complaint in his voice.

"There has been so much to do, my darling," Lara replied. "We have now restored the balance to the worlds, and the darkness has retreated. There remains but one thing to do, and I will go off today to see to it. Then I thought you would be pleased to learn that Marzina is coming home briefly."

"What did she do?" Taj asked.

Lara laughed. "Does a visit home necessarily mean your twin has committed some fault, Taj? Perhaps she just grew homesick and wanted to see us."

"Nay, I know my sister. She has done something to outrage our grandmother Ilona. I knew she would eventually. Marzina is always in a great hurry," Taj said.

"And besides, Mother, she was here for my coronation, so she couldn't be homesick."

"I have underestimated you, my lord son," Lara told him with a smile. "Aye, she has indeed proven to even my doting mother that she is not quite ready for the responsibility of her magic. She will visit with us briefly, and then will go into the care of the Daughters of the Great Creator for a year or more to hopefully learn self-discipline and restraint. When the High Priestess Kemina says Marzina has learned these virtues Prince Kaliq will take her as a student, and train her in the magic arts himself. Her talents are far beyond my mother's tutoring."

"What did Marzina do that Grandmother Ilona banned her from her kingdom?" Taj asked, curious, and both Gare and Sinon leaned eagerly forward to learn the answer, too, having heard all the previous discussion.

"The nature of Marzina's crime is of no account to Terah or its welfare, my lord Dominus. I think we shall leave it at that," Lara told him. "Oh, I see the cook has baked us fresh raisin bread this morning." Reaching for the loaf, Lara cut a slice for herself and buttered it lavishly. "And baked *pomme fruits* with honey! I am ravenous." She smiled at the three boys. "How are your studies coming?"

"We are learning the history of Terah," Taj said. "Just before the time of Usi the sorcerer. Do you think he was as terrible as he is portrayed, Mother?"

"You should know as my son that there is both light

and dark magic. Usi's magic was evil," Lara told her son. "His descendants rule the Dark Lands. And there is even a female line of his descendants in Hetar, Taj. Aye, Usi was the darkest of sorcerers."

Taj turned to his two companions, who did not know of that dark time in Terah's history. "When my mother came to Terah and the men heard her voice, they were astounded, for they believed their own females dumb and speechless. It turned out this sorcerer had cursed the men of Terah with his dying breath. While they thought their women had become speechless, it was actually the men whose ears had been stopped up to their voices. It was my mother's magic that changed all that, and my father fell in love with her then," Taj explained proudly.

Lara smiled, remembering her earlier days in Terah. Remembering its proud Dominus, Magnus Hauk. Now Terah was ruled by his son. For a moment she recalled Taj's coronation just a few weeks back. The family and the few representatives from the various cultures of Terah had come. The Lord High Ruler of Hetar, however, had not come, for he greatly feared to leave his kingdom for even a day. The first day of the celebration had honored Magnus Hauk, his life and his accomplishments. On the second day of the festivities, at the exact hour of Magnus Hauk's death, the crown had been set upon Taj's head by both Arik, High Priest in the Temple of the Great Creator, and his female counterpart, Kemina, the High Priestess. The third and final day was given over in celebration of the new Dominus. All of

Terah had feasted and rejoiced at the peaceful transition between reigns. Then their lives had again picked up the daily rhythm of their world once more.

Summer was coming. Gare and Sinon begged the Domina to be allowed to remain with Taj. And Taj wanted his friends with him. They would all go to visit in the New Outlands in late summer and early autumn, remaining for The Gathering. Reluctantly, the parents of the two young Fiacre clansmen gave their consent. They could see the advantage for their sons, and for the Outland clan families in the years to come.

Lara returned to Hetar. She was not yet ready to inform the Lord High Ruler of Hetar's most recent escape from the darkness. Hetar needed to be reformed, and the only way that was going to happen was if Jonah and his minions still believed they were in danger. She appeared in his privy chamber to discover him enthusiastically fucking a dark-haired female he had bent over his worktable.

"Give me your juices, Aprika," Jonah panted. "Give! Give!"

"Oh, my lord Jonah, it is too much! Too much! I die!" the female cried dramatically. "Oh! Oh! *Ohhhh!*"

He grunted, stiffened and then sighed gustily as he stepped away from her, drawing down his robe. "You may go now, Aprika," he said coldly.

The female arose slowly, and, turning, put a hand upon his arm. "My lord, did I not please you?" she murmured. "You said last night that I pleased you." Then she gave a shriek of surprise as her eye met Lara's.

"Go along, girl," Lara told her in a kindly tone. "Your master is a pig who takes pleasures from little slave girls like you, but rarely gives them back. Good morning, my lord Jonah. You are well, I see."

The girl gaped at Lara, then scuttled from the room without another word.

The Lord High Ruler of Hetar strolled around his worktable and looked at the faerie woman. "She is our sex slave," he said. "And my wife was too busy taking pleasures with our two male sex slaves to attend to my needs this morning."

"You really must be firmer with Zagiri, Jonah. She will not respect you if you are not," Lara told him. She almost felt sorry for him but that she knew he was a coldhearted man. "Sell Aprika, and one of the male slaves. Then see that your wife receives and gives pleasures only with you. The slave you keep will be for special occasions, or when you are away inspecting the new roads that are going to be built," Lara said.

"We are building new roads? Who is to build them, and from where is the coin to come, Domina?" he demanded to know. He was feeling irritable. Aprika had not satisfied him at all. Despite her reputation he found her boring. Only his beautiful wife could please him completely. He was a fool, but he actually loved Zagiri, and was terrified she would one day realize she had married a man old enough to be her father, and despise him for it. Or fall in love with another, younger man.

"The coin will come from the taxes you collect from the magnates for their unconscionable profits in these hard times. Odd that they should profit while the rest of Hetar suffers. The workforce will come from the general population who need jobs," Lara told him, breaking into his thoughts.

"The magnates don't pay taxes. They claim no profits," Jonah protested.

Lara laughed. "They lie as well as they cheat. Did you not enact a new law that says they must pay taxes. And instead of taking a percentage of their profits if they have none we shall take a percentage of their losses. The bigger their losses, the bigger the tax to be collected. That should end the lie about no profits. You know they have been cheating you, and you allowed it so your own sin of greed might not be brought to public light."

"You are harsh, Domina," he said.

"You are this kingdom's leader. Behave like a leader!" Lara snapped back at him.

"What of the Hierarch?" Jonah wanted to know.

"I will attend to him next," she said, and then Lara disappeared from his sight.

Jonah swore softly beneath his breath. The faerie woman was very irritating, but now he realized from where his wife got her fire. Lara was right. He would sell Aprika and Casnar this day. As for Doran, they would keep him. Jonah had actually come to like Doran, and he was more talented than his companion. His mind turned back to the Hierarch, who had been silent of late. What could he be planning? Jonah wondered.

Cam, however, was planning nothing, for he did not know what was wanted of him. Ciarda had been strangely absent in the last few days. Cam was beginning to become very frightened. He was trapped in Hetar, and his face was now recognized by every man, woman and child. He could not walk out into the streets for fear of them touching him, begging for his blessing, asking when it would all be all right again. He was actually beginning to wish he were back herding cattle in the New Outlands when Lara appeared in his small chamber.

"Aunt!" he cried.

She saw his fear and smirked inwardly. "Well, Nephew, you seem distraught. What is the matter?"

"Where is she?" he asked her. "Where is my Darkling?"

"The Dark Lands have a new Twilight Lord on its throne. Ciarda has been chosen to bear his heir. The mating has already taken place. Lord Kolgrim has no further interest in you, Cam. Ciarda's powers have been stripped from her. Women in the Dark Lands are not expected to be ambitious or intelligent. They are expected to accept their inferior position. Ciarda is now learning her proper place, Nephew."

"Then what is to become of me?" he shouted at her. "What happens to me?"

Lara heard Andraste begin to hum softly from her position in the scabbard on Lara's back. "You are the Hierarch," Lara taunted him mockingly. She was so tempted to leave him here to be unmasked as the fraud he was.

His bravado crumbled. "You know I am not," he said, low.

Lara nodded. "Aye, I know, but you will have to continue this charade, Cam, for a little while longer. Hetar needs hope, and the Hierarch represents that hope."

"But I have no powers," he said. "What can I do?"

"You will do precisely as I tell you," Lara answered him. "And if you agree to my terms, Nephew, I will see to it that a Shadow Prince stands by your side, invisible to all eyes but his own kind. It is this prince who will perform the miracles that will be attributed to the Hierarch. And Hetar will walk the road to recovery."

"Why do you care what happens to these people?" Cam queried her. "They sold you into slavery. They persecuted the clan families for centuries. Is there any good in them, Aunt, that you would help to save them?"

"There is good in everyone, Nephew, even you," Lara told him. "Yet there is also wickedness. But the light must prevail, Cam. Now, will you agree to my terms?"

"Aye, I will. I just want to go home to Rivalen," he admitted.

"You will, and soon," Lara told him.

"And you will keep your promise to me? You will give me Anoush to wife? Land? Cattle?"

"Land and cattle I will gladly give you, Cam, but remember I have said it is Anoush's decision to wed you or not. If she will have you then I will have you," Lara said to him, and she smiled.

"Then let us do what needs be done," Cam said. "I find I am eager to return to my own life and leave this Hierarch behind." Aye, he had had enough of magic folk, and power games. He had been a fool, but no more! He would have wealth and Anoush.

"So it shall be," Lara told him.

CHAPTER EIGHTEEN

IT WOULD HAVE been easy for Lara and her allies to simply correct the problems that Hetar had burdened itself with, but they did not. The lesson would not have been learned had they done so. At Lara's direction Cam walked through the streets of The City to the palace in the Golden District. He was garbed in a simple long white robe, a black rope girded about his waist, leather sandals upon his feet. His young face was smooth shaven, his short dark hair, which had become ragged in recent days, trimmed neatly, his blue eyes resolute. He trusted that a Shadow Prince walked with him, for his aunt had promised him that he would have a companion to perform the small miracles he needed to perform to reassure the people of The City.

And they came forth to greet him. Touching his robe, calling his name. His heart beating furiously, Cam smiled, stopped to touch an infant held out to him. "Blessings, my child," he murmured with a soft smile before moving on. "The Celestial Actuary be with you all," he called to the crowds that followed him to the gates of the Golden District, where they were barred from entering.

"Hierarch!" a voice in the crowd called out. "Let us come with you!"

Cam turned. "Nay, my brother," he replied. "This is a journey I must make alone. Wait for me here. When I have spoken to Lord Jonah I will come again to you." Then, turning, he was passed through into the Golden District by the guards, whom he blessed as he passed them by.

Nicely done, Hierarch, a voice next to his ear said.

Cam started, surprised. "You really are there," he whispered.

I am, and at the palace you will speak my thoughts to Lord Jonah, was the reply.

"May I ask who you are, my lord Prince?" Cam inquired, politely nodding and raising his hand in blessing to the woman with the two children who passed him by.

I am Kaliq, the invisible voice told him. *Now, do not address me again, Hierarch, for those you meet as you reach the palace will think you mad to be speaking to yourself.*

Cam nodded but, as no one else was approaching him, said softly, "Thank you." Then he walked on until finally he came to the palace.

Recognizing him instantly, the guards knelt for his blessing, and then allowed him to pass by. A servant notified by a runner from the main gate of the Hierarch's approach hurried forth to greet the Hierarch and lead him to the Lord High Ruler, who was waiting in his privy chamber. As much as it irritated Jonah, he knelt for the Hierarch's blessing, but feeling a little burst of energy from the hands placed upon his head soothed his pride.

Arising, Jonah invited the Hierarch to be seated in a comfortable chair by the fire. He signaled to a servant to bring Frine and cakes. Then Jonah sat down, asking as he did, "How, my lord Hierarch, may I be of service to you?"

"The High Council must be called into session, my lord," the Hierarch said. "Summer is half over, and we have much work to do before the Icy Season sets in again."

"Can you not make a miracle, my lord Hierarch?" Jonah asked him slyly.

"What lesson would you or your people learn from that, Lord Jonah?" the Hierarch asked him. "Hetar has brought itself low. Now you must pull yourselves up by your own efforts even as you brought yourselves down by your own efforts."

"But what can the High Council do?" Jonah wanted to know.

"It can follow the path that I lay out for it to follow, my lord Jonah. All the council members are currently in The City. Summon them now to the council chamber as I have bid you to do!" Cam was astounded by the words he was speaking and the commanding tone his voice had suddenly taken on, but then he remembered that Prince Kaliq had said it was his words that the Hierarch would speak.

Jonah stood up immediately, bowing to Cam as he did. "At once, my lord Hierarch," he said. Going to the door of his privy chamber, he opened it and called to Lionel, his secretary, "Summon the members of the High Council to the council chamber immediately. The Hierarch waits upon them!"

"At once, my lord," Lionel replied.

"We will wait here until they have all come," the Hierarch said. "I find this little fire pleasant, for this late summer day holds a hint of the autumn in it." He picked up his goblet and sipped the grape Frine as he closed his eyes in apparent meditation.

Well done again, Prince Kaliq said, but only Cam could hear him.

Jonah sat silent across from the Hierarch, studying the man. He seemed ordinary enough, Jonah thought. And yet...

When an hour had just passed a knock sounded upon the door to the privy chamber, and Lionel stuck his head into the room. "My lord Hierarch, my lord Jonah, the High Council awaits your coming."

"All of them?" Jonah wanted to know.

"Aye, my lord, all of them," Lionel replied.

Without a word the Hierarch arose, and, jumping back, the secretary held the door open for him and for his master as they passed through. Then Lionel ran quickly ahead of the pair, slipping into the council chamber by an almost hidden side door so he might take his place behind the chair of the Lord High Ruler where it was his duty to listen, and remind his master of anything he might later forget.

The guards at the main door snapped to attention and flung open the double doors for the Lord High Ruler and the Hierarch.

Cam raised his hand in blessing to them, and smiled as he passed by. Then he took Jonah's marble seat, relegating him to a smaller chair next to him with a gracious nod. Cam had almost gasped aloud when he felt himself being gently pushed before the Lord High Ruler's thronelike seat and then held in place as his head was made to nod in Jonah's direction. He almost laughed at the look of outrage on the Lord High Ruler's face, which was quickly masked as Jonah nodded in return and took his assigned seat. The council chamber was silent. All eyes turned to the Hierarch.

Cam felt his two hands being raised. "Greetings, and blessings to you all," he said. "I have asked Lord Jonah to require your presence this day because it is past time we began to plan the restoration of Hetar. With summer almost over we must work to rebuild the infrastructure of both The City and the provinces."

"And where are the materials to come from for this rebuilding?" the Forest Lord Enda wanted to know. "We will not allow you to deforest our lands as the emperor once did. Our woodlands, with the aid of the faerie Lord Thanos, are just beginning to thrive again."

"Surely you have certain areas where the trees can be thinned," the Hierarch said. "Harvest those areas for us, and trim the lumber. As for the rest of the wood we will need, ships are already on the way across the Saggitta carrying lumber for this endeavor."

"And who is to pay Terah for their lumber?" Clothilde of the General Population wanted to know.

The Hierarch smiled benignly. "Why, the magnates will cover the costs, taking the gold from their outrageous profits. I will personally go to each of them to collect each share. The hovels in The Quarter must be repaired as swiftly as possible. Squire Darah—" and the Hierarch turned to the governor of the Midlands "—can you gather enough thatch and workers from your province quickly?"

"The harvest must be brought in first," Squire Darah said. "It is amazingly bountiful this year, and we will be able to feed all at reasonable prices."

"Excellent! But can you spare enough men to teach some here in The City that art of thatching?" the Hierarch asked Squire Darah.

"That I can do, and gladly!" the governor of the Midlands answered.

"We have men to rebuild," Councilor Mikhail said. "And if the Midlands or any of the other provinces need our aid there are men to spare."

"And who is expected to pay these men for their labor?" Cuthbert Ahasferus asked sourly.

The Hierarch turned his blue eyes on the man. "Your guild will be assessed their share, as will the magnates. Sir Philip, Sir Anatol, your Crusader Knights have a large treasury that has lain untouched for years. You will bear the cost of the repairs to the Garden District. Everyone in Hetar must have a sound, dry habitation by the start of the Icy Season. Let us cease now for today. You will all be required to remain here in the palace until we have entirely completed our business. Lord Jonah will see to your comfort, and that my wishes are obeyed precisely. Tomorrow we will meet in midmorning to discuss the fair distribution of foodstuffs until the markets can be reopened. There is also a matter of the Mercenary Guild and the Crusader Knights to decide."

"What matter?" Peter Swiftfoot wanted to know.

"Your futures," the Hierarch replied mysteriously, and then, blessing them, he disappeared from their sight.

The High Council gasped, astounded at this.

"Where did he go?" Master Rupert of the Midlands wanted to know.

"Can there be any doubt now that he is who he says he is?" Prince Coilin said. "Only someone with great powers could disappear like that."

Prince Lothair hid a smile, for he had seen Kaliq toss his cloak about Cam and then disappear.

"Well, I for one will be glad to have Hetar get back to normal," Lady Eres of the Pleasure Women's Guild said. "Without our former prosperity there is little business these days. Only by the careful management of our Pleasure Mistresses have we been able to survive these last few years."

"Aye," Maeve Scarlet from the Guild of Pleasure Mistresses agreed. "I will be happy to see things returning to normal."

"We must do better than we have in the past century," Councilor Mikhail said quietly. "It was our own negligence that caused us to fail as a society."

"I do not see what we did that was so wrong," Aubin Prospero spoke up.

"You do not comprehend that greed for more and more profit caused our kingdom to fail?" Mikhail replied angrily. "You are not shamed to see hunger and want sweep our people to desperation? Despair is not wrong? Ignorance is not wrong? Perhaps, Aubin Prospero, if you lived among the people instead of being insulated from them in the Golden District, you might understand what has happened to Hetar. Do you ever venture into the streets anymore except to scuttle like a rat to your counting house?"

"You are as insulated as I am in the Garden District," Aubin Prospero shouted back at the councilor from the General Population.

"I haven't lived in the Garden District since I was twenty," Mikhail, son of Swiftsword, said. "I own a small house near The Quarter where I was born. I know the people for I am one of them."

"Your words border on sedition," Cuthbert Ahasferus blustered.

"So speaks one of our greatest profiteers," Lady Gillian said softly.

"My lords! My ladies! Enough!" the Lord High Ruler

spoke loudly above the din of the council chamber. "The council is dismissed until tomorrow. As the Hierarch has told you, you are all my guests."

"I need to send word to my wife," Aubin Prospero said.

"A messenger will be dispatched to each of your homes to inform those there of your whereabouts," Lord Jonah told them. "No personal messages will be carried for any of you, and the guards will be made aware of my order."

"Do you not trust us?" Aubin Prospero demanded to know. "Has it come to this? Would you side with a stranger over your own kind, my lord?"

"The Hierarch was always expected to come to Hetar in time of great trouble, my lord," Jonah said. "Have you so lost faith in everything and everyone but yourself and your profit that you would ask such a question of me?" Turning, he murmured to Lionel, who nodded, and hurried off. "Each of you will be escorted to your own guest chamber by my guards. You will remain there until your names are called. I will see you at dinner, my lords and my ladies." And, turning, Jonah departed the council chamber.

The two Shadow Princes waited with the others until they were escorted off to their own chambers. Silently they communicated with one another, and as soon as they were left in their quarters they each transported themselves to Shunnar, where Kaliq and Lara were waiting for them.

"We cannot remain long," Lothair said. "Lara, my beauty, it is good to see you." He kissed her cheek with a smile, causing Kaliq to glower.

"Aye, we have all been *requested* to remain at the Lord High Ruler's palace tonight. Our merchant friends are very angry," Prince Coilin said. "We must return in time for dinner with the Lord High Ruler." He chuckled.

"Jonah seems to have found faith all of a sudden," Lothair noted, grinning. "What did you do with our Hierarch?"

"I took him back to the little room he so modestly inhabits. He was quite relieved to find himself there, for now that the Darkling has deserted him he is very nervous of being found out for a fraud. I advised him to eat lightly and rest. That on the morrow I would transport him back to the council chamber," Kaliq said.

"Your exit was quite dramatic," Coilin murmured.

"It caused a brief discussion on faith in the Hierarch, which of course degenerated into an argument between the merchant representatives and the Lord High Ruler," Lothair said, grinning. "And then Lord Jonah virtually locked the council away until the morning except for a dinner over which he will preside. The merchants protested, for they will have wanted to warn their fellows of what is to come. Jonah didn't give them a chance."

"What lies ahead is a huge task," Lara told them. "We will use our powers to help the people of Hetar gain their goals by the Icy Season. They will not know that we aid them. They will believe that they have done it themselves, and it will give them a sense of accomplishment and national pride. They will then be ready for the next step in their rehabilitation."

"What did you mean, Kaliq," Lothair asked, "when you had the Hierarch tell them he had plans for the Crusader Knights and the Mercenary Guild?"

"The Mercenaries have always had but one task. To be the foot soldiers for war, or for guarding the caravans of the Taubyl traders. When there is no war to fight or traders to protect, they sit about idly drinking in the taverns of The Quarter, dicing, and expecting to be paid nonetheless. This cannot continue. Each Mercenary must be taught a trade, and put that trade to good use supporting himself and his family when his services as a Mercenary are not required. The wars of the last decade and the sicknesses that have swept Hetar have cut its population in half. But as long as Hetar insists on living as it always has no progress can be made.

"As for the Crusader Knights, they, too, must change. They have lost many of their members in these futile wars, and to illness and old age. And times being what they have been, they have not replenished their ranks. Perhaps the time has come to dismantle them."

"Nay," Lara said. "The Crusader Knights must remain. They must be rebuilt, but on a smaller scale I will agree. Should there ever be a war again it is these men who are the leaders of the armies. They are needed. The opportunity that they offer at their tournament for any who can meet their requirements is necessary, as well.

Had my father not sought that opportunity he would have remained among the ranks of the Mercenaries, and I might never have had the opportunity to seek out my own destiny among this world. Surely you must see that, Kaliq."

"But they serve no purpose except in war," the Shadow Prince said.

"Then we will find a purpose for them that they can practice in times of peace, my lord," Lara said. "Oddly many are artisans in their spare time, but of course only for their own amusement. What if those talents were turned to profit?"

"So speaks she who was born in Hetar," Kaliq teased. Then he grew a bit more serious. "A warrior who turns from killing to beauty. There is an odd balance to it, my love. I like it! But they will resist, of course."

"If they are told now there can be no new tournament to replenish their ranks, that the Crusader Knights will become a thing of the past until they can change, they will grumble, but will change," Lara said. "We did promise a new tournament next year."

"You grow cleverer with each passing year," Lothair complimented.

"Nay, my lord," Lara teased him. "With each passing day."

The three Shadow Princes laughed aloud, and Kaliq said, "I have always considered modesty a lesser virtue, my brothers."

"We must return to our guest chambers," Coilin said.

"It would not do to be called for dinner, and not be there." And he was gone.

"He's right," Lothair agreed, and he, too, disappeared.

The following day in Hetar the High Council met again with the Hierarch presiding over them. The Lord High Ruler's wife had slipped into the council chamber out of curiosity, for she had never before seen the Hierarch except from a distance. A deep blue veil covering her head, Zagiri watched from a corner in the rear of the room. There was something about the Hierarch that was familiar, but she could not quite put her finger on it. Still it troubled her, and she could not shake the feeling.

That night as Zagiri lay in her bed with her husband she considered the Hierarch. "Jonah," she said, "just who is this Hierarch? Where does he come from, my lord?"

"The legend only said that the Hierarch would come when Hetar was facing a time of terrible trials," he answered her.

"Is he mortal? Or is he someone from the magic worlds?" Zagiri persisted.

"I do not know," Jonah said. "Why do you ask me?"

"He seems familiar to me," Zagiri responded.

"Then he is probably someone from your mother's world whom you may have once seen," Jonah replied. "I feel better knowing that."

"Will he stay in Hetar forever?" Zagiri wondered.

"The Hierarch? Nay. When he has set us on the right

path again it is said he will disappear back to wherever he came from." Jonah rolled over, and took his wife into his arms. "Come, and take pleasures with me, my golden girl," he said to her. "Your pretty head should not be filled with questions about the Hierarch. I will always take care of you." And Jonah kissed her ruby-red lips passionately, fondling her breasts as Zagiri reached out to stroke his manhood with her now very skilled fingers. But her mind was still filled with thoughts of the Hierarch.

And then several days later it came to Zagiri in a flash of memory. The Hierarch reminded her of her mother's wicked nephew. She could not remember his name, but she knew the Hierarch looked exactly like him. She had seen him her last summer in the New Outlands tending cattle in a meadow near the village of Rivalen. And later at The Gathering. Zagiri understood that the Hetarians believed those people who had once inhabited the Outlands were savage, undisciplined, ignorant barbarians. Hetar would have enslaved them when they annexed the Outlands. But her mother and her allies had rescued the clan families, and resettled them in Terah with the blessing of Magnus Hauk.

Zagiri knew that her mother was revered by the clan families. She also knew they were not what the Hetarians believed they were. They were agrarian by nature, but highly intelligent. There was even one small clan family, the Devyn, who were the poets, the bards, the keepers of the clan families' verbal history, which they would recite and sing each year at The Gathering.

What if this young man who was known as the Hierarch was actually the nephew her mother so disliked? An Outlander. The outcast member of the Fiacre clan family. Did her mother know if he was? And if he was, did it mean her mother was using this Fiacre male to wreak her revenge upon Hetar because Zagiri had run away and wed with the Lord High Ruler of Hetar? Did Lara mean to embarrass Jonah and the people of Hetar by foisting this fraudulent Hierarch upon them?

Or was it merely a coincidence that the Hierarch looked like her mother's nephew? Was he actually who the Hetarians believed he was, a savior come to help them in this terrible time of trouble? A member of the same magic kingdoms to which her mother belonged? And were her mother and her allies aiding him? Certainly the Hierarch had not caused any harm, although she had heard from her husband and those about her that he was proposing radical changes to Hetar's traditions.

Zagiri did not know what to do. As *First Lady of Hetar* was it not her duty to bring her concerns to her husband? Yet she knew Jonah well enough by now to understand he would use any information she gave him to his own advantage, and not necessarily in Hetar's best interests. Zagiri wanted her husband to be the same kind of strong and benevolent ruler her father had been. And he could be under her influence. She had not really wielded that influence to date, but she was no fool.

Jonah adored her, and by being clever she could bring out the best in him. Until now all the women in his life had encouraged the darkness in him to flourish.

Zagiri needed to speak with her mother, but she knew that Lara was still angry with her. A year had passed since she had let herself be magicked to Hetar, and in that time Lara had not once contacted her, or sent an emissary to her. Zagiri felt a tear slip down her cheek as she realized how much she missed Lara. She hadn't wanted to disobey her mother, but those few meetings with Jonah on the Dream Plain had sent her tumbling headlong into love with him. She didn't understand why she had fallen in love with this Hetarian. He was not a young man and his character could hardly be considered noble in either thought or deed. But love him Zagiri did. So much so that when he had sold off two of their three sex slaves she had freed Doran. Then to her mother-in-law's double fury she had set the former sex slave up in his own business. The Pleasure Mistresses of The City were delighted, for Doran was an excellent trainer of new Pleasure Women. He would soon be a rich man.

For the last two months Zagiri's only lover had been her husband. She had ceased taking the herbs to quell pregnancy and she prayed for a child. Her stepson, Egon, was becoming a fine young man with her mothering. He held no resentment toward the young stepmother just a few years his senior. But Zagiri had begun to long for her own child. Perhaps a daughter. Now, however, she had other things to think about. Hidden within her own little privy chamber, and swallowing her pride, she called out to her mother. *"Mother, Mother, hear my call, and come to me from out yon wall."* She waited. Again she cried out to Lara. *"Mother, Mother, hear my call, and come to me from out yon wall!"* Still Lara did not come.

Zagiri felt tears welling up in her eyes. Never before had Lara behaved so coldly to her. And then for a brief moment she grew angry. She would tell Jonah that she believed the Hierarch to be a despised Outlander. Then reason set in once more. *"Prince Kaliq, hear my plea. Cease all else, and come to me,"* Zagiri said, and to her enormous relief the Shadow Prince appeared to her. "Oh, my lord!" Zagiri cried. Then she burst into tears, flinging herself into his arms.

Astounded by this unexpected outburst, Kaliq comforted her. "What is the matter, Zagiri?" he asked her, drawing a silk square from his sleeve, and handing it to her so she might wipe her eyes. He waited for an explanation.

Zagiri finally managed to control herself, but she clung to the silk square he had offered her. With a final sniff she moved out of his embrace, saying, "Thank you, my lord, for answering me. I called to Mother twice, but she will not come. I must speak with her, my lord. *I must!* It is very important."

"Tell me what it is about, Zagiri," Kaliq said quietly.

"It is the Hierarch, my lord. I think I know something

about the Hierarch," Zagiri told him in a whisper. "I really need to speak with Mother."

Kaliq nodded. Lara was still angry at Zagiri. She had heard her daughter calling to her, but she would not answer her. And when Kaliq had scolded her Lara had stalked off across his garden. He could, of course, bring her here to Zagiri now. His magic was far stronger than Lara's. But the Shadow Prince knew that the walls had ears in Hetar's royal palace. When mother and daughter met again there was likely to be a loud argument. Wrapping his cloak about Zagiri, he said, "Come!" And when he flung back the garment they were in Shunnar in his garden.

"Where are we?" Zagiri gasped. "Is this your palace, my lord? Ohh, you must take me back! I should not be here."

"Of course I will take you back, Zagiri," Kaliq told her calmly. "But your mother remains angry at you. I might have brought her to you, but I think you know that everyone in Hetar would have heard her outrage with me and with you if I had. Better the pair of you work out your differences here than in your little privy chamber, Zagiri."

Seeing the sense in his words, Zagiri nodded.

"Good! Are you ready for me to bring her to you?" the Shadow Prince asked with a small smile, and Zagiri nodded again. *"Lara, come to me now,"* Kaliq said. She did not appear, and he was not of a mind to play games with her. Zagiri could not remain long else she be discovered missing. His deep blue eyes narrowed, and with a snap of his fingers he brought Lara into the garden.

"Kaliq!" she cried, outraged, and immediately disappeared.

The Shadow Prince snapped his fingers twice this time, bringing her back.

Furious, Lara attempted to transport out of his sight again, but she discovered that she couldn't. "What have you done, you villian?" she demanded to know.

"Your daughter has come to make peace with you, and tell you something of import," Kaliq said in a stern voice.

Lara turned to walk away. If she couldn't use her magic she could use her feet. But to her shock she couldn't move her legs. "Kaliq!" she shrieked at him.

"I have rooted you to the spot where you stand, my love. Now greet Zagiri," he told her.

"I will not forgive you for this, Kaliq!" Lara threatened him.

He did not answer her.

"Mother, please," Zagiri pleaded. "Please speak with me. I am sorry I made you angry running away, but I really do love Jonah. I know I can make him a better mortal. He loves me. Jonah has never loved anyone in his life but himself, but he loves me."

Lara remained stone-faced and silent.

"Mother, I believe I recognize the Hierarch. I think he is your nephew. Do you know that? Are you helping him, or are you using him to harm Hetar?" Zagiri said.

"What would happen if Hetar learned that a despised Outlander was calling himself their Hierarch, Mother? Surely you do not hate Hetar that much."

"Have you told Jonah?" Lara asked, speaking the first words to her daughter that she had in over a year.

"Of course not," Zagiri said. "I wanted to speak with you first to obtain your advice in this matter."

"You want my advice now?" Lara asked scornfully. "You did not want it before you ran off and married the Lord High Ruler of Hetar when you were expressly forbidden to do so by your brother."

"My brother who spoke the words of Terah's Shadow Queen," Zagiri snapped.

"Kaliq, release me!" Lara said angrily. "Will you allow me to remain here, and be insulted by this viper I spawned?"

"I am not a viper!" Zagiri cried. "I am your daughter. Born of the great love my father had for you, and of the love you had for him."

"I wanted the best for you!" Lara said to her daughter. "I did not want you to wed a man almost three times your age, Zagiri! A man of such incredible ambition that he stole another's wife, and then stole a throne. He wed you so that Terah would be forced to come to his aid if he needed us. When you are no longer of use to him what will happen to you, Zagiri? What will happen to my child?"

"He loves me, Mother. He really does. When he is

with me he is different," Zagiri said. "There is light in him. I know it!"

"I hope for your sake you are right, Zagiri," Lara told her daughter.

"Forgive me, Mother, for hurting you," Zagiri said softly.

Lara shook her head.

"Have you stopped loving me, then, Mother?" the young woman asked.

"I will always love you," Lara said and her green eyes filled with tears.

"Then forgive me," Zagiri begged, and she knelt before her mother, her golden head bowed.

She didn't want to, but Lara could not help it. Reaching out, she caressed her daughter's head. Lips pressed tightly together, she attempted to keep the words back, but finally she could not. Bending, she kissed Zagiri's head. "I forgive you for running off, but I cannot forgive you for marrying that man," she said.

Rising, Zagiri hugged her mother. "You will get used to him eventually," she said mischievously.

Unable to help herself, Lara laughed. "No, I won't!" she replied firmly. "But I do love you, Zagiri, and we shall not be parted again."

"Oh, thank you, Mother!" Zagiri cried happily.

Kaliq smiled from the shadows where he had retreated while mother and daughter had settled their differences. Zagiri would never understand the deep hurt she had inflicted upon her mother, but it had been un-intentional, and at last they were reconciled.

"Now," Lara said, "this matter of the Hierarch. I could lie to you, Zagiri, and you would believe me. But I will not lie to you. The Hierarch is my nephew Cam." Then Lara explained to her daughter how the Darking Ciarda had ensorcelled Cam for her own purposes. And of how the magic world that championed the light had foiled the Darkling, but in doing so had left the Hierarch the mere mortal he was and helpless.

"Hetar needs to face its weaknesses, and then rebuild itself again. We might do it for them, but they would learn nothing from their mistakes then, and expect the magic kingdoms to help them whenever they failed. Instead we speak through the Hierarch, telling them what it is they need to do to rebuild their own kingdom. Their legend says the Hierarch will come in their time of trouble, and lead them back into the light. We have seen to it that happens, Zagiri. Had we left Cam to be discovered for the fraud he is the magnates and the Merchants Guild would have kept on squeezing every last drop of profit from the people.

"And, too, Hetar and its peoples would have resented any open interference from the magic worlds. This way the Hierarch gives them a direction, and a plan to follow. In doing so Hetar feels a sense of national pride and accomplishment, Zagiri. This is the way it should be in the mortal world. Mortals are eager to succeed. It makes them unique among the different races of beings. You cannot tell your husband the truth about the Hierarch," Lara finished.

"I know," Zagiri replied. "He would not understand, Mother, but I do. I will keep the secret. Tell me one thing, though. What happened to the Darkling?"

"The Twilight Lord decided she would make him a good mate," Lara said. "As such she is not permitted to leave the Dark Lands without him."

"Oh," Zagiri replied. "Then she will not bother Hetar again."

"It is unlikely," Lara told her daughter.

Kaliq now stepped from the shadows, smiling. "I must put Zagiri back in her own privy chamber before she is discovered missing. I am happy to see that you two are reconciled once more."

"Mother?"

"Yes, Zagiri?"

"Give Taj, Marzina and Anoush my love," the young woman said, and she hugged her mother.

"I will arrange for you to visit soon," Lara replied. "Your husband will find he owes me many favors, and I will certainly want to collect from him."

Zagiri giggled, which made her mother smile.

"I will send you back," Kaliq said.

"Thank you, my lord," Zagiri responded, and, impulsively, she kissed his cheek, blushing as she did so at her own daring.

With a wave of his hand and a chuckle, Kaliq returned Zagiri to her own world.

"She called to you when I would not answer her?" Lara said to him, rather intrigued by her daughter's foresight.

"Be glad she was clever enough to do so, and not run to Jonah," Kaliq remarked.

"I cannot believe that she loves him," Lara said. "I have never found anything lovable about Jonah. Still, I will admit that I have seen he loves her. Perhaps she can influence him to the good. Perhaps that is her destiny."

"Perhaps," he agreed, and his arm slipped about her waist. With a sigh Lara leaned against him, and, turning her heart-shaped face to his, kissed him softly, tenderly. "My brothers are correct when they say you are my weakness," he told her.

Lara turned to face him, and took his handsome and ageless face between her two hands. "It would seem only fair since you are my weakness, my lord," she told him, kissing him back, her lips warm against his.

He did not wait, but transported them to his bedchamber, smiling into her eyes as she magicked their garments away. Lifting her up, he buried his face between her breasts, tasting the salt of her slightly damp skin with his tongue.

Lara smiled down at him, hearing his thoughts as he touched her. *My faerie woman. Mine!* She twined her fingers through his dark hair as he slowly lowered her, walking as he did so, setting her upon his bed. Now it was he who cupped her face between his hands, smiling down into her green eyes. *My Shadow Prince. Mine!* Lara silently said to him.

They fell together onto the bed. Their lips met in a fierce and passionate embrace, one kiss blending into another and another and another until they were both dizzy with desire. He lay upon his back as she explored him with her lips and tongue. She nibbled on his nipples, pushed her tongue suggestively into his navel, licked the length of his torso with her hot little tongue. Her hand closed about his love rod, which needed little encouragement for his lust was high. Lara bent and kissed its tip. Then she mounted him, her shapely thighs pinning him, absorbing his length slowly, slowly, until she had completely sheathed him. Then, leaning forward, she offered him a breast.

Kaliq's mouth closed over her nipple with a snap. He sucked hard on it as Lara began a gentle movement upon his rod. His tongue licked around the nipple over and over again. The movement increased the tiniest bit. He sucked her again, then, unable to help himself, bit down upon the tender flesh. Her sheath squeezed him tightly, and he groaned and their eyes met. His fingers caressed her breast, then, taking it in his hand, he squeezed it and all the while his mouth never left her nipple. Taking his other hand, he pushed two fingers into her mouth, and with tongue and lips she played with them.

Kaliq's lust was near to boiling over. *Enough, my love,* he told her.

"No!" she said aloud and nipped at the fingers between her lips.

In answer to her, he quickly rolled her onto her back, pulling his fingers from her mouth as he did so. "Now, my faerie woman, I have you at my mercy," he told her, laughing as her legs clamped about his torso. "The time for teasing is over, and the time for pleasures begins." Lara's arms slipped about him, and, pulling his head to her, she kissed him again as he began to move upon her.

She closed her eyes and concentrated upon the size and length of him as he plumbed her depths until she was dizzy again with the delight he was engendering in her whole body. She clutched his rod tightly within her sheath, sighing as he groaned. Her fingers dug into his muscled shoulders, and clawed down his long back. The pleasures he offered her were so intense that Lara found herself close to losing consciousness. Then the inner storm began as her sheath began to spasm and Lara cried out as the pleasures overwhelmed them both. She slid into a heated darkness that enfolded her, wrapping her in warmth and contentment as he cried her name aloud.

Afterward as they lay sated with each other Kaliq said, "I want you to make Shunnar your home, my love."

"I cannot," Lara answered him. "Not until Taj is grown and ruling on his own. You know that I cannot leave him now, Kaliq."

"I know," he admitted with a sigh. "But when you can, Shunnar should be your home, not Terah."

"We have much to do before that can happen, my lord. This business with Hetar needs to be finished. And Anoush must be awakened, Marzina taught self-discipline lest she become a danger to herself and others and my son grown and wise enough to govern without me. There will be time for us eventually, my dearest Kaliq, but neither you nor I are apt to neglect our duty, are we?"

"Nay, we are not," he admitted. "Will you come to me when you can, my love?"

"Aye, I will. You are the only creature, mortal or magic, to truly understand me," Lara said softly. "But you must remember always that I am faerie, for I would not hurt you deliberately, Kaliq."

"I know that," he told her, pulling her back into his embrace, and Lara sighed happily with the knowledge that whatever happened Kaliq would always be there for her.

IN THE DAYS and weeks that followed Hetar began to heal. By the time the Icy Season returned all in the kingdom had warm, dry shelters. The Hetarians were proud of what they had accomplished in those few months. Even the magnates and the Merchants Guild had stopped complaining about the monies they were spending, for they saw a future of fresh profits for themselves as the people became prosperous once again. It was time for the Hierarch to leave Hetar.

He did so at Winterfest in a dramatic fashion that would be remembered for years to come. The square was overflowing, for the Hierarch had announced several days prior that he would leave them on the last night of Winterfest. The crowds jostled with one another for a glimpse of the Hierarch. People hung from the windows of the buildings about the main square. They stood or clung to the rooftops. Children were held up for the Hierarch's blessing as he made his way into the crowds that parted for him, and stood upon the painted platform that had been raised up for this occasion.

"I will not come again, my people," he told the Hetarians who stood listening to his words with upturned faces. "Follow my teachings. Be kind to one another. Profit is a good thing when not carried to extremes. I have shown you how to restore your traditions so that they fit the times in which you now live. You have already demonstrated much progress in the rebuilding of your kingdom. I came but to guide you, but it is you who must, who can and who will restore this land by your own good efforts. Hetar is capable of great things, my children. I give you all my blessing," the Hierarch said as he lifted his hands to encompass the crowds below, above and around him. Then to the gasps and cries of his audience he began to rise up. "Farewell!" he called out to them as he appeared to float away.

And those there in and about the main square watched, astonished, until the Hierarch had disappeared completely from their sight. A feeling of euphoria filled the air with his passing. All night long the people of Hetar celebrated the Icy Season, the Hierarch and each other. Frine flowed freely. There were stalls selling little hot meat pies and skewers with roasted vegetables. The Pleasure Houses were busier than they had been in months. Everyone agreed that Hetar's difficult days were behind them. They were well on the road to recovery, and the High Council would see they remained there.

As for Cam of the Fiacre, no one was more relieved than he to be returned home to his village of Rivalen. His last few months in Hetar had been very frightening, for he had never quite believed that his aunt would really aid him. Each day he had been required to perform as the Hierarch the Shadow Prince Kaliq stood invisible at his side, putting the proper words in his mouth, creating the miracles he was required to perform. Still, until he actually found himself back in his own environs he had never believed he wouldn't be betrayed. He appeared in Sholeh's hall with Lara even as the morning was beginning.

"Go and find your bed, Cam," Lara advised him. "I will return this evening, and we will speak with Sholeh together." She gave him a quick smile and was gone before he might question her further about Anoush.

Returning to Shunnar, Lara sought out Kaliq. "I need a favor of you, my lord," she greeted him.

"What would you have of me, my love?" he asked her.

"I do not wish to lie to Cam when he accuses me of turning Anoush's heart from him," Lara said. "When I awaken her I need your aid in this matter."

"Before I agree," Kaliq said, "I must look into Cam's heart to see if he truly loves her. We cannot in good conscience separate true love, for if we do neither lover will ever find real happiness, Lara. You know this to be so."

She sighed, nodding. "My instinct tells me he is the wrong man for her, but even my natural talents may be flawed by his parents' crime. Look into his heart, Kaliq, and I will abide by your decision in this matter," Lara said.

The Shadow Prince took his crystal globe from the place where it sat in the garden absorbing the sunlight by day, and the moonlight by night. Holding it in his left palm, he passed his right hand over it. *Show me if your heart is true. Or loving you the maid will rue.* Finally, after gazing for a brief time, Kaliq indicated to Lara that she should look into the globe herself.

She peered into the crystal and then said, "His heart is black as pitch." Then she sighed. "In a strange way I am sorry," Lara said.

"I will contact the Munin, and have all recent memories of Cam removed from Anoush's memory," Kaliq said. "Your instincts are sound, my love. When it is done we will awaken Anoush together."

"Aye, and in time perhaps my daughter will find a man who loves her with a true heart whom she will also love," Lara replied.

Kaliq called his friend the Munin Lord Satordi to him. He explained the situation, and together the two stood by Anoush's bedside while Satordi gently extracted the girl's recent memories of Cam from her head. Those memories were also excised from the clan families. The Munin were the magical folk who had dominion over the memories of all beings. When memories were lost it was the Munin who found them and stored them away. They were also adept at taking memories if needs be.

"Store them carefully in a hidden place known only to you," Kaliq said.

"It will be done, my lord Prince," Satordi replied, and he was gone.

Kaliq then went to find Lara. They transported the girl by means of their magic back to her own home in New Camdene. Anoush would never know of her kidnapping and rescue while she slept. Gently they awakened her, undoing the spell that had put her to sleep those few months ago.

Anoush opened her blue eyes, yawned, stretched and then sat up. "Mother! My lord! Why are you here? How long have I slept?"

"For several months, my darling," Lara said. "You fell ill of a fever, and magical sleep was the only remedy for it."

"Mother, I had the oddest dream while I slept," Anoush said. "A handsome young man came and stood by my bedside. He stroked my hand, and said no harm would come to me for we were kin, and he could allow no harm to touch his kin. Isn't that strange?"

"And what did this young man look like?" Kaliq said

in an amused voice so as not to alarm the girl, for he had heard Lara's soft gasp.

"He was tall, and fair with golden hair just like yours, Mother, but his eyes were a dark gray," Anoush replied.

"So, Mistress Anoush, you dream of handsome golden-haired men when you sleep," Kaliq teased her, chuckling.

Anoush giggled, sounding very girlish. "Maybe I will meet him one day, my lord," she said. "Do you think I will?"

"Ah, my child, I suspect it was nothing more than a dream," Kaliq told her, patting her shoulder. "As you were forced to sleep for so long I am glad you had such pleasant dreams to keep you content."

"Mother, would you ask Gadara to set up my bath? And would you and Kaliq remain to eat with me?" Anoush asked. "I want to know everything that happened while I slept. Have you spoken with Zagiri? Has she come home yet? And how is Marzina? And my brothers?" She stood up on wobbly legs, but remained upright.

"Of course, darling," Lara said. Then she and Kaliq left Anoush. Finding Gadara, she told the servant that Anoush was awake, and would want a bath. "And we will remain for the morning meal." When Gadara had hurried off Lara turned to Kaliq. "How did he dare to reach out to her?"

"Be glad," Kaliq responded. "Kolgrim has sent you a message through Anoush. He has told you that he will never harm the other children that you bore, my love. This is a good thing, Lara. Though you will not acknowledge him, he acknowledges his siblings as his blood kin through you. It is sad, for what he really wants is his mother."

"I know! I know! Do you not think it has pained me beyond all to have to deny him? Dark though he may be, I see a glimmer of light in him. I want to reach out to him, but I know I cannot. Must not," Lara said, her voice trembling. "For a time I could forget the twins I bore Kol. And then the Darkling unknowingly raised the specter of that past I have struggled to forget. Kolgrim and Kolbein are my sons. But I will never say it aloud again, Kaliq. I must live with those memories that I would sooner forget. But when you tried to spare me those remembrances I knew something was missing, and demanded them back from the Munin."

"My poor love," Kaliq said, taking her into his arms to soothe her.

"It is all a part of this damned destiny I have been ordained to live out," Lara told him, half laughing. "This spirit whose powers are greater than all of us put together certainly seems to have a great sense of humor." She moved from his arms. "I am all right now, my good lord. And I find I am hungry. I hope Anoush hurries with her bath."

When Anoush finally entered the hall they sat together at the High Board, and devoured a fine breakfast of oat stir-about with dried apple, sweet spices and heavy cream; rashers of bacon; hard-boiled eggs; fresh baked bread; butter and a jam made from last summer's apricots. They drank apple cider. As they were finishing their meal Cam burst into Anoush's little hall. Lara grew pale.

"Anoush! You are awake at last!" he cried out to her, and he strode forward to stand before her High Board.

"Cousin, you were not expected," Anoush said, "but I welcome you to my hall. May I offer you some cider? Have you eaten?" She rose from her place, and stepped down from the High Board to greet him politely.

"Anoush, I have come to ask you to be my bride!" Cam said.

Anoush looked astounded. Finally she said, "Why would you think I would marry you, Cam? We have not known each other since we were children."

Now it was Cam who wore a surprised look upon his handsome face. "But last summer you fell in love with me," he said.

Anoush laughed. "Nay, Cam, I have never been in love, and I could certainly never fall in love with the man whose parents were responsible for my father's death," she said. "Are you mad, then, to think such a thing?"

Cam turned briefly from Anoush. His blue eyes fastened upon Lara. "You have made her forget me!" he shouted.

"Nay, Nephew, I did not," Lara replied. She rose now from her place at the High Board, and came to stand by her daughter's side. "For your aid in pushing back the darkness I promised you land and cattle."

"You promised me Anoush, too!" he cried angrily.

"I said you could ask my daughter to wed with you, and if it pleased her I would agree," Lara responded.

"You have tricked me!" Cam said furiously. "Well, Aunt, if I cannot have Anoush no other man shall have her!" And he drew his dagger from its place on his waist, leaping forward, his arm raised for the attack.

Lara quickly pushed Anoush behind her even as she drew Andraste from the scabbard on her back, taking a defensive position, her sword before her. "Leave this hall, Cam!" she ordered him. "Leave it, and all will be well." She jumped back as he leaped forward, his dagger lashing out at her, tearing her shirtsleeve, scratching her arm.

Andraste began to sing in her deep voice. *I am Andraste, and I will drink your blood, oh son of Adon the slayer!*

Cam was not deterred. "Kill me if you can, faerie woman," he shouted. "If I do not kill you first!"

Lara felt a wave of dizziness sweep over her as a stinging pain began to burn her arm where he had cut it. The knife was tainted, she realized. "He has poisoned me, Kaliq!" And then with a burst of faerie strength she raised her sword, and with a single swift stroke sliced Cam in two from his head to his groin. The twin halves fell apart even as Lara crumbled to the floor.

The Shadow Prince jumped forward, gathering the

unconscious Lara into his arms. He disappeared before Anoush's wide, terrified eyes, reappearing in Shunnar shouting for his fellow princes to come at once. "Poison!" he cried to them.

At once the one called Nasim stepped forward. He lifted Lara's arms, sniffed and then quickly tied the arm at either end of the wound with silk cords he drew from the air. Then he began to press firmly upon the wound. Dark matter spewed forth, followed by a bilious green, and finally a clear fluid that preceeded her pale lavender-red faerie blood. Nasim sighed with relief, as did the other Shadow Princes surrounding them. Then he dressed the wound. "She will live, Kaliq, but she will be weak for some days to come. It was the right arm, praise the Creator! Had it been the left the poison would have reached her heart before I could stop it."

"What happened?" Prince Eskil asked anxiously.

Kaliq told them. "She and Andraste killed her attacker," Kaliq said.

"I trained her well," Prince Lothair, who had once been Lara's sword master, said proudly.

"Take Lara to her chamber," Kaliq said to no one in particular. "I must return and reassure Anoush her mother is all right. And there is the matter of a body to dispose of, as well, I fear." He immediately disappeared, reappearing in Anoush's little hall.

The girl still stood in shocked silence. She turned, wide-eyed, to the prince.

"Your mother will live," Kaliq said.

Anoush relaxed visibly. Then she said, "What on earth ever made Cam think I would marry him, my lord? As a child we were friends briefly, but it was nothing more than that for me."

"Your mother promised him land, cattle and a house in return for his aid. He gave it to us, and performed well," Prince Kaliq said. "And he did indeed ask her in my presence if he might have you to wife. Your mother told him such a decision was yours alone to make, but if he asked, and you agreed, she would not stand in the way. I realize now he didn't fully understand what she meant."

Anoush nodded. Then she said, looking down, "I wonder if we shall ever be able to get the blood out of the stone, my lord." Her head came up again. "Give my mother my love, my lord. I will come to see her soon."

"She is in Shunnar," he said, and then disappeared from her sight.

He had transported himself directly to Lara's chamber in his palace. Drawing up a chair, he sat by her bedside for the next few hours. She was paler than usual, but her breathing was even and steady, to his relief. And then to his great joy her dark eyelashes fluttered, and she opened her green eyes to meet his ardent gaze. Kaliq caught her small hand in his two big ones, and, bringing it to his lips, kissed it fervently. "Nasim says you will be all right. He got the poison out in time," he told her. "It will take you several weeks to recover, however, and you are going to remain here in Shunnar.

I will send word to Terah so the young Dominus will not worry. You can trust Corrado to guide him in your absense, my love." He kissed her hand again.

"Where is Andraste?" Lara said weakly.

"She didn't leave your hand until I got you here," he said. "She is with Lothair for the interim. She needs honing, for slicing Cam through dulled her. Lara, you cannot leave Shunnar right now. You are weak. You need to be taken care of until you are strong again. You cannot go!" Kaliq told her.

Lara's eyes grew misty. He was crushing her hand, but she would say nothing, for the concern on his handsome face, the desperate love in his eyes told her all she would ever need to know about him. He did indeed love her. She would never doubt it again. "Oh, my dear lord," Lara said. "You will not so easily get rid of me this time, Kaliq. Not this time!"

Not ever! the Shadow Prince told her in their silent magic language. But then he spoke the words aloud as if to reiterate them. "Not ever, Lara, my love. *Not ever!*"

* * * * *

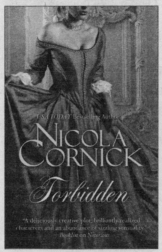

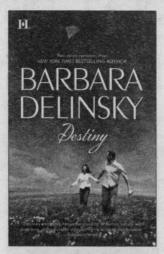

REQUEST YOUR FREE BOOKS!

2 FREE NOVELS FROM THE PARANORMAL ROMANCE COLLECTION PLUS 2 FREE GIFTS!

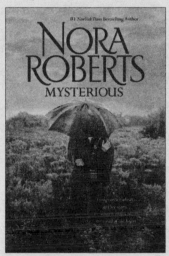

BERTRICE SMALL

(limited quantities available)

TOTAL AMOUNT	$ _____
POSTAGE & HANDLING	$ _____
($1.00 FOR 1 BOOK, 50¢ for each additional)	
APPLICABLE TAXES*	$ _____
TOTAL PAYABLE	$ _____

(check or money order—please do not send cash)

To order, complete this form and send it, along with a check or money order for the total above, payable to Harlequin HQN, to: **In the U.S.:** 3010 Walden Avenue, P.O. Box 9077, Buffalo, NY 14269-9077; **In Canada:** P.O. Box 636, Fort Erie, Ontario, L2A 5X3.

Name: _____
Address: _____ City: _____
State/Prov.: _____ Zip/Postal Code: _____
Account Number (if applicable): _____
075 CSAS

*New York residents remit applicable sales taxes.
*Canadian residents remit applicable GST and provincial taxes.

HARLEQUIN® HQN™
™ www.Harlequin.com

PHBS0912BL